COMRADES

a novel

by Georgiana Hart

Materialist Press

ACKNOWLEDGEMENTS

A special thank-you to the members and friends of the Progressive Labor Party, to the writing group for their efforts, and to the people in my family for their patience.

Published by: Materialist Press
                121 Oakland Terrace
                Newark, NJ 07106-2301

Copyright 1991.   Materialist Press

No portion of this book, except quotes for the purpose of this review, may be reproduced by any means, without written permission from the publisher.

LIBRARY OF CONGRESS CATALOGING IN PUBLICATION DATA

Hart, Georgiana. 1941

    Comrades

ISBN 0-9617820-1-3

In memory of comrade Alfredo,
who was killed by the Mexican police

Preface

The pages of <u>Challenge-Desafio</u> in the appendix cannot relate the story behind-the-scenes within the Boston summer project. This novel, however, describes a strictly fictionalized version of relationships among the volunteers. For example, many more young people were involved than is depicted here. The real biographies and dramatic political development of the one hundred seventy-five volunteers must be left to the reader's imagination. The book attempts to illustrate that political struggle and deepening personal ties within the Progressive Labor Party and the Committee Against Racism* determine the growth of the party which, in turn, measures the success of these historic events.

----

* The Committee Against Racism (CAR) was formed in 1972 by the Progressive Labor Party as a specific organization to fight what they saw as the main contradiction in the U.S. working class. The name was changed officially to INCAR, the INternational Committee Against Racism, in 1977-78.

Prologue

The year was 1974. When school began in Boston that fall, a group calling themselves ROAR threw rocks and bottles at black children boarding buses. ROAR, Restore Our Alienated Rights, was founded by Louise Day Hicks and others opposed to school integration. Nine out of ten members of the Boston School Committee belonged to ROAR.

Hicks, a member of the House of Representatives for two yars, became chairwoman of the Boston School Committee in the mid-sixties. During her term the committee blocked integration of the public schools by resubmitting plans the State Board had already rejected. One plan included a proposal to "notify at least 11,958 Chinese and Negro pupils not to come back to Boston schools." Hicks was named woman of the year in 1964 and outstanding citizen by the Boston City Council in 1965.

Boston was a city like many cities of the early seventies. The banks' policy of district redlining prevailed. Whites could not get a mortgage to buy a home in a "changing" neighborhood. The workers in some of Boston's industries were ninety-seven percent white and three percent black; those in others were three percent white and ninety-seven percent black. In 1970, two hundred ninety-six Boston teachers reported that no textbooks were available. Three out of sixty-eight schools had gym facilities. Integrated PTA's were actually illegal in the Boston schools, but segregated PTA's were allowed, whether mainly white or mainly black.

South Boston Crowd Attacks Black as Tensions Rise

By JOHN KIFNER
Special to The New York Times

BOSTON, Oct. 7—The crowd was milling around the intersection at South Boston's Old Colony housing project this afternoon, glaring and jeering at the police, when someone saw a black man, his car stuck in the traffic jam on Dorchester Street.

"There's one, get him!" came the cry, and suddenly dozens of people were running. "They're going to get him, people in the back were shouting and the rest of the crowd was in motion.

The attack on the lone black man pointed up the ugly tension building up as Boston entered its fourth week of court-ordered busing for school integration in South Boston, the tensions are not only racial but are developing into confrontations with the Police Tactical Patrol Force, some of whose members broke up a bar there on Saturday night.

Elsewhere in the city, white students stoned buses carrying black students to Roslindale High School this morning, and the incident led to 18 arrests. A black delegation demanded tonight that Mayor Kevin H. White get Federal protection for the schools.

In the outbreak of violence on Dorchester Street, the

Continued on Page 20, Column 4

Andrea Jean-Louis trying to escape from a group of antibusing demonstrators yesterday afternoon in South Boston. He was attacked after his car was caught in traffic jam.
Associated Press

In a separate incident:

Black man pulled from car, beaten by 4 in S. Boston

Oct 23

A 48-year-old South End black man was dragged out of his car and beaten by four white males at Broadway and M streets, South Boston, this afternoon, according to the City Hall Information Center.

The victim was identified as Colly Seaborn, of Worcester street, the South End. He was taken to Massachusetts General Hospital where he was treated for lacerations of the head and left forearm and released. Police said baseball bats were used in the assault. No arrests were made.

On Oct. 7 an angry white mob dragged a Roxbury black man out of his car in South Boston and beat and stomped him before he was rescued by police.

Earlier School Story, Page 3.

100 persons from New York and New Jersey protest 'racism' in Boston schools

More than 100 persons, mostly from New York and New Jersey, gathered at the corner of Franklin and Washington streets in downtown Boston yesterday, then marched to City Hall Plaza to protest what they called racism in Boston's public schools and the school boycott.

The rally was sponsored by the Committee Against Racism, an organization of students and teachers with chapters on 40 campuses, according to the Boston chairman, Albert Leisinger, a part-time mathematics instructor at Boston State College.

Tony Ntukogu, New York area chairman, called the rally and march a freedom ride in the tradition of the bus rides of the 1950s and early 1960s which protested segregation in the South.

Speakers at the rally condemned what they called the racist practices of the Boston School Committee and attacked Boston City Councilman Louise Day Hicks and School Committee Chairman John Kerrigan.

At the urging of the various speakers, the sign-carrying demonstrators frequently broke into such chants as "Hitler, Hicks, same old tricks."

Addressing the rally, Leisinger said it is racist on the part of Mrs. Hicks to call Roxbury a high-crime area and base an appeal for a school boycott on that claim. "The only high-crime area in Boston is the office where Louise Day Hicks sits. Except maybe, Kerrigan's office," he said.

He urged all races to unite to protest racism.

x x x

Union Square in January of 1975 looked to Russell Brown as it must have looked for the past fifty years. Communists held May Day rallies here until after World War II, he recalled. Now all that remained this icy January afternoon were bank buildings, poor folks huddled out of the wind and the store, S. Klein On The Square. Knowing the Progressive Labor Party leaders were responding vigorously to the horrors of Boston, Russell felt proud. But soon, surrounded by the tan marble walls and floor of the old building where they were to meet, he sensed that--despite the civil rights movement and the party's activities around the Vietnam war--not much had changed.

At that special meeting in early 1975, the communist Progressive Labor Party leaders proposed that the May Day march that year be held in Boston. Follow-up meant a summer project of people from other cities. The thrust of activities before the march would support the busing movement. Among the members at the meeting there was immediate disagreement.

Russell was among the first to speak. "I'm no racist," he said, "yet I don't think we have to support busing. After all, it's the Boston politicians who set it up. Why should we back something they started? It's phoney integration if you ask me."

Coralee Heatherington, a parent from Boston, agreed with Russell. "I know what you're saying. I feel like these crooks are trying to trap us into fighting one another. We should let parents decide where they want to send their children. Some of these places are miles out of our neighborhoods."

Russell then confided to Coralee, who was sitting next to him, "I enjoy walking my kids to school."

"Why not demand that the same money be given to black schools as to white schools?" someone suggested. "They can tear down the old schools in black areas. Build new ones."

Inez Siqueiros, who led the meeting, answered by reminding everyone, "On June 21, 1974, when Judge Garrity handed down the ruling on busing, he also enjoined the School Committee from constructing a single new school building or addition to an existing school!"

"We've been through that separate but equal

AMALGAMATED MEATCUTTERS SEEK NEW LOCATION

FOR UNION HALL

October 15, 1974: The Amalgamated Meatcutters Packinghouse Division, Local P575, no longer meet in their Andrews Station, South Boston, headquarters. Their meetings, held on the second Tuesday of every month, concluded in violence this August and September. As white and black union members left the hall together, they were attacked by a group of unknown assailants. "There weren't many of us at the summer meetings," the union reported. "But even so, they waited to jump us when almost all the guys had already gone."

The local has been known for its insignia displayed on the front door: a black hand and a white hand clenched together. After the September meeting, graffiti appeared on the union hall door. The October meeting was well-attended, and there were no physical attacks. However, when the men emerged from the hall, they found that cars of the black members had tires slashed and windshields broken.

"Some call it racism. I call it union busting," one of the officers stated in the interview. He refused to give his name but disclosed that the union had received two letters warning them of the attacks. "'Break up or get out' was what they said," the union officer reported. "Along with a whole lot of stuff your newspaper wouldn't see fit to print."

business in New York," said Frank Donovan, who taught music in the High School of Art in the Bronx. "So long as you're separate you'r going to remain unequal. Then the so-called better schools begin to deteriorate. In order to win any improvements you've got to unite the parents of many backgrounds. Integration can no longer be simply a moral issue."

Arms went into the air. Inez picked the first one. Tom Wycoff spoke from a corner of the room. He was a transit worker, a big, powerful man. "I think we have to consider the people we're bringing. I mean, I'm scared, and the people we'll bring with us on May Day don't know Boston. The shit is really going to hit the fan."

"We're all afraid, but look how ROAR attacked the meatcutters' union," said Coralee. "Those of us living in Boston, we don't have a choice."

"We can be a real support to you Boston folks," Norberto Mendez told Coralee. He spoke in Spanish, and his words were translated by Inez. He was a pruner of grape vines, coming just for the meeting this winter weekend from Wasco, California. "I plan to be there for two months this summer as part of our project to drive ROAR completely out of town!"

What he didn't add was that he was thinking that the white people in Boston--and perhaps blacks like Coralee herself--had been living with segregation for too long.

Another woman sitting near Russell didn't voice all her hesitations, either. Nikkia Porter, who spoke after Norberto, conveyed mainly enthusiasm. "I'm going to use my vacation time to spend in the summer project."

The problems of Boston seemed to her, however, so unlike those of the integrated area of Manhattan where she had chosen to live. She recalled the leaflet written by some women in Dorchester that had been passed around at the beginning of the meeting.

WE CALL ON RESIDENTS OF DORCHESTER TO FIGHT FOR WOMEN'S RIGHTS

The neighborhood of Dorchester is no longer secure for women! For the past two weeks single women involved in community affairs have been accosted on their way home. Many of you Dorchester residents know these women who have been active in affordable housing rent strikes. Then last night a group of pro-abortion women called "Our Bodies Our Right to Live" met in the second floor of 222 Tonawanda Street. They were attacked physically, the mimeograph machine and furniture broken. One woman was hospitalized and received nine stitches to her head! The assailants, from ROAR, said abortions kill innocent babies, mainly of black women on welfare.

All women, though, deserve to have the choice of a safe medical procedure. There have been recent serious illnesses and two deaths resulting from "back alley" abortions. You have all seen the lines of women waiting for "medicine" at a certain location. You have all known women who could not afford or were otherwise unable to raise an infant in proper circumstances. What we are asking is the right to a healthy life for all women and the children we choose to raise.

It is true that the majority of poorer women are blacks--with the lowest paying jobs or no jobs at all--whose health and very lives are being affected. However, those of you involved in the rent strikes have seen how cutbacks in city-subsidized apartments have raised the rents for everyone. Planned Parenthood facilities benefit many minority women who can least afford hospital abortions. But the clinic we seek will mean healthy choices for middle-class and white working-class women as well. Planned Parenthood for young people and pre-natal care are included in the proposal for the clinic.

Coalition for Women's Rights and Affordable Housing

Nikkia thought the leaflet apologetic in tone. But what struck her most was the crass nature of the attack on women. What happened in Boston can't happen here, she told herself. Nothing can change the Upper West Side.

The others in the room, looking at Nikkia as she spoke about using her vacation to go to Boston, couldn't guess at the conflicting notions going on inside her head. Nikkia stood tall, almost five feet nine, and her confidence in the proposal for a summer project seemed to be conveyed in her posture. A few years back she had been with one of New York City's first professional black ballet troupes; her calves and legs were still firm; her spine held the poise of someone ready to dance. Now she worked as a rehabilitation therapist at Metropolitan Hospital. She missed dancing, but the theatrical life style was in contradiction to her growing political ideas.

Nikkia listened to the final speaker, Cyril Waddell, a man who had grown up in England. "I tell you they can be beaten. In London, before World War II we had this guy Mosely who wanted to be the Hitler of England. And Britain's rulers allowed him free rein. Mosely's group led bigger and bigger demonstrations to recruit more right-wingers. One day--it was in June--they even rented double decker buses.

"The Communist Party was the only group organizing people to fight the fascists. My father organized with them. They went house to house in working class districts. They got the people to come out. Of course the first thing everyone realized, the bobbies--that's the cops in England--protected those fascists. But in numbers, the workers were more. The streets became a battleground. Thousands of men and women tipped the buses over! My father helped beat the fascists that June day, and they never raised their bloody heads in a demonstration again."

Cyril reinforced the immediacy of the situation. As Nikkia herself heard his words, she also felt an uncomfortable sense of missionaryism. The conditions of her own integrated job and comfortable apartment building made Boston seem like another country. But she voted with the one hundred thirty-five people in the room to hold May Day in Boston. And she planned to request vacation time for the summer project the very next day.

Nikkia and Russell both left the meeting early, each for his/her own reasons. "We're going to a birthday party," said Russell, "and it's mainly for the kids, so it's early. The little boy of a woman my wife works with."

"Pat's gotten to know a number of people since you guys moved here," said Nikkia. "She comes to most of the city-wide meetings, too, but this is only the second time I've seen you since October. Will you be going to Boston this summer?"

"I could get some days off," said Russell, "but they won't give Pat any time. Other nurses have more seniority. There's the whole question of our children. I really couldn't be gone."

"Boy, that job of yours. Pat has been telling me." Nikkia was sympathetic.

"My club's been struggling with me to quit and get a day job," he said. "I can't seem to bring myself to take anything right now for less pay. I feel uncertain I'd get anything better the way the economy is."

Nikkia opened the door to the street. Tiny snowflakes scattered sideways in an icy wind. "Brrr," Nikkia wrapped her arms around herself. "I can't wait for May Day! See you there, anyway."

Russell didn't want to show his uncertainty about going on May Day. Beside him, Nikkia seemed so strong and determined. What he said was, "Taking a whole day to go to another city means a lot of hours to ask someone to watch our four children."

Nikia felt unable to argue. She wanted to help, to relieve his whole state of affairs, but the questions of her own personal life were answered. She said simply, "Hang in there."

The New York Times

THE WEEK IN REVIEW
Sunday, April 27, 1975

The International Committee Against Racism Announces

BOSTON '75

A Summer Of Struggle, A Lifetime Of Commitment, A Call to Action

JUNE 1-AUGUST 31

The Steering Committee of the International Committee Against Racism (CAR) calls on students and other interested people to join our Freedom Summer Anti-Racist Action Project in Boston, Mass. Its purpose is to give a national/international focus to the anti-racist struggles going on in that city. Summer volunteers will work under the leadership of Boston CAR. Together, they will prepare the way for a strong grassroots movement that will unite blacks, whites, and other minorities to fight for quality, desegregated education and to fight against the racism being used to wreck the busing program.

The struggle will have a programmatic focus. Our aim is to select seriously committed people, students and others, but especially students, who will work on commuter campuses. Student volunteers must register at these schools in order to be effective. Some people may get jobs. A few may be assigned to community organizations. Others will talk to workers at plant gates and in union halls. The main focus will be on working with Boston students, parents, and teachers, especially those from ethnic communities like South Boston and Roxbury.

A CAR subcommittee (Boston '75) will co-ordinate all activities. Two one-week anti-racist schools will be opened at the beginning of June and July to prepare our volunteers for the correct ways of interacting with the Boston community. The key strategy is alliances with existing rank and file forces already mobilized against racist attacks. The result will be solid citywide CAR chapters and other rank and file anti-racist groups, tremendous experiences for our volunteers, and the growth of CAR itself. Only in such a united, rank and file, multi-racial, mass movement can we defeat racism—in Boston and elsewhere.

Why Is Boston Freedom Summer '75 So Important?

Because the power structure has kept Boston in a turmoil. Anti-racist actions are swept under the rug while pro-racist activity resembling fascism is given top billing. Boston is the international/national expression of racist ideas published by Jensen, Hernstein, Banfield, and others to justify the failure of the system. Moreover, Boston racists are totally organized by political forces more dangerous than those in the South. The Boston School Committee, President Ford, other politicians, and even the U.S. Supreme Court abet the anti-busing resistance.

Furthermore, racism is preventing working and middle-class people from getting a decent school system to replace a poor one. Racism is keeping blacks, whites, and other people from fighting back against unemployment and the cutbacks which are ruining health, education, and welfare in the Boston area. Boston Freedom Summer '75 will especially help many white Bostonians to begin to understand that racism hurts them, and that without multi-racial unity, there is no decent life for anyone. CAR BELIEVES THAT WE CAN REACH THE SILENT MAJORITY OF WHITE ANTI-RACISTS AND BRING THEM INTO OPEN STRUGGLE. By hindering the attempt to bring even further racial turmoil around the '75-'76 busing program, we will greatly improve our chances of creating an international movement against racism.

MOST OF ALL, Boston is the test of whether or not racist mob violence similar to FASCISM, combined with political racism, can succeed in stopping the desegregation movement. CAR says with its summer project, THE RACISTS ARE GONNA FLUNK THIS TEST!

THE ENDORSERS OF BOSTON '75 INCLUDE: Madison, Wisc. Chapter of Women's International League for Peace and Freedom, Pan-Hellenic Council, University of Wisconsin (Madison), Ad Hoc Committee, AFSCME Local #1 (Madison, Wisc.); University Student Senate, City University of New York, Day Student Government, Bronx Community College, N.Y. *The Communicator*, Bronx Community College, N.Y.; Associated Students, California State University at San Francisco, Associated Students, California State University at Los Angeles, Graduate Student Association, UCLA, *University Times*, California State University at Los Angeles.

To Contact the International Committee Against Racism:

NEW ENGLAND
Boston '75
896 Huntington Ave., Apt. #1
Boston, Mass. 02115

Phone to be installed after May 5. Dial (617) 555-1212 for information. Ask for Committee Against Racism.

NEW YORK
P.O. Box 904, Brooklyn, N.Y. 11202
(212) 783-6790

MIDWEST
P.O. Box 03017, Detroit, Michigan 48203
(313) 964-4202

SOUTH
804 E. Ash, Little Rock, Arkansas 72205
(501) 666-0048

NORTHERN CALIFORNIA AND NORTHWEST
855-C McAlister, San Francisco, California 94102
(415) 826-1860

SOUTHERN CALIFORNIA and SOUTHWEST
3084 Manning Avenue, Los Angeles, California 90064
(213) 839-0451

CANADA
P.O. Box 363, Station E, Toronto, Ontario, Canada
(416) 922-5046

THE INTERNATIONAL COMMITTEE AGAINST RACISM
Co-Chairperson: Prof. Finley Campbell
Director, Boston '75: Prof. Bill Iverson

CHECK WHERE APPROPRIATE AND MAIL TO ONE OF THE CAR REGIONAL HEADQUARTERS LISTED ABOVE.

_____ I want to participate in BOSTON '75.
_____ I come from the Boston area and can provide housing for _____ people.
I need housing for _____ spouse and _____ children (indicate number).
I am interested in organizing _____ on the job _____ on campus _____ in the community.
ENCLOSED IS MY CONTRIBUTION OF $ _____
Make checks payable to Boston CAR.

Name _____
Address _____
City _____
State _____ Zip _____
Area Code/Phone _____

LOCAL UNION 1010
United Steelworkers of America

3703 EUCLID AVENUE
EAST CHICAGO, INDIANA 46312

(219) 398-3100

HENRY J. LOPEZ
  PRESIDENT
JIM O'CONNOR
  VICE PRESIDENT
YVONNE PORTER
  RECORDING SECRETARY
JAMES ALEXANDER
  FINANCIAL SECRETARY
ROBERT FLORES
  TREASURER
C C CRAWFORD
  GUIDE
WALLY HARTMAN
  INNER GUARD
FRED JENKINS
  OUTER GUARD

TRUSTEES
JESSE TORRES
BUDDY HILL
MARY M HOPPER

June 18, 1975

Local Union 262
United Electrical Radio & Machine Workers of America
538 Dorchester Avenue
South Boston, Massachusetts

Dear Brothers and Sisters:

The attached resolution was read and passed at our regular local union meeting of June 5, 1975.

This is to inform you that Local 1010 fully supports those who continue to fight racism and the anti-busing campaign in South Boston.

Fraternally yours,

Yvonne Porter
Recording Secretary

mk
attachment

cc: Amalgamated Meatcutters and Butcher Workmen of America
    Local Union P 11 and Local Union 575

    Committee Against Racism
    Boston, P.O. Box 836
    Roxbury, Mass.

TO THE RECORDING SECRETARY, LOCAL 1010

Whereas the racist anti-busing campaign is continuing very strong in South Boston, to the point that union halls with black and Latin workers have ceased meeting because of vandalism and racist attacks on those workers.

Whereas Louise Day Hicks has formed ROAR (Restore Our Alienated Rights) nationwide to continue the spreading of racism not only in Boston but throughout the country. And that this organization actively integration of schools and encourages attacks and vandalism of minority workers.

Whereas an organization named CAR (Committee Against Racism) was formed to fight the anti-busing campaign. This organization is fighting to build 25 new schools, hire 5,000 unemployed workers in the schools, hire hundreds of teachers, especially minority teachers, expand the bilingual program, indict Louise Day Hicks for conspiracy to violate the civil rights of school children and integrate the schools and parents meetings.

Whereas our local has sent letters to the local AFL-CIO and the Boston AFL-CIO and our own international with no response.

Be it resolved that our local sends letters of support and solidarity to the South Boston locals who have been forced to close their doors to their union members.

The following list are the addresses of the locals and CAR:

United Electrical Radio & Machine Workers of America
Local union 262
538 Dorchester Ave.
South Boston, Mass.

Amalgamated Meatcutters and Butchers Workmen of America
Local Union P 11 and Local Union 575
626 Dorchester Ave.
South Boston, Mass.

Committee Against Racism
896 Huntington Ave.   Apt #1
Boston, MA 02115   (617) 277-0232

Chapter 1

Half her life seemed to be spent waiting, if not for one man, then for a subway, Nikkia thought. These goddamned local IND trains. The posters on the gray walls waited with Nikkia. Seagrams 7 in the half gallon. A movie ad about one good cop against the world.
A blast of warm air came to her face as she stood on the subway platform. This was one of the few heated stations, Nikkia thought gratefully. She was unaware of the damp cement walls, and while waiting for the train, stared at the water puddles between the tracks without seeing them. Her thoughts went back to the room she had just left. There, men and women in the Progressive Labor Party were ready to ask friends to march on May Day in Boston, despite their own questions.
Nikkia's mind went over Russell Brown's situation and his arguments on the busing issue. Would she want her kids to be bused miles away? Those Boston politicians must have spent days, she thought, just figuring how to get people to scrap over the deteriorating schools. Allright for her to spend a couple of weeks there this summer. But that city of sharp racial divisions was not an environment she'd choose to live in. Partly in contrast to the problems of Boston, Nikkia was looking forward to the quiet of her own apartment and her boyfriend, Lawrence. He would be so glad to see her. He'd hold her securely.
Russell's predicament continued to bother Nikkia, though. He really was stuck on being in the house. Nikkia sympathized with Pat's concerns. Too bad Russell can't work out of his home, while looking for a better job, as Lawrence does with his editorial skills. But then it might become harder for the poor guy to ever leave the house.
Take Lawrence, for example, she told herself. He

rarely goes out except to interview for articles. Only tonight, Wednesday, he's waiting for me at my place. Like every Wednesday night, Nikkia thought. Will we ever resolve whether to live in his apartment or mine? When we get married, we'll have to decide.

The train came, and there was no heat on it. Forty-second Street, fiftieth, fifty-ninth. Nikkia's thoughts were on another poster in front of her, some new male actor she'd never heard of. Lawrence was better looking, with his full, glistening afro and hazel-colored eyes. Women stopped to look at him on the street, and Nikkia enjoyed seeing that. She nagged at herself: twenty-nine years old means it's time for you to get married. Thirties is pushing it if you want to have kids. He loves you. She gave herself these arguments as the train passed seventy-second, seventh-ninty, eighty-sixth, ninety-sixth; she had been riding this train forever.

One hundred third Street. Out! Up the stairs and past the smell of urine and hamburgers. On the street, wind that makes the snow hurt. Did I remember to put my keys in my pocket so I won't have to dig for them? Yes. Open the door. The elevator is out of order again. Walk to the 1234567th floor. Open the door. Lawrence, where are you? Nikkia asked herself.

He never called out to greet her, and so she felt foolish calling his name. She saw him lying on her bed, watching television. He had on a soft, yellow sweater and faded jeans. He looked at her with calm eyes. Nikkia went over, taking off her coat, and lay on the bed beside him, putting her arms around the soft sweater. Lawrence held her firmly.

Nikkia raised her head to look at his small nose and profile. Curly lashes, watching television. "It was a good meeting," she offered.

"They're always good, to you." He moved one of his legs so that it lay between hers.

She questioned herself: Did she usually respond so mechanically? "They mostly <u>are</u> very positive."

"How many decisions did you make tonight?" He continued to focus on the TV set. "Or did you go there to rubber stamp a decision that essentially was already made?"

"We agreed to have May Day in Boston, if that's what you mean." Nikkia tried to get beyond Lawrence's competitiveness--that's what she figured it was--with the leadership of the party. Lately she made more of an attempt to get him to view the ideas involved. "But this busing issue is a tough one. There was a lot of disagreement. The whole idea of racism can no longer remain a moral question, but rather one of survival of the white children, too, in the crumbling schools."

"That's the only time whites become involved, when it's their own skin."

Nikkia remembered there was a time when she, too, thought along nationalist lines. "Most of the white people at the meeting weren't even from Boston."

"But you're still going to have the march, even with half of you in disagreement. And when there's a revolution you'll run off and get killed, whether or not you understand why."

"If only you could see how people debate these ideas during our meetings. You snipe at me, but you never come to anything."

"All I would do is argue. I have to be perfectly honest with you. I would only join in activities the better to convince you to leave." He kissed her forehead by the hairline. "I'm afraid for you because I love you."

"It's hard for me to see how you could continue to love someone who is so mindless she'll act without thinking," she teased. Nikkia didn't want to argue. She knew he was trying to make amends. But she couldn't let pass the remark about her lack of understanding.

"You go to the same old rallies whenever the leaders say."

Nikkia felt the warm pressure of his fingertips in places on her back. She didn't doubt his love for her. But lately she had discovered something more about Lawrence. His thoughts held two--sometimes three--images of her. One, where she formed part of a pattern that linked the party's activities, the need for party leadership and her involvement. And then he knew a separate Nikkia, the person whom he first loved. At the same time he cared deeply for this woman who had grown with an inner strength he did not associate with the party, the woman who stood before him now. When he felt caught in the middle of these, his own impressions, he lashed out in every direction, as he was doing tonight.

Nikkia struggled to sit up, "I'm becoming a part of the leadership here in New York. And black and hispanic women are on the international committee."

"It's all image. Big business is starting to hire black executives. Next we'll have black mayors and blacks running for president. Think that'll change anything?"

"Why do you think that's what the party's like? You want to ignore the fact that people change within the party, build close ties with others. I think you're starting to believe the cynical magazine copy you write!"

Lawrence moved easily, like a cat, taking his arms from her to lean on one elbow with the other arm resting on a bent knee. His hand no longer touched her; the long, graceful fingers curved in the air between them. For the first time he looked at her. "That hurt," he said quietly.

She wanted to touch him.

He continued, "You know that life to me is more than meetings and marching. Yet you want to degrade my hopes for us. You're telling me I'm turning into an advertisement for Arrow shirts."

Nikkia smiled, appreciating him.

"I want us to get closer together, and the party moves you more in danger."

Nikkia could think of nothing to say. She was no longer angry. His simple words left her ashamed instead. A sadness for him, for herself, made her cry.

"You're tired," he said.

It was late. She had to work the next day. Nikkia got up to undress. When she came back from the bathroom, the light was out. There was only the green glow through the room from the television. Lawrence was already under the covers.

She slid over the cold sheets to reach the warmth of him. His lean arms went around her. They fit her body. Her leg slid over his. He warmed her feet. The curves of his body met her ankle here, and there. His hand felt her lower back. She knew the slimness of him and the contrast of his skin that was more textured than her own. Then his hand moved between the top of her legs where the skin was most smooth, and the lower parts of their bodies met. For her, there was only the feeling of him.

x x x

Nikkia heard the alarm clock the next morning. She lay there for a moment and thought about when she would request vacation and who she would talk with that day. The bed felt cozy, and the idea of talking with people about going to Boston made her insides quicken.

"Do you have to go in today?" Lawrence made a face.

"Of course."

"What do you mean, 'of course'?"

"Let's not start the day by arguing. You know I don't like to take sick days unless I really have to. I never know when I might need them to do something else."

"It's enough you work every other weekend. Your life is not your own."

"Look, I don't mind going to work. I mean I hate the set up; the hospital stinks. But I actually enjoy seeing the people there. I'd go nuts staying at home."

"But I keep telling you, you're too good for this kind of work. You've told me how you sometimes clean up people's behinds, even when there's an aide around."

"I don't mind."

"But you know that I mind just the thought of your doing that. These are our hands!" He held her hands then. "When you could be a model. You need to start a part time career that'll help us raise the children together. How often I wish I could do this writing part time."

Nikkia didn't want to talk about a modeling career at all. They'd been over and over that. Of course, he would keep insisting as long as there was a grain of truth in the need for her to work part time eventually. The hospital had no part time physical therapists. "You know what I think of modeling. I like working with people. Real people."

He spoke in a softer tone. "Some people who model are stupid. Not you. It would pay a lot of money so you could spend time with our children. Other people need to spend the time at work away from their children. You wouldn't be like that. Some even go to their jobs in factories or hospitals--I'm not saying you do this--in order to turn off their minds so they don't have to think."

"Working with my hands _is_ thinking," she said, taking her fingers from under his. "I don't dwell on myself. There are too many patients to work with. And talking with them about their problems is a kind of therapy, too. I get them to think. What about you," she countered. "What do you have on your mind?"

"Us. I spend a great deal of time thinking about you." His voice was resigned and a little sad. "I think about us even while I'm writing. Where we're going. That takes most of the energy I have."

Nikkia felt a squirming somewhere inside her. She didn't think about their relationship much at all. It was too painful to contemplate, the contradictions in their political lives. She attributed his lack of understanding to his constantly working alone. But she couldn't criticize the fact that he did have a steady income, when so many black men were on the streets. And he liked his work as much as she liked hers.

Many men would try, physically, to stop their women from going out and organizing. Lawrence had never done that. Other men felt the need to run around. She never had to worry about that with him. Most of the people in this country didn't share her politics yet. So how many _men_ would she find who wanted to get married, who also shared her love of music and dance? Nikkia's answer was that she had to win over this one man's viewpoint. And surely, wasn't it her belief that people changed?

Yet she had held off moving in with him. Their original wedding date had been postponed by six months. As close as she felt to him, it seemed to her that he guarded something about himself that she had to know before she decided. But for some reason, her taking a day off work to steal time together didn't seem to help their relationship. Twice before, she had given in to his plea, 'I need more time alone with you,' and they had argued most of the day.

At this moment, this morning, Nikkia decided to talk very soon about Lawrence with Cyril Waddell. Cyril was one comrade in whom she confided easily. She needed another viewpoint. He and his wife, Karen, had met and talked with Lawrence at two social events. Nikkia also decided to speak with Bonita, her best friend at work. Perhaps Bonita could come over and relax with the two of them for an evening, without the distractions of a movie or the ballet.

"OK if I ask Bonita over for dinner soon?" Nikkia took a uniform from the closet.

"Why not?"

But before Nikkia even got in the door at work that day, she heard pressing news: The hospital had just laid off several hundred workers. Everyone was talking about it. Nikkia spoke at length with the elevator operator. He had been hearing all the reports. Hermel Jones was a stocky, well-built West Indian man. Nikkia liked his face, with his smooth, rounded forehead, gleaming darkly.

"After Mayor Beame and the city council met last night," he said, "the city told the hospital administration to send telegrams to the laid off workers. It sounds like the hardest hit were housekeeping and the aides." Nevertheless, he was distressed, "Which of us is going to be next?"

When she arrived at her fourth floor, Nikkia immediately looked for Joe Nesbitt, a housekeeping worker. He had been working at Metropolitan longer than anyone, and he knew everything that went on. His wife was sick and lately had taken a turn for the worse, so Joe had not been in as usual every day. Nikkia looked in the porter's closet. No one was there.

She went down the halls looking for his mop and pail cart. There wasn't one housekeeping worker. Nikkia ran up the stairs to five. Here was Henrietta, lively with small spectacles.

"Where's Joe?"

"I haven't seen him. Did you hear that some of us were sent telegrams this morning not to report to work?"

"They didn't want people to come in and get upset together here," Nikkia thought aloud.

Henrietta told her, "Some came in anyway. They're downstairs in the emergency room."

Nikkia was distracted and did not respond to that information. "Joe had too much seniority for him to get laid off. I'm going to call him at home."

She had five minutes before she had to report to work. Joe's wife answered the phone. "No, he's not here. He didn't get no telegram."

Nikkia didn't want to worry her, who depended so on Joe. "I'm sure they're not even considering him, with thirty-five years. I'll call you later."

She took the stairs back down to four. There, at the end of a hall she saw Joe, his back to her. Joe's immediate supervisor, Caruthers, faced Joe. Beside them, the elevator door stood open, and Caruthers held it open with his foot. Nikkia couldn't approach Joe now. Better to stay out of sight until Caruthers left. She could barely hear them talking.

"Anybody who leaves the men's shower room wet after thirty-five years on the same job . . . I ought to send you to the eye doctor."

Joe said, "A patient just left the shower."

His voice was so low, Nikkia had to cup her ear to catch the words. She felt her heart pound in anger.

"Mop it up immediately. If . . . so tired from your second job you might pay more attention to this one."

"I have no second job." Joe's voice was angry now.

What was Caruthers getting at?

"You know, playing nursemaid to your wife."

Too much. Nikkia remembered that Joe's wife had Alzheimer's. Caruthers was going too far.

"Leave my wife out of your filthy mouth, you son of a bitch."

Nikkia walked quickly toward them. But Caruthers was steering Joe into the elevator. "Insubordination. Downstairs to the main office." The elevator door shut before Nikkia could get halfway down the hall. She was shaking.

Slowly now, Nikkia went to the nursing station. "I'm here," she announced. "But something's happening downstairs." She looked around the station. A panicky feeling. "Where's Bonita?"

"We got a call. Her and Bennie's told not to come in."

"Oh shit." Nikkia's hands were sweaty. "Hey, Henrietta told me a lot of housekeeping workers are waiting in the emergency room. What's happening?"

"I dunno. I came in the front."

"We'll cover for you," said Lily, the assistant head nurse. "Go downstairs and find out what's going on."

"Watch out for Miss Jenkins," advised Candy, an LPN.

"Is there something I can do up here?" It was

Steve Tobias, the ward clerk.

"Yes. Please. Yes. Call Bonita and Bennie. Tell them both to come to the hospital. Go to the E.R."

"Don't be too long." Carol, the head nurse.

Instead of waiting for the elevator, Nikkia ran down the stairs. Through the basement and past the kitchen. The engineering office. Up a back ramp that led to the emergency room.

The head housekeeping suspervisor, Masterson, was standing in the middle of a group of two dozen men and women. "For the third time, I don't know what you're all doing here. Weren't you sent telegrams not to come in?" Masterson was a black man, and the people surrounding him were hispanic and black as well. But Masterson wore a white shirt and a tie with the crest of the hospital. "Go back home and wait. I'm doing what I can for you."

"Don't you go home," Nikkia shouted from the back of the emergency room. She surprised herself. "Stay in the E.R. Picket. They're scared to death to see you here. That's why they sent telegrams."

She knew she would get a corrective action for this. Perhaps even fired today. But if she could get other departments to support housekeeping . . . She just needed a little time.

"You don't know what you're talking about," Masterson yelled. He pulled up his pants by the sides of his belt. "We ourselves weren't told by the city until last night."

"You've been planning this for months," said one of the women closest to Masterson. "I've a mind to call in a few people I know who're still at home." She started toward a phone booth.

"We'll get up a petition inside now," Nikkia called to them. She could see a couple emergency room security guards. Masterson waved to them. He pointed to the woman at the phone. He pointed toward Nikkia. But she had gone.

"We're wasting our time talking to Masterson." A very thin, pale man announced. "Let's picket right here."

They pushed IV poles and stretchers toward the walls, into the examining rooms. They joined arms. Security formed a broken ring outside their circle. Patients waited in wheelchairs and on stretchers. No one moved. No one had been prepared for this.

Nikkia, meantime, could hardly think straight. The organizing was all so spontaneous. It would fall apart unless she could gather support inside. She began making plans. First, she had to call someone on the party's city-wide steering committee. From a basement phone she dialed Inez first. She wasn't home. Cyril; can't call him at work. Next try Gloria Luzon.

Gloria answered with a murmur. She was an aide in another hospital. She was off that day.

"I'm sorry if I woke you," Nikkia hurried. "But this place is really jumping. Two hundred people-- housekeeping, aides-- mostly black and hispanic, were laid off by telegram so they wouldn't start a rebellion together at work. They came in anyway, some of them. They're in the emergency room, and they're not budging!"

"What's your plan to get more people involved?"

"I'm going to start a petition and try to get some people to join them. What else?"

"Try to get people you know best to help you write it."

"I got you. I try to do too much by myself."

"Many of us do." Gloria was understanding. "Let me ask you another question, though, how've you planned to raise the Boston march in all this?"

"Damnit. Everything's happening at once. The connection isn't obvious."

"I disagree. Sounds as if racism is a major factor in both the New York hospitals and in the busing issue. That's clear to me."

"They won't see this has anything to do with busing," Nikkia argued. At once, she could see from the phone booth that Miss Jenkins herself was coming down the hall. Two security guards walked beside her. They went toward the elevator, not seeing Nikkia.

"I gotta go. Thanks." Nikkia hung the phone with a crash and found a door beside the kitchen. PLEASE KEEP CLOSED. FIRE DOOR. Nikkia opened it, pushed it shut again and ran up the stairs. She reached the nursing station on the fourth floor before Jenkins.

"I have to tell you all," Nikkia's breath came gasping. "They're picketing in the E.R. Jenkins'll be here any minute to try to catch me coming in late. Masterson saw me downstairs. We have to start a petition, get people down there . . ."

"That sucked, sending people telegrams," Candy spoke angrily.

"Hold it. One thing at a time," said Lily. "You got it right, though, this administration is disgusting."

Nikkia remembered something else, "You haven't heard it all. Caruthers got on Joe Nesbitt's back even before we started work this morning. Insulted Joe the way he cares for his wife. Joe cussed like Caruthers knew he would. He's probably been suspended."

Candy punched her fist at the nursing station wall.

Nogales, the unit orderly, was looking out of the corrugated window. He saw Jenkins and the advancing security guards. He said, "Madre. La puta! (whore)."

Jenkins and the guards got to the station door. They hesitated. Perhaps they sensed the angry mood of the six people inside. Miss Jenkins, six feet tall in her flat shoes, seemed nervous. She opened the door and motioned the guards to wait.

"Porter," she pointed at Nikkia. "You didn't report on time for work. You were away from your unit."

"Oh yes she did," said Candy. "She got here early. It's just that we all--me especially--wanted to know what was going on. I still want to know!"

Before Jenkins could say anything, Steve talked, "We have no housekeeper on the entire floor. The patients are asking me for room cleaning. I want to know if Joe Nesbitt is fired or what."

Unprepared for their questions, Jenkins glanced from one to the other, her eyes then directed to Carol Rydell. "He's under three day suspension."

But the head nurse had her own problems, "We're short staffed with Bonita and Bennie gone," she challenged. "I can't function here in ortho with only one male orderly."

"We're calling a state of emergency," said Jenkins. "Under the contract you'll have to cooperate."

She jabbed her finger in Nikkia's direction. "And you, Porter, have a corrective action. This makes your second. One more and you're fired. I'll call you down when it's ready. Right now I'm needed in the E.R." And Miss Jenkins swept out the door.

Lily went over to Nikkia. "She was afraid to take you down herself." She put her arm around Nikkia.

"I've known her a long time. When she's really scared she takes security with her everywhere." Lily chuckled, "Well, almost everywhere."

She's going to be even more afraid when we join with housekeeping," Nikkia stated. "What did Bonita and Bennie say? Did you reach them?

"Bonita was dressed, about to come down on her own," said Steve. "Bennie's too afraid. I tried to tell him he'll feel better here . . . ."

"He's a real loner," said Nogales.

Carol looked at the clock. "Dietary will be here noon with the trays," she said.

"Let's all of us wash and feed the ones who can't do for themselves," Nikkia suggested. "We'll talk with them about what's going on. Nogales and I can set the tractions, and then I'll need all your help to write this petition."

Steve pulled an old manual typewriter from under a shelf. "I'll start on it right now. And there's carbon paper between the med order sheets."

Lily was much more cautious. "The bigwigs who tell Miss Jenkins what to do aren't afraid. We don't want the rest of us to get in trouble, too."

"We're already in trouble if two hundred workers are laid off." Candy spoke sharply.

Carol said, "I know the layoffs affect all of us. But honestly, it's the city that told our administrators what to do. And you can't fight city hall."

"City hall would like to think we can't," put in Nikkia. "Ask yourself, why did they demand layoffs with only eight hours' notice?"

"They're as scared as Jenkins," said Nogales.

Nikkia spoke again, this time with increasing confidence. "Let me tell you about the Boston city hall. They handed down busing in the same sudden way. They hoped black and white would fight each other over the crummy schools. At the same time they froze the school budget because bigger and bigger chunks are coming out of health and education to cover the Vietnam war deficit.

"Like in Boston, just when New York's hospitals get worse and worse, city hall eliminates jobs, hoping we'll argue over what's left. They figure by laying off black and hispanics first, the rest will be glad it's not us. Especially us black professionals and the white workers."

"I know some other Filipino nurses are relieved that they're not getting laid off," said Lily.

"Our petition should say what's going on elsewhere," Nikkia said. "We want people to understand why it's happening and that there's a pattern, not just to sign their names."

By the start of the first lunch break, the petition had reached the rehab building and the Martha Graham pavillion. It read:

"We protest the layoffs of the two hundred aides and housekeeping workers at Metropolitan Hospital. Hundreds more jobs of mainly black and minority workers were lost today throughout New York City. This is a racist act by City Hall to cut the budget.

"Workers in other cities throughout the country are being affected. For example, the Boston politicians cut the school budget and pit whites against blacks over the busing issue. We are all made to pay for the billions spent in the Vietnam war, and the recent losses in the auto and oil industries. Instead of fighting each other over these budget cuts, we choose to support our brothers and sisters.

"We the undersigned demand:
    Immediate rehiring of all workers;
    Payment for all days fired;
    No corrective action for any picketers."

The last line, underneath the space for signatures, read "JOIN THE LINE IN THE EMERGENCY ROOM NOW!"

During the first lunch break, thirty-five workers came to the emergency room. They were stopped from joining the picket. Then the security guards pushed the picketers out to the sidewalk. City cops surrounded the ring of guards. The picketers themselves numbered twenty-seven housekeeping workers and aides.

But on the outside, more workers from the hospital came to support. They stood in the street and blocked the sidewalk, cheering, "JOBS NOW!"

Gloria lived near the party headquarters. She had talked with comrades there after Nikkia called her, and a leaflet had been prepared. Gloria and a few comrades passed out the flyers to workers and passers-by. The leaflet explained the situation and the need to get rid of the whole system. Their voices joined the chants against the mayor.

"BEAME SAYS CUT BACK; WE SAY FIGHT BACK."

Nikkia had the last lunch break. She counted at least one hundred housekeepers and aides who had come to the hospital. Workers from this lunch crowded around them. Passers-by stopped, too. They filled the sidewalk to the corner of the block. Nikkia found Bonita among those supporting the picketers.

"You made it," she hugged her friend. "Have they said anything yet?" she indicated a group of administrators standing by the door to the emergency room.

"No. The cops try to push us back further. That's all that's happening."

"A hundred sixty people signed the petition already."

"METROPOLITAN WORKERS SHOW: RACIST LAYOFFS GOTTA GO."

The breath of the picketers made vapor in the air. From their position at the emergency room entrance, Caruthers, Walker and Jenkins took down names of workers who had come out.

"Just like when we were in school," Bonita said. "If you didn't behave, the teacher wrote your name on the board."

"Like boot camp," said Nikkia.

Joe Nesbitt came up beside Nikkia. "I didn't see you," she cried.

"They had me sitting inside all this time. Believe me they're upset. And they're scared."

"That bastard Caruthers," said Nikkia. "I saw what he did."

"I laugh at them," Joe told her. "They're small people."

Bonita nodded. She looked at Joe, fully five feet three, wearing thick boots, his white moustache frosted. "And you have the attitude of a giant." Nikkia looked at her watch. "I have to go. Meet you both out here after three."

But at two o'clock the administration informed all the workers that most of the two hundred would be rehired. Bennie was not. Joe Nesbitt was not.

"We're going to keep fighting until everyone is rehired," Nikkia said to Steve and Candy. And on the swing shift once again the pneumatic tubes carried messages:

"We must get all jobs back."

Then was sent around, "Demo at noon tomorrow."

Someone replied, "Tomorrow <u>morning</u>."
And so the fight continued.

x x x

When Nikkia met Joe outside at three o'clock, she didn't know what to say to him. "I'm sorry."

"I know you are," he said.

"I want to tell you that Steve, Henrietta, Candy and I are going to Caruthers' office about it tomorrow." Nikkia was afraid Caruthers wouldn't see them, but it was worth a try.

"I'd like to kill the motherfuckers myself. Excuse me."

Nikkia felt a rush of warmth and closeness at the same time she wanted to cry. She hugged him, "We'll all bury them together one fine day."

Nikkia then saw Bonita talking with a group of other aides. To Nikkia, Bonita had an ageless kind of face. Her full mouth added flexibility to her years. She could easily be twenty, or forty. When she spoke, her warmth made everyone feel good. Now she greeted Nikkia, her hands in front of her. "Hello, my friend."

"We all know about your petition." said Marylea Hopkins, one of the aides.

Nikkia shook her head. "It was people being out here that made the difference."

"Administration told us the picket lines only hurt the cause of us workers," laughed Marylea.

Bonita smiled. "They said the petition came after they had made their decision."

"Listen to this," Candy joined the little group. "Jenkins says to us, 'That rabble rouser, Nikkia Porter. She's trying to use you all to get ahead.' As if <u>they</u> haven't been using us for years and years!"

"Next they'll be saying it's your fault we got fired in the first place!" said Bonita. This last comment seemed very funny to the group of women. They stood laughing, holding onto each other.

"We need to celebrate," said Nikkia to Bonita. "Lawrence and I wanted to have you come over for supper sometime anyway. Why not tonight?"

"I'm starved," said Bonita.

They got on the subway, and Nikkia spoke above the rattle of the train. "Listen, it was a terrific day. You were really good."

"Thanks. I really enjoy showing up racists for who they are. They hate being exposed." Bonita chuckled, then asked, "Why do you suppose they hired me back and left Bennie out? We work on the same unit. It doesn't make sense."

"I think that initially they got rid of you because you're my pal. Notice they laid off all the more militant workers." Nikkia nodded toward her friend. "But then you fought back. They have to figure, what's less trouble for them in the short run. Bennie, he stayed home. It was easy to pick him off."

"Right now, for just the opposite reasons," Bonita laughed, "they must have been afraid to fire you!"

The train became very crowded at forty-second street. The two women continued to talk, but now with people standing between them. It wasn't until they got off at one hundred third that Nikkia felt she could ask, "Why don't you join Progressive Labor? You already contribute money to the party."

"I see the need to have a leading party, but I feel us blacks have to get ourselves together first. Or we'll get swallowed up."

"You know, Lawrence thinks that way, somewhat. I try to convince him otherwise." Nikkia continued to talk as they walked around a woman with a baby stroller. "The party knows we blacks, especially women, have a great understanding. We can give terrific leadership, on our jobs and in the party itself."

Bonita looked thoughtful but didn't say anything.

Eagerly, Nikkia described the Boston summer project. "I've been asked to spend time up there. It would be great if you could join us."

"I'm listening," Bonita said, taking a sideways step closer to Nikkia. But she wanted to move the subject back to Lawrence. "Do you think Lawrence is jealous of your time?" she asked. "Do you think chauvinism has anything to do with it?"

"Could be. Working closely with people takes a lot of my time. But he thinks too highly of himself to be jealous. I think it's deeper than chauvinism with him."

Bonita fingered an earring, sliding it back and forth through the hole in her ear. "He's scared, or something."

"I think he's afraid of what I'll get into. But

what really gets me is when he says we make decisions blindly, as if I haven't thought through the ideas myself. Yet he won't come see how we all discuss things."

"That helped change my mind about a communist party, being invited to club meetings and seeing what they're like," Bonita said. "I learned that communism means many people dealing with politics, not obeying one dynamic leader."

"Lawrence has no time for meetings or political involvement. His own writing is so time-consuming." Nikkia thought a moment. "But he feels he owes it to other blacks to make a success of himself. And he's careful not to be a cutthroat with the competition out there. He even tutors a few of the younger black editors."

"So why does he stay in love with someone like you, who's so active?"

Nikkia looked over at the island of bushes and dried grass that separated the Broadway of the upper West side. Downtown and uptown traffic rushed to the left and right of the cemented island. "I think partly because he feels he can't be active now himself. Lawrence has traveled a whole lot, and he's very aware of what goes on in the world. He wants change. But he does nothing about it. He's his own contradiction."

"Don't you feel lonely living with someone who doesn't share your ideas?" Bonita asked.

"He does understand the need for revolution. He was active at one time, too. But he doesn't see the need for a multi-racial party and sometimes puts the party down."

He puts you down, Bonita thought. But she didn't want to hurt her friend. She decided it would be better to ask questions than to give advice.

"We've talked about all the things he isn't: He's not your typical male chauvinist. He doesn't step over others on his ladder to success. Can I ask what attracted you to him in the first place?"

"We met in the ballet. Lawrence and I danced in the same company until I was twenty-four and he was twenty-eight. After we both quit, I kept up with some of the exercises, though I don't work out half as much as I used to. Dancing, like Lawrence, is a part of me. I haven't met anyone in the party who is as sensitive, shares my taste."

The idea of sensitivity, Bonita thought, was a notion of Nikkia's that she didn't like. It made her a bit of a snob. But Nikkia seemed to have a blind spot whenever the term came up. "Tastes can change," Bonita offered instead. "I didn't use to like Mexican food. Now I can't go a week without it."

"It's not the same," said Nikkia, staring at the traffic signal. But she thought about Bonita's remark. "I hear you," she said as the light turned green. "I get your point."

"Let me stop in the bakery there," said Bonita. "I feel we deserve a treat for dessert."

Nikkia opened the door to the sweet, warm air. "I think all the stuff for a main dish, lasagne, is home already," she thought aloud. "We're going to have a real feast."

While they waited for their number inside the bakery, she added, "We don't get a chance to talk enough at work. I tell Cyril Waddell my problems sometimes--you met him at the last meeting of the Committee Against Racism--but I don't see him every day like I do you."

"We've talked," Bonita reminded her, "But lately more about what's been going on with me. Jeez, with everything that's been happening, I haven't told you the latest: my sister finally got her own apartment. And Saleem is going to move in with me over the weekend!"

"Hey, that's cause for a double celebration!"

The elevator in Nikkia's apartment building stopped dead on the fourth floor. "I hate to get in this thing. You never know where it's going to stop. On Sundays it doesn't work at all. It knows the super isn't around on Sunday."

They walked up the remaining stairs. "I always think, when this happens in my building, what do the old folks do with their groceries . . . those high-rises with twenty some stories . . . ."

Nikkia turned the key in the lock. "Sometimes they don't eat." There were no lights on in the apartment. Her happy mood changed. Where the hell was Lawrence?

"Hi. We're here."

"I'm in the living room." He stayed there while they took off their coats.

"You did a lot to this apartment since I saw it

last."

"Thanks. Come on in the front room. I got a beautiful Navajo rug and this huge plant."

Lawrence remained with his feet stretched on the couch as they came in. The TV set was on. "Hi," he smiled.

"You remember meeting Bonita at that dance."

"Of course." Lawrence got up and shook her hand. "Can I get you some coffee, a drink? It's cold."

"All of the above." Bonita laughed. "Did Nikkia tell you what happened today?"

"You just walked in. How could she tell me." Lawrence smiled to show he hadn't meant anything by the remark.

"She might have called you from the job." Bonita sat opposite from Lawrence on a chair and straightened her spine, not leaning back.

"I didn't have time," Nikkia said, apologetically.

Bonita waved her arm in a dismissing motion. She began to talk, Nikkia filling in. As the two women spoke, one remembering to say what the other had forgotten, they wove the story.

At one point Lawrence asked, "Don't you think it's better some people get laid off than all your wages cut? That's what Beame said, that the city doesn't have the money."

"They have the money. They just bought the old maritime building across the street." Nikkia hated it when Lawrence played devil's advocate. They'd discussed this issue before. "But you're right in the sense that the whole country's in financial trouble."

"Don't we still have the highest standard of living in the world?"

"Who's this 'we'?" Nikkia asked him. "In this country millions of people live in shacks. If you mean by standard of living more boob tubes, more murderous automobiles, you know damn well that half of those are really owned by the banks." She felt herself getting angry, repeating an old argument they'd had months ago. "You watch, one day they'll make us buy this apartment just for the privilege of paying rent!"

"She's not only a Marxist but a prophet, too." Lawrence smiled at Bonita.

Ordinarily at this point, Nikkia knew, she'd go into a rage. Maybe she _had_ exaggerated; however, that was no reason for him to be insulting. But lately, in getting angry with him, she always seemed to lose. It was a lot easier to fight with Miss Jenkins! Now with Bonita here, she decided to find a reason to leave the room.

"Let me start supper."

Nikkia boiled the water and laid the big lasagne strips in it. The sausage was frying. Moving away from the stove and its crackling fry pan, she could hear for the first time what Lawrence and Bonita were saying in the living room.

"Bonita, what do you think communism is?"

Nikkia could hear only parts of Bonita's reply. "Equality . . . even though everyone won't be alike. People will have to decide who gets what, since there won't be any money . . . ."

"Don't you know that the party's really going to make all the decisions?"

Nikkia had heard him say this time and again. But now his voice sounded colder. Nikkia felt like an observer on her own life.

"Nikkia wants you to join the party," Lawrence said. "It bothers me that your friendship should result in politics."

Did Lawrence think she wasn't able to hear? Nikkia paced in the kitchen. Then she stood in relever position, on her toes with her arms stretched above her head, fingers touching, shaking. The tension felt good, but her insides hurt. He must hate her. Or think that Bonita was awfully stupid. Or both.

"Are you implying that Nikkia's using our friendship?" She heard Bonita say slowly.

"That's not what I said," Lawrence replied.

"If she to con me by being friends," Bonita went on, "she wouldn't argue with me so much."

"I meant it another way. You misunderstood, and I can't blame you," said Lawrence. "It's me that has a limited definition of friendship."

Then Lawrence turned on the stereo, and she couldn't hear the conversation any more. She went to the window and rubbed her forehead on the glass. Cold. A chill passed through her skin, like icy wind, making the fine hairs move.

Was he deliberately playing music so that she couldn't hear? Did he know she had heard part of the conversation? Did he know, too, that she wouldn't run, accusing, into the living room? Had she always been so wrong about him?

Or was he angry, too? Did he love her so much that he was afraid for her? Didn't he care what he did if only to move her away from her politics? Her friends?

The sun set, big and red-orange. Larger than it was when it was high in the sky. Somewhere, she thought, she had read that the setting sun only looked big in relation to the skyline. Why was she thinking about that now?

She watched the sun set and then calmly laid lasagne strips in the pan. Ricotta cheese. Tomato sauce. Sausage slices. More lasagne. Mozzarella cheese. As she continued the homey tasks, her stomach unknotted. She put the pan in the oven and came into the living room, smiling. "Hi. Aren't you people tired of talking about politics?"

"I was just telling Bonita," said Lawrence, "I've been in love with you since the first time I saw you dance. And I can't ever look at you without picturing you dancing." He directed his last comment to Bonita. "I'm thirty-three years old, and never wanted to marry anyone else."

Bonita's face turned up at Nikkia, and she smiled, a little half-smile. "That would make it hard to say no."

If Nikkia hadn't known her better she would not have recognized this play smile. "You bet it is," she said. And the relief of understanding between the two of them made her laugh aloud.

Nikkia looked at Lawrence, there on the couch. His dark green crewneck sweater and white shirt contrasted against the rust-colored couch. His healthy, deep almond skin. Nikkia still thought him good-looking, but there was something about the tightness of his face she hadn't noticed before. Was that the way his face had always been? She thought, we'll have a nice dinner. Relax. I won't even bring up May Day tonight. She kept the conversation on a movie they'd all seen. And when the lasagne was done, they moved to the table.

As she pulled her chair in Bonita looked around, glancing first at Nikkia, then at Lawrence. "You mentioned a couple times lately this Boston march, the summer project . . . ."

"Don't look at me," Lawrence said. "I've been trying to persuade Nikkia not to go. It's too dangerous with those thugs walking around."

"It's not that I'm not afraid," said Bonita while they ate. "But it seems to me somebody has to stand up to these creeps. The cops aren't going to, or they would have stepped in when they beat up that West Indian fellow in Boston."

"You're sure right," Nikkia's mouth was full of lasagne. It was good and spicy-hot. She swallowed. "During the rise of fascism in Europe, Hungary and Austria, the cops did nothing against the roving bands of Nazis."

Lawrence laid his fork on his plate. "The communists and left-wing parties in those countries were bigger by far than Progressive Labor. How do you expect to win with your little group?"

Nikkia and Bonita looked at each other. Nikkia spoke, "It's not strictly a numbers game, though numbers count."

"Look what we accomplished today, starting with a few to give a little leadership." Bonita put a whole cherry tomato in her mouth as if to indicate she was finished speaking.

Nikkia completed the thought. "The Communist Party of Germany was huge, but they relied on the legal system, on elections. They were even winning in the polls but didn't lead people early enough to smash the Nazis in the streets." She gave this little lecture mostly for Bonita's sake, for she knew that Lawrence was aware of the information.

"That's how Hitler won. He rigged elections, walked into office, and the communists weren't prepared to do a damn thing."

She helped herself to a second helping of lasagne. Bonita took seconds also. Lawrence could eat no more. He left some on his plate.

Nikkia tore off another slice of garlic bread. It was still warm. She no longer remembered the chill she had felt in the kitchen.

"This has been one of my happiest days—confrontations and all," said Bonita. "Maybe <u>because</u> of the confrontations."

"I was just thinking the same thing," smiled Nikkia.

Bonita left Nikkia's apartment by eight o'clock.

Her boyfriend, Saleem, worked the swing shift. She wanted to get some rest in order to be up to tell him all the news of the day. As soon as the door closed behind her, the phone rang, and Nikkia was busy until after eleven with calls.

Lawrence worked at his portable electric typewriter all the while. When Nikkia came into the bedroom, he stretched and smiled contentedly. Nikkia was feeling satisfied, too, with the plans for tomorrow. She didn't want to spoil the day, their shared mood. But she could not simply forget what she had overheard him say to Bonita. She sat on the edge of the bed to prepare herself.

"I have to tell you I didn't like the way you were talking with Bonita tonight," she said. "Not only when you were taking the side of the <u>New York Times</u> about the layoffs. But also when I overheard you treating her as if she couldn't grasp communist ideas. That I was manipulating our friendship."

Lawrence turned the chair to face her fully. "Now that you mention it, the way you make friends has been bothering me for some time. You don't choose friends like I do, or like any normal person does. You pick people who're militant or people who will let you fight their battles."

"I prefer people who fight their battles with me." Nikkia tried to keep her approach light.

"But how much can you have in common with her background? In fact, most of them at the hospital don't share your experiences. And most people in the world don't share your cultural sensibilities, or aren't as bright as you. Except perhaps for the doctors."

"Are you saying that most workers have an inferior intelligence?"

"Not ninety-nine percent. But the vast majority. Certainly the ones in the position of aides and housekeepers. You make contrived friendships with them so the person will join the party. That's manipulation. It's not natural."

Nikkia felt her mind twisting in the contortions of his arguments. She searched for the secure feeling she'd had minutes ago, when she'd entered the bedroom. The strength of her friendship with Bonita. She thought how she needed the party as well as friends with political awareness. Like she needed air and food.

"Who made you the judge of what's natural? Lack of unity among working people--that's what's unnatural."

"I'm talking about you, who I love, not masses of workers."

Nikkia always felt defensive when he brought up the issue of love. To him it was so simple. To her, so fragmented.

When she didn't respond, he continued. "I think about this all the time, as I've told you. Writing gives me space. I have this luxury more than others. More than you, you admit that. My whole concern--and most of my success--is bound up in our life together. I asked Bonita because I'm concerned for you."

Nikkia listened, partly believing him.

"I wanted to know what she thought. So that you wouldn't be disappointed in her and disillusioned, eventually, in the movement. Most of the people who were involved against the war, for instance, have gone on to get good-paying jobs. Within the system!" He indicated the typewriter. "I mean for corporations, not just free-lance."

When she started to interrupt, he put a finger to his lips. "I'm not saying <u>you</u> should. I don't even insist that you go into modeling. But I just want you to be aware there are lots of choices between being a ballerina and a communist. I could live with them all, so long as it was you. It's your future happiness I'm thinking of."

Now Nikkia had to talk. "What I'm doing right now makes me happier than I've ever been. And I would feel this way if Bonita weren't my friend. Can you understand me and not your idea of my happiness?"

"Your happiness. What <u>I</u> think is best for you. I know they don't always coincide," he laughed at himself. "I get pretty stuck in my little paper world."

She smiled, too. Her anxiety seemed to have evaporated. "And our friends might be very distinct, and that would be all right with your notion of my happiness?"

"Of course."

"My struggles on the job. You won't feel you have to instruct me in how to think politically?"

"For thousands of years, people have fought their battles." Lawrence sounded old to Nikkia, not only in the words that he said. "And many good and intelligent people have died."

He seemed so sad, as if he were mourning those very people, that Nikkia moved to stroke his cheek. While perhaps she didn't agree with him, she realized with a quiet confidence, at least she understood him better.

Chapter 2

It was early morning of the May Day demonstration. A security squad for the march assembled around an open flatbed truck containing sound equipment. They waited in front of Boston's Columbia Point housing project for the buses from other cities, scheduled to arrive that morning. The year, 1975.

Thirty-nine Progressive Labor Party comrades and friends on security wore red wool hats and red T-shirts. The police had already searched them and told them they could carry nothing in their hands, not even banners on a stick.

About a quarter mile away--in a park which lay over a hill--gathered another group of about one hundred men. They ranged in age from fifteen to fifty. They belonged to ROAR.

The Progressive Labor squad sent scouts to the park every fifteen minutes. They noted ROAR's position and numbers. The type of weapons, and how many: ROAR held chains, baseball bats and metal poles. Between nine and ten thirty in the morning the number of ROAR vigilantes grew to two hundred. So far, they stayed in a clump of trees at the edge of the park, waiting for the right moment to attack.

Boston's police, about fifty of them, also held a position that morning in the project's parking lot. The three groups formed an irregular triangle: the sound truck stationed between ROAR and the police. Buses from other parts of the east coast and the midwest were not due until 11:00 AM.

Cyril Waddell, who was one of the squad's co-captains, listened while the leading comrade from New York, Inez, outlined the situation: "You know, the police have been working with ROAR. Do you suppose they'll try to get us in a squeeze?"

Cyril rubbed at his large, sweating forehead. A brown clump of hair stuck straight up from the pressure of his hand and the moisture. His full face looked tense, his mouth in a line. "I don't think so. These bloody cops know the people in Columbia Point will be watching them. I don't think they want to expose themselves so early."

Inez was thoughtful. "They just might let ROAR attack us first and then come in." She crossed her arms, round and muscular in the T-shirt. "In fact, I think they'd love to come in while ROAR was attacking our sound truck. That way, there'd be no center for the buses to mobilize around when they arrive. We'd all be sitting ducks."

"Unless we meet the ROAR attack before they get here." Nikkia spoke. She was the other co-captain of the security squad.

"That's it." Cyril drew a diagram in the gravel with the toe of his shoe. He pointed halfway along the leg of the triangle from the sound truck to the park. He drew in the road alongside the park, where the march would go. "Most of us will have to meet up with ROAR first. We'll run up over the hill. We need to leave at least fifteen people to guard the sound truck. The surprise is the key."

"Surprise is all we have," said Inez nervously.

"I feel ready," Nikkia stated. "I'm just not sure our comrades will take my lead." Her sense of Boston's being someone else's problem had almost disappeared during the events on her job. But she had suggested Russell Brown take more responsibility for the May Day march and had argued for his co-leading security. Up until this morning her judgment seemed correct, and then Russell called to say he was sick.

"You know that the people on security trust him best," Nikkia continued. "He had two separate get-togethers with them. Then he backs out from yesterday's practice session and doesn't show up at all today. Even Pat doesn't believe he's that sick."

"I know. He's been in real low spirits lately. But they all have confidence in you. You'll be smashing." Cyril encouraged. Then he admitted, "My own knees are knocking together."

A scout came from over the hill that hid them from a view of the park. She didn't wait to catch her breath. "They're starting . . . to move out of the trees."

Boston Sunday Globe

per Co. ® * * * SUNDAY, MAY 4, 1975 Tel

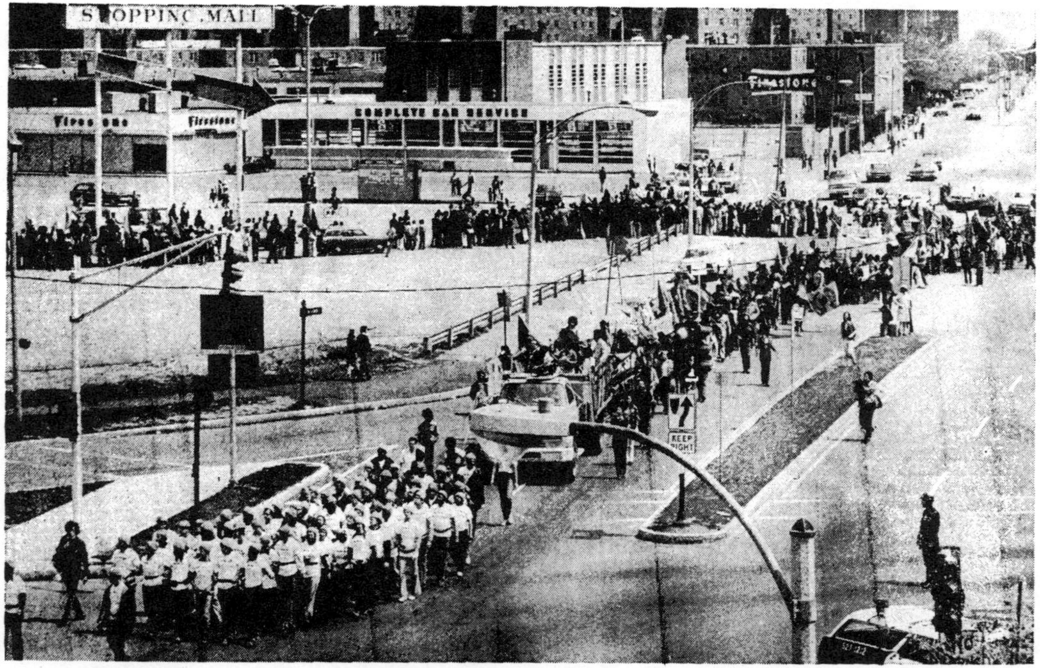

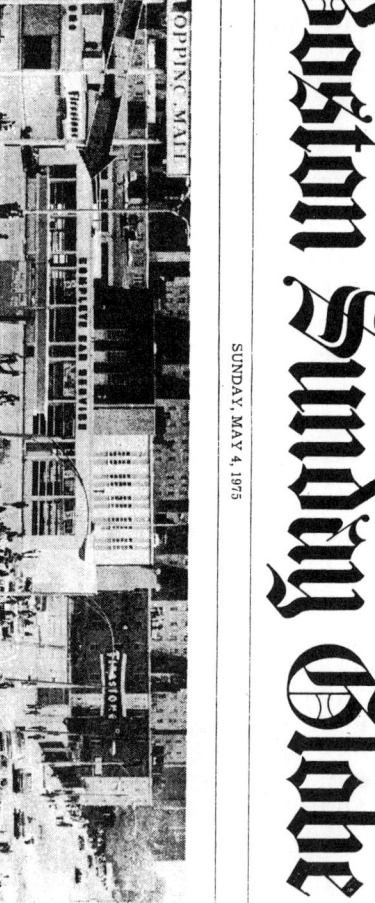

Progressive Labor Party members wind through Bayside Mall and down Day boulevard to start their march against racism. (Ted Dully photo)

Clashes mar May Day march in S. Boston

"Now listen everybody," Inez gathered everyone around. "These bastards hope to get us in a trap. Their friends in blue would love nothing better than to break up our sound truck, too. And they--not us--would greet the buses. And turn them right around.

"Instead, we've got to meet ROAR. They'll be scared shit seeing a bunch of red hats coming at 'em." Inez paused to collect her thoughts. "The sections should get together. Carole, Norberto, keep guarding the driver. Sections E and F, stay where you are by the sound truck. When I yell 'charge', A, B, C and D go straight up the hill. It's the last thing they expect."

The red hats and T-shirts moved with an awareness of order. From the sound truck where Inez stood, it seemed that everyone knew exactly what to do. They looked to her like a real army.

To each other, people spoke of their inward jitters. "I've never taken a baseball bat away from anyone in my life." The speaker, a medical student, had clear brown eyes and an athletic build.

"At least you're tall." The woman next to him with curly blonde hair happened to be shorter than five feet.

One dark-haired woman spoke to her, "You got to get on top of them. Pull them to the ground." She clenched her fists. "I'm scared, too. But they'll never stop their shit unless we stop them."

Another scout ran up to the sound truck. "They're crossing the road! In two shakes they'll be down the hill!"

At that moment Inez shouted, "CHARGE!"

Twenty-four people in red wool caps ran up the hill. The police by the housing project signaled to each other. Behind the hill the nearest ROAR group couldn't see the communists yet. They swung their bats in readiness.

At once, out of nowhere and over the hill came what seemed like waves of red hats and T-shirts. They had no bats or chains. But they swung long garrison belts.

A few people were still taking the belts off their waists. It was frightening to watch the belts being wrapped around fists. The big metal buckles slashed high then low in the air.

Seeing them, some of the ROAR men didn't even try

to cross the road. They didn't want to get a belt buckle in the face. They ran. More red hats came in close formation.

Then one of the vigilantes' bats connected with a wool hat. A lot of blood ran from under the hat, staining it a different red. Two people in red T-shirts jumped the vigilante. He went down.

A woman wearing a red T-shirt picked up the bat, swinging. The few ROAR men nearest her jumped aside and scattered. None of them waited to help their buddy.

The plan was for three red hats to attack one of the ROAR vigilantes. A group was getting another one down. Not far from there from behind a bush, crack! went a bat. And more blood. The woman in the red hat was dazed, lurching back.

Another group of three went in to hold the bat before it could swing again. One pushed the back of the vigilante's knees with her shoulders. The guy went down, and a third person in a red hat kicked him between the legs.

More of the ROAR group turned and ran. Some ran clear out of the park.

A belt buckle cut into the cheek of one ROAR man. He dropped his metal pole, eyes wide. Another vigilante saw this. He gripped his bat firmly--by the wrong end--and stumbled in his haste to get back across the road.

Two men then struggled over the metal pole, swaying back and forth. The blood of one was running over his face, but he hung on. He had lost his red hat. But that would have been no protection against the billy club that now came down on the back of his head. He let go of the pole. The thug who had been fighting him over the pole now had hold of it and swung the metal across his ear. Two cops hit at his arms and legs with their clubs.

Cops were all over the place. They held the arms of a few men in red hats, arresting them.

At the same time, the comrades could hear, "BACK! BACK!" It was Nikkia yelling to them to retreat.

The police grabbed one here, one there. Most of them were able to run, though, back over the hill to the sound truck. And there, on the main road to the parking lot, Nikkia could see a line of four or five chartered buses, one behind the other, full with

people.
"The New York buses are coming!"

Progressive Labor Party members set out from Bayside Mall. (Ted Dully photo)

Chapter 3

Russell never felt at home in Brooklyn. Not that he expected more of this neighborhood. Here was where people like him and Pat were meant to live. No house on the block was special, all of them two-family frame. There was a lot less room than in the one-family brick they'd rented in Pittsburgh. But Russell was earning more money then. His whole life spent in Pittsburgh--the steel plant, the smokestacks, the hills of the city, his friends--all now seemed as unreal to him as Brooklyn.

Yet, when he looked down their block of Avenue Y at four fifteen each morning, he felt loneliness for his friends at the plant rather than the vacantness of a sleeping Brooklyn neighborhood. Russell worked nights, seven forty-five until three forty-five in the morning. He imagined anybody's block might feel as deserted at that time, but the houses themselves appeared as strangers, closed and quiet, impossible to know.

After the last round of U.S. Steel layoffs, many of his pals couldn't afford to stay and had left Pittsburgh. Even other members of the party had had to leave during the energy crisis of the early seventies. For each of them there had been a plan, and for Russell and Pat their moving to a party center seemed most sensible. Russell's wife, Pat, being a nurse, could work anyplace. While apartment hunting, they could live for a week or two with Vitoria and Tony Morese, comrades whose children were married. The main idea was for Russell to be around more comrades to help overcome his depression at being unemployed.

"Bullshit," said Russell. "I'm not depressed. You're outa your minds. I gotta figure different is all. These are different times." But in his mind, from day one of the layoff, he'd been scared to death. He didn't want to admit to Pat or anyone how frightened he was at losing his place as a respected communist.

With Pat working at Pittsburgh Children's Hospital, the loss of income produced no immediate panic. Others were worse off, weren't they? That was one reason he was a communist, after all, because no one's job was secure under capitalism. Very privately, he would admit that he was losing a skill for which there were no longer enough jobs. He would not allow his mind to dwell on his worst remaining fear: with no future as an organizer in steel, he might lose himself.

Each morning after the layoff he woke with the sense that there was a hole instead of a floor beneath his bed. He tried to quiet his nervous stomach by saying very little. "No sense complaining." But the hole remained inside him during the day. The less he spoke to Pat and to his friends the harder it became to say what he thought. His fear grew into an ugly thing, to bury out of sight. From time to time his armpits prickled, but he could live with that.

On the other hand, watching their small savings disappear, Russell had had it with waiting for the steel industry in Pittsburgh to turn around. His muscles, once huge from working the blast furnaces, had turned to flab from disuse, then to fat. He watched the company lay off people with twenty years seniority, about to retire. Everyone got severance pay--several thousands of dollars--but it got used up quickly when they couldn't find another job in six months or more.

Pat tried to get Russell to use the severance pay to finish college, but he wouldn't. "I've got three and a half years to go--that's too long. And I don't know what I'd finish taking up," he said.

"Go in for teaching. You're so good with children. Somehow we'll live on my salary. Maybe your parents'll help out."

His parents waited a long time before replying. They didn't want to touch their one hundred thousand dollar deposit certificate. They claimed they had no other income. Russell knew better. They had put through college his youngest brother, who had always done better in school. What could he do, he asked himself, get pissed? Like when he was fourteen years old? He shrugged his shoulders.

So Pat and Russell paid some of their bills with the severance pay. As if on cue, their secondhand refrigerator broke, and a new one took the rest of the money. For twenty-six weeks Russell collected unemployment.

At first he looked for work every day. But he was in the third lay-off group. Any job that was worth anything had been taken by the others before him. Then he gave up looking.

He was used to organizing with the guys on his job. Now his friends were scattered during the day. Some of them had found work at opposite ends of the city. Two guys became fast food managers from 4:00 to 12:00 PM. They had less and less in common, it seemed. His best friend, Leo, moved to Chicago. The other fellows, who like him weren't able to find a job, seemed ashamed and unwilling to get together as much. One day McInerney actually hung up on him.

Day followed day in what seemed a different Pittsburgh. He missed the familiar work habits almost as much as seeing his friends regularly. The morning coffee--there didn't seem much point in it to him anymore. He began to watch TV until three or four in the morning to try to avoid thinking about his job.

Even so, every World War II movie about the Pacific front made him remember those movies taken by U.S. Steel of the new Japanese processes. How angry he and his friends, Quigley and Barnes, had gotten at those films! The foreman showing the movie had told them that in Japan the new Basic Oxygen Furnaces didn't leak carbon monoxide. "Why do we get stuck with furnaces that're out of joint?" Quigley had bellowed. Everyone was well aware that the company had put alarms all over the place when the furnaces became faulty. The trouble was, by the time they sounded someone was already dead.

With his eyes on the WWII movie, Russell saw in his mind a day on the job when water had gotten trapped under the slag in one of the old troughs. The instant the molten iron hit that water, the water turned to steam and caused tons of slag to erupt. The burning slag completely covered a fellow, Merv Valentino, incinerating him. Another man by the name of Kendall was blown away hundreds of feet by the blast.

The very next day they had seen a company film about the new furnaces in Japan. They were told that, after all, the Japanese did not spend so much money defending democracy in Vietnam and so could afford new furnaces. His anger rose, and Russell came out with some openly communist leaflets showing why the rulers chose to spend their capital on a war for cheap labor and natural resources. He pointed out in conversations and in leaflets how, under communism, safety would be primary. Equipment could be put underground. Hoods that didn't leak carbon monoxide would be installed. When plants were remodeled, men and women would be retrained. While they learned new skills, they'd receive the same food on their tables because the wage system would have been abolished.

Russell's position wasn't popular. Nearly all the men disagreed with his raising communism. Then management fired him. But unpopular though his radical notions were, evidently the men needed Russell, his ideas about unity and his militancy. For they walked off the job until he was rehired. Russell had been very proud of his friends, and of himself, back then. Now such good memories only became painful because all trace of that life was gone. No matter how late he slept after those late TV nights, his every problem still loomed. He finally made up his mind to move from the city he'd known for all of his thirty-four years. Of course, once in New York, there remained the problem of finding work.

It seemed natural that Pat begin job hunting first, being an O.R. nurse with a skill in demand, while Russell worked at unpacking. That turned out to be the right decision, for after a physical exam following her first interview, Pat started work the very next day.

Meantime, in the job of straightening their second floor apartment of the two-family house, nine-year-old Al was a big help. And one of Russell's younger sons, Marvin, although only six, already had an organized mind. He had numbered the boxes back in Pittsburgh: one through fifteen for the kitchen, and so on. Four year old Jerry entertained little Tammy for long hours. The helter-skelter furniture and boxes made wonderful children homes. Sometimes Russell joined in the play.

The living room became a great campground with upside down chairs as tents and box mountains. Each child could have his own tent or move chairs together with the couch for two or three or everyone, including Russell. They always had lunch on a mountain top. It was more interesting than regular rooms and much more fun than school or work. In fact, they were quite surprised at Pat's being angry when on the fourth day she came home to find them still playing in the living room, none of them wanting to put it to order.

And so on the fifth day, Russell took their children to P.S. 193 to register them in school. There was a pre-kindergarten, mornings only, and that would be great for Jerry. Quite suddenly, the apartment seemed empty with only two-year-old Tammy, as empty as the indoors can be with an active toddler. And it wasn't as relaxing in the apartment as in the Pittsburgh house.

Perhaps that was partly because Russell's big lounger was gone. There simply wasn't room for everything they'd had. It was his own suggestion to get rid of it. He'd felt good about giving it to Hank, the old custodian at the Y in Pittsburgh. But now he missed it. Tammy used to be able to nap right in it, Russell recalled, while he read or dozed. These days she didn't seem to want to give him a rest without that chair.

He spent hours just watching her tire him out. He got to know her better than the boys, although at first he thought it would be impossible to get to know a girl so well. "What do you do with a girl?" he had asked himself.

Tammy--Tamarinda--was the only girl, and the baby, in a family of boys. But she remained bald until she was one and one-half years old. "What a healthy-looking baby boy," said strangers to Tamarinda in Russell's shopping cart. One day he found a lacy hat to go with a gift outfit, and he dressed her up. She looked like the old comedian, W. C. Fields. And so he took off the hat. Yet it pained Russell now to remember that Pat had defended Tamarinda as the most perfect, beautiful baby. These days, Pat seemed to regard Tammy as more without fault than anyone else in the family, including Russell himself.

"Tamarinda never smiles," Russell used to complain. He would tickle her tummy, like he had always done with the boys, and she wouldn't laugh. When they got her she was eight months old, and for the first six weeks afterwards, Tamarinda would cry when Pat wasn't holding her. Nursing at Pat's breast seemed to be the only cure for the colic, and later for cranky moods.

"You can't keep her on breast milk forever," said Russell.

"I was lucky my milk didn't stop completely after Jerry. You've got to give an adopted baby every chance." Pat was firm on this. "Tammy was so skinny when we got her. Remember how she thrived."

Russell couldn't deny the fact that Tammy had been underweight when they met the plane from Rio de Janeiro. The veins protruded along her scalp. She was on some Pet milk formula. She vomited most of that. Pat's closest friend in the O.R., Elvira, pronounced that Tammy wouldn't make it.

That all seemed like a long time ago now to Russell. But he remembered exactly what happened when the Pittsburgh children's hospital changed their weekend policy. They forced even the operating room nurses to work every other weekend on the floors. When Pat had to work weekends, Tammy wouldn't stop crying no matter what Russell did. Trying to keep Tamarinda quiet with the small supply of breast milk Pat left him, even along with the solid food, was impossible. He would switch her over to regular milk, but somehow Pat would always discover the difference. "I can tell by her stools," she said.

Russell was beginning to wonder whether adopting a baby outside the state adoption agencies had been such a good idea.

"It's the only way to get a girl in Pittsburgh," Pat had said.

Again, she was absolutely right. The adoption agencies had few girls. If one came up for adoption, she would go to a family with no children that wanted a girl, not to one that already had three boys. And paying a lawyer twenty thousand dollars was out of the question. Even if they had had that kind of money, so large a sum would have gone into the purchase of a house. Pat wasn't an impractical person.

When Russell started dating Pat, her parents told him how they had been amazed at the way Pat could think for herself at a very early age. They bragged how she could read before she entered the first grade. Her father drove a truck, and her mother was a nurses' aide. Of Pat's six brothers, recalled Russell, not a single one of them graduated from high school. They were all so proud of their girl.

Pat's mother and father hadn't exactly come right out and said that she and Russell should have a girl, but each time Pat became pregnant, Pat's mother made one of her prophecies: You're carrying high; that's just like a girl." And when the boy would come, Pat's mother spent every cent of her salary for weeks, as if every boy were the first. She did the same, in equal proportion, for all the girl and boy children her sons had, and she never could figure Russell's parents' attitude toward money.

Not one of the grandparents, however, agreed at first to the notion of adopting a child from another country. And when Pat initially raised the idea with Russell she didn't expect him to see her point of view. "You grew up with all brothers and were right in the middle. You might not understand my feeling. I'd like to adopt a girl without trying our luck again."

But Russell had understood.

Now that Tammy was almost three years old, Russell still felt they had made the right decision. Being in the house with her alone all day long let him see things about her he hadn't known. Her sense of fairness, for example. He suggested coloring a picture to surprise Mommy, and she brought him two. "'Prise you, too, Daddy!"

That first week in the Brooklyn apartment was hell, though, for Pat and Russell compared to the constant companionship of Vitoria and Tony in their orderly place. Russell had forgotten to put everything up higher--the way they had their plants and books in the Pittsburgh house--and he had to buy childproof locks for the low kitchen cabinets. Fixing a clogged drain pipe while managing the children the second day in the house took Russell sixteen hours.

But Russell wasn't looking for daycare for Tammy just yet. He felt they couldn't afford it now like they had on weekdays in Pittsburgh, though it would mean company for Tammy. He decided that he could make up for the past half year's unemployment by caring for Tammmy himself during the day and being home after school for the other children. He told Pat and the Brooklyn comrades that he had trouble settling for any job that paid less than steel. But after almost a year off the job, the truth was that with every passing day, he was losing more confidence in his organizing ability.

The people in the party suggested he get a job in the post office, where they had a concentration of party members. One of the women in the party, Jeanine, lived in the Flatbush section of Brooklyn and was home with her small baby. She offered to watch Tammy when he went to the main post office. Russell could find no more excuses.

Jeanine suggested he go immediately. "The economy's rotten," she urged, "soon the post office will even stop taking on temporaries." However, that night Russell came down with the flu. He could do nothing but stay home with Tammy for over two weeks. Then the very day he made up his mind to go the post office they announced a hiring freeze.

Hearing of Russell's discouragement, Tony invited Russell over for a beer. "You shouldn't feel obliged to grab the first thing that comes along," Tony stated. "These small metal shops, for instance, don't pay anything,"

Tony sensed but didn't mention the fear behind Russell's delay at the post office. He anticipated that Russell might take a job where he'd be very isolated. He'd say it was for the money, but it would be out of personal insecurity, to be "doing something." This was what Tony remembered he himself had done after the first time he'd been fired. What he said was, "I'd like to offer to lend you some cash till you get a job where you can use your organizing skills."

"Absolutely not," said Russell abruptly. He reminded himself of McInerney, but he couldn't help it.

"OK, man, OK," said Tony, not wanting to press Russell. Here was a guy, Tony thought, who was a crackerjack union organizer. If Russell didn't know firsthand the importance of getting into a good situation, Tony felt he couldn't hit him over the head with it. "But we all know that getting something halfway decent could take a couple months."

One week longer was too much for Russell. After the post office experience, he became afraid he might never take home a paycheck again. Stubbornly, he took a UPS job loading trucks at night, six nights a week. This meant he would be unable to come to regular party meetings for awhile, he knew. But the pace wasn't too demanding, and the two guys on his platform seemed OK.

Pat was surprised he took the job. "I can still get the children ready for school and save money with no day care for Tammy." What he didn't foresee was something Pat pointed out right away. "How are you going to get to know these guys away from the job?" He told Pat, the people in his party club and himself that it was only temporary.

What Russell also couldn't know was how he would react to working all night. Even though the house was quiet, he couldn't sleep when he got home at four-thirty. His feet were cold from hefting boxes outdoors, and they seemed to keep his whole body awake. So the hours from four-thirty until seven were often restless.

He didn't want to get up and read or watch television. The thermostat was turned down at night in the house, and he felt guilty turning it up just for himself. To heat up the rooms took an hour anyway. But Russell took some comfort in lying in bed awake next to soundly sleeping Pat. He forced himself to block out the larger, troublesome thoughts: the loading platform, with just a couple guys, made a lousy organizing situation; he was making two-thirds of Pat's salary. Little things seemed to climb into his consciousness, though. Unpleasant things, like bells to awaken his nerves.

Russell had a lot of hours those early mornings to think about the times his parents had disappointed him. One incident that hurt occurred when his mother refused to let him bring Tammy over to the neighbors. "They won't accept her," she said out of her own prejudice. He took her anyway but still got upset thinking about his mother's attitude. Then Russell would go over the times he had yelled at his own children the day before. He felt badly that his impatience was beginning to be a part of the morning routine.

Pat had to be at the hospital by six forty-five, and she kept her fresh uniform over the ironing board in the living room so as not to disturb him at six. She worried when he told her he couldn't get those first few hours of sleep. Russell got so he pretended to be asleep. As luck would have it, he was often just relaxed enough to doze off when the alarm rang at seven.

Or he would waken to the sounds of Al and Jerry

fighting. Jerry usually woke without an alarm. He would leave Tammy asleep in the room he shared with her to see what Al would be up to. From the bedroom that Al and Marvin used, Russell would hear, "Jerry's standing on my clothes."

Marvin tried to stay out of it. He was six and already reading on a third grade level. He left his and Al's room early, dressed and ready for breakfast. He didn't enjoy the play-fighting, and in fact had never wanted to tag along with Al. Pat suggested a system of taking Jerry's clothing out the night before and putting it in the living room. There, sometimes Russell could get Jerry dressed separate from Al. But Tammy often woke up at this very moment, in some way aware that she was alone.

Then Russell had to stop everything and change her and keep one eye on her so she didn't get into anything. Already, at two and one-half, she could climb further and faster than any of the boys had ever done. Mostly, Russell told Tammy "no," trying to ignore the yells of Al and Jerry.

By eight-fifteen the boys were out of the house, and Russell was ready to sleep. But Tammy wasn't, and from his spot on the couch Russell's inner clock jabbed him alert to check on her activity. He would find it easiest to play with her. She loved ball. She loved sock puppets. And then, gratefully, he would watch her ease into her morning nap. If it weren't for her naps, he thought, he would totally lose it. At eleven fifteen, he had to leave to pick up Jerry from pre-K, and so his morning sleep had to be a nap, too.

Many mornings the nap dream would be the same. He was lying in a sunny field surrounded by a forest. He dozed on the grass and lazy clouds touched his eyelids. Then always he felt, or heard, the danger of men he could not see. They were walking toward him from within the forest. He never saw them but he had to run.

There was nowhere to go but toward the forest. He couldn't find a path. His feet twisted in underbrush. His body grew heavier. He ran until he had no breath. He had to hide somewhere--a bush, a tree--the place was different each time. But he could go no further.

He hid. These agents would kill him if they found him. He sweated. That was worse than the running. While he waited sweating, under the bush, one eye in his dreaming mind could see his exposed feet. Or if he was behind a tree, his dreaming eye could see parts of his body sticking out beyond the tree.

They found him. As he knew they would. Never--for the life of him--could he foresee this when he first began to run. So it was with relief that each day when they found him he woke up. Now all he had to think about was picking up Jerry. And each day taking Tammy to meet Jerry, he forgot about the dream.

On their walk to P.S. 193 Tammy would bustle beside him with her little swish-hip movements. He carried her across the one busy street. This was their most active time--he was too tired to go outside with her earlier, though she seemed to enjoy the cool fall weather. But this walk they had to take, and they made the most of it.

"See the doggy in the car. Whose doggy?" Russell would lift her up so she could see inside a parked car.

Tammy often saw things he did not, "Man doggy." She pointed to a neighbor walking toward the car.

Garbage at the curb was most interesting to her. "Bargage," she called it. Tammy swish-swayed to the piles of plastic bags, olive-green garbage cans and stacked kitchen chairs. She noticed the formica shell of a television with the screen missing, "EEEVEE."

Sometimes they brought home a treasure, like the small doll dresser they found with two drawers missing. But that third drawer could be opened, shut, opened, to make a dolly bed, a place for pennies and to hide Daddy's keys. Daddy was so surprised each time he found them in the little drawer.

They stretched the five minute walk to fifteen. Russell moved slowly during their short walk to Jerry's school. His world was a twilight of sounds. The noise level he perceived became shaded to protect his overtired brain. He had to look carefully as they crossed Broad Street, not trusting his senses. Once at the schoolyard, he let Tammy run ahead in all her energy, to meet the jumping Jerry.

Russell almost resented the intrusion of Jerry into the little twosome, for Jerry commanded all Tammy's attention. Sometimes he would tell Jerry to run ahead to spy for cars at each corner so that he and Tammy could prolong their "fun time" together. If it had rained, there would be just time for their quick game of finding the first worm and placing it gently back on the grass.

The trip home took much less time. "What's for lunch?" Jerry asked this question every morning as the three of them paused at the door while Russell fiddled with his keys. This inevitable question seemed to mark the day. And, in a way, it was a signal for Russell to move from junk food to serious eating.

His continuously over-tired state made him crave quick energy. He found himself wanting snacks he'd never liked. He used to hate Twinkies. The sugary sponge over sugar-creme made his teeth slide. But now he couldn't wait to open the cellophane and touch the domes of moist cake. He ate them every day as soon as Tammy was asleep in her morning nap; otherwise she would want bites, and they weren't good for children.

Chocolate cupcakes with filling he reserved for the job. He would be exhausted, and thirsty, and the thought of biting into the hardened chocolate icing and smelling the chocolate rich cake beneath made him almost insane with wanting. He had to have a cold Pepsi with them, sometimes two packages of cupcakes.

The thought of cupcakes make his ham or bologna sandwiches seem a mere prelude, like a cigarette smoker's meal before the first deep inhale. He gulped his sandwiches, they were incidental. And bags and bags of cheese doodles and potato chips sustained him in-between.

A large bag of barbecue chips, Russell supposed, could be compared to the way a six pack of beer or a bottle affected certain people. Finishing one might make you over-filled or even nauseous. Yet you found that the next day you had to have another. After the first bite of the tangy barbecue or the roll of his tongue around the salty coating of cheese, Russell had to keep eating. There never was enough in one bite except a crisp crunch, some air and the hint of food. After eating the whole bag, rather than being satisfied, he felt bloated with sewer gas.

It took Russell's body several hours to recover from the snacks at work and mid-morning. His need for real food again came most sharply when Jerry asked him for lunch. He was happy while preparing food for the children.

Today, as he spread peanut butter on soft white

bread, the pressure made a bigger dent than usual and tore the sandwich. The ripped bread seemed in a strange way to make Russell sad, and he looked out the window, down to the back yard. But the glass was filmy with soot and rain streaks, and he could barely see the outlines of the children's swing set and playhouse. The thought of washing the window made him shake his head, no.

"What's the matter, Daddy?" asked Jerry.

"Nothing." The soup sputtered in the gas flame as it boiled over onto the burner. Russell turned it off. "Shit."

"Ooh. Daddy said a swear," Jerry crooned.

"You'll have to wait to eat your soup in a few minutes after your sandwich, kids," Russell pretended to ignore them. "I let it boil over."

"Ah, Daddy," said Jerry. "It won't be no good."

"You're going to eat it," Russell said, through his teeth. And then, more softly, "I'll have some, too, and you'll see it's OK."

With lunch over--Russell ate two helpings of everything, including two apples--he could begin to relax a little more. He read and dozed, while Jerry and Tammy played. Then at two, they all napped. Tammy and Jerry in their room, Russell on the couch--in case either of the two wandered out.

Russell was usually so tired by this time that the minute he put a handkerchief over his eyes he only knew black sleep. But sometimes he had time for a last cheerful thought. Pat would be getting home right after Al and Marvin. Which was the most pleasant to think about? Seeing her, energetic and happy; having her lift the weight of the children from his mind; or, contemplating almost four hours of real sleep.

Chapter 4

The fifth bus from New York City arrived at Columbia Point. At this time the ROAR forces were still scattered throughout the park. And as for the police, their fifty men--who they thought would be enough against a lesser number of unarmed women and men--were also dispersed. The comrades had done their job.

Some of the comrades were being held in the police cars. Ten in red hats were arrested. Not one member of ROAR. Cyril took with him two demonstrators to go and find out in which precinct the arrested comrades would be. More police cars and a police van pulled up. At the same time four other New York buses drove into the parking lot. The crowd numbered more than eight hundred.

One of the doctors in Progressive Labor told Inez she could see no serious head wounds, although there was a lot of blood. That was the nature of head wounds, she said. Only one person would need stitches, Frank Donovan, who had been hit by the metal pole. The doctor announced to everyone that he was on the way to the hospital and had been damn lucky.

The short blond woman took off her red hat and used it to wipe sweat from her face and neck. She turned to the medical student next to her, who had been by her side before the charge. "Once we started running," she said, "I didn't have time to be scared."

"When I saw you run, I wasn't afraid, either," he laughed.

Nikkia overheard their conversation. "And you're among the most advanced comrades. You'll have to help us convince a lot of people to take a militant stand around the question of busing before they come to the summer project. Most folks in and around the party aren't won to the need for violence against ROAR."

"If we don't convince them," the blond woman answered, "ROAR will."

Before Nikkia could respond, Inez asked her to begin organizing the march formations. Nikkia passed the directions to the rest of the security members: six abreast, arms linked. While getting into their rows, the marchers talked. People in one row related the story about the fight. "They didn't know what they'd find over the hill." "The ROAR guys reeked of booze something fierce." And, "You should have seen how many turned and ran!"

Buses came one after another over the next half hour: Atlanta; Washington, D.C.; New Jersey; Philadelphia; Detroit and Chicago. Many people had been on the road all night. One thousand seven hundred fifty marchers in all.

More individuals from ROAR appeared, too. Gradually they all came out of the woods. They lined the road from Columbia Point to the area of greater Boston known as Dorchester.

Much of Boston's police force had been delegated to motorcycle duty. They revved their engines. More police arrived to stand along the ridge of the hill and along the road beside the park. And there were some on horseback, as if to protect the nearly two thousand marchers from a hundred fifty individuals from ROAR.

Five people from the other cities joined Inez on the sound truck. They led the marchers in chants.

Other security forces had been organized in each city's area prior to the march. At this time they put on their own red hats and joined the Boston-New York forces at the front and rear of the march. Others helped organize the growing line of marchers. There were some disruptions before the march got started.

One man who appeared to be drunk shook his finger at the Philadelphia banner, "BE BOLD. CRUSH RACISM." He was firmly turned aside by three security people.

A woman dressed in a turban and long African dress swept up to the line of marchers. Two men walked behind her and out of the way of her flowing garb: She was like a boat with a wake. The woman got next to the line, surprising Nikkia who stood on security. Nikkia had been assigned to stay near some of the people she knew: Steve Tobias, Bonita, Saleem and Joe Nesbitt. Pat, Russell's wife, stood between Bonita and Steve.

The woman with the turban pointed a finger at Pat. "You, Whitey, where do you think you're taking my brothers and sisters?"

A security marshall from Boston approached Nikkia and whispered, "She's in the NAACP. I was at a meeting of theirs around the Andrea Jean Louis affair. She'll try to heckle the march. Ignore her, if that's possible, because we're about to start."

Nikkia nodded, "Stay near and alert five or six more security. I'll make a decision if we have to get rid of her, physically."

The woman continued to direct her efforts at Pat. "We don't need you to fight our battles for us."

Pat clenched her fists, looking at Nikkia out of the corner of her eye.

"And you, sister," the woman addressed Bonita. "We've been watching you. Get away from the line. They want to make this march look integrated. Get smart."

Bonita narrowed her eyes. She kept her arms linked to Pat and Joe. "You're no sister of mine," she said sharply. "I saw you over there earlier talking with the police. Get back with your buddies."

Suddenly, before Nikkia could stop them, the two men accompanying the woman formed a wedge so that she could get between the rows of marchers. Surprised at the push, the people in the row in front of Bonita and Pat turned their heads. Their arms remained linked. The woman made one more step so she stood directly in front of Pat. She spat in Pat's face.

As one, the Boston marshall and Nikkia grabbed the woman's arms. Steve tried to pull away from Pat, to help. "Let security handle it," Pat cried. "That's what they want, to get the line fighting them."

Nikkia's knee came up quickly and hit the woman's stomach. The woman made a grunting sound and spat again in Pat's direction. The marshall from Boston held her arms. Nikkia hit her in the face with one closed fist. The other marshall twisted her arm as Nikkia pushed her chin. The woman's head snapped back, her turban fell off and she went down. Nikkia lost her balance and fell also, hard on her side.

At the same time, six marshalls grabbed the two bodyguards. The men went without a protest. Meanwhile, the woman got to her knees, reaching for her turban among the legs of the marchers. The turban, its insides stuffed with tissue paper, rolled further away in the wind. Half crawling, the woman scrambled after it.

Two marshalls helped Nikkia to her feet. "I didn't know what she was up to at first."

"It's the costume," said the Boston marshall. He smiled, "It's amazing how we tend to respect a uniform."

"I sure didn't see her talking with the cops," Nikkia said to Bonita. "That was right on."

"I notice those things," Bonita said.

A member of the medical team brought Nikkia some antiseptic and a gauze square. Her arm was badly scraped and some gravel had gotten under the skin. The nurse cleaned her arm. Nikkia grimaced.

For a moment, Bonita left Pat and Steve to see how Nikkia was. "I'm impressed," she told Nikkia, "that Pat didn't break up the line and take her on right there on the spot."

"She's a very disciplined person," smiled Nikkia.

"As I watched you handle that woman, I remembered seeing her cozying up to the police. She was trying her damnest to hold back progress. I realized how it really matters to me that I'm a part of the force moving workers forward."

Nikkia looked at her friend. She felt proud, hearing Bonita say things that had taken her, Nikkia, years to realize. And now the person saying these words, was also her close friend.

"I think," Bonita continued in her careful way, "I should join the party."

Nikkia looked at her, and blinked tears away. "That's great!" She gave her friend's shoulder a little push.

"We're starting!" The chanting began again.

"FIGHT FOR COMMUNISM. POWER TO THE WORKERS!"

The marchers moved out, straight for the hill, the road, and the city of Boston. As the beginning of the march crested the hill, they could see the ROAR youths behind the cops. Some of them stayed behind the bushes in the park. They threw rocks at the marchers.

The marchers dodged. Marshalls on the sound truck passed out cardboard signs to those marching. Bonita read the CAR trade union demand that was printed on the signs, "30 hours' Work for 40 Hours' Pay." It meant a step forward in the long battle for a shorter work week. She recalled the history behind the very first May Day, the workers who were shot down fighting for an eight hour day.

The New-York Times

NEW-YORK, TUESDAY, MAY 4, 1886.

BLOODSHED IN CHICAGO

INITIATING THE EIGHT-HOUR FIGHT WITH BROKEN HEADS.

FIERY SPEECHES INCITE LUMBERMEN AND OTHERS TO ACTS OF VIOLENCE—THE FREIGHT HANDLERS' DEMANDS.

CHICAGO, May 3.—The eight-hour movement spilled its first blood to-day, and Joseph Vojtek, a lumber shover 18 years old, was fatally wounded, and a dozen more strikers, with bullet holes in their bodies, represented the result of the first encounter. There was a collision at McCormick's Reaper Works between a mob of 7,000 or 8,000 anarchist workmen and tramps, maddened with free beer and free speech, and a squad of policemen. More than 500 shots were fired and hundreds of windows in the works were stoned. There are broken heads and bruised bodies all through the lumber district

of which he said that during the last three months and three weeks the earnings of the company had decreased $358,823, as compared with the earnings of the same period last year. By the end of the month the decrease would have reached $400,000, and in all probability before the end of the year, through labor disruptions and disorganized trade, the decrease would reach $800,000. Nearly every employé had experienced a decrease of from 10 to 20 per cent. In its earnings. The laboring classes, therefore, in view of these concessions, had struck at the wrong time. The only outcome of this movement was that they would remain out, lose money, injure their families, and return to their old places at the same rates.

The men listened quietly to Mr. Jeffrey's remarks, thought they saw at once what the reply of the company was. When he had finished, all the men, to the number of 150, quit work, marched over to the headquarters of the Freight Handlers' Union and joined that organization. The Michigan Central's men remained at work and will not go out before Wednesday night, when the company has promised to reply to the demand for an advance of 25 cents a day or 1 hour. The Baltimore and Ohio freight handlers worked, along with the quota given the company till Friday to reply to a demand for higher wages.

THE GRÆCO-TURKISH CRISIS.

SPEAKER H[...]

A CHANGE IN TH[...] OF TH[...]

ALBANY, May 3.— [...] varied the proceed[...] night. Ex-Speaker [...] chair and Speaker [...] down into the well. [...] nificent picture of t[...] rested upon the repr[...] the entire Assemb[...] most artistic pieces [...] crayon, faithfully [...] as he is to-day, after [...] 16 years, the longest [...] lot of any citizen of [...] standing erect, his r[...] gavel, which was pr[...] Speaker who preside[...] old Capitol, that of [...] It will never be d[...] most conspicuous o[...] trails. The artist [...] attitude that illus[...] perfection. As th[...]

While she marched, Bonita thought about how a thirty hour work week in a hospital would create four six-hour shifts, more jobs. Then a rock struck her signboard, and she put it closer to her face. The cardboard shielded the other marchers, too, as they held it against their heads.
"THIRTY HOURS' WORK FOR FORTY HOURS' PAY!"

WATCH OUT!—Demonstrators use placards and hands to ward off rocks and bottles being thrown from Old Colony Road.
Staff Photo by Mike Andersen

A skinny, young white girl came running and giggling up the line with a big rock in her hand. She got ready to throw it, and when two marshalls stepped toward her, one of the cops put his arms around her. As he led her away, she screamed after the march, "I'll get you, you fucking commie bastards."

The line crossed over a bridge. Below the bridge, ROAR forces were throwing rocks up. They had no aim, throwing as they did from under the bridge. The cardboard signs stopped the few rocks that found a target in the line of marchers.

The heaviest rain of rocks landed on the motorcycle police who were nearest the side of the bridge. They revved the engines on their machines and tried to duck. The rocks hit the cops' helmets. They drove off the bridge. But not in single file order. They ran into each other, bumping motorcycles. The marchers laughed.

"SMASH RACISM. DEMAND BETTER SCHOOLS."

The march passed through a long stretch of vacant land. To the marshalls alongside this seemed like the perfect place for an ambush, with no place for the demonstrators to run. But they noticed that the ROAR men appeared to be equally afraid of open spaces, and there were no incidents.

At last, the march entered the integrated area of Dorchester. Some people who had been assigned to sell the Progressive Labor Party newspaper, <u>Challenge</u>, left the line at this time. They heard a shout, "That's the way!" The marchers looked up to a welcome sight: Boston residents leaning from their windows.

"THE WORKERS, UNITED, WILL NEVER BE DEFEATED!"

Their chants rang off the apartment houses. Here, ROAR would not openly attack the marchers. Only handfulls of jeering men stood in the doorways of the occasional corner taverns. The marchers, every one of them, felt victorious. As they continued through a shopping section, here and there, people joined with them to the end.

Ahead was the park where the march would stop, and where a food truck held box lunches. Nikkia stepped over to the side for a moment to look at the long line of marchers. The red flags, satin and shining, glowed, "FIGHT FOR COMMUNISM." Yellow banners saying "30 Hours' Work for 40 Hours' Pay," bounced along. Many people on the march were young--some had brought children although asked not to. Others were older. Nikkia spotted Joe Nesbitt.

He turned around his cardboard 30 For 40 sign. On the other side he showed her a large picture of Karl Marx he had carried during the march. Nikkia grinned.

"I had my most restful days off. My wife is glad I got fired. She thinks we're well rid of the place." He confided. "I been figuring to get back at Caruthers."

Nikkia knew Joe's being fired had been eating away at him since January, but she had not been able to get a group of people to confront Caruthers. "There's not a worker in the place that doesn't want you back and Caruthers fired. And they have long memories," she said. "We're not finished yet."

The march entered the park, still in formation.

"HITLER, HICKS. SAME OLD TRICKS."

The security squads formed a giant circle around the marchers, who now began to spread out, and sit down, on the hill. Kids were draping the red flags around their backs. The sun shone through the young leaves.

Some of the security passed out the box lunches and soda. An auto worker from Detroit gave a talk from the sound truck. He talked about how the UAW leadership worked with the General Motors bosses to push through the layoffs of thousands of auto workers.

Nikkia handed a carton of lunch boxes to Pat and Steve. As she did, Pat said, "Did I get a chance to say how terrific you were?"

"I think it's harder to do what you did," said Nikkia. "You managed not to get into it."

"By the way, I'm sorry about Russell today," said Pat. "I still don't know if he really tried to get a baby sitter."

"He's got to decide to quit that job." said Nikkia.

"I'm going to light a fire under him," Pat smiled. "He doesn't know it yet, but I called my mother. She's agred to come live with us in July, if I can just get Russell to go along with my great plan."

"What's your proposal?"

"That he spend a whole month in the Boston summer project!"

PLP Leads Charge vs. Fascists

BOSTON, May 3—A gigantic blow was struck against fascism in the U.S. when over 2,500 workers and students, evenly divided between black, Latin and white, celebrated the historic international workers' holiday of May Day in a militant march through working-class Boston.

Led by communists in the Progressive Labor Party, members of PLP, Workers Action Movement (WAM)—who also endorsed the march—and a score of caucuses and unions, all sent the cry of "DEATH TO THE FASCISTS!" ringing through the skies over Boston which has become the cradle of a mass-based fascist movement centered around Louise Day Hicks' Nazi organization, R.O.A.R. (Restore Our Alienated Rights).

The marchers had picked Boston for the annual East Coast May Day march this year because it symbolizes in name and in fact the rise of a fascist movement around the busing issue directed against black working-class families but intent on destroying the unity of all workers, diverting us from fighting on the real issues of jobs, for 30 for 40, and against racism itself.

The leadership given by communists in PLP was signalled by the call to "Fight for Socialism!" which was pointed out as the real and ultimate answer for workers oppressed by capitalism and threatened by fascism. Many workers and students either joined, or expressed the desire to join, PLP or PLP study/action groups. The marchers, the majority of whom were not PLPers, graphically understood the life the leadership provided by communists and communist ideas in the fight against fascism. And they understood how communists carry on the militant tradition of May Day by directing the organized strength of the working class against the most virulent section of the class enemy, for on this May Day, 1975, the fascists were routed in their own back-yard.

Part of a simultaneous May Day effort that saw marches take place around the continent, in Detroit, Houston, Toronto and Los Angeles, the Boston marchers began arriving in the assembly area at Columbia Point, adjacent to South Boston (the home of R.O.A.R.) at about 10:00 A.M. from Boston itself and as far away as Durham, N.C., Washington, D.C. and Baltimore, as well as later on from New Jersey, Buffalo, Connecticut, Philadelphia, Long Island and New York City. (According to the **Boston Globe**, May 4, "Police estimated that 2500 persons eventually marched.")

BOSSES DENY PERMIT FOR SOUTH BOSTON

The Boston PLP had applied for a permit to march through South Boston, where the Hicks-Kerrigan fascists have made their home base (organizing a national R.O.A.R. organization in 11 states from there). However, Boston's rulers feared the working-class unity-against-fascism message that might get across to the workers of South Boston, many of whom had greeted PLP and WAM members in March and April leafletting for May Day. So they denied the permit, "offering," instead a route through downtown Boston where absolutely no one would see or hear the marchers.

The March organizers refused to accept this dead-end, appealed the ruling, and thereby forced the City to issue a permit for a march through the area adjoining South Boston, along Columbia Road through Dorchester, a combined white, integrated, and black working-class area, all of which was plastered with May Day posters.

However, scores of workers and students **DID** break the ban on anti-fascist demonstrating in South Boston by picketing Hicks' home in the rich section of that area earlier in the morning. Then they proceeded to the main assembly at Columbia Point. It was then that the biggest battle of the day took place, in which the fascists were routed, despite the presence of hundreds of cops, armed to the teeth.

While organizers were setting up the sound system and making preparations to receive the thousands soon to arrive, scouts on a hill nearby sighted about 75 fascists—out of a group of maybe 200—moving towards the assembly area with clubs, baseball bats and sawed-off hockey sticks. They raced to alert those in the assembly area.

March leaders immediately recognized the fascists' plan, obviously coordinated with the cops (who were applauding the fascists as they made their move): to attack the early marchers and give the cops the pretext to move in with swinging clubs, smash the sound system, and use the melee as an excuse to cancel the march as an "incitement to riot." (This was mentioned as a warning shortly afterwards by the police chief in the area to a March leader.) Then the rest of the fascists' supporters could take over the entire Mall assembly area and "greet" the main body of buses soon to *(continued on page 3)*

(continued from page 2)
arrive with rocks and prevent the marchers from even assembling, much less marching. But this May Day the fascists' plan was not to be.

The March leaders, especially the communists in PLP, had organized to meet the fascist threat, having recruited many members and friends in the preceding weeks into a Fighters Group which would defend the march in a militant, organized way. As the scouts arrived with the message of the impending fascist attack. Derek Pearl, a leader of PLP and WAM, took the mike on the sound truck and alerted the gathering Fighters Group: "Attack! Attack!" (See "Battle of Columbia Point").

FIGHTERS

The heroic action of these Fighters had maintained the security of the assembly area. However, the cops attempted one more foray. About 75 on motorcycles began encircling the still small group of 100 or so early arrivals near the sound truck. At that point Pearl led the workers and students in the singing of the international communist anthem, the Internationale, and the union song "Solidarity forever," as well as militant chants of "Death to the Fascists!" This united the people in a tightly-knit manner, in defiance of the cops' attempt to terrorize them. After 15 or 20 minutes, these uniformed fascists gave up and left the immediate assembly area.

Soon afterwards the main body of buses began arriving, hundreds streaming off to hear the results of this early battle and inspired to make this May Day one to remember. The Fighters Group grew, the workers and students formed into ranks six abreast with arms linked, and, with contingents of Fighters at both the front and rear.

With a sea of red flags flying smartly in the breeze on a warm, sunny spring day, the marchers stepped off in spirited fashion chanting, "Death to the Fascists!"; "30 Hours Work for 40 Hours Pay!"; "Men and Women, Black and White, Workers of the World Unite!" and "Fight for Socialism!"

ROCK THROWING

With 50 Fighters in the lead, the March approached the very hill and overpass on which the early battle had been fought. Several hundred were on the other side, including some of the fascists who had just been smashed. All they left was some cowardly rock-throwing—from a goodly distance—which landed harmlessly at the marchers' feet or on cops' heads!

The six-abreast formation never broke ranks. The Fighters Group and marshals alongside the March continued giving leadership according to plan, emboldening the marchers who were facing a constant stream of harassment from cops on motorcycles constantly gunning back and forth along the route of the march with sirens screaming, trying to terrorize people. But this May Day these militant workers and students were not to be denied.

MARCH WAS A VICTORY

As the March wound its way for 2 3/4 miles up Columbia Road, bystanders began applauding, drivers of cars gave the clenched fists and honked their horns in salute. Many onlookers joined the march and hundreds bought **Challenge-Desafio.** As the march reached the integrated area of Dorchester, the rock-throwers gave up in despair over the discipline and determination of the marchers.

Scores of residents waved from apartment windows. An entire group of Spanish-speaking workers and their families came out in the street to clap and join in a chant in Spanish. An elderly Irish woman, right next door to a smiling black worker, threw out her arms as if to embrace the black, Latin and white marchers and began applauding vigorously.

By the time the marchers reached Franklin Park, the final assembly area, with the knowledge that the fascists had been defeated, the cops were prevented from canceling or breaking up this May Day. Fear had melted into the collective strength of thousands linking arms in solidarity and fighting fascists in an organized way.

The final rally heard revolutionary songs, and two main speakers, John Harris, leader of Boston PLP, and Prof. Finley Campbell, chair-person of international CAR. Harris drew some of the lessons of this historic May Day, pointing out that the fascists' attempt to drive the anti-fascists out of Boston had been turned around, and that the success of the march meant that a new movement could be organized to unite black, Latin and white workers against fascism and for jobs. He welcomes all those present to join PLP as the revolutionary communist party who will lead this movement.

Two points made by Campbell stood out. He drew a contrast with another clash "on a bridge" at Selma, Alabama, and this one "on the overpass and hill" adjacent to the early assembly area, pointing out that at Selma the philosophy of pacifism and "turn-the-other-cheek" had enabled the fascist Alabama cops to slaughter mis-led black and white workers and their families. But here, the idea of **TAKING THE OFFENSIVE** with an organized fighting strategy had routed the fascists.

RED ARMY

This point, of taking the battle to the enemy, was underscored when he recalled that on this day, May 3, "exactly 30 years ago virtually to the hour, the Red Army entered Berlin after chasing the Nazis half across Europe and meted out the only punishment one can give to fascists—death!" The point was cheered mightily by assembled workers and students.

The 2,500 marchers then returned home, proud of the manner in which they had carried forth the glorious tradition of May Day, and confident they had added a chapter to that heritage that would put one more nail in the bosses' coffin on the road to smashing their profit system completely.

Chapter 5

Russell slept all the way to Boston. Nikkia, Bonita and he left New York on July 11 after supper, and with last-minute packing, Russell hadn't closed his eyes since the previous day. Nikkia insisted he lie down on the back seat, and as soon as they got on Flatbush Avenue he began to snore.

The cheaply rented car had seemed adequate for the three of them. When they reached the lights of Hartford, though, the car started to run slowly on the incline of every hill. Nikkia was nervous. Bonita and she decided they would waste even more time if they pulled into a gas station. They had rented the car from a small company, and they knew there weren't any branch offices except in Boston. Their mood had been holiday-spirited, but now Nikkia hoped only that they'd make it there that night.

To Nikkia Boston itself began to seem like a city full of problems. "It's not a place I'd want to live in, with all that segregation," she said to Bonita. "Nothing compared to New York."

"Maybe I'm not as crazy about Manhattan as you are," Bonita said. "I've noticed some folks there think that the type of people in their area will never change. Greenwich Village, for example, used to be a great place for poor artists. And then, Bingo! You can't afford to move there."

Bonita kept glancing at the speedometer as they went up a hill, and Nikkia didn't answer while they both watched it go from fifty to forty to thirty.

"Inez showed me where, in the 1960's, the banks in Mattapan--that area of Boston south of Dorchester--actually drew a circle on the map around what was an all white area." Bonita spoke intently. "They worked with real estate speculators to scare the whites out, buying up homes cheaply with HUD funds. Then they turned around and sold to blacks at inflated prices. The banks and real estate investors made out like bandits."

"That's what they call redlining, and it can't happen on the Upper West Side," said Nikkia. "You've got people living in rent-controlled apartments for years. Their neighbors are already black and hispanic. They aren't about to leave, no matter what. Nothing can make New Yorkers do what they don't want to do."

They cruised down a hill now, and the car ran as if nothing had happened. Both women relaxed somewhat, although they still anticipated the next incline.

"What about if there's no jobs? That changes the picture," said Bonita. "People hadda have both man and wife working to afford those high mortgages in Mattapan. When somebody got laid off, the banks foreclosed. The bankers got all that HUD insurance, right in their pockets."

"You've got some memory. I don't even remember that discussion. My mind must have been elsewhere." Nikkia sought for an explanation. "You in Brooklyn have seen a lot of changes in the last five years."

Bonita shifted one leg underneath her and stretched it. The foot had grown numb. "You've been a communist all that time," she said. "During that period, Lawrence kept you thinking in a backward way."

"Don't blame him," Nikkia said. "He's someone I choose to spend a lot of time with." She looked at her watch. It was eleven o'clock at night. They should have been in Boston by now, Nikkia realized. Glancing at her friend across the seat, Nikkia saw the same youthful face she had known for three years. Somehow she'd been more aware of Bonita's changed attitude toward the party than how her own life had moved. "I'm the one who carried the ballet in my head for so long. Do you have any idea what that's like?"

"I never gave it a thought," Bonita shook her head. "I can't get past looking at a dancer's graceful legs and arms. I think how my own body doesn't move like theirs."

"You could, if you exercised for six hours a day." Nikkia spoke in a matter-of-fact tone. "Imagine being aware of your every muscle, constantly toning them up. And what for? To repeat the same movements people have done for centuries.

"African modern dance troupes were just barely coming into their own about the time I quit. You had more freedom of expression, but would work only six months out of the year. So realistically, we're talking about working in classical in the late sixties to early seventies. That's what people paid real money to see."

"But I think it's beautiful, like going to see an old statue."

"Think about it. How would you like to be one of those statues?" Nikkia sounded bitter. "You have to love seeing yourself in the same positions, year in, year out."

"That's true," conceded Bonita. "Especially what the men have to do. Yet, it's fascinating; they're so strong, and so graceful . . . ."

Russell snored in the back seat. Both women laughed.

"And so stuck on themselves," said Nikkia. "It comes with the package. That's why you've got to stay into it one hundred percent. Or get out."

Bonita was silent a moment while they inched up another hill and watched for signs of Boston. She turned around and looked at the sleeping Russell. "He's going to turn into a statue, too, from all the housework and childcare year after year."

Nikkia smiled, "But for some reason nobody will pay half the price of a ticket to the ballet to watch a housewife's tired body."

They arrived at Coralee's house after twelve-thirty. "Only three hours longer than I thought," Nikkia said sarcastically. The Boston streets seemed strange, with more three-family houses than in New York. She felt tired in a nervous way that made her irritable. And Coralee's house, where Russell would stay, was only their first stop.

The wooden frame house looked small from the street. Getting out of the car, Nikkia peered up the narrow walkway that separated one house from the next. As did every other house on this block, the front of Coralee's house had five windows. Many more windows stretched on the side to the back. The windows looked directly on the neighbor's windows. They each blazed with light.

Nikkia reached over the seat to nudge Russell, somehow annoyed he hadn't shared the anxiety of the drive. But when he rolled over, blinking into the car's interior light, she felt sorry, seeing the red wrinkles of sleep his jacket sleeve had left on his face. She hesitated to tell him that there didn't appear to be a restful corner in the house.

"They've got every light on waiting for you."

When the three comrades rang the doorbell, they couldn't tell if it worked. Noise and music came from the back of the house. After they knocked, and knocked again, though, the door pulled open. There stood a toddler in diapers, with small rows of braided hair, shirt smudged with a sticky substance. "Ay dah!"

Russell picked the child up, "What are you still doing awake at this hour, little lady?" He put his hands over the child's eyes, as if to close them.

"Peek," said the toddler, pulling Russell's hand down.

"She's just raring to go," said Nikkia.

"You mean <u>they're</u> just raring to go," said Bonita. In the doorway to the living room she could see another toddler without a shirt. He pushed aside an older boy in shorts to see who was at the front door.

The older boy, wearing shorts and one sneaker, took charge. He walked the little girl to meet the guests. "This is Shukyyirah," said the boy, putting an arm around the second toddler. "And that one you've been calling a girl, that's Muhammed-Ahmid."

"Sorry," Russell said.

"It's all right. Everybody thinks Shukyyirah's a boy, too." He rubbed his hand over the toddler's tight curls. "Cuz she's so rough." He sniffed, "Shukyyirah. You stink."

"The names!" said Nikkia, trying to ignore the odor from the toddler. "I'm glad I didn't have to grow up having to spell them."

Russell looked down at the little girl. "I thought I smelled something," he said. "Could you bring me a diaper?"

"Sure," said the boy, already half-running.

"Hey, what's your name?" Russell called after him.

"Me, I'm Adam!" He darted to the next room and disappeared.

"Russell, you don't even know if Coralee wants somebody else to clean up the baby," Nikkia said.

"Somebody's got to do it, right?"

Nikkia shrugged, and she and Bonita took Russell's two bags. They followed Shukyyirah, who waddled after Adam. In the living room were two couches, in leopard-print velour. A matching leopard chair shared a low wooden table with one of the couches. On the other couch, a mound of sheets stirred, and someone pulled a cover over his head.

"Oh! Shhh!" Bonita whispered.

"Nothing wakes up Tyrone." Adam, their guide, came back into the room with a pamper. "He stays here sometime. He's used to our noise."

Russell took a newspaper off a pile on the wooden table. He spread it on the floor and took off Muhammad's pamper. "You have a cloth or something?"

Adam produced a round plastic container of Wipe-'ems. Nikkia turned her head. "Where is Coralee?" she asked.

"<u>Everyone's</u> in the kitchen making sweet potatoe pies." said Adam. "C'mon."

He led Bonita and Nikkia into what might have been a dining room. Laundry piled high on the table. No chairs stood next to the table. The only other piece of furniture was a high, glass-doored cabinet with china cups and saucers and many sets of salt and pepper shakers. Next to the cabinet was a swinging door that Adam pushed open. And there was the kitchen, and everyone.

"Nikkia!" Coralee threw her arms open wide. Her round stomach, was covered with flour. The long braids of her hair clicked with blue and white beads as she moved.

"Coralee!" Nikkia finally felt the relief of the end of a journey. She hugged Coralee, who smelled of nutmeg and cinnamon. "I thought we'd never get here. The stupid rental car." Nikkia backed away to be able to look around the kitchen. For the first time she noticed that small tin plates covered every surface in the kitchen and even lined the top of the refrigerator.

"We're making pies for the bake sale tomorrow," said a girl about eight years old.

"That's Fay, my biggest helper."

"Your onliest helper, you mean." corrected Fay. She had been rolling dough. Accusingly, she waved her hand, covered with flour, at four older children sitting on chairs that matched the dining room table.

"We are <u>so</u> helping," yelled one older girl. She pushed Fay, and Fay pushed back, getting flour on her sister's blouse. "Who do you think took all the skins off them potatoes! Look what you did to my blouse!"

"You're full of it, Fay! We did all the hard work, mashing and stirring." Two gangly boys, around thirteen or fourteen, got up from where they'd been watching a TV in one corner of the kitchen. "She thinks she's the onliest one around here who can make crust and that makes her some kind of a big deal." The shorter of the two fellows spoke.

"Them are my twins, Thomas and Timothy. Just starting to grow," Coralee looked up at Timothy. "They don't look alike, but they sure do eat alike!"

"Yeah, they been eatin up the batter as fast as I'm trying to get it into the shells," complained Fay.

Coralee appeared oblivious to the arguing. "Where is Russell? He's the one supposed to be staying here. I've got to get you two directions to Yvette and Don's place."

"They don't have any children," Nikkia smiled at Bonita. She added, "Russell's changing Shukyyirah."

"He'll find plenty of other things to do around here tomorrow outside the house," Coralee winked at Nikkia. She then dug through a drawer by the sink, and produced a crayon and scrap of paper. Using the side of the refrigerator as a writing surface, she began to draw directions to the address where Bonita and Nikkia would go to stay.

The two women waved to the children in the kitchen as they left through the swinging door. Coralee called after them, "Remind Don; we're meeting at Field's Corner for signatures at ten o'clock."

"All right, Timothy, Thomas, get yourselves away from that TV and fill the pans on the counter. Renee, you better go find out where your baby went to." Coralee shouted then, "Timothy turn off that TV!"

With the television off, Coralee could hear shrieks from the living room. Furiously, she pushed Fay in her rush to go see what was the matter. Fay began to cry. "I'm not helping anymore!"

"It *is* almost one-thirty in the morning," said Renee.

"Nobody does anything else until this is finished," Coralee paused at the door. "Renee, stop combing your hair in the kitchen. How many times do I have to remind you?"

In the living room, Russell held Shukyyirah's ankles while she sat and bounced her bottom on his head. She squealed in delight. Adam and Muhammed-Ahmed rolled on the floor with laughter, oblivious to Coralee coming into the dining room. Russell continued bouncing Shukyyirah.

Coralee's voice was angry. "What's going on in here?" She thought to herself, isn't it obvious to this guy Russell that there's a lot to be done around here?

"Hi. Sorry we were so late." Russell wasn't sure why she was upset. "I'm the main one horsing around."

Coralee wanted to shout again. Instead, she picked up Muhammed-Ahmed and scolded him. "Your mother hasn't come for you yet? I suppose you'll be here the weekend." He whimpered when she mentioned 'mother,' his happy mood gone.

"His mother's a real party goer," explained Coralee. "Muhammed-Ahmed is my oldest son Rudy's boy. He's the one in the national guard whose room you'll take. With Adam. Muhammed-Ahmed's there, too, but he'll sleep in Adam's bed. See, my son used to take the boy most of the time, and now Darlene's in the habit of just leaving him . . . ."

"These kids should be in bed," said Russell quietly.

"That's fine for <u>you</u> to say," returned Coralee. "You haven't seen my kitchen."

Russell looked at the sleeping form of Tyrone. He looked at the pile of laundry in the dining room. "I guess you could use some help," he admitted. He lifted Shukyyirah from his head.

Renee came through the door from the kitchen, and Shukyyirah wiggled restlessly in Russell's arms. "Hi," Renee waved a hand at Russell and stretched. She announced, "I'm going to bed."

"Oh no you're not," Coralee stated. "Nobody is going anywhere until those pies are done and out of the oven and the kitchen cleaned up. Russell is here to help. You can just hold onto Shukyyirah like you're her mother for a change.

"Russell, you can take the one batch that's ready out of the oven and put them on the back porch. And Adam put the ones that are ready to go in, to bake." They marched into the kitchen, one behind the other. Russell came last, slowly shaking his head.

In the kitchen, Timothy and Thomas wrestled on the floor. Fay watched television, her arms folded across her chest. The boys bumped the table in their play, and two pans, crust and filling, splattered against the stove.

"Timothy. Thomas! Get up!" Coralee grabbed their arms, and with a strength that surprised Russell, lifted them both to their feet. "I've had it! You've done nothing but cause trouble!"

"Oh oh, guys, you're going to have to clean that up." offered Russell.

"They're not capable," Coralee told him. "Fay, you know I wanted that television set off."

"I don't care," said Fay. "I filled all the rest of the pies while the boys did nothing." The dried tear tracks through her flour-streaked face made her look to Russell like a sad clown.

Muhammed-Ahmed, free from Coralee's arms, went over to play contentedly in the spilled crust and potato mixture.

"Well, mom," Renee balanced Shukyyirah on one hip and flung out her other arm in a gesture. "I hope you're happy now that you've got us all in here."

"Sit yourself down and be quiet," said Coralee, her lips drawn. "These boys think they're two years old, and they've got to be punished like two year olds. Fay! get that child out of that mess and clean it up!"

Russell wondered what Fay would do. He watched her bend down to Muhammed and pick him up and wash his hands. He wanted to clean up the spilled pies but worried that Coralee might have something else in mind.

Renee shifted her baby over to the other hip and sat down in front of the TV, where Fay had been. A slightly burned smell drifted through the kitchen.

"What's the matter with all of you?" Coralee shook the arms of the boys without letting them go. "Am I the only one around here with a brain in their head?"

"The pies are burning," said Adam. "Do you want me to take them out?"

"You'll burn yourself." Coralee stood next to the oven and could smell the overdone pies, but she was bound by her anger at the twins and held their arms all the tighter. They both twisted to get away, their faces in pain.

Coralee pulled the boys to her and stared at

Russell. "You don't know what it's like with teenagers. One minute they think they're men and the next minute they're whining little boys."

Russell was afraid to contradict her. "It's tough to grow up these days," he said.

"It's a lot tougher to be a single parent," said Coralee. "Right now I've got to take these two and pull their pants down like babies and use my hairbrush. Do you think that's easy?"

"I never said it was," answered Russell. He was beginning to feel an ache in his legs. He recalled the long ride in the car, where for six hours he had slept almost unconscious, with bent knees. The thought of the pies yet to be baked, and the ones already burning made him desperate to move. And yet, he had no idea what to do first.

"Forgive me, honey," said Coralee. "But I'm about to say something I don't mean because I'm angry," Coralee looked tired and disgusted. "I don't want to have another child to take care of this month. You're going to have to see what needs to be done around here and do it."

"All right," said Russell. His very physical discomfort brought a solution to his mind. "You're the one who knows what has to be done around the kitchen with the pies. What do you say I take the boys upstairs and talk with them?"

"They don't understand words! They knew better than to wrestle in the kitchen with all this food around! What they understand is the feeling of pain!" All her frustration seemed now to be directed toward Russell. "If you want to be a real help you can try to save those pies."

Defeated in what he felt he knew best, Russell put one hand on the table, for support. Perhaps he didn't know much about teenagers, but he realized he knew even less about cooking.

Coralee was not one to wait for his next suggestion. "Fay, get the hot pads. Show him where to put the pies. Renee, turn off that TV and watch both the babies--not just your own." Coralee's voice was still angry, but controlled. "Adam, hand Fay the unbaked pies when she's ready. And while you're just standing there, put the last of the dough into those two pans that fell. Do I have to remind you to rinse them first?

"Now you, Timothy and Thomas, I have a little lesson for you," Coralee was angry again, and she bumped the kitchen door open with a slam of her hips.

"No, Mom!" Thomas protested.

Adam looked after them, and then they were gone. Fay had already opened the oven door and blew at the smoke.

"It's only batter got on the racks and burned," she said with a little smile.

The relief that Russell was feeling he could sense in every other person in the room. His hand moved, almost without his thinking, up to his forehead. "Private Russell reporting for duty to General Fay," he saluted. "Where do we stack the ammunition, Sir?"

Adam responded quickly, "TenSHUN! Right face!" he handed Russell a pan with crust and pointed to the remaining potato batter.

Grinning, Russell realized that brother Rudy must have been teaching Adam some of the drills.

Renee looked up first at Fay then at Russell. "Hey, I wanna ask for a leave to get these privates to bed."

"Permission granted," said Russell. "Okay, general?"

Fay smiled, preoccupied with a hot pie in each hot pad mit. She set them down on the porch shelf and came back in, her hands empty, but with the smile still on her face. "Okay, private Russell, Sir!"

x x x

Russell woke to a brightness like midday. He looked at the tan window shade, strange to his eyes. The unfamiliar window made him wonder where he was, and he remembered finding his bed in the dark, and throwing off only his outer clothes and sleeping in his underwear. He sat up. His watch said eight o' clock.

Across the room in the other single bed lay Adam, a knee up and one arm around another little mound that would be Muhammed-Ahmed. The house was quiet. Russell could hear his own watch ticking and the separate breaths of the two boys.

Careful not to disturb their sleep, Russell picked up his sneakers and duffle bag from the floor at the foot of the bed. His own house was never so quiet on Saturday morning, and he enjoyed walking right into the bathroom without having to wait.

He took a shower and rinsed out his underwear and socks and put them on a drying rack in the bathtub. Thinking about the pies he helped make and getting to know the children made Russell feel at home. He missed Pat, who would be making Saturday morning pancakes, the sound of her brisk steps giving him energy. But the rest of the rooms in this house remained silent. He wished Pat were here.

And then he was sharply hungry. He got the idea to make pancakes himself and then wake everyone. The thought made him happy, and he pictured the ingredients he would need. As he went down the stairs, the fellow on the couch rose to stand and stretch. "Hi, you must be Tyrone," said Russell. "I came in last night."

"Good to meet you, man." As Tyrone stretched, his hands touched the ceiling. He was very tall and slender. A bleached birthmark on his face and neck made him look older, but Russell remembered he was a friend of Rudy's, and that would make him about nineteen.

"I gotta go to work," said Tyrone. "I can walk it from here. Coralee lets me stay here. Alls I do at home is wash up these days. I don't get along too tough there."

"You have to have something in your stomach," said Russell. "I was just going to make pancakes."

"Hey, that'd be great." Tyrone took two steps toward the kitchen, and his long legs brought him ahead of Russell. The kinetic energy of his body seemed to vibrate to his fingertips. Russell took strength from watching him, the way he did from Pat. He looked down at his own stomach, though, and realized how his swelling midriff made him feel old and slow. Perhaps he could even lose weight up here. He decided he would have just one pancake.

Tyrone was already getting out milk and had found the baking powder. He evidently knew his way around. "What do you do that you have to work Saturdays?" asked Russell.

"A moving van company. Mostly it's local." He put on water to boil for instant coffee.

"I do loading, too. UPS." Russell said. He remembered where the flour was from last night. Meanwhile, Tyrone had gotten two eggs from the refrigerator. "You really know where things are around here."

"I'm like part of the family. Been stayin here one or two nights a week for years. All Rudy's friends usta hang here, too, before Rudy went in the National Guard. Coralee's great that way." Tyrone poured milk into his coffee and added three heaping spoons of sugar. "One day I came here, and there were four complete strangers sitting on the couch. Two women, a man, and a kid."

Russell listened to Tyrone. He finished stirring up the batter and watched the sun make a windowpane pattern on the floor. He couldn't resist opening the door to the pantry and looking at the rows of individual pies cooled. The sweet smell of nutmeg filled every corner.

"Coralee tells me, 'These people don't have any place to go.'" Tyrone took a sip of his coffee. "So these four stay here the whole weekend; I couldn't believe it.

"Coralee fed them and everything. They refused to lie down on a bed but sat on the couch the whole time except to go to the bathroom. Couldn't speak one word of English. French, or somethin. But Coralee understood them all right. She sees what somebody needs, and they've got it! By Monday they were gone," Tyrone snapped his fingers, "just like that."

Before Russell could respond, the kitchen door opened. Timothy and Thomas tried to walk through the door together. "Quit shovin me," quarreled the shorter Thomas.

"Here comes trouble." quipped Tyrone.

"Guys. Good morning," Russell saw they both wore pajamas that came above their knees. Timothy wore a short-sleeved shirt open to his chest, and Thomas had on no shirt at all. The boys' chests and legs were muscular, and bony and solid. "How'd you like to help make pancakes?" suggested Russell. Then he changed his tone to one of firmness. "But first, Thomas, go upstairs and put on a shirt. Any kind of a shirt, I don't care. A T-shirt, for instance."

Thomas was so surprised, he opened his mouth and then left for his bedroom without a word.

"I think you shocked the shit out of Thomas," said Tyrone.

"I didn't mean to scare him," Russell said. "I just don't like looking at somebody's hairy armpits in the kitchen."

"Don't get me wrong," said Tyrone. "I think it's good for kids to have something expected of them. That's been one of the problems since Rudy, Senior, died--that was less than two years ago. It's been too much for her."

The kitchen door slammed open, and Thomas, Muhammad-Ahmed and Adam came in together. Adam accused Thomas, "He woke me up."

"If I'm gonna have to help make breakfast, you're gonna have to work, too."

"That's not fair. You didn't do a darn thing last night. Fay and I did all the cleaning up."

"Nobody tol' you to do it all. Just because Russell's new around here, you want him to think you're the big man."

"Not _true_! You're the one who sits around like some king. Most of the time doin nothin!"

"You stop talkin about Thomas doin nothin," defended Timothy. "Him and me cleaned our room last Saturday, and you never had to clean the bedroom while Rudy was here."

"Hold it," Russell said. "Nobody's accusing anybody else of being lazy. But let me ask you, everybody's hungry, right?"

"They're always hungry," said Tyrone, indicating the twins.

"Look who's talkin," stated Timothy. "You're always eatin around here. And you're not even a part of the family."

"That's none of your business you little punk. You shut your face." Tyrone lifted Timothy off the floor by his shirt collar. "I pay Coralee every week, and you never mind how much, either."

Timothy, held up by one of Tyrone's hands, sputtered and wiggled, his face a dark red-brown. "You better not hurt my brother," said Thomas. But he didn't come around to Tyrone's side of the table.

"Do you want me to jack you up, too, Thomas?" asked Tyrone.

"Just you try it," said Thomas. But still, he moved no closer.

"Cool out!" yelled Russell. "We're all a family right here, like it or lump it."

Slowly, Tyrone let Timothy down. Taking the boy's shoulders in his large hands, he set him firmly on a chair.

Thomas came and sat beside his brother. Russell continued, "Me, too, I'm going to be a member of this family for the next month." He put a forearm up on Tyrone's shoulder. "And by the way, I'm paying your mother for staying here. But that's not the point. We're all going to be sharing this kitchen and all the housework."

"Goodie," said Adam.

"Yea! Yea! said Muhammad-Ahmed, looking up to Adam for approval.

"There's a lot of differences among us in this house," said Russell. "Three of us have jobs. Some of us are still in diapers."

"Pie-der," said Muhammed-Ahmed, lifting his shirt so that he could see his pamper.

"Two of us are mothers and two of us are twins," Russell paused. "But all of us have stomachs, and food has to be fixed, and we all wear clothes that're somewhere in that big pile on the table."

"Me and Fay folded those clothes and put em away last time," said Adam. "I'm not doing it again."

"Somebody's wet clothes are on a rack in the bathroom so's I couldn't take a shower," said Timothy.

"Those are mine," Russell said. "I'm sorry."

"Dripping stuff can only be put in there at night."

"O.K. I didn't know. See. You've got things to tell me, too. Let's get back to cooking breakfast."

"Juice," said Muhammed-Ahmed.

"I'll get it for him," said Tyrone.

"The rest of you aren't little kids," Russell continued. "If all of us share the work, nobody will have too much to do."

"I wish I had a job like Tyrone," said Timothy. "Then I wouldn't have to do nothin around here. I'd just sleep and eat and pay my money every week."

"Oh no you don't," said Tyrone. "I was around here before senior died, and he wouldn't let me pay. After he passed, Rudy took over the house, more or less. Then nobody did it when Rudy went in the service. I insisted on paying. But I didn't know where to begin with the chores. And Coralee seemed to be getting mad all the time.

"So I just tried to stay out of her way." Tyrone put the tips of his fingers on his temple. "I'm gone working seven days a week. I won't be able to cook for the family. But I sure can do my share of anything else."

"I don't know how to cook," said Thomas. "That means I'll get stuck with all of the dirty work."

"You guys can learn how to cook," Russell said. "It's something men and women can do. Like taking care of the babies."

"I'm not gonna watch Renee's baby," Timothy stated. "Renee doesn't even act like a mother her own self."

"You never took a care of her," said Thomas. "I did. My friends used to tease me like she was my kid. And I don't mean to have no kids until I got me a job. An that's when I quit doin anything around here."

"You just said a lot," Russell frowned. "You mind running that by me again."

"What'd I say?" asked Thomas. "I just said I'm not gonna do nothin."

"No. no. Where you got teased by your friends."

"Most everything anybody said made me mad after Dad died." Thomas would not look at Russell and began to fiddle with the carton of milk. "I don't know why Renee doesn't get out of the house completely. Or give away that baby to somebody who wants one."

"Whoa, fella," Russell held up the palm of his hand. "We don't want to talk about anybody who's not here. Let's stick to this business of men and boys taking care of babies, no matter whose they are. Babies are everybody's job. We were all babies once upon a time."

"Not him," giggled Adam, pointing to Tyrone.

"Believe it or not," said Tyrone, "I was a runt."

"Anyway, I'm sorry you got teased, Thomas," said Russell. What d'you think you should've said to your friends?"

"That it's not my damn baby!" said Thomas.

"How about, 'I'm helping my sister.'?" said Russell.

"I get too mad," Thomas said. "Them guys made me mad."

"I got real mad at some friends of mine lived by us in Pittsburgh," said Russell. "Just after I got laid off, and I was pretty sore about not working.

They were getting together a baseball team, and I told them I didn't have time. I thought they were ribbing me because then I didn't have nothin <u>but</u> time. I even cussed em out. Can you imagine that?" Both twins were looking steadily at Russell. "Now wasn't that stupid? My best friends!"

"So then what'd you do?" asked Thomas.

"I apologized. And I said why I got so mad. Then you know what they told me? They knew it all along."

"Well these guys that live around here knew Shukkyirah and Muhammed weren't mines." Thomas got angry all over again. "These guys did it deliberate."

"Lotsa kids today walk around mad," said Russell. "They think they got no future but to get their heads blown off. If they can get somebody else mad they don't have to think about it for awhile. That doesn't mean you have to be their dummy."

"They knew damn well it ain't your kid." said Timothy. "And you knew they knew. That makes you stupid."

"I couldn't help it," Thomas said, pushing his body weight off the chair with his hands, restlessly.

"Now you can," said Timothy.

The kitchen door swung open with a bang. Coralee stood in the doorway with her hands on her hips.

"I had nightmares about this," she yelled. "It was hard enough to go back to sleep after Muhammed-Ahmed woke me up at four o'clock. Then I dreamed that all the other people in this house were sitting around waiting for me to make breakfast. Just the thought of it woke me up. And sure enough!"

"I was just . . .," began Russell. He looked at the pancake batter in the bowl.

"This is ridiculous," Coralee said. "You all knew we had to be at the shopping center at ten. It's after nine and there's barely time to scramble eggs. I bet we don't have an egg in the house after last night. And didn't nobody think to go out to the store this morning."

"I was going to make pancakes," said Russell. "There's enough eggs for that."

"But not enough time to fry them for ten people," Coralee stated. "Thomas, you've been up. Do you have to wait for somebody to tell you to go to the store? Would you just sit there and starve to death if somebody didn't come and wait on you?"

"You're not picking on anybody else," pouted Thomas. His lower lip came out further the more he thought about being insulted. "Fact, I don't care if I ever do eat again around here." He got up and ran around Coralee and out the kitchen. "See if I will!"

"Now you really did it," said Timothy to Coralee. "He was . . ."

"Don't you sass me, young man," Coralee pointed a finger at him. "You're going to the store."

"I want pancakes, not eggs," said Timothy. "He said that he would make pancakes," indicating Russell.

"I want pancakes, too," said Adam. "We never have pancakes around here any more."

"See what you started," said Coralee to Russell. "You know that we've got all these pies to load into boxes and put in the car, too."

"Your mother's right, kids," said Russell. He was truly surprised so much time had passed since he'd gotten up. "There's really not time." He wished there were some way he could make it up to the children, but he felt defeated by the whole situation: the unfinished discussion, the half-started breakfast, the pies.

"I'll make French toast," he suggested. "That takes less time and not many eggs."

"I need you to help me load the pies," said Coralee. "They'd be all over the floor if we left that up to the kids." She shook the twin's arm and gave him some change. "Timothy. The store."

"Hey, get me a pepsi and chips, Timothy, O.K?" Renee handed him a dollar bill.

"Get it yourself," said Timothy. "I'm not your servant."

"Mother. He knows I can't leave Shukyyirah. She's not dressed. I can't take her."

"Just go, Timothy, and cut it out with your lip," said Coralee. "Renee's not dressed, either, and we've got to get out of here."

Timothy glanced over to Russell, who, resigning himself to a breakfast of coffee, said nothing now. He looked back to Coralee. "I'm just getting eggs," Timothy said. "Renee can damn well eat what we do."

"I've got to get to work," said Tyrone. He took a big swallow of coffee and slung an arm out to Russell. "Catch you later, man."

No sooner had he left than Coralee handed Russell

a carton and instructed him on how many pies would fit inside. The box held exactly as many as she said it would. And one by one, the cartons were stacked in the car. Fay scrambled eggs, Timothy made toast, and Renee fed the two toddlers. Only Russell and Coralee were to attend the bake sale, and after they ate they went right out to the car.

A woman across the street waved to them. "Hey Coralee, you opening a stand at the flea market?" she laughed.

"You know me better than that! It's our bake sale for the Committee Against Racism," shouted Coralee. "Come help us!"

"I'll buy one offa you. Right now," called the neighbor. She ran over, producing a small coin purse from her dress pocket. She took out some folded dollar bills. "Keep the change."

"This is Lucille," said Coralee. "She makes the best chocolate brownies. I can't tell you how many she baked for us last fall."

A teen-age girl came out of the house two doors away before Coralee was able to start the car. "Don't drive off," she said, "I told you I'd come with you, and it looks like you're forgetting me." She was still pushing an afro comb through her hair and then stuck it in the back. Russell noticed that as she looked him up and down, her eyes were a striking light brown.

"Una Blakney. My other daughter," said Coralee. "Her mother and me delivered Una and Renee on exactly the same day, and I think I adopted her."

"Coralee knows all my secrets," Una giggled as she got into the car. "Mmmm. I can smell these pies. You really outdid yourself, Mom."

As they drove down the street, an elderly man yelled to them, "Hey, baby!"

"Hi, Demetrik! Go home to your wife before she steps out on you!"

"Sara says to save one of them pies for her."

"Better come get it now; they'll be all gone."

"He used to work in the shipyards," said Coralee, as they pulled over to the side of the road. "He was the strongest man in his shop."

"Mrs. Heatherington!" An albino boy, about eleven, waved from a stoop.

"Johnny!"

Other people waved and called out "Coralee", even as they got more than a mile from the house. Russell had to comment. "Everyone knows you. I feel like I'm with a celebrity."

"If you had lived in this town all your life . . .," said Coralee, shaking her head so that the beads rattled against each other.

"I lived in Pittsburgh," he said. I knew everyone on my block because we had a block association. And the guys at work. But that was it, really."

"She's never home, that's why." said Una. "At least never when Rudy Sr. was around to keep the pot on the stove, so to speak. He was some cook."

"Sometimes I still think he's gonna be there in the kitchen when I walk in," Coralee's voice was husky. "And I get this shock when I just see it empty. Or just one of the kids standin there." Coralee blinked, and Russell put his hand on her sundress sleeve.

They got to Field's Corner, a subway stop and shopping area, and there was a table set up with the CAR flag of black and white fists. Bonita and Nikkia waved. Nikkia was talking with a college-age fellow who seemed to be arguing with her. Bonita stood with a woman who was signing the petition, and had put down her shopping bags to do so.

Una arranged the pies in an attractive display while Coralee and Russell unloaded the car. "Maybe I shouldn't bring this up now," Russell said to her, "but there's been so many people around. I've wanted to ask you, couldn't you use some help with your children? You have so many friends. I bet they'd pitch in."

"They all got their own problems, believe me," said Coralee. "The comrades up here are great, too, and they do things with the kids quite often, but nobody knows what it's really like. None of them has to live with those teenagers."

Russell was somewhat hesitant to speak his mind. He got along well with the guys at the mill by always being up front. But he'd been tight with them for years and barely knew Coralee. Yet, with only a month to be here, he considered he had nothing to lose by being honest right away with a comrade. "I don't think you talk with them, any of your children, enough. You're always screaming. Orders."

"Look. You can handle them so great? It's all yours," said Coralee, handing him a big carton.

Russell was sure he'd gone too far. But before he could say anything more, Don Hofler came up to help them unload. To Russell, Don's young, tanned face appeared rested and carefree. "How did you ever do all this, Coralee," Don cried, putting out a hand to Russell but looking at Coralee. "You're amazing."

When they were alone again, Russell said to her, "You do accomplish an awful lot. And I'm not saying people don't have confidence in you. In fact, long before I met you there in New York, I'd heard of you and what friends you had in the community."

"But maybe I oughta stay home more, is that what you've been trying to say?"

"No. I came here in the first place to learn more about gettin out of the house, myself," Russell admitted.

Coralee set down the carton she held. "Can I tell you something personal?" she asked. "I love my children. More than anything. But I _like_, even better, the people I've met and made friends with outside the house. Now maybe that sounds strange, yet it's the truth."

"But you could like your children more than you do, I think. They're really good kids," said Russell. He was finding it hard to express himself.

"Feel free." Coralee picked up the carton again. "If you think you know better how to deal with teenagers. For a month, they're all yours."

"I'm not saying I know so much," said Russell. "But perhaps . . ."

"That's what I thought," said Coralee. "You don't really want the responsibility either. Well, you know something? Neither do I. But I'm stuck, and if you can come up with a solution, you're welcome to it."

The way she spoke, Russell didn't feel either welcome or competent. The bake sale and the gathering of signatures pressed upon them. He was handed a clip board. And the instant it was in his hand, a middle-aged, balding man with very thick glasses asked Russell if he were a resident of Dorchester.

"No, but this issue of more money for schools concerns me, as a parent," Russell said off the top of his head, having no time to think. His initiation into the anti-racist busing campaign had begun.

Chapter 6

"And you, Nikkia, how many signatures did you get today?" Don asked at the end of the rally.

"Oh, a page or two," said Nikkia.

"Don't let her get away with that," Bonita cut in. "She always gathers a lot of signatures or sells a lot of papers whenever she goes out, and she never likes to say how many."

"We have to keep a record," Don stated. "This is a campaign."

"All right. Forty-five."

"That's a lot." He wrote the figure in a yellow pocket notebook.

Nikkia had noticed that Don carried a little spiral notebook with him wherever he went. He had a separate one for shopping lists, which he took when they went to the supermarket. Everything about Don seemed small and neat to her. His and Yvette Hofler's apartment had been immaculate, Nikkia recalled. Neither one of them seemed to neglect a corner of their place.

"Why don't you like to report your numbers?" Don pressed her, "Numbers are important, though not everything."

"It goes back to the fact that I used to dance professionally," said Nikkia, reluctantly. "Talking about how many papers I can sell or the number of signatures seems to me like competition. The ballet is very competitive in the worst sense. Since I left, I try very hard not to call attention to myself."

"I've heard there are few companies," Yvette remarked. "For black dancers the competition for jobs must be fierce."

"Try one black swan in Swan Lake!" said Nikkia. She felt an unconscious tightening in her abdomen, like she got before an audition. Here was at once the discomfort and the excitement she worked hard to forget. Usually her one line remark about black ballerinas was sufficient to bring a chuckle and to ward off further inquiry into the subject.

But Yvette was insistent. "I can't understand why someone like you would leave. You were successful. You made money. Wasn't the glamour irresistible?"

They were walking toward Don and Yvette's apartment. Don had wanted to go there for lunch. He was not one to spend money on what he called "brown bag places," when you could make better sandwiches at home. Feeling the hot sun on her face and arms, Nikkia was reminded of the dance theater lights. "There is nothing like performing," she said. And for a moment Nikkia could not see the streets of Boston, recalling the admiration of hundreds of people looking at her, her body. Sure of her condition and confident of her movements, she drew the minds of people to her fingertips and along the perfect arch of her back and extended leg.

Don noticed, "You seem to carry that world with you, still."

"She even drives a car with good posture," said Bonita.

"And I crack my neck when driving is tough," Nikkia felt somewhat relieved to relate to the present. "My tension used to go to my neck when I would work at memorizing an exercise. I still feel all my stress in my neck, and a part of me will always be a dancer."

"Here's our street. It's right around the corner from the CAR office." Don seemed to enjoy having them stay. Yvette, too, had been waiting up for them the previous night, beside the couch bed turned down and ready with fresh sheets.

"It's good to have you here," said Don. "I get so involved in studying during the year that it's hard for me to keep a balance with political work, seeing people."

Nikkia looked up at the three-story stone building with curved front rooms on each floor. This was the third time she'd entered the door, and the smell of the cool tile of the entrance foyer already seemed familiar. She wiped her face with both hands, and the feel of sweat reminded her of smooth makeup oils. Involuntarily, she held her hands from her clothes, so as not to stain them.

The four of them entered the apartment, and

Nikkia watched the sun wave shadows of leaves on the polished wood floors. This place was clean, almost too immaculate, she thought, with blond pinewood tables and couch and chair upholstery the color of sand. The only bright colors were in a huge abstract wall painting above the couch bed. In many shades of blue and green with white. The painting made Nikkia envision a snow scene that seemed to raise the entire room to a cool ski mountain.

Yvette turned on the air conditioning, and joined Bonita and Don in the kitchen that was visible through a large entranceway from the living room-dining room. Nikkia herself couldn't help standing just where she was, gazing at the painting. Something in the colors or the close feeling of the snow--she was sure it was snow now--made her aware of another human presence not shown on the canvas. Someone, the artist perhaps, became a necessary ingredient to the painting, if only to witness this plane of snow on a cold sunny day.

Seeing the painting captured Nikkia into the mood of an observer, and she began to look at the entire apartment with a certain curiosity. She felt the differences between this and her own apartment. No rugs cushioned the dustless floor. She would have preferred more color, more softness. And yet Nikkia appreciated the change from the crowded nursing station, the dark of her Manhattan apartment. The very wood of the floors seemed to invite her bare feet, and so Nikkia took off her shoes.

She knew she should walk to the kitchen to help with the lunch preparations and yet she still couldn't become a part of the bustle and chatter. She needed the time to move from New York to Boston, and Nikkia asked herself what made this apartment different from Manhattan living space. Certainly there was more window area; you had to have money to pay for a sunny New York City apartment. Everything seemed much lower; there was more access to the sky. But that was to be expected. Manhattan could not hold so many millions of people without stacking them on top of each other. Nikkia had long ago accepted that.

She watched the three others making friends in the kitchen--the small-boned Don; Yvette, petite with her thick mass of long, dark-brown wavy hair; Bonita, a part of them already, slim arms and body able to move gracefully between and around them. The three made a dance. Now to the refrigerator, then to the cabinets, reaching, turning. Herself becoming a part of that dance, Nikkia knew what made this apartment so different from her own: the kitchen. There was space for more than one person to work together with others. In her own kitchen, two or even three people could eat at the little table, but the stove and sink area demanded that cooking and cleaning up be done by one person, alone.

"I'm glad to see you take off your shoes," said Yvette bringing out a plate of sliced ham and cheese. "You should feel at home."

"I feel something more than at home," Nikkia responded. For the first time that day, she thought of Lawrence. The newness of the apartment, her tiredness last night and their busy morning had filled her mind. Only once or twice she had wondered what he might be doing. Usually when she was away from him--and they often spent nights in their separate apartments--she missed his physical presence throughout her body. In this fresh scene, this particular apartment, she found she did not want his negativism. He would be as out of place as a layer of dust on this polished floor. She simply could not imagine him here at all.

As she sat down at the table Nikkia chose a chair that faced the painting, and it was then that she realized Lawrence had not shared looking at it with her. She could not explain to herself why that thought made her happy, but it did.

"I like that painting," she said to Yvette.

"Don would be pleased," said Yvette. She turned to take a pitcher of juice from Bonita's tray. "He painted that during winter break instead of studying for finals."

Nikkia could feel her face show her amazement at Don's being an artist. She quickly looked down at the table, running a finger along her placemat. I must be careful, she thought, not to offend Don by saying he didn't strike me as being creative. The others sat down then, and she accepted a plate from Don. Yvette moved into her line of gaze. "You are surprised," she said.

"I wouldn't put it that way," Nikkia stated.

Yvette laughed softly. "When I first met him, I was amazed to find out he painted. I expected artists to be a little crazy, and messy."

"I forget neatness when I paint," Don said, joining them.

"He confines it to that room," Yvette pointed to a closed door that Nikkia had thought was a closet. "There's a skylight put in by a previous owner of the building. He's come back here and bought a couple of Don's paintings."

"He liked some of my more experimental work," said Don.

"You should both see the mural of the summer project he's painting with three of the high school students," Yvette told Bonita and Nikkia.

"I'd like to see that," said Bonita. "Coralee was telling me there's a dance tonight. Is the mural at the CAR office going to be part of the decorations?"

"It'll have to be, even though it isn't finished yet," said Don. "It seems the city of Boston has conspired not to let us rent a hall. We've tried the Y, a couple of private places and three churches. Some of the ministers are afraid because ROAR has been so violent. We're also sure the city officials have threatened a few of the places that we could afford. At first they agreed, then later backed down."

"The tables fold up; we'll make good use of the space at the CAR office," added Yvette.

"What can we bring in the way of food?" asked Bonita.

"I had planned to make a vegetable dish," Don said.

"Nikkia makes great lasagne," offered Bonita.

"That's right," Nikkia chuckled, remembering the evening Bonita had spent with her and Lawrence. "I do!"

The doorbell rang. Yvette appeared startled but Don moved to press the buzzer that opened the front door lock. "It's Norberto," he said. "He wanted to go canvassing for an hour this afternoon and make sure some friends of ours were coming to the dance." Don went to open the door to their apartment and peered down the staircase.

"Norberto's already made a difference in our work," Yvette told them. "He's made a commitment to work with us this summer; even got a job to send money home since he left his family for this time."

"Like Russell," said Nikkia. "But Russell found

himself an even bigger family here."

"No rest for the weary," said Bonita, just as Don came back in the room, with the man called Norberto.

As he came through the doorway, Nikkia noted how quietly he walked, compared to Don. Norberto walked straight to their table without hesitating in the living room. Nikkia tried to look directly into his eyes, and he didn't look back. But she felt, rather than saw, that he had noticed her. She had always been able to sense when people's eyes had been on her, if only for a second.

His hair was black, his skin light brown, and his face had the complexion of a young man though Nikkia could see worry wrinkles. He wasn't tall, like Lawrence, nor did he look like him in the slightest, but Nikkia knew that her own skin prickled in an excitement she had not felt lately with Lawrence.

"Hello," she said. But Norberto was looking at Yvette, and they began to speak Spanish.

Then, Yvette introduced him to Bonita and Nikkia, and he shook their hands. Nikkia noticed nothing special in his handshake nor in his steady gaze at her own eyes. She shocked herself by the thought that already she wanted something more intimate from him, like another movement of his eye, to tell her she was special to him. And she felt embarrassed, but her shame didn't touch the excitement.

Norberto's clothing, she realized, didn't attract her. He wore a cotton shirt that seemed too big for him, a khaki print, rather faded. The shirt was loose, worn over his jeans that had no particular style. Wide leather sandal straps crossed the tops of his feet, and Nikkia saw that his toenails were as neatly clipped as his fingernails. She wished at once she could stop noticing details about him. His hands weren't as tapering and long as Lawrence's, but his fingers were slender, and she liked them.

"He wants to do some visiting right away," said Yvette. "He's been urging us ever since he came, right after May Day, from California. Norberto says the visiting is the most meaningful part of our campaign. And I must say, he's tireless. The rest of us tend to knock ourselves out on the mechanical aspects of the work, signature getting and such."

"Where did he learn English?" asked Nikkia.

"That's the amazing part of it. He didn't before

he came here in April. But he's becoming fluent. He has learned enough to get across the ideas of the busing situation. And he understands everything you say."

Nikkia could think of nothing to ask Norberto.

Bonita asked, "You work in California?"

"Yes. I did." Norberto spoke the word 'did' carefully. "My wife, Silvia, and my sons work now."

Nikkia still felt too shy to speak to him. She thought of the fact that he had children old enough to work, and that would make him close to forty. He looked thirty. Then Nikkia just realized he'd told Bonita he worked in California. "He speaks English very well," she said,

"No," said Norberto.

"He knows how to say a lot about himself, because everyone's been asking him," explained Yvette. "He got fired from Lucas & Sons, one of the biggest growers near Delano. We don't think he'll be able to work again, with the grapes at least. His family may have to move." Yvette placed a hand on each of Norberto's shoulders. "This summer project makes good use of his leadership."

"Which of you would like to go visiting with Norberto?" asked Don. "Yvette and I promised we'd set up for the party tonight. Norberto says there are four families who would probably bring other people to the dance, and they should be seen today."

"I'll . . .," Nikkia began.

"Oh no. You drove all that way last night, and you've already had lots of experience in this sort of thing," said Bonita. "It's time I started getting to know people. That's what we're here for, aren't we?"

"I think she's right, Nikkia," said Don. "And you did say you'd make lasagne."

"Oh, that doesn't take so long," said Nikkia, thinking both she and Bonita could go with Norberto.

But Don looked at his watch and said that it was already close to three o'clock. Realistically, he stated, Nikkia had to stay.

Bonita and Norberto prepared to leave, and Nikkia saw that Bonita was getting him to smile at her attempts at Spanish. She noticed that his teeth were somewhat uneven and very clean. Their slight crookedness made his mouth interesting, and Nikkia closed her eyes before she could trace his lips with her eyes, for that would be wrong.

As Norberto and Bonita walked out the door together, she felt a burning sensation that she knew as jealousy. How stupid of me, she repeated to herself. He's married. But Nikkia also felt a strange sadness, as though she might not see him again.

When she began to make a shopping list for her and Don, Nikkia remembered they would all be going to the social that night. A dance, actually, hadn't Coralee and Don said so? Suddenly it didn't matter to her that Norberto was married. She would be able to look at him. He would certainly be there. In fact, Nikkia decided, she would make a point of asking him to dance.

Chapter 7

Bonita spoke in Spanish with Norberto as they got into the party's old Volvo. "My mother is from Nicaragua. She didn't like for us to speak Spanish in the house. I used to do it anyway and get my little brothers and sister in trouble. She would smack me!"

Norberto laughed. "I understand you. Sometimes children learn best the things they are told not to!"

A pocket dictionary lay on the car seat. Bonita turned the pages as Norberto started the car. "I was wondering how to say this word," said Bonita, continuing in Spanish. "Reactionary."

"It's the same as in English, reaccionario," said Norberto.

"I don't know exactly what it means," Bonita said carefully. "I've been embarrassed to ask Nikkia."

"It means people who are afraid of change," said Norberto. They were travelling through streets that were more run down than Don and Yvette's neighborhood. "But you have to know why a person has fear, and that could be many reasons. So I never use the word, myself."

"Oh that's good," Bonita laughed. "Then we'll understand each other perfectly."

Norberto stopped the Volvo in front of a dirty wood frame house. "This is South Boston," he said. "Or almost. One of our comrades, Lennie, is afraid to go door to door in his own neighborhood. Poor white people afraid of change." Norberto pointed to the rest of the block.

Garbage flowed from overturned cans into the street gutter. Some large piles of bottles and paper filled the sidewalk in front of the frame house. Someone had made a path around the pile that led to the side door. The front door was nailed shut with a big X made of boards. A sour smell came from the garbage. Bonita turned her head, but a breeze brought the same odor.

In the middle of the block children jumped on mattresses. They ran, and flipped in the air and landed on both feet. Bonita closed her eyes. She envisioned broken glass around the mattress, and the children falling on it. When she opened her eyes, Lennie stood before them.

A cigarette hung in the corner of Lennie's mouth, and he squinted one eye from the rising smoke. He was tall. Bonita guessed him to be about seventeen years old.

As he stepped forward to walk with them, Bonita could see that what she thought at first was a smooth hair style, consisted of a pony tail that extended halfway down his back. Lennie said, "I'm ready." He carried a clipboard.

"You are not ready," said Norberto.

Lennie pulled the cigarette out of his mouth. To Bonita his movements suggested a toughness that went beyond superficial show-off.

"I need your help," said Norberto in Spanish to Bonita. "The people we're going to visit will judge Lennie by his long hair. I can give you an example. When Chavez's organizers came into the fields where we were working, they wore their golfing shorts. We farmworkers have to cover our legs even when it's one hundred ten degrees because of the poisonous pesticides. We looked upon the organizers as men who had never worked for the growers and who still did not have to work. That's the way people view kids who keep their hair long these days. I told Lennie that the next time we went out he was to get a haircut, or he could not go."

When Bonita began to translate, Lennie held up his hand. "I know what he just said," Lennie told Bonita. "You don't have to translate most things. With the Mexican women from Chicago here and my Spanish course last year, we've been talking in both languages for two months."

"Is there anything more you want to say to him?" Bonita asked Lennie.

Lennie took a drag from his cigarette before replying. "I'm just a high school kid from South Boston who's in the party. I think it's O.K. for other people to know right away that I don't stand for the system. Those guys in shorts, paid union organizers, everyone knows they're for the system. If people want to think I don't work my twenty-five hours a week by judging me on how I look, that's their problem."

Perhaps, Bonita thought, when Lennie grew his hair that year in high school, he had the need to demonstrate his strength to the world. And for the first time Bonita understood the story of Sampson.

She began to translate what Lennie had said. Norberto stopped her, indicating he already understood. He looked annoyed. The party had discussed individual attitudes since March. Norberto was sure Lennie knew, for example, that most of the volunteers had to change their own prejudices. Some people from New York still had to overcome a certain disdain for residents of white segregated areas. The volunteers petitioned in integrated pairs or groups as the most obvious way of presenting CAR's ideas. The question of a neat personal appearance seemed clear--except to Lennie--as everyone worked at getting to know people in different parts of Boston.

For his part, Lennie had brought fifteen teenagers, black and white, along with their parents, to the May Day march. His junior year of high school, '74-75, he had written and directed a musical play called, "The Bus from Nowhere." The play made fun of the freezing classrooms and low college entrance statistics from segregated schools.

Bonita had heard earlier in the day from Don and Yvette that the play had been a resounding success. But she knew that the black students at Lennie's school still could not attend after-school activities for fear of being attacked. She also knew that Lennie admitted the need to break down racism in his own neighborhood. But despite the fact that in 1975 many workers still associated long hair with young people who didn't want a job in the "system," Lennie still refused to cut his hair.

"It's like asking blacks to change the color of their skin," he said in Spanish to Norberto, flipping the cigarette out of his hand. With that, he turned and went to a house directly across the street. Norberto shrugged and followed Lennie. Bonita followed more slowly.

A man in an open blue work shirt came to the door before Bonita could join them. "Nobody's home," she could hear the man shout before he slammed the door.

"I shouldn't have gone there," Lennie told them.

"He's a grouch."

At the next two houses, no one responded, though at the second one a woman peered at them from behind a curtain.

"A big family lives here," Lennie announced at the fourth house. Bonita heard a note of optimism in his voice. A girl who had evidently just washed her hair opened the door.

"Hi, Lennie," she said.

"This is my friend, Sharon Pittsfield," introduced Lennie. "Sharon, I want you to read our petition about making the schools better."

Sharon was pretty, with round brown eyes and clothes that seemed too big for her, Bonita thought. She would be even prettier if she gained a little weight.

"My dad says we can't sign nothin." She studied Norberto. "He's heard about the petition. He says you're a bunch of hippies that want to sit around and smoke dope."

"Sharon, you know how I changed . . . ."

"I know. And I know you told me communists don't want to steal our house . . . ."

"Get the hell away from the door, Sharon, and that no-account!" A woman's voice came from inside.

"I gotta go." Sharon's eyes rested on Lennie. They were sad. She shifted her gaze back to Norberto and then to Bonita and bit her lip. Her eyes became worried as she twisted her thin arms with helplessness.

"You gonna keep the door wide open to those wet backs and beatnicks?" screamed the voice.

"I'm really sorry," said Sharon. Bonita could see she was afraid, but not of them.

"SHARON!" She quickly closed the door, but they could still hear the shouting.

Lennie spat on the sidewalk. "Her old lady's a boozer, and she's got nerve to call us that crap." He strode away so quickly that Norberto ran to catch up. And Bonita paused to look back at the house.

When Lennie rang the next doorbell, neither Norberto nor Bonita caught a glimpse of the woman who answered. "Get off the streets and find a job," was all they heard. Lennie crossed the street diagonally then and headed straight for his own house. Norberto followed him.

Before Bonita realized Lennie was going home, Norberto and Lennie had disappeared inside Lennie's house. She quickened her pace so as not to be left alone in this neighborhood.

Just as she was about to step around an old tire, a large dog, skinny-ribbed with swinging teats, grabbed a loose bag of garbage. The dog shook it, breaking the bag, and then began to pick through the refuse. When Bonita moved toward the house, the dog growled.

Bonita stared at the dog until it looked up at her. "Listen, mama," said Bonita. "Things are tough all over for mothers. But if you don't let me go on my way, those fellas aren't going to be able to settle the argument that's comin'."

The dog put her muzzle back into the garbage and, ignoring Bonita, attacked the contents of the bag.

Bonita hesitated again, seeing no buzzer at the side screen door. There was only a thin aluminum frame with no place on the door to knock. She didn't want to wait too long behind Norberto and Lennie, either, for she realized that no one else in the house knew who she was. So she walked in, hoping to find Lennie and Norberto right away.

Alone in the kitchen stood a woman as tall as Lennie. She was ironing. Her pouchy face looked as if she'd been sick recently. Deep lines cut through her face from her nose to her chin. Brown spots of age showed on her cheeks, but perhaps, Bonita thought, they were freckles. She saw dishes piled in the sink and pots sat on the stove, but there was no smell of cooking. Instead, the sour odor from the outdoors blew through the kitchen.

"Just walk in, do ya, without knocking?" said the woman, who must have been Lennie's mother. "Come right into the house of complete strangers."

"You must be Mrs. McIntyre," said Bonita, feeling that to be apologetic wouldn't make the situation easier. She held out her hand. "I'm Bonita Simpson."

Mrs. McIntyre didn't smile and clicked her tongue on the roof of her mouth. But she put out her hand, too. "At least somebody's got some manners around here. My son goes out without saying where he's going and then he storms back in. And Norberto, too, is acting like I'm a fly on the wall until I cough and he turns around and says, 'I'm sorry, Mrs. McIntyre.'"

"Your son's upset." Bonita decided on a direct approach, knowing that Lennie's mother wasn't in the mood for a lot of empty words. "Norberto didn't want him to go to his friends' houses to talk with their parents about the petition and the dance tonight until he cut his hair. He went anyway and got thrown out."

"I could've told you that. I know what the neighbors think of him and all the rest of his friends. Some of 'em ain't even from here."

Mrs. McIntyre put her hands on her hips. Bonita noticed that her hair, which had once been a reddish brown, was now mostly gray and white. "You here from someplace else, too?" She blocked the doorway to the rest of the house.

"I'm from Brooklyn," said Bonita.

But before she could continue, a boy about eight came in behind Lennie's mother. "What's for dinner?" he whined. "I'm hungry."

"Get outta here," snapped his mother. And when he didn't budge, she gave him a sweep of her hand. He hung on the door. "You see," Mrs. McIntyre said to Bonita, "This son of mine was going to go to a brand new school one block away. Instead he's being bussed to Roxbury. You tryin to tell me you'd sit still for that?"

"The court order for busing also stopped the building of any more schools." Bonita stated. "We can't fight each other over a rotten situation."

"These're my kids you're talking about. For a long time we've known the schools are lousy. But some kids make it." Mrs. McIntyre indicated the open door where the eight year old stood listening. "Lennie stands a chance to go to college. I don't want <u>him</u>"--she pointed to the young boy--"working in a paper bag factory like his mother."

Bonita felt intimidated but tried to think of the right thing to say. "Schools have a built-in flunking scheme: grading. They say it's a normal curve for some kids to get F's. Even in the suburban schools. <u>Especially</u> in the catholic schools."

"I know you commies don't believe in God." Mrs. McIntyre seemed ready to argue religion.

Bonita decided against it. "The system stinks from the top down," she said. "You and I have got to fight for everything we have. But so long as those few people are there at the top, this government allows them to do as they please with our labor and our children. But we can't get rid of them unless we do it together."

"Not with me," said Mrs. McIntyre. "I don't associate with ni . . . bums."

Bonita saw she was getting nowhere. "I work in a big New York hospital as a nurse. Really a nurse's aide. And nothing else but a complete turnaround of priorities makes any sense. You should see what the hospitals are getting to."

"My sister, Alice, is a nurses' aide. She tells me all about the hospitals. Some of the other aides are damn lazy." McIntyre licked a finger and touched it to the iron. It sputtered. She unrolled a shirt from a pile of sprinkled clothes.

Bonita wondered how to ask this woman, who obviously didn't want to talk anymore, if she could join Norberto and Lennie in her house. Somehow, she felt better saying nothing.

"You'd better go into the living room and set yourself down," said Mrs. McIntyre. "Those boys are either asleep or have knocked each other senseless."

Bonita wanted to laugh, but Mrs. McIntyre wasn't laughing. She began to iron as if Bonita had already left the kitchen.

The hallway was dark. Lennie had his back to Norberto in the next room, where a weak lightbulb burned in the overhead fixture. The room had red curtains over the windows and the shades were drawn. Lennie was fiddling with the dials on a radio while Norberto was talking.

He was saying, "Back in the sixties it was very popular to have long hair. But even then, people thought these guys didn't work. And that's what your neighbors think. You can't get a good full time job if you look like that." Norberto spoke now in a mixture of Spanish and English. He had discussed these things before with Lennie and knew the words. He tried to get Lennie to laugh, "Under communism, no one will care about how long your hair is because _everyone_ will have to work."

Lennie didn't change his expression of disgust. "So maybe I'm teaching people now not to discriminate about looks."

"Open your eyes, Lennie: blacks in Roxbury and whites in South Boston. Irish whites in Charleston.

They hang their problems on each other. Nobody blames the bosses. Your one funny play--although that was good--isn't going to convince people of the need to overthrow capitalism. Getting to know people will. But you're not giving them a chance to understand what a good brain you have underneath that pony tail."

"This block has a lot of drunks. Most of the rest don't wanna work. Some are junkies. You don't want them under communism. No way."

"Are all of them so hopeless?" asked Norberto. "Even Sharon?"

Lennie turned up the music. He had gotten more into himself and his music since school let out, Norberto thought. He was such a good kid, too, reminding Norberto of his own Wilfredo: stubborn yet sensitive, both impatient and soft-hearted. Norberto also felt the kind of helpless block he had in arguments with Wilfredo. The more he pressed, the further away grew his son's responses.

The eight-year-old boy had come into the room and was watching quietly. This promised to be more exciting than waiting for his mother to iron while his stomach rumbled.

Bonita listened through the song, "Who's Makin' Love With Your Old Lady?" and she wondered if Lennie had a girl. Maybe in addition to his hair being a sign of distinctness, he felt more attractive with it long. His face was a lot like his mother's, flat, with freckles and small clefts on either side of his mouth. She began to talk then, to tell a story about herself. She had told her younger brother and sister this story over and over because they kept asking, until it no longer bothered her to tell it to a stranger. "Lennie; I used to steal stuff. I used to steal a lot from stores. And I never got caught."

Lennie put down the volume of the program and turned around. "So," he said.

"I never had any money; I gave it all to my mom what it didn't take me just to live on. And so I stole clothes and makeup." Bonita added, "I'm good at it."

Lennie appeared concerned. "But you could have got caught," he said. "And then you could lose your job. You're not a minor," he said seriously.

"Exactly," Bonita said. "But I didn't care because I would see the sweater or skirt, and I would already imagine it being mine. With me, it wasn't the thrill of getting away with something. It went beyond that. As soon as the picture of my new self was in my head, I couldn't stop."

"I'm that way with music," said Lennie. "When I hum a song I've made up, the sound begins inside my head. I can't help myself." He felt disarmed by her openness. Not many people in the party treated their own feelings as public property, especially in front of him, the youngest comrade in Boston. "I don't mean to escape from people. The music is there already. It's impossible to stop it. I want to go to my room and play it."

"Now it was different with me and pot," said Bonita. "I found I could stop doing that. When Nikkia said the party separates ourselves from the potheads, it made sense to me. Not only because it's illegal. But there're a whole lot of people we want to get to know who don't smoke, who don't base their relationships on that."

"Exactly," said Lennie. "Also with me. I found marijuana made my clarinet playing worse."

Bonita nodded her understanding, and then she said, "I kept up the stealing for a few weeks after I joined the party."

"What happened?" asked Lennie.

"I never told Nikkia. No one knew I went on doing it. I'm not going to tell you that I was suddenly afraid of getting caught. I wasn't. But I thought about why I needed the clothes, to look better, to make me more confident. I didn't think I'd stop wanting clothes just like that, but I said to myself, 'Why not start going to thrift shops?' I thought maybe I could shop carefully and look even better," she stopped talking for a moment and then said, "Why do you have to wear your hair long?"

"I really don't know," he said. "But it's a part of me. I feel that cutting it would be, you know, betraying my own self."

"What does your mother say to you about your hair?" asked Bonita.

"Oh, she hates it. Definitely," said Lennie. "She's always bugging me about it. But not as much as you guys."

"I had a little talk with your mother there in the kitchen," said Bonita. "I got the impression there are lots more things about you she really cares about. I don't think she really gives a shit about your hair."

Hearing the word 'shit,' the eight-year-old boy made a phoney gasp and put his hand over his mouth.

"You know I like you," said Norberto. "You're able to draw so many of your friends to our ideas with your music. I would be very sad if you stopped being active and left the party because your own thing was more important to you. Don't you think you'll be able to play the clarinet as well at the dance tonight if your hair is short?"

Lennie laughed a harsh, embarrassed laugh.

"I think you'll be able to play better," said the eight-year-old boy. "Sometimes when you play and you forget to stick your hair in a rubber band, you have to stop to push it out of your eyes."

"Shut up, Patrick," said Lennie, "Just tell me where Mom's sewing scissors are."

"I know where. Upstairs." Patrick vaulted over the railing and ran up the steps two at a time.

"You're not supposed to hang on the railing!" Lennie yelled automatically. "You broke it once already!"

No sooner had Lennie closed his mouth than Patrick was back. He avoided the last group of stairs by swinging over the bannister once again.

"You know you shouldn't do that. You think just because there's company here . . . ."

With a smile, Patrick handed Lennie the scissors. And before anyone said a word, Lennie grabbed a handful of his hair and cut. The sound of his hair between the scissors went right through him. He was furious for a moment as he stared at Norberto and Bonita. They didn't make him mad, though, he realized. Sharon's mother! Lennie gritted his teeth. That fucking bitch! He cut again. And again. Then he was able to pull the rubber band out easily. "There," he said.

Now, Lennie's hair looked horrible to Bonita. The three bunches had been cut at different lengths, and his hair stuck together where he had grabbed it. She felt a pain for him and a little guilty. More than anything, she was very proud. She wanted, in some way, to make him feel better.

"It's hard to get the back yourself," she said so that they all could barely hear her. "If you'll let me touch it up. I went to beauty school when I was eighteen." Bonita hoped he wouldn't see through this little lie. She had cut her brothers' hair at home for years but had never taken a lesson.

Lennie dragged over a chair and sat so Bonita could reach his head. She pulled up a window shade to let in more light. And very quickly, Bonita trimmed the hair to just below his ears. Then she lifted the sides by combing with her fingers, and it stayed, having been trained back by the pony tail.

"You've got beautiful waves up here I couldn't see before," she said. And she cut a stray wisp on each side, working quickly, knowing he wouldn't sit still for long. His hair fell naturally in place. He looked like a picture Bonita had seen of nineteenth century schoolboys. The overhead light now caught the red in his brown hair.

"I've had enough," said Lennie abruptly. "Let's get out of here." He grabbed his clipboard from off the radio where he'd left it.

Norberto saw that Lennie looked at himself in the mirror above the couch. "Buen mozo," he said with a smile that showed most of his very white teeth.

"Lucky for you I'm so handsome," Lennie retorted.

"Boy do you look better," Patrick said in a hearty voice. He bent to pick up the long hair and to play with it.

Lennie glared at him. "I told you to shut up."

"We'd better go," said Bonita, putting the scissors down beside Patrick. "Could you put them away, please, because your mother wouldn't like it if she couldn't find them."

Patrick continued to play with the hair, making a braid of sorts.

"Now, please," said Bonita.

Patrick gathered up all the hair first, finally the scissors and took them all upstairs, perhaps to create arrangements of his own.

In the kitchen, Mrs. McIntyre had long since started a wash. The machine was so noisy she couldn't hear the three comrades come into the kitchen. She saw them only after they passed her ironing board on their way out the door. Norberto paused to pat her shoulder, and she looked up to see Lennie slam the screen door behind him. "Oh my god!"

Lennie's mother rushed to the door and yelled at him, "Don't forget to be back here by six to take

Patrick over to the church." She hesitated, "Your hair looks swell."

Lennie waved one hand and kept walking toward the Volvo.

Mrs. McIntyre held the door to let Bonita and Norberto go by. "I don't know whether to bless you or curse you," she said without a smile.

Bonita couldn't help laughing this time. "Don't do either one," she said.

Boston Evenin

PLUS: **CALENDAR**

Vol. 207, No. 170 © 1975, Globe Newspaper Co.　　　THURSDAY, JUNE 19, 1975

Black family greeted by violence on moving into Hyde Park home

By Bob Sales
Globe Staff

Deanna Hammond's first impression of her sister and brother-in-law's new house in Hyde Park was admiring, maybe even a little envious. Then she met some of the neighbors.

"I've never been attacked by white people before," Mrs. Hammond, a native of Jamaica, recalled.

It happened Monday when Mrs. Hammond and her husband, Winston, were helping their in-laws, Elaine and Kenneth Daley, move into their $35,000 brick and shingle duplex near the Milton line on Washington street, in the middle of a white, residential neighborhood. Both the Hammonds and the Daleys are black.

When the two families arrived, they were greeted by a group of name-calling, rock-throwing teenagers and young adults who tore out sections of their picket fence and threatened the Daleys' well-being.

Mrs. Daley, 33, a soft-spoken mother of three, suffered a broken backbone Monday night when, she said, she was struck by a rock or bottle hurled at her when she was returning on foot from a nearby supermarket.

Mrs. Daley, also a native of Jamaica, was shocked by the welcome her family received. She said they did not inquire about the neighbors, the neighborhood, the school, the park or the pool across the street when they looked at the house.

None of that seemed important at the time.

"We'd been looking for three bedrooms for more than a year," said Mrs. Daley, who previously lived in an apartment in Roxbury. "This was just what we wanted. Three bedrooms. It was perfect."

The Daleys took title to the house last Thursday, using their life savings as a down payment. Their troubles started within a few days.

Early Saturday evening several windows were broken and one section of white picket fence on the side of the house was torn out. On Sunday night, another window was broken.

"We decided then that we'd have to move in Monday," said Mrs. Daley. "We couldn't leave it unoccupied. They would tear it down."

On Monday afternoon, a crowd of teenagers and young adults gathered on Washington street when the Daleys and their relatives started to move in their belongings.

The crowd hurled racial taunts and curses at the family. Mrs. Daley recalled one youth, about 20 years old, with brown hair over his ears, shouting: "You'd better get out of there or they'll burn that house down with you in it."

HYDE PARK, Page 3

Gov. Michael Dukakis and former Gov. Francis W. Sargent at Home for the first time since Dukakis took office. (Paul C...

Chapter 8

"The Daley house has been hit again," Zack Jerome announced. Someone broke Mrs. Daley's collar bone."

Zack came up just as Russell, Coralee and Una were packing up from the bake sale. There were some leftover pies that could be eaten at the dance that night. They had told everyone else to leave and were putting the card table in the trunk, when Zack arrived.

Zack Jerome was one of the permanent residents and leaders of the Boston work. He had been active in the civil rights movement in Mississippi. His going door to door in the town of Almira was so effective that one day he found a crowd of three hundred following him down the street. "Where do you think you're going?" asked a nervous chief of police. "Why, down to City Hall to register for the vote," said Zack. "You can't do that," the chief said. "You'll need more men than you have to stop us," said Zack. And then Zack told the growing number of people that they might have to fight. They soon became more than five hundred, and they did not have to fight.

In his slow, careful way of speaking, Zack explained to Russell the situation of the Daley family. "We've been taking shifts to help guard their house. This week some of Winston Daley's relatives came to stay with them, and the worst incident happened last night, when none of us could be there."

Russell had heard about the Daley family back in New York. They had bought one of the houses in the Hyde Park area near Matapan. This was one of the few areas of Boston with many "middle class" single family homes. Bernadette and Winston Daley had come to the U.S. from Jamaica ten years ago. They and their two children, Benjamin and James, had been living on the third floor of a three decker frame house in Dorchester. Winston worked as a process engineer at a chemical plant, Bernadette as a lab technician. Bernadette was tired of climbing the three flights with the children, and they could well afford their dream of a private home.

On the second night in their new house they were wakened by ROAR members throwing rocks and bricks through the windows. Then the shouts of "Go back to Africa, black bastards," could clearly be heard. The next day they found the sidewalk had been spray-painted "Niggers go home." In the following weeks, every window in the house had been broken at least once. Keeping up with repairs--seventeen windows--had cost them hundreds of dollars. But they accepted CAR's offer to help only when Benjamin, three years old, got hit by a rock in his sleep.

Russell couldn't imagine how he would react under similar circumstances. He thought of himself sitting in his own living room and seeing a brick crash in. Never to know when it might happen again. To have to arrange the children's beds in the center of the room, or in the corner furthest from the windows. He could never be sure of his children's safety! Imagining his own kids in danger, Russell didn't think he could stick it out anywhere.

He wanted to take the Daley children in his arms, to comfort Mrs. Daley and to bring them all to some place safe. At the same time he knew they had to take on those vicious cowards.

"I'd like to go there," he said. "And take Timothy and Thomas with me. They're old enough to help out. I don't expect these racists are brave enough to attack in broad daylight."

"Timothy and Thomas'd only start a fight with each other," said Coralee.

"I think they need to get out and feel useful," Russell was insistent.

"They need to develop some responsibility around our house first," said Coralee. "I won't trust them until they've proven themselves."

Zack decided to stay out of the argument. He knew Coralee and her children very well. But since Russell was living in the house, and Zack had heard about Russell's way with children, he thought some changes might occur. So instead of getting into the disagreement, he looked over the petitions to see where the signers lived. He thought about the fact that there were racial battles going on in most of the districts on any given day this summer.

Russell felt compelled to bring others to the Daley house with him. But he didn't want to argue with Coralee, either. And so, instead of answering Coralee right away as he wanted to, he let his mind wander.

And his eyes took in the four pies. Gradually it came to him that he often ate without hunger. Why, at UPS he had indulged in the kinds of rich snacks he would never have been able to stomach at the steel plant! There, where survival itself had become an obsession to him, his all-consuming ned had been not to eat but to organize. He realized, now, months later, how much he missed the men at the mill.

Russell half-listened to Coralee and Zack making plans for driving to the Daley's, and his mind drifted. Right this minute he was sweating as much as he did when he walked around his work area at the mill. The burning seemed to come from inside his body rather than outside.

Russell's body seemed heavy to him as well, as if he were actually wearing the fiberglass coat, shoes and gloves with their aluminum reflective surface. His legs moved slowly as he put away the last table. He seemed to be wearing the protective leather pants, too. Maybe he was tired from writing on a clipboard and standing in one place for two hours. He sniffed, and then he knew of something else that made him remember the mill. The sulphur stink in the Boston air this humid summer day was triggering his whole body to react as if he were still at work in the plant.

The city pavement stretched off in the distance like a craneway for the open hearth furnaces. Russell breathed deeply, a habit he developed to try to rid himself of the mill's pollution every chance he got outdoors. The sulphur stench persisted, he remembered, in the long span between taps of the molten slag. Then they repaired the runners where the iron would flow uncovered. Russell thought of those hours when nothing much happened. At such quiet times even the open hearth became like his own living room. Actually, they all spent less time in their own living rooms than beside the furnaces!

Weird, how relaxed they became, he thought, as if there were no quick danger anywhere. A kind of mental weight let him and everyone else pretend nothing could ever happen and made him want to do less and less to fight back, as he had been feeling at home lately. He could sink into the rug beside the couch, trying to stay awake. The healthy urge to fight back became a dream.

He thought back on how he, Quigley and Barnes had been the core organizers, as well as Morales, who knew the guys who worked on top of the coke ovens. In his flash of thoughts, Russell remembered trying to convince the white guys who were electricians or in the control booths to strike with them, and of them saying no. Their own loyalties dated back to World War II when there had been two unions: one white, one black. Then in the late sixties, instead of building new plants, the bosses offered incentive pay for tonnage produced, to divide the men. This division hit back on the electricians who got no incentive pay while black men in operations made more.

The strike of 1970 was more successful than the previous ones. They forced the building of the first Basic Oxygen Furnace in the country. But because the process took less time, Barnes and other men were laid off. Soon the company introduced continuous casting, and steel wasn't wasted in forming the ingots. Since there were no more ignots, they didn't have to be reheated. And the men who had transported them to the rolling mills were unnecessary, so there were suddenly no more of them, either.

Before the strike, Russell's club had tried to persuade him to run for shop steward as an open communist. Until the layoffs, though, he didn't fully understand that the reform of more efficient Basic Oxygen Furnaces, or B.O.F.'s, essentially would mainly mean fewer jobs in the steel industry. Finally he did agree to bring out revolutionary politics. And, after that, there was the work of pulling together an election slate.

On the slate were men from mill rights, who repaired the furnaces; men in operations, who ran the furnaces; and men like Quigley from maintenance, who repaired the brickwork. Russell knew that none of the guys in the control booths would vote for a communist slate, let alone agree to run on one with him. But he found it exciting to plan the campaign and fight the anti-communism that came about. More than he realized, however, he was expecting to win. When their slate received only twenty-five percent of the vote, he took it very hard.

Russell smiled to himself now, standing on the corner in the city of Boston, thinking how personally he had taken the defeat! Pat and his club reminded him repeatedly that the party's politics had advanced. Barnes, who helped the campaign by holding meetings in his home, even joined the party. A new chapter of the Committee Against Racism was formed. But Russell had felt a subjective loss. Why didn't a majority like his ideas? They all worked in the damn plant. He looked at the number who had voted against him and felt that he had done everything he could to change their minds. He could not get over the feeling that he had lost.

Then the company started to build continuous casters, and it seemed that everyone but Russell forgot about the election as they bid for the new jobs. Now that the dual, racist union system had been eliminated, black and white alike put in their bids. But the criterion of seniority meant that the jobs filled up according to the same segregated pattern. Russell recalled their CAR leaflets, which pointed out that blacks were first fired and therefore always had low seniority.

One of these high seniority positions was that of strand operator. A strand operator pushed lubricating powder onto the mold of the caster. Russell recalled the man named Douglas who got one of these jobs. Douglas had the opinion that nobody else could gauge the flow from the tundish as well as he. Douglas went along with the seniority system all the way.

It happened that one day the steel was too cool coming out of the ladle. The man opposite Douglas, Herb Kretchmer, had to take the shroud off so everything could be moved. No one new had been hired yet to work as spotter, so Douglas couldn't see Kretchmer when he went to move the ladle back. Douglas moved the ladle in the wrong direction. The steel, which was cold enough to plug up but still molten at two thousand degrees, poured over Herb Kretchmer.

Douglas called in sick the rest of the week. When he came back he apologized to Russell and others. No one knew how to answer him. Now Russell shivered in the heat, for he had been working in the caster that day and had heard Herb's scream.

As U.S. Steel built more B.O.F.'s, more men got laid off. Some guys came up to Russell and said they were sorry they hadn't voted for him, for he had been right. Russell's club again struggled with him to get out of his rut and spend more time with friends away from the job. The CAR chapter grew by ones and twos.

At that time, Russell remembered, the smaller American steel companies closed. The Japanese and Swedish and German steel processes moved ahead still more efficiently, so the U.S. companies were forced to cut costs further. More continuous casters were built so that the steel would get pre-molded into three ready-to-use forms. Billets of four by four inches were more malleable for I beams than the huge ingots had been. This, in turn, led to more layoffs.

But certain jobs, like Quigley's in maintenance, could not so easily be eliminated. Bricks constantly needed repair in the B.O.F.'s, as well as in the blast furnace ladles. Quigley was a bricklayer. A little wiry man, he had dreams of running his own limousine company. With the incentive pay, he bought a limousine. But he continued organizing the CAR chapter at the plant six days a week. Sundays he reserved for polishing and running the limo.

The bricks Quigley worked with were made of silicone. Quigley was always careful to wear a mask, especially when ripping out the old brick. Most men didn't wear their masks for the same reasons Russell didn't wear his. It irritated his face, got sticky and hot.

Russell remembered well the day Quigley fell out unconscious, for the third time in one week. He was a young guy, too, only twenty-nine. He went to the hospital and was back again in a month. Russell himself had been in the hospital fourteen days that year. Pleurisy and double pneumonia. He knew that whatever was wrong with Quigley was from the hot gases and the dust in the air of the caster. None of the masks were foolproof. But nobody could prove it. And Quigley got no compensation.

"Why do you come back?" he'd asked Quigley.

"Same reason you do. The money. How else can I raise my family and keep up two cars for me and my wife to work?" With the gasoline crisis of 1972 Quigley still kept the 1970 Lincoln limousine, but it stayed in the garage. He had snuffed a laugh, "Some people eat to live; others live to eat. I work to keep on working!"

Quigley had silicosis. He didn't die suddenly as had Valentino, Kendall and Kretchmer. Russell remembered Quigley's slow death, for he had been with him at the time he died. When the diagnosis turned to tuberculosis, his weight had gone from one thirty-five to seventy-five pounds. He was embarrassed to spit the blood into a tissue in front of his wife, Irma.

Going back and forth from the hospital, Russell composed leaflets calling for accurate diagnosis of all silicosis cases which affected the bricklayers. And for compensation for lung cancer of the guys on top of the coke ovens. At that time Irma told Russell that she and Quigley had decided to sell the limo and give the money to the Committee Against Racism. The struggle at the job was still going on when Quigley died. Russell and Irma insisted on staying in the room while the nurses washed Quigley's wasted body.

Seeing him naked, Russell recalled the story Quigley had told him of hearing shots in the lobby of his apartment building in the middle of the night. Quigley had rushed into the hall without a stitch of clothing on. He so startled the intruder that he dropped his gun. For some reason, Russell chose this moment in the hospital room to remind Irma of that story. While Irma's round face smiled for the first time that day, the nurse in her surprise dropped Quigley's ID tag on the floor. Russell picked it up and carefully tied it, according to the hospital requirement, onto Quigley's left great toe.

Russell began to pant from the hot summer sun and the thoughts of the mill. He looked up. The sun was white hot like steel ready to be poured into ingots. He could not look at it, and as he put his head down there came again the sulphur smell of the tapping process. His eyes stung from the salt of his sweat and tears of anger.

Chapter 9

"Russell, what do you think?" Russell heard Zack's voice as it broke into his memories. "Timothy and Thomas might be too young to be going with us to the Daley house just now. But they could do the leafletting work at the subway stops in the morning. Those kids need a plan for the whole summer." Zack looked at Coralee, asking for her opinion as well. "Right now I think they could watch the smaller kids while we bring Renee."

"We can all go in one car and leave yours at Coralee's," suggested Russell, still partly lost in his thoughts.

He noted how Coralee seemed to take to Zack's suggestion. Had he been too ready to get into a tug of war with her this morning, as well as last night? Was that because her habit of shouting scared him?

There was no time now to wonder about how he could act differently, for they had to drive both cars to Coralee's first, and Una was making plans to go with them. Russell listened to the easy conversation between Zack and Coralee. They were talking about the Daleys.

"You know that family's got my praise," Coralee was saying. "I used to have a prejudice against West Indians. But I never seen anybody stand up to those dogs better than Bernadette and Winston. There I go, insulting the animals again."

Zack chuckled from his belly and got into his car. "I bet that family never saw a stick of dynamite like you, either!"

Russell noticed how Coralee shrugged off the compliment, and he saw that she was confident of her strength. But something made her afraid to manage her own children, something that made him want to argue with her. Not finding the answer, he suddenly became tired of the whirl of inner questions and memories.

"What are your plans for the summer, Una?" he asked. Her animated face consumed his thoughts for the entire ride to Coralee's. There, they picked up

Renee and dropped off Zack's car. On the way to Hyde Park Russell took in the sights like a tourist. Through block after block of Dorchester Russell saw three-deckers exactly alike. One block would have black children playing baseball-wiffleball at the curb, with black men trimming the bushes and fixing their cars. The next block had white children running after a dog and white women washing cars and pushing laundry carts down the sidewalk.

The scenes reminded Russell of the segregation in the steel plant in Pittsburgh. At the coke ovens you saw only blacks at the top, where it was most dangerous, and whites in the larry cars. The control room jobs were for whites and maintenance jobs were for blacks. Russell's thoughts shifted back to the three-deckers. Watching block after block of divided people went through him like the sawing of a dull knife.

Russell knew that here in Boston right after the 1850's, discrimination against the Irish had been the strongest. He had read something of the history of South Boston since he'd volunteered for the roughest detail of the summer: the big projects on A, B, C and D streets. These projects, where the elevators and incinerators no longer worked, had replaced the stinking refuse of burned out hundred-year-old two-flats. The signs on shop doors a hundred years ago had read, "No Irish Need Apply." So men got jobs on the waterfront. It was said that near those piers there had been more bars per square mile than anywhere else in the world. Today, once again, jobs were scarce, but now ROAR was trying to organize Irish in the projects of South Boston to keep out the blacks.

Russell tried to imagine himself as a Southie, which many South Boston residents called themselves. He felt sure that, like them, he would have tried to get out of the projects. He might have modeled his life according to the lectures from his teachers about the need to get ahead. But he never had been good in school and had gotten D's by paying as little attention as he had to. Perhaps, Russell told himself, that was where he'd developed his ability to tune out the world in his own living room.

He might have learned how to get ahead, though, and to improve his life somewhat. He would have left the projects for the three deckers on these streets.

Here, tree branches had been hacked away to make room for overhead wires, whereas the projects had no trees at all. Of course, if he got a clean job like Winston Daley, he would have chosen a house in Hyde Park with soft grass for the kids.

He could see himself making a move like the Daley family. If he were black, lots of houses would be available to him now. Many of them were in neighborhoods that had been all white, but now whites couldn't buy there because of the banks' redlining policy. He could see Pat narrowing down the final decision to two houses. She had good taste in these matters. The whole family could have their say after that. The kids would be excited.

The move would not be like the step down his own family had just made, from a house to an apartment. No, when the kids got inside a two-story house, right away they would run up and down the stairs. What fun to have their bedroom on a whole 'nother floor!

He pictured the back yard with a tall cottonwood tree, so restful that he longed to lie in bed on a summer night and listen to the leaves moving. On a similar summer evening . . . he could almost feel the rock crash through the window and hit his face. He could not know the Daley's physical pain, but he understood the deep surprise. A sadness came then, a hurt that spread through his chest.

"This is Hyde Park," said Zack.

Russell could see the difference for himself. As he had imagined, the streets were green with maple trees and clipped grass. What he noticed first, though, were giant elms that grew between the sidewalk and street and rose unobstructed by wires. The houses were rather close together but looked cool. Looking at the calm Saturday afternoon, Russell felt a sense of relief and ease.

A man mowing his grass looked up and saw three black women and a black man in the same car with a white man. Russell stared back and waved. The man scratched his head.

"The Daley house is around the next corner."

Without seeing the house, Russell could feel a pounding of his heart. His hands became sweaty. The ache of hurtful surprise came back as they rounded the corner. There he saw three police cars, parked haphazardly. They drove closer, and he saw a group of men and women, about a dozen of them. Then he heard them yelling, and he became afraid. He could make out their faces finally, ugly with anger. Spotting Coralee's car, one of the women stuck up the middle finger of each hand.

Zack pointed to the Daley house. "Shit, look at the swastika," said Coralee, indicating the side wall.

"They must have spray-painted that last night," said Una. "It wasn't there yesterday when we visited the Daleys."

Renee began to cry. Russell put his arm around her and studied the house. It was small, about six rooms. Every window on the side that faced them, upstairs as well as down, had been broken. A blue Chevy sat in the driveway, and all four tires had been slashed.

Russell felt no more brave than Renee. But the sight of the broken windows and the swastika and the car resting on its hub caps made his teeth clamp down, one jaw against the other. He leaned up to touch Coralee. "Let's get out of the car. We're not doing anybody any good sitting in here."

Zack explained to Russell, "We can't leave the car on this street. Last time they smashed our windshield. And the cops didn't lift a finger. I'll park it on the next block."

"I'll go with you and walk back," said Una. "You should't go alone."

Renee looked at the jeering crowd as she got out the back door. Taking his arm from around her, Russell could feel her wanting to retreat to the car. She cried more loudly and covered her face.

"Nigger lover!" shouted a voice from the crowd."

"What a baby," said Coralee. "If I'd a known you were going to act like this, you never would've come along."

At that moment, Russell felt strong enough to walk over to the knot of people and take them on by himself. He focused on Coralee with an effort. "It doesn't help to belittle her," he said evenly.

Zack pulled the car away, and the three of them remained alone in the street. "I suppose you're right," said Coralee. She led the way around the nearest police car to the Daley house.

Two cops leaned on their car, seeming not to hear

the shouts of the crowd twenty feet away. They also appeared not to see Coralee and Renee, for only when Russell passed the squad car did one of them say, "I wouldn't bother with this mess if I were you." They made a move as if to stop him.

"I work with Mr. Daley," said Russell.

While they approached the house, a car pulled up. A man got out and opened the trunk. He lifted a tire out and rolled it half way up the short driveway. Winston Daley came out of the front door then, and Russell could see that he resembled the man who had just driven up.

"Get the fuck inside, or we'll cream your ass." Another voice from across the street.

Winston ignored the threat and rolled the tire the rest of the way toward his car. When he turned around, Coralee waved to him.

Winston waved back and smiled. He was a slim, slightly stooped man with a Roman curve to his nose. Russell waved back. Moving closer to the house, he could see black paint on the sidewalk, "Niggers suck dick."

Russell extended his hand to Mr. Daley even before he reached the driveway. "I'm Russell," he said, "Friend and comrade of Coralee."

More timidly, Renee held out her hand. "I'm Coralee's daughter," she said. "I'm so sorry." And she began to cry again.

Winston awkwardly took her elbow. "Child," he said.

"I haven't seen her cry since she was a baby," said Coralee, somewhat ill at ease.

"You just don't know," Renee stated flatly, through her tears.

"The first night I cried, too," admitted Winston. "But when my son got hit with a rock through a window, I got mad. Then we all got determined. We bought plexiglas. And we called you.

"My wife was even more determined to call you when the cops did nothing about the Pages' little girl being chased down the street. Some nut with a torch." Winston rubbed his head as if to erase the memory. "Excuse my manners. This is my brother, David. David Daley."

David's nose also curved. His arms and legs were slim, too, but he had a firm little belly. "I'm awfully glad to meet you," David said. "What this older brother of mine doesn't tell you is that shatterproof plastic windows set him back thirty-three dollars a pane."

Russell whistled, and he and Coralee followed David to the open trunk of his car. They took out two more tires and rolled them to Winston's car.

Just then, Una and Zack came into view. They all could hear the yelling, "Black bastards!"

"As long as it's just words," said David to Zack.

The men across the street screamed louder. "We want the big nigger."

"Don't worry 'bout my reacting," said Zack to those close to him.

The screams became a shrill pitch with the words no longer distinguishable to the people in the driveway. With the women and men all working, they quickly placed the tires on the car. David's wife, Eunice, called and beckoned to them from the kitchen window, and they went inside. David introduced them to Eunice and Winston's two children, Benjamin and Gabriel, who Russell guessed were both under five.

Now that he was in the house, under a kind of seige, Russell began to assess the people he was involved with. He didn't hear the conversation around him. Many times his co-workers had accused him of not paying attention. For instance, during the crucial tapping of the blast furnace, Russell would be busy absorbing the moods of others around him. He couldn't help it. He watched their actions as though they were the changing elements and not the molten iron and slag.

Renee, he noticed, was coming out of herself, having built three-year-old Benjamin's confidence in her. That was important for Russell to know. If something happened, Benjamin could be calmed by Renee. Children were so quick to trust, Russell thought. It took years of experience to undo that trust and a long time to rebuild.

He didn't know Eunice. But her calm voice and the solid set of her shoulders and arms reassured him. She seemed to say to him that she was the one who took charge of her own household. This meant that if they all had to act, that she could be the one to talk her husband into action. Russell watched Eunice find utensils for what he smelled as a goat curry. He was fascinated by the manner in which she handled herself in a kitchen that was not hers, with strangers she had never seen. It seemed to Russell that Eunice had managed to keep the trust one had had as a child. She would listen to Zack if it became necessary.

David talked and joked a great deal. He seemed to Russell to be nervous, for he laughed too much. But he appeared to be a very proud man, who would not take kindly to following another man's ideas. And so Eunice would guide him.

In those moments, Russell got to know Coralee a bit more, too. He seemed to be able to understand her better here than while she was relating to her family. He remembered her telling him that while she was getting to know the community and its movements, that she had given over the workings of the family to her husband. She had said that he often remained in the kitchen, while all Coralee's energy flowed into the streets.

Why Coralee was happier outside her home he could not say. Perhaps she took her family somewhat for granted simply because her husband had done everything. In any case, Russell sensed that she resented the detail of a household and had no patience for fitting the tiny gears of a family together. He predicted, though, with a sense of relief, that Coralee would fight side by side with him and Zack. An invisible yoke bound the three of them. He only had to remember not to nip at her sense of political priorities. Or she would turn to fight him instead.

Right now, Coralee was speaking about this neighborhood, "The folks here will not come out like they did with us in Roxbury. There, they had seen us rally, and they understood it was in their interest to get out there with us." She pointed around the room, "But here, people think of their house more as protecting them from invaders. Now we could be the invaders as well as ROAR. So they would have to have a reason to want to unite with us."

Coralee faced Zack with a short smile, "Me and Bernadette--Mrs. Daley--went around already, door to door, on this block. You told us to wait until a couple of white comrades could go with us. But I didn't want to wait. We did it when Winston wasn't home, because he never would have let her."

She hurried on to explain, "You were right, a lot

of people wouldn't even open the door, seeing two black women through the peephole or around their living room curtains. But most did open up. And a lot of them said they hated, really hated, ROAR's attacks on black children and others. Not that all of them were ready to do anything about it. But two people told us they thought busing was important and that they would help in some way." Coralee added somewhat defiantly, "Because we <u>asked</u> them to help and not just to sign the petition."

Zack chuckled, his deep laugh. That was his way of showing Coralee he appreciated, even admired, her doing something he would have hesitated to do. "We usually organize going door to door with whites and blacks together," he explained to Winston. "Not that white comrades are needed for protection in areas like this. We do it to demonstrate the character of CAR."

"I know that," Coralee retorted. "But sometimes you can't wait for everything. The way I felt after that second window breaking, when Ben got hit in the head, well, it was good that Winston wasn't home to try to stop us from going around to all the neighbors."

Zack didn't reply, and Russell felt the same admiration he realized that Zack must have had. They both listened to Coralee admit her deliberate planning.

"I think you did the right thing," Russell said, finally. But Coralee didn't acknowledge him. Maybe, Russell thought, she didn't need to hear his encouragement. But more likely, Russell thought, she probably took him for granted, as she did her family.

"I would have tried to stop you, and Bernadette," Winston said. "As much as I like you, Coralee, I wouldn't have stepped up to the houses around here, either. You might say I was becoming afraid of people."

Winston added somewhat timidly, "We grew up with the idea that American blacks were lazy. I never thought a black American woman would turn out to be my motivator."

"I got rid of that prejudice right away coming to this country," said Eunice. "I've worked in many kinds of jobs--toy factories, cleaning houses. You tend to notice more about society the lower the job you have."

"You can't say I don't know what's happenin'," Winston was quick to say. "Why, I can see that with a force of people like this," he pointed to Russell, Zack, Coralee and himself, "we could take on the whole system."

"Brother mine," said David. "You always were a hothead."

"But you can't argue with his notions," said Eunice. She looked out the window then. "One, no, two of the police cars are pulling away just now."

Renee joined her at the window. "But most of that crowd is still out there--all men--with a pile of beer bottles."

"That's all right," said Winston. "I feel safer without the cops around. You never know who they're going to take off to jail. They've never arrested the vandals. At any rate, no matter what the cops do, I've got to keep on with our life. I'd best be going to the hospital to visit Bernadette." He took up a rolled bunch of newspaper that had been on the kitchen table. The scent of fresh cut roses came to them as he lifted the top flap. "She thought I chose this particular house because of the rose bushes. They remind me of home."

Russell got up. "Let me go out there with you at least."

"I think we should all go," said Zack.

"Won't more of us provoke them?" argued David.

"Maybe," Zack replied. "But they're more likely to jump one or two people thinking they've got the advantage."

"The children will be all right with me," Renee said. She had folded paper hats for both boys while the rest of them were talking.

Eunice agreed.

Outside the sun was still hot. But the five-thirty light slanted, and Russell could hear the rhythmic chirps of catbirds singing the day to a close. He felt relaxed. The sound reminded him of when he was a child, satisfied with a day of summer play. His mother would have supper ready.

While in this mood he contemplated that it might be a mistake to get into it with ROAR. They couldn't keep up this seige forever. The city would see that busing as a solution was unrealistic. The money that was being spent on buses could go for new schools.

Russell wrapped his arms around his chest, thinking of his own children. No child should be bused into danger. His own arms felt like his mother's—safe.

No sound came from the nine men across the street. Their women had retreated. As Winston opened his car door, the first bottle smashed behind the rear tires. "Scum!" said Winston, slamming the door shut and kicking the broken glass away from the tires.

A second, broken, bottle came higher than the first—Winston didn't see it coming—and splintered on his hand that held the roses. The rolled package fell, and roses scattered on the driveway. Winston's hand, slashed by the glass, dripped blood on the cement where he stood, unable to think or move.

The two cops in the remaining car kept their windows rolled up for the air conditioning. The driver rested his arm on the steering wheel.

Eunice ripped at her headscarf and wrapped Winston's hand. He shook his head as if to clear it, and another bottle crashed at Eunice's feet. It all happened in less than five seconds.

Across the street the nine men moved closer together. The tallest, in plaid shorts, seemed to be in charge. A fat, bald man and a guy with a baseball hat worn backwards moved to the front.

Between clenched teeth Zack stated, "We have to deal with these shitheads. We don't have a choice. They'll trash the house."

"I think the other cops left to give them that chance," said Coralee. "They know the people on the block would question why so many cops didn't bust up a fight."

"Maybe there's not going to be a fight," said Russell.

"What the hell do you mean?" Zack asked.

"They've been throwing crap. They're too chicken to engage us one to one."

"All the more reason why we got to," argued Zack. "Our line is, they'll grow unless they're stopped. Didn't we learn from Nazi Germany, or what?"

"This isn't the thirties." Russell said.

While they talked, David moved slowly toward the house. Zack spotted him and turned to Eunice. "We're going to ask you to take some leadership in this," he said. "Are you willing?"

"All my life I've been doing it," said Eunice.

She picked up a broken bottle by the neck. "Where do I begin?"

"You can start by keeping David here. He's headed for the house, and with fewer of us it's more dangerous."

With her free hand, Eunice grabbed the tire iron that dangled from Russell's fingers. "I'll tell him I'll break both his legs if he doesn't," she said, and stomped toward him as though she meant every word.

"Coralee, you'll be in charge of the group with Una, Eunice and David," Zack glanced over at the two of them arguing. "If we can get him to join us."

Zack handed two of the car jacks to Russell and Una. "Russell, you'll be second in command to me as Eunice to Coralee. But," he added, indicating Una, "we are all leaders here."

"I'm ready," said Coralee. "We should go single file across the street before forming our groups. We'll be less of a target. I can start if you make sure about Eunice and David."

Just then a brick shattered Winston's car windshield. The men across the street moved closer, as if on signal.

Russell watched Coralee start across the street. Una followed close behind her. And then Winston. Russell sensed his own feet moving. He walked because Winston was in front of him, but something kept telling him it was the wrong thing to do.

A barrage of bottles crashed furiously in the street and on both cars. They just missed the moving men and women.

The man in the baseball hat and the fat man in front had blackjacks. They crouched, advancing into the street. Russell saw in more detail now the seven men in back of those three. Most of them were taller than any one of his friends. They each had a baseball bat or a club. But one T-shirt had the words, EAT ME. Another had the insignia of Harvard University. The man with plaid shorts stood next to a man whose shirt was open to the waist. Russell couldn't make the link connecting these guys' appearance with any serious intent.

The man with the baseball cap swung his blackjack to Coralee's face. She blocked it with her forearm. Before the guy could swing again, Una and Winston were on him.

Winston swung a heavy car jack on his target with a fury. He pictured this man hitting his wife's jaw. He no longer felt the pain in his own hand.

Russell hesitated. He knew he made an easy mark standing still, but he couldn't move, forward or back. Suddenly there seemed to be too many ROAR guys all around. He looked for Zack.

There he was, urging David forward. Eunice ran straight into Russell. She shouted, "Come on!"

In that moment, Russell knew what to do. He and Eunice should get on this closest man in plaid shorts. Russell had the jack raised in his hand. David and Zack would be right up with them. But again, he wavered.

None of them noticed the cops get out of their car.

Eunice moved in to slash the fat man's face with her bottle. She was stunned by the amount of blood. The man in the plaid shorts shielded his own face and stepped closer to Eunice. She swung back the tire iron. The man with the baseball cap turned to run, bumping the guy in plaid shorts. He side-stepped and swung his bat to hit Eunice.

Before Zack could take a step toward Eunice, the two cops grabbed him. They hit at him. He wrestled. They handcuffed him. He shouted to Russell, "Fight on!"

Russell sensed that everything depended on his decision now. He could see that his group was still outnumbered. Two of the thugs still held bats. Another man picked up the blackjack that the fellow with the cap had dropped.

"Retreat!" Russell yelled.

"You're crazy!" shouted Coralee, for she was looking into the faces of ROAR. They had been surprised at the vigorous fight back. They were shocked at the sight of angry women. Even the man in plaid shorts hesitated, his bat still poised.

Coralee could see Una and Winston stop, undecided, on hearing Russell's order. She heard a siren wail. She could tell the ROAR men heard it, too. One of them, with the blackjack, took courage at the sound. He got behind Russell. Coralee shouted, "Watch your back!"

The warning came too late. Something hit Russell, hard, on the back of the head. Dimly, he saw both cops get Zack in a chokehold and drag him to the squad car. The real danger pounded through his head for the first time.

Russell knew only one thing. The goons must not gain ground toward the house. The children and Renee would become their territory. More cops would be coming any minute. He yelled, "Don't retreat toward the house." But the command was confusing to Eunice. And David didn't know which way to run.   The squad car left with Zack, its siren screaming.

Four ROAR men, including the man in plaid shorts and the two in printed t-shirts, started for the house. Then they saw Una and Coralee. The two women had got together, back to back. It was in both their minds to defend the house. They swung their weapons wide. The men altered their course.

They all could hear more sirens, louder now. A neighbor peered out his front door.

Hearing the police cars, the two ROAR men in T-shirts began to circle away from the scene entirely. More neighbors came out. One of them yelled at the man in plaid shorts about to hit Una, "Hey, you!" The man stopped. He ran around the side of the house.

Russell watched the scene with a numb sensation, as if he were dreaming. He felt the back of his head. Finding a huge knot, he looked at the hand that came away covered with blood. His only thought was: I should have fought. We'll all be arrested anyway.

He realized he was beginning to think less and less clearly. He weaved unsteadily toward the others. "Winston, get in your car. With Eunice." He tried to make sense. "David! The children, and Renee. Go to the hospital."

Then Russell remembered, with a leaden feeling, that Coralee's car was way over on the next block. The sirens became much louder. He panted, "We have no time to make it to our car."

Now he was dizzy; he leaned heavily against Coralee. Una took his other arm. They watched Eunice, Winston and David run to the car. Renee came out of the house, shooing the children in front of her. Then they all drove away in David's damaged car.

"I can't believe this neighborhood; nobody did nothing." said Coralee, more to herself than to Russell. "We're going next door," she nudged Russell. "The woman's name is Priscilla Chambers. Her car is in her driveway, so I know she's home."

Coralee held Russell from falling. Russell began to vomit, with Coralee and Una supporting him on their arms. Somehow, they walked quickly along the walkway to the pink stucco house that Coralee had visited that week. Squad cars pulled up to the Daley house. The police ran into the Daley house just as a woman opened her front door for Coralee. The sight of Russell made Priscilla Chambers cry out.

"I saw the terrible things they did all night to the Daley people," Miss Chambers said. She was at least seventy-five years old, Russell guessed. He saw that she had very blue eyes.

"We may have to stay here for awhile," said Coralee. "We'll be arrested if we don't. Do you mind?"

"That head of his needs our attention right away," said Miss Chambers with a practical tone to her voice.

Afterwards, Russell didn't remember anything of that evening. He figured that they stayed for several hours. The last memory he had was that of seeing a large blood stain on Miss Chambers' parlor couch and hearing at the same time the rhythmic song of the catbirds.

Chapter 10

A light scent of soap followed Norberto out the door of Yvette and Don's apartment. Nikkia imagined for a second Norberto washing his clothes with a bar of soap at night by hand. Then the phone rang, and the sharpness of his features drifted and blurred until she couldn't recall what he looked like. All that remained was her desire. And with a start, Nikkia thought that the call might be Lawrence.

Yvette spoke into the phone, "Who is at the Daley house now?" she asked. "Did anyone besides Mrs. Daley get injured?" Nikkia remembered that Yvette's reports to the steering committee meetings in New York had been very thorough. At this moment, Nikkia envied Yvette's concentration on the particulars. Her own thoughts were still pulled to thoughts of how the warm afternoon sun would feel on her flesh as her fingers played on Lawrence's silky skin.

Nikkia couldn't follow the phone conversation easily any longer. She saw Lawrence's face, where Norberto's had been, to accompany the powerful physical longing that so often came over her on a midafternoon. That was when she enjoyed most making love with Lawrence. And it was in the afternoon when she was most moved by something within her to go to the studio, to do her best workout. Her extensions and balance would be at their peak. Sometimes only Nadeen, an instructor, and she would be there.

By performance time, Nikkia's legs and arms moved smoothly, but the inner pulse was gone with the afternoon sun. Audience contact and the night were incidental to her, she realized, whereas for most of the other dancers, that was where their lives began. They strove to do their best in the show, where they could prove to the critics and to the other dancers who was better. Nikkia herself did not live for that acclaim because she had already danced her best, alone.

Perhaps the applause hadn't mattered, she thought

now, because from the beginning the ballet was her mother's idea. That might have been why she was able to quit. Yet she knew the real reason she had left dancing and could still remember the exact moment she had made up her mind. Nikkia recalled the details while Yvette's voice on the phone faded into the background.

It was in August of 1970, while some members of her company were enjoying an after theater party at the apartment of a brother and sister of the wealthy Gaynor family, Jeff and Iona Gaynor. . . .

x x x

Nikkia wasn't uncomfortable. On the contrary, Jeff and his sister always made her feel quite at home. Certain select dancers--the most attractive or the best--were chosen to grace the Gaynor apartment's twelve rooms. Nikkia hadn't entered most of those rooms, sprawled atop one of the older buildings on Sutton Place. So that Jeff and she wouldn't be bored, Iona had just redecorated the penthouse in Chinese lacquer.

Nikkia remembered being startled by the gleaming black finish with its gold flowers. In the leisure room stood a waist-high Chinese vase that Nikkia realized must have been worth at least one hundred thousand dollars.

"What did you do with the Iroquois pottery and the bead wall hanging?" Nikkia had asked that night as she entered the leisure room. It was one of the largest rooms in the apartment, the only one with a fireplace. Previously, Adirondack style furniture had blended with the antique Indian artifacts. Soft cushions in mimic Iroquois design had padded the rough-hewn couches and lounge chairs. In the fireplace, with an opening five feet high, a fire always crackled for the pleasure of guests and for Jeff as well, because he loved it. He kept the room cool enough, even in the summertime, to enjoy the orange-red hues of fire.

That night the flames glowed as warmly as ever, but Nikkia couldn't believe that the brown and white pottery she liked to stroke was gone. "I donated all of it to the American Indian Museum," Jeff had answered. "And now everyone can see it."

Because she liked Jeff, Nikkia tried to understand why someone would alter his surroundings, changing them as you would a tablecloth, when they were filled with memories. She found the deeply carved, antique Chinese rug elegant, however, with its cream and red pattern. And the silk cushions with red and yellow threads inviting to touch. The wall tapestry, too, haunted the room with a presence of sculptured gardens five hundred years ago.

Maybe she could get used to this room. There wasn't as much lacquer furniture here as in the dining hall they had just left. But the Iroquois art had made her feel at home, and it was obvious to Nikkia that these elegant Chinese furnishings could only be part of the lives of a very few.

As usual, Jeff had singled her out that evening. Nikkia knew he was not trying to prove he could make acquaintance with a black person. Theirs was a real friendship, which seemed to stay above the dancing and drugs and frivolous escapes to one of the bedrooms the Gaynors had designated for guests. On summer evenings, Nikkia liked best to be outside the confinement of any of the rooms, lovely as they were, and to stand with Jeff on one of the terraces, watching the lights on the Queensboro Bridge.

They would laugh at their city sensibilities. "Look at the cars on the FDR Drive," Nikkia would say. And she would smile, for Jeff already was looking at them. "They relax me, just as if I were looking at a river flow."

"You and I prefer the lights and things people have made, to watching a river," Jeff responded.

Jeff enjoyed the streets of the city and the contrast of sky and buildings. He accepted and loved the limitations of Central Park and a roof garden. One day, Nikkia and Jeff walked more than one hundred blocks, completely around Central Park.

In contrast to Jeff, Lawrence was strictly an indoor person who required air conditioning and taxi cabs. He noticed only the dirt and litter in Central Park. Nikkia knew he would have gotten sick to his stomach rather than have lunch, as she did--on the Central Park grass, protected from the ants by Jeff's sports jacket--drinking French wine wrapped in a brown paper bag. Lawrence could not understand Jeff's propensity for lovers of both sexes, either.

Never once had Nikkia even pictured herself

sleeping with Jeff, though he was not physically unattractive. She thought he had a pleasant enough face, like that of a young boy, always closely shaven. His blond hair was soft and neat. Neither did Nikkia mind that he was somewhat overweight for his five feet ten inches. His wasn't the flushed fat of one who drank too much. Jeff simply ate too much good food. She could accept his stomach. What she could not love was his mouth.

A peculiar articulation stiffened Jeff's mouth. Beginning at the age of four, Jeff had learned six languages from private tutors. He was also taught how to be polite and proper in those languages. His lips were controlled, even when he laughed. Yet his smile and his kindness, Nikkia knew, were genuine.

Nikkia considered herself then an expert in judging the depth of emotions of the wealthy families across the country who hosted their ballet company. She was in the company from 1963 until 1971, which included part of the civil rights movement. Then, the response of most whites toward her was limited by their uneasiness around a black woman. As a guest in the homes of patrons of the ballet, sometimes for an entire weekend, Nikkia was often put in the position of an observer.

Until the last two years, she found it possible to accept the proprieties extended to her. Nikkia amused herself with the discovery that people who were more recently wealthy, within two generations or so, showed a rather icy politeness because of their insecurity. One prominent Atlanta family didn't speak to her at all. The drunk woman on that Texas ranch one winter, had actually attacked her.

Jeff Gaynor, Nikkia knew, was incapable of such rage. But neither was he completely content surrounded by Iona's furnishings or inside his own body. For some reason, he had never been able to commit himself to a person of the opposite or the same sex. He had known two lovers for five years, a cellist and a sculptress. Nikkia sensed his ambivalence toward his own body, held in place by his careful, firm cupid mouth, and could not sleep with him. He, in turn, had never asked.

But once, sitting with him in Central Park, she felt closer in friendship than she did with Lawrence, who lately seemed only able to relax in passion with her.

Nikkia had met Lawrence in June of 1964 while they were both on tour with separate companies in France. Four years older than her eighteen years, Lawrence decided this was to be his last season dancing. He was going to college. "There's no future in dancing," he told Nikkia bluntly. He had injured a tendon that season, and he needed no more convincing. A more serious injury, he told her, and a dancer could be out for many months or even years. He had seen it happen. He himself had gotten ahead by replacing another black man who had strained a ligament. "We owe it to ourselves, not just as individual blacks, to get on top in some other field and stay there."

It was Lawrence who convinced her to spend their brief two week vacation in late 1964 organizing for the vote in Mississippi. He brought Nikkia to a movement that allowed him to vent his own anger: the Black Panthers. For the first time Nikkia saw in Mississippi the body of a black boy who had been lynched. His genitals had been cut off and shoved into his mouth.

Nikkia remembered many of the faces of the organizers. At that time the Black Panthers had white members as well as black. Members of the Progressive Labor Party were in the leadership as well as people in the Communist Party and blacks who believed in a separate nation-state. Lawrence introduced her to Zack, who had taken up residence in Mississippi the year before.

They made a good pair, Lawrence and Zack. Lawrence was the speechmaker. Zack was better at talking one to one with people. He got them out into the streets. In the brief two weeks that Lawrence and Nikkia spent in Almira, she also noticed a more fundamental difference between Zack and Lawrence than their outward abilities to speak with people.

Zack saw voter registration as only one way to unite blacks with whites. Voting itself, he told Nikkia, simply could be a means to deceive them into thinking the system would work for them. He conveyed to people that militancy worked toward bettering conditions and that ultimately revolution would be necessary.

Lawrence, by contrast, made his speeches motivated by a more personal fury. Nikkia thought he still felt guilty on looking back at his dancing career. It was as if he couldn't forget the sense of his own betrayal. He had mentioned to her many times that he should have quit the company before taking over another black man's leading role.

Two years later, the three of them renewed their friendship in New York City. Zack did community organizing while working in the garment center of Manhattan during the fall and spring of '66 through '67. Nikkia spent two hours out of every day gathering signatures on a referendum for complete withdrawal of U.S. troops from Vietnam. She attended study groups with Progressive Labor, trying to understand the reasons behind imperialist war. Lawrence became an economics student. In 1967 and '68, Nikkia took college courses in the mornings. She and Lawrence were both present at the Columbia University sit-in, but for different reasons.

Lawrence stated that his political demand was to separate the university from connections with imperialist investment. Nikkia, however, now understood that the role of the university was to train a certain elite necessary for the U.S. to maintain worldwide control. Lawrence came out of the confrontations with a determination never again to jeopardize his final grades. At that time, however, he encouraged Nikkia to follow her political ideas. He only suggested that she continue to limit the amount of time so she could continue dancing. On the other hand, he saw himself as furthering the cause of all blacks by his own academic advancement. Their politics, as well as their careers, separated. But their loyalty to each other persisted.

In the summer of '68, Nikkia's mother, Rosemary, came to visit from North Carolina. She met both Lawrence and Zack. She preferred Zack. "That man Lawrence thinks he's better than ordinary folks," she told Nikkia. Now and again, Nikkia wondered if her life would have been very different if she had developed more than a friendship with Zack. Perhaps she had stayed with Lawrence, Nikkia once thought, because her mother disapproved of him.

Her mother also told her then that she wouldn't be able to mix her interest in politics with a dancing career. "I'm afraid you'll end up doing something foolish," she had said. "You'll spend time in jail, and they'll throw you out of the company."

She frequently reminded Nikkia that she had had

to work two jobs in order to keep Nikkia with New York City instructors. She guessed Nikkia hadn't even considered that for her to ride the train four days a week from East Orange public school to New York was yet another additional cost!

All through high school, Nikkia would come home from New York City at ten in the evening, and Rosemary would not be home yet. When she got up in the morning, her mother was already gone. At night, she was often hungry and would open the refrigerator to find only eggs, milk and mustard. The milk was made from powder and in a glass jar. Nikkia would pour it on cereal for her evening snack before bed.

Five evenings a week her mother worked late, and the two of them would eat their sandwich dinners away from home. Rosemary ate peanut butter every day, for lunch and dinner, on cold toast. "It's protein," said her mother. Nikkia's meals were more varied but just as simple: a fried egg sandwich, or cheese and fruit, or any weekend leftovers. The only time they had hot meals, with a chance for leftovers in the refrigerator, was on the weekends.

On Saturdays and Sundays, Nikkia would cook. Rosemary would allow Nikkia to shop and spend more money for these meals. "So long as I'm not out there comparing prices, I don't mind that you buy something I wouldn't have."

The first thing Nikkia noticed about Lawrence's habits, when she met him in France, was related to food: He ate expensively. He had four courses if they ate out, and he carried his love for French cooking to New York City. Lawrence often cooked when they ate together, and Nikkia was astounded that together they spent as much for one meal as she and Rosemary did on their food budget for a week.

In the years she lived with her mother, Nikkia would make an event of the Sunday meal. She put flowers in a vase or a lace cloth on the formica kitchen set. She also saved impressions about people she'd seen during the week, who were riding the train or sleeping in the train station. She or Nikkia would make up stories about the love lives of other students and their instructors. They became so detailed that Nikkia would believe them herself.

Those Sunday afternoons were the only time Nikkia and Rosemary talked, for all day Saturday Nikkia worked as a clerk in the local Shop Rite. Saturday evenings they were both too tired to do anything but watch television. During Sunday dinner, they would chat and look out the kitchen window. They could see only the cement court which connected the back doors of each half of the hundred-unit apartment building. Their living room windows also showed this courtyard that was used to store garbage cans. While Nikkia told her made-up stories, the two of them looked outside and pictured a more beautiful scene.

So every time that Nikkia visited Jeff, she thought how her mother would love his roof garden of fruit trees and terrace vegetables. In the soil brought up to the southeast section of the terrace grew asparagus, four kinds of lettuce, and tomatoes. The particular evening that Nikkia left the dance company for good, she listened to the hard rain outside and wondered if the tomato plants would survive. And as she and her mother often did when the weather was nasty, she thought about people with no homes.

She glanced over at Jeff. His smooth face carried no problems. What was there for him to worry about? Nikkia asked herself. The fire that night didn't seem warm enough.

x x x

Nikkia, reminiscing in the Boston apartment, thought about her mother while the air conditioning was making sounds like rain. And she had thought of Rosemary that particular summer night in New York as the rain beat on the small window squares of Jeff's leisure room. Before her death in 1968, Rosemary got so she hated the rain.

x x x

It was long before that, before Nikkia graduated from high school, when her mother started to be more anxious about everything. After a time, she could not even be happy about Nikkia's recitals. She would worry over the expense of the costume and the extra carfare. Her stomach began to bother her, and she had trouble keeping her food down. "You're doing this to yourself, Ma," said Nikkia. She wanted to stop her dance classes, but by then she had been offered the job with the company.

Her mother's skin turned darker. She had weak kidneys, the doctor warned her. She finally stopped working two jobs just as Nikkia graduated from high school and began full-time with the New York City Ballet Company.

In that first year, 1963, hearing about the civil rights movement, Nikkia felt self-conscious about her privileged position. She was constantly reminded that it was much more than her mother's early recognition of an exceptional talent that made her a dancer. Sheer sacrifice had bought her years of trained practice. Nikkia had been sure from the beginning that one or two blacks in a dance company could not signify opportunity for all blacks who wanted to dance. The lack of opportunity, in turn, made her skeptical about a voting drive that offered a choice of candidates from another class of society. But she never shared these doubts with Rosemary.

By the time Nikkia became active against the Vietnam war, her mother had to stop working altogether because of her health and had to move in with Nikkia's aunt in North Carolina. But her mother's prediction about the contradiction between dancing and revolutionary politics remained in Nikkia's mind.

While gathering signatures in the morning, Nikkia met hundreds of mothers whose sons were in the war or already dead. Often she worked out alone in the exercise room, and evenings, she performed. The hot lights kept her from feeling contact with any individual in the audience. Afterwards, the company members in the performance would have to go to a party. The only thing Nikkia cared to talk about was the world beyond the United States. Yet their hosts--some of them Democrats--would be the very people who had put Johnson into office. And their money told his advisors exactly what to do.

Jeff had been thirty when the war began. By 1970, he still thought the U.S. involvement in Vietnam was all a mistake. His sister was less liberal and wouldn't listen to Nikkia's arguments. But no matter what Nikkia said to Jeff, she realized that his life had not changed at all because of the war. Not like the lives of the thousands of people who she'd met on the streets during the petition campaign. The war wasn't causing him sleepless nights, the way Nikkia herself was often troubled.

Nikkia felt frustrated talking with Jeff that one evening, and she was also thirsty. She had excused herself for some orange juice. Her mother would have told her that water was perfectly good to drink, and her mother always made the point that it was free.

"I don't know if there's anything in the refrigerator," Jeff had mentioned absently, staring at the August fire across the room. "Ask the caterer." But there had been a big crowd around the bartending woman. Everyone must have been drinking screwdrivers, Nikkia thought, for there were several cartons of Tropicana in the trash, and she could see no more next to the seltzer bottles. She wanted an excuse, anyway, to go to the kitchen. She needed to leave the lacquered room.

The kitchen was bright white and narrow. At one centered counter, a thin young woman in black and white uniform arranged a platter of artichokes. She didn't look up, and Nikkia squeezed around her with an uncomfortable sense that she should be helping. The woman's fingernails, Nikkia noticed, were long and red, the only color in this room. Neither was there the relief of a window in the kitchen. It was a place for unwrapping delivered food packages. The bag for garbage in one corner was enormous, and the thin woman started another before leaving the kitchen with the platter. The stove looked to Nikkia exactly as it had on her first trip to this kitchen six years ago--unused.

A large Subzero refrigerator stood next to the round breakfast table. Jeff and Iona probably never ate here, Nikkia thought. They went to either the Green Door Cafe or Lillian's on First Avenue. To Nikkia, the kitchen walls suddenly seemed too close, and she felt herself breathing as if she needed air. She thought the refrigerator might give her relief when she opened the door. She tugged with one hand and then both, with all her weight. The door opened.

Nikkia stared at the inside of the refrigerator. The metal shelves gleamed. Gold letters--MEAT BUTTER EGGS FRUIT VEGETABLES--announced organization to the owner of this refrigerator. A lone jar of Poupon mustard occupied one shelf. Nikkia's thoughts flashed back to her mother's refrigerator and the terrible emptiness. Her mouth felt dry, and her head throbbed.

She wanted to cry. It was as though she had just ridden the train alone from New York to come home, except that at home the mustard was French's.

Nikkia didn't know whether to be sorrier for herself or for her mother, who had worked so hard so that she might stand here alone in this kitchen. The soothing tears would not come, though the pain of sadness lay somewhere below her heart. The hurt reminded her that she missed her mother terribly. But then, Nikkia realized with hot flush, she had always missed her. And Nikkia pushed the door shut.

When she closed that bottom portion of the refrigerator, it occurred to her that there would be ice in the freezer compartment above. This thought made her lick her dry lips and shake her head as if to free it from the weight of the headache. She would fill a glass with ice and put in water and drink that and then put in more ice and more water and carry some back to Jeff and sit down and talk about her mother.

Quickly, Nikkia pulled open the freezer and took out two ice blue plastic trays. One tray had one cube in it, and the other was empty.

"Lazy bastards," Nikkia stated out loud. The young woman, coming back in the kitchen, turned to stare at her. But Nikkia's dismay had already turned to anger. Anyone who could use the next to last ice cube, without filling either tray, Nikkia thought, could not be truly considerate. Or had probably never carried a full, dripping tray to the refrigerator, having to mop the floor afterwards. Someone else followed behind Jeff and Iona, cleaned up, shopped, served the food and threw out the leftovers. With shaking hands, Nikkia took the trays to the sink, found a plastic glass and put in the one cube and filled the glass and trays with water. By the time she got back from replacing the trays in the freezer, the one cube had melted.

She drank the water. The liquid wet her mouth and throat, but she was still angry. She didn't know exactly why--after all, the bartender had seltzer and ice cubes--but it was partly directed at Jeff, and she couldn't go back to him now. Nikkia saw a door at the back of the kitchen, went over and opened it. As though she had had this plan in her mind for weeks, she walked through the door, out into the hall and pressed the button to the elevator that belonged to the penthouse. She went down to the street and through the glass lobby. Outside it was raining lightly now. A good night for walking home, Nikkia thought, and for making a decision to leave the pretend world of dance.

Her immediate decision in 1970 to apply for scholarship money to go to college had been as positive as her joining the party a year previously. She had already taken many courses in the mornings. By going summers she could finish in two years and be working as a physical therapist. Three major decisions within one year, then, when Nikkia added them up. Not the worst year for her by a long shot.

x x x

She felt confident relaxing in Yvette and Don's apartment that hot Boston afternoon. Thinking about those three good decisions now took her mind off Lawrence.

When Yvette got off the phone, she and Don debated who of their friends might be asked to speak with the neighbors in Hyde Park. On this question, Nikkia couldn't help them. Instead, she asked if they needed any provisions for the apartment, and she welcomed the opportunity to walk to the store.

The deep feelings Norberto had aroused in her made her want to sort out her emotions. She had left Lawrence's arms less than twenty-four hours ago. It was unnerving that another man could bring out such intense desire. Was she so fickle, so shallow? With how many men was she capable of making love?

The hot, heavy air outside made her gasp. She wasn't ready for the heat nor for an accompanying physical need for Norberto. Walking the streets, with no apartment ceiling over her head, Nikkia felt as though her wanting had no limit. She could see the supermarket at the next corner, and she stopped in the middle of a block of three-decker buildings to savor the new excitement within her.

Orange flowers with black centers clustered in a front yard waved stiffly, erect with life. Through the space between two houses she could see a back yard vegetable garden. It was all green, except for the two rows of white-gold corn tassles and the browning leaves of climbing beans. Norberto works in the vegetable fields of California, she thought. Sweat covers his body under layers of clothing that protect him from pesticides, like all workers in the fields. She thought about touching the sweat on his smooth, brown shoulders. This feeling she had about Norberto and the vegetable fields should be dismissed as romantic, she told herself. Yet she couldn't negate the profound need that went deeper within her than fantasy.

Without her being aware of it, she kept staring at one vegetable: the biggest head of cabbage she had ever thought possible. It lay in the middle of the vegetable bed. It had big fat leaves, one after the other, fuller and darker green. The outside leaves spread full to the summer sun.

Nikkia didn't know how long she'd been staring, but something made her look away from the garden up at the house. A man in a third floor window stared down at her. She felt herself jump as if she'd been doing something wrong. How long have I been here? Nikkia tried to force herself to think of shopping and moving on to the store. Still, thoughts of Norberto pushed to her mind, and only when the icy air conditioning of the store penetrated her skin did she begin to sort out these thoughts.

Be realistic, she warned. In front of you is a list of food to buy. And when you return to New York, a man waits there for you. He wants to marry you, too, after years of your waiting for him to make a commitment. Or am I the kind of woman who's afraid? Nikkia asked herself. Am I afraid that he'll leave me, and I'll have to raise children on my own like my mother?

Maybe. Maybe. But there are no guarantees of any sort in this life, Nikkia realized. She also knew she wasn't so insecure as to get married for the sake of having a ring. She wasn't even enthusiastic about the ceremony itself, though the party afterwards would be wonderful.

And Lawrence was not a bad choice. He at least understood her political commitment, though he didn't agree with it any longer. And how much time would it take to meet someone else? Nikkia wondered. And then to break them into the habits of a household and her own sexual comfort? Lawrence knew her body so well. She was lucky. Many married women never achieved a satisfactory sexual arrangement. While she was thinking these reassuring thoughts, Nikkia chose ingredients by going down each aisle, methodically.

The time spent waiting in line brought her more sobering notions. After all, Norberto **was** married. That was the reality, far more than her imaginary thoughts of the sweat on his body. It was ridiculous, this flight of passion, leading nowhere. The sooner she stopped fantasizing, the healthier she would feel. His wife is real, and she loves him, Nikkia told herself again. He has children. There is nothing I can do to alter a whole family, she continued, and I don't want to.

Back outside, Nikkia took in the hot air, and this time her head was clear. She felt happy to have straightened out her ideas and to have finished the shopping. If I had gone visiting with Norberto and Bonita, she thought, I would have built up material for an entire system of illusion! Walking back through the three-decker block she didn't even glance at the vegetable garden.

When she returned to Don and Yvette's apartment, Nikkia found them talking intensely. It sounded as if there had been another incident at the Daley home, this time involving comrades. Gradually, she learned that Russell had gotten hurt and Zack arrested.

"There is a consideration now," said Don, "that the dance might put too many of the volunteers in danger. If the police want to make a mass arrest, we would be making it awfully easy for them."

"On the other hand," said Yvette, "I feel Don tends to be overly cautious. I think the morale of everyone will be helped by the social that we've already planned. It would be even more disheartening to remain separated after we and the Daley family have been through so much."

"Oh, I agree with you," Nikkia responded. She was still pleased with herself for her time alone and was anxious to meet the other people who were in the project. "It'll be good for everyone to hear what happened. Maybe we can get someone from the Daley family to speak." The very real problems facing other Boston families came full into Nikkia's thoughts. It felt good to be free of her own petty worries: Who is more appealing, one man or another? Nikkia scolded herself: enough, already!

When Yvette and Don left to help set up for the dance, Nikkia made the lasagne and put it in the oven.

Then, on impulse, she decided to call Lawrence. She put a couple of dollars under the phone cradle and glanced at the digital clock. Three minutes, she told herself.

"What's wrong?" His voice was distant, almost cool.

Nikkia thought, of course, he's worried about me. I'm to be his wife. Out loud, she said, "Nothing. I just wanted to hear your voice. A family named Daley got their house smashed up and the woman her collar bone broken by the ROAR thugs." She decided not to tell him about Zack's arrest or mention Russell's head injury.

"You don't have to remind me that the criminals in ROAR remain free to roam the streets," said Lawrence angrily. Then he added, "I can't help but be skeptical about your program for busing little kids to places far away from home."

"Maybe you can come up for one weekend to see for yourself what we're accomplishing." Nikkia spoke quickly, not wanting to spend this time arguing. There were two minutes left. "Right now, I just wanted to let you know I miss you. There's a dance tonight." She added, "Don't worry, we've even organized security at our social events."

"I've been imagining the worst. I'm counting the days, and I've arranged a research project to occupy my time. I have a good chance of getting a feature next spring in Fortune magazine."

"On what?" asked Nikkia. At this long distance, she preferred to keep him talking about something he enjoyed.

"Mortgage rates and the stock market," he said. "I'll be practically living in the laps of some Wall Street brokers."

Nikkia glanced at the apartment as if it would offer her something to say. "I'm staying in an air conditioned place," she said finally. "It's all Danish modern. You'd love it."

"I'm sure," he said. "Just come home in one piece. I want all of you back here with me," he spoke in his measured phone voice that she knew so well.

"I love you," she said.

"I love you too, now be careful," Lawrence returned.

Nikkia hung up the phone with the feeling she

wanted to pick it up again and start over. She told herself, he cares for me. Most women would give their eye teeth to be in bed with him. He wants to marry me. He's faithful. He doesn't stop me politically. She talked to herself while the lasagne baked.

To pass the time she walked around the apartment and then stood in front of her favorite painting of the snow scene. She stretched and thought about how glad she was to have made three good decisions over the years: to marry Lawrence, to go to school for physical therapy and to join the party.

It had been the result of her relationship with her father, Morris, rather than her mother, that helped convince her to join the party. When Nikkia was seven years old, he worked in a metal filing cabinet shop and tried to go to night school. His reading and writing skills allowed him to pass a high school equivalency. There, his math teacher encouraged him to go to college. But he failed every remedial English course offered at the college level. He was ashamed thereafter of being an uneducated man. He quit school and stayed with the metal shop. Then, when they laid off half the workers and hired Haitians, Morris started working in the Pabst brewery. It paid a little more, and he was happy.

He bought Nikkia little extras each week. Sometimes it was a pair of socks with kittens on them. Or a bookcase that he painted pink. Because he was used to being able to buy her some things, it hurt him when the brewery cut back and he was the first to get laid off. He began to drink with the unemployment money. And then he began to use the money her mother had saved for Nikkia's dancing lessons.

Somehow, she could never blame her father, and she still cried when she thought how her mother threw him out when she was twelve. Nikkia had tried to keep the family together then by holding her father's hand and her mother's at the same time. When Nikkia was thirteen, her father died.

She remembered how her father had thought he was special with his math ability. He never tired of telling Nikkia that he had won prizes when he was a boy. Then he found out he was a failure in English. Nikkia always recalled this when her mother told her she was a genius as a dancer. She knew the word could only be self-deceiving. Any day someone who was an even greater "genius," perhaps someone more ambitious, could come along. Or discrimination might throw her out of a job as it did her father.

Her father's situation made Nikkia realize many things. She observed that when blacks were laid off her father's job, white workers failed to react and unite with blacks. Then, she read that all the white workers were laid off when the brewery closed. She discovered that the system, not white people or her father (as her mother claimed), was the enemy. And she saw throughout the war that white soldiers were being killed, too, so that Vietnamese might die.

With her father gone, there seemed to be more money than before--the bills got paid on time--but Nikkia felt more alone. At age thirteen, she tried to fulfill her inner needs by dancing. But her artistic accomplishments somehow didn't bring satisfaction.

Now she knew that she probably wouldn't have stayed with dancing after her mother's death in '68 if it hadn't been for her friendship with Jeff. He treated me like an equal, she remembered, if only because he loved the dancing so. Why couldn't my father have had one-one hundredth of Jeff's money so that he might have stayed around to become my friend, too? Today, Dad is gone and I never saw Jeff again after I quit dancing. I wonder if he missed me. He never tried to call, and I was too embarrassed since we had so little else in common. I wouldn't have known him if it weren't for dance.

An odd thought occurred to her, that she would not have known a man like Morris, either--with so much potential and such a sad life--if he weren't her father. Here I am missing him, she thought, and he's been dead sixteen years.

Lawrence, whose parents died when he was very young, saw me through my mother's death. He also stayed with me through the dance, through the politics. No wonder he's afraid for my safety. He's afraid to lose me. And like him, I have no one else. Nikkia sat with her legs stretched out, bending over so that her forehead touched the floor, and cried.

Chapter 11

The doorbell rang, and Nikkia was glad for the sound. She got up and pressed the buzzer, happy to know there was another person coming up. With a second thought, she realized it could not be Yvette or Don since they had keys. She ran to the bathroom and looked at her puffy eyes and ran cold water, putting her whole face under the faucet until she heard the knock on the door.

"I'm Darlene. You must be Nikkia." The young woman was very fat and wore loose jeans as though she had recently lost weight. She had light auburn hair and medium brown eyes. Her face was pleasant. Nikkia thought her attractive, because her forest green T-shirt set off her eyes and skin tone. Embroidery sewn on it showed a beautiful design. "I've come from the office to give you and the lasagne a ride to the dance. Don thought you'd probably be ready."

"You bet I am," Nikkia answered. Not only did she welcome a visitor, but it gave her a lift to be in the company of this young person. She put on a red gauze skirt and matching peasant blouse that made her feel cheerful and festive.

"I love that," said Darlene. "I can't wear bright red myself. That looks like a dress. I'd like to be able to wear a blouse tucked in one day. I'm trying to lose weight. There's a boy I like in the project. His name's Lennie. I'm from Albany." Darlene talked without waiting for a response.

It was evident to Nikkia that Darlene was lonely, too. She felt like a big sister with her New York City clothing, her years of working with the party and her permanent relationship. It was a relief to have something to offer.

"You could wear a narrow belt sometimes," she began. "Wait, I think I have an emerald hair comb you can have for tonight."

"You have such a good figure," said Darlene.

"It's just habit." Nikkia tried to switch the conversation back to Darlene. "Where did you get your sense of color?" And as they drove to the dance she let Darlene know how she, in turn, respected Darlene for having become interested in politics at an age younger than herself.

Darlene held the door open to the clubhouse and helped Nikkia carry the heavy lasagne inside. She pointed to a table at the far end of the room. As Nikkia's eyes grew accustomed to the darker interior, she could see someone in the back on a ladder and a number of other people working to decorate the office. Don and two other women, neither of them Yvette, were painting a mural. On it, three workers held a flag with a black hand and a white hand in gripping handshake. They straddled a building that looked like Boston's city hall.

"Hi everyone," said Nikkia. Her eyes gazed around the room and then up the ladder. There on the top rung was Norberto. Nikkia was glad she had already set down the lasagne. Norberto wore no shirt, and the sweat on his back made his skin shine under the light. His arms were lean, but more muscular than Lawrence's. His stomach muscles, as he bent and straightened, held firm and knotted. They were the muscles of hard work. Nikkia's throat became thick, and she held the ladder as if to steady it for him. But it was to keep herself in balance and still be able to look up at him a moment more. "Can I hand you anything?" she offered.

"Oh no. I have it all on the what-do-you-call-him top step," Norberto said. And so it wasn't necessary for her to look up any longer. Nikkia swallowed and glanced around to find Darlene. She felt as if the room had become stuffy, and she was angry with herself for not being able to control her physical reactions. Her mouth was as cottony as it got when she made love.

"Are there some paper cups for the sink?" she asked Darlene.

"Just a few. We have to go out in awhile and get more paper goods."

Nikkia was about to volunteer herself to go out now and get the things when she remembered she had promised to help set up. She was torn between wanting to stay in Norberto's presence and wanting to leave so she wouldn't have to think about him. Darlene chose that moment to ask her help with the card tables.

"I'll be living here the whole summer," she said. "I think I've lost fifteen pounds already since June. I'm working in the Freedom School."

Nikkia focused on Darlene. She thought how worthwhile it was for young people to be working with the Boston children. They had missed so much school this year because of the violence over busing.

"What's difficult for us in the Freedom School is to visit the parents of the children when school is over. We tend to feel our job is done at the end of the school day!" Darlene continued, "We have to get the parents active so there'll be an organization to carry on when we go home."

"When I was your age," said Nikkia, "I was all wrapped up in myself and how to make my dancing perfect. I was the youngest ballerina ever asked to join the New York Ballet Company. The rest of the world didn't exist for me."

"That's a part of the world no one else knows," Darlene said admiringly.

Nikkia didn't want to talk about herself any longer. From this angle she could see that Norberto had almost finished hanging a SMASH RACISM JOIN CAR banner across the middle of the ceiling. His back was to her. She wanted to pull up a chair and watch the curve of his shoulders. Nikkia noticed that he had not positioned himself so that he could look at her. Still, she had had the distinct impression he had <u>seen</u> her earlier in Yvette's. But since then it was obvious that she was more attracted to him than he to her. The thought made her nervous, so she decided to ask Darlene something. "Tell me about this Lennie," she asked. "Is he from Albany, too?"

"No. He's from here. You'll meet him. He's gonna play saxophone at the dance. He's got this beautiful red-blonde hair that, when he takes it out of a pony tail, falls all over his back. He's beautiful!" Darlene smiled in a way that wasn't silly to Nikkia. "Do you know he wrote this anti-racist play for his senior class last year? He let me read it. The dialogue was so hilarious. Other parts were serious. He can say some really heavy things in a very funny way."

Darlene looked expectantly at Nikkia.

Nikkia hoped for Darlene's sake that this Lenny didn't have a girl friend. And even if he didn't, her weight was going to be a barrier. Somebody like Lennie, a performer, had to be very conscious when someone else was at least eighty pounds overweight. Nikkia couldn't help wishing that Darlene had already lost the weight. "What kind of vibrations do you get from him?" Despite herself, Nikkia was reminded of her own situation.

"He said he's not going with anyone," Darlene's eyes twinkled, and she was really pretty. "I asked him."

Nikkia smiled and shook her head, thinking that if she herself were overweight she might not have been so bold. "I mean vibes toward you," she pressed.

"I'm not sure. I think he's shy or something. He doesn't come on to me at all. But he did let on he didn't want to hurt anyone because he recently broke up with some girl." Darlene looked hopeful. "He even said that he would like to be friends. I guess that's something, huh?"

"I knew someone once who I always remained friends with," said Nikkia. "But that was because both of us wanted it that way." She thought of Jeff and how his weight and her toned muscles helped keep them as friends and not lovers. She considered that Lennie might see Darlene as being "safe" to be friends with because he wasn't attracted to her.

The phone rang. Nikkia answered. It was Lennie. He told Nikkia that he and others had been picking up some of his classmates for the dance. Seven or eight men pushed the kids out of the van and stole it. Lennie only had a bloody nose, but a boy named Kareem had been hit on the side of his head with a baseball bat, and he had been taken to the emergency room. Two adults from the Freedom School, themselves teachers who lived in Connecticut, had driven off after the van with a station wagon full of people. Four of them were parents of the children from the van.

"Who's with Kareem?" asked Nikkia.

"His mother and sister."

Lennie went on to say that he and three of his friends were about to take the metro to the CAR office. He said they were starving to death.

Nikkia then saw a young man in shorts come in the front door with a platter of spaghetti as large as her lasagne tin. He was followed by a man with a salad bowl and a tall woman with a restaurant-sized tin of fruit salad. "We just might be able to save you some food," she told Lennie.

"My sax was in that van," he said.

"Oh no, I'm so sorry." Nikkia began to feel angry thinking in whose hands Lennie's instrument lay. Then she said, "I'll tell Darlene here what happened. I know she'll wish she had been there to help."

"Let me speak with her," Lennie asked. And Nikkia was happy to give Darlene the phone.

A family pulled up in an orange Vega. In the hatchback they had stacked cases of soda. Nikkia went to help carry them in. She made out an old refrigerator near the back table. Opening it with one hand, she held a case of soda with another. "You're strong," said a voice. As Nikkia's eyes grew accustomed to the dark corner of the office once again, she saw the voice belonged to Norberto.

"I'm in good shape," she answered, pleased that he'd said something to her. Then Nikkia became angry with herself. Why did she have to say such a stupid thing in response?

"I can see that," he said.

Nikkia had never in her life felt at such a loss for words. Darlene handles her conversation with Lennie much better than I do with Norberto, she thought.

"I used to dance," she added and was immediately uncomfortable. That wasn't the sort of thing which would impress a farmworker. Better he should know nothing about her past until they had spent more time talking. What was he thinking? She reminded herself silently. He's married.

"But I quit." As soon as Nikkia said that she wanted to kick herself for telling Norberto what must have been obvious. She should have asked him something about his children, she thought. I <u>already</u> told him I used to dance.

"It's a whole different life," Norberto said.

Of course it is, Nikkia thought. It must seem like a big waste of time to this man whose entire family has to break their backs in the fields. She forgot the positive attitude that she had known in the afternoon, which was based on her decision to stop dancing. Instead, Nikkia felt ashamed of her past.

"You're right. I had to be a dancer all day long." She felt the need to explain herself and so started to tell him about the hours of practicing and the mandatory socializing. Gradually, a happy feeling of release came as she talked, and the happiness increased with every word. She had no control over what came out in talking with this man, who listened without interrupting.

"Perhaps it was a sacrifice, to put aside people's admiracion."

In using the Spanish word that was so like English, he had put his finger on her most vulnerable point of contention with Lawrence: her decision to become a health worker. He felt she needed a career that would give her status and admiration. "Very important for us blacks to maintain our pride," Lawrence would say. And when she would tell her reasons for seeking a hospital job, they sounded weak and defensive in Lawrence's presence.

"Oh no, no. Not a sacrifice to me at all." And this was the truth as Nikkia described herself more clearly, away from Lawrence. "I knew where I was going; I knew I'd be much happier working in a job around many more people, people in all kinds of work, from cleaning to therapy."

Nikkia felt the joy of her decision that she was unable to share with Lawrence. Her happiness bubbled from her body's center. She looked across at Darlene, laughing and talking. She thought with amazement, I must look as happy.

Seeing Darlene, though, Nikkia feared for the hurt Darlene might experience. And then she stopped talking for she thought: but Norberto is married.

"What's wrong?" Norberto asked.

She wanted to tell him. She had been talking so freely that it didn't seem right now to withhold. She had been healing the years of criticism she'd gotten from Lawrence, and she needed to feel better.

But she couldn't tell Norberto how she felt about him, that he was powerful for her because of who he was: an honest man who was for the working class and as physical as she. It was a relief to know her needs could be met, but she could never tell him that he might be one person who had what she needed. "Nothing is wrong," she said. But it was all wrong.

Nikkia looked around. In a matter of these few moments, the social had taken on a party atmosphere. Now, sixty or so people crowded the two-room office. Don and Howard, one of the teenagers from the Freedom

School, took over the food arranging and serving. Norberto and Nikkia found themselves speaking with a woman bringing in more food, who had three small children who attended the Freedom School. Her name was Maureen McGovern. "Like the singer," Maureen explained. Nikkia was curious as to why a white woman would stay in a neighborhood where only blacks lived.

"I didn't stay. I moved in," said Maureen. She had large brown eyes and shoulder-length hair. Her make-up was carefully applied. She was thoughtful. "You've got to look at the way people treat you. I've had white friends and black friends. I never thought white neighborhoods were no better. I looked at it this way: the apartment was bigger for the amount of money than in South Boston. Once I got to know the people--I have a lot of new friends now--why should I move?"

"You're like me," said Nikkia. "I wouldn't want to live in a place where there wasn't integration. Even if I had to be the only black." Nikkia thought of her dancing and said, "I used to work in a place with all whites, and I think people respected that. Of course, one woman hated my guts."

"I've learned there's good and bad with any color skin," said Maureen.

"Am I good or bad?" asked a man with a salt and pepper afro that was receeding in the front. He put his arm around Maureen.

"You're a little bit of both," Maureen said. "See, I lived in Roxbury for ten years now." She looked at Nikkia. "And Glenn and I have been together for five. If he was to leave me tomorrow, I'd stay put right where I am."

"She sure doesn't let me feel like I'm a protector." Glenn seemed a bit sorry, to Nikkia, that Maureen wasn't dependent on him.

"That's the way it should be, between men and women," Norberto nodded to Maureen, not asking her to affirm his statement. And then he walked to help Don carry a garbage can full of ice and soda.

Nikkia heard a Latin rhythm start, and Glenn asked Maureen to dance. She had promised herself that the first dance Norberto would be comfortable with, that she would ask him. Now she looked in the direction where he had just walked and couldn't see him. She walked around, pretending to study the murals.

Then she was at the front door. There, outside tying a bundle of trash, was Norberto.

Nikkia inhaled the night air, walked over to him and put her hand on his shoulder. "I'd like to dance with you," she said.

"I can't dance the new dances," he told her.

"It's a merengue," Nikkia smiled. But she was afraid. Was this his way of saying no?

"That's good," said Norberto.

"Come on in," Nikkia held out her hand.

He didn't take her hand but walked beside her. Nikkia was thinking that the music would probably be over by the time they got back in. But the record was still playing, and the dance floor was crowded. "Let me wash my hands," Norberto said.

He's stalling, she thought. Yet he wants to be polite. It seemed to her that he was gone at least five minutes. Nikkia pulled her fingers through her hair, and her fingers got stuck in the humidity-tight curls. Now here he came toward her, and the fingers of her right hand were caught in her hair. Nikkia jerked her hand out and took some hair with it. She swallowed an "ouch," and held out her hand to Norberto.

Norberto moved into her hand, and his whole body moved behind his own hand. Already, he seemed to be dancing. His grace took her by surprise, and Nikkia wasn't ready to begin moving when his arm went around her back. She was very sensitive in the middle of her back, and the heat from his hand seemed to penetrate and turn her spine to liquid. He moved back several steps, dancing, his upper body never moving. Somehow, Nikkia had expected him to move toward her. She tried to pull him toward her. In her nervousness, instead of moving with his body, she stepped on his foot.

"Oh my gosh," she said. "I'm so sorry." She couldn't possibly tell him that never in her entire dancing career had she stepped on her partner's toes. Rather, her ability to anticipate her partner's moves was one of the assets that made her in demand. She was never so bound up in her own performance that she forgot her partner. None of that mattered now. Clearly, her relationship with Norberto was one where she sought him, she knew, and it made her clumsy. She lost the rhythm so completely now that she stepped on his other foot.

He seemed hardly to have noticed. They stopped

dancing. He held himself away from her, but his hips still moved slightly. Nikkia thought, that's one of the problems. I am not special to him, so that the dance inside him doesn't stop because of me. He is truly married to someone else, and I feel alone and awkward. But she found that now his legs were moving in such a way that she could begin to follow.

"You're not one of those people who wears shoes with highheels," he said.

Nikkia realized too late that she had stepped on his bare toes. "I forgot you're wearing sandals!" Nikkia felt her neck and shoulders stiffen. He was still dancing, though. She wanted to follow his movements, but all she could see in her mind was her foot on his bare toes. She felt as if she were one of her own patients learning to walk all over again. Her neck was growing more stiff and even painful now, and she could not dance any longer.

"We have to stop," she said, and she was almost crying. "I get a pain down my neck into my shoulders when I feel . . . when I've been driving a long time, and I drove a long time last night." She had this trouble only when she became upset, she recalled. Muscle strain had little to do with it. "My neck gets a spasm."

"What can you do for it?" he asked. He was really concerned. His question was so earnest that it made her care for him on an entirely new level.

"I get someone to rub my shoulders," she said softly. "Would you please?" But as she spoke he was doing it. The thumbs of his hands worked deep into her neck muscles.

Nikkia thought to herself, her back and arms relaxing. He's done nothing to put me ill at ease, even though I've been so awkward. He allows me to let myself go. Norberto makes me feel as though I share the space where he moves.

From the corner of her vision, Nikkia saw Darlene run past her to the door where someone waited outside. It was Lennie. Nikkia watched them talk animatedly. Nikkia smiled as she saw Darlene run her fingers in friendly fashion through Lennie's hair. She thought: that's what I need right now: a friend, a comrade, without the physical pull of sex working on me. Like Jeff--without his life style, his superficiality. But Nikkia knew that Darlene, too, felt the added excitement of sensuality with Lennie. And as of yet for Darlene it wasn't returned, as her own was not. Then Darlene was waving to her, and to Norberto, to come outside.

"Lennie says one car of six people drove off after the van. As soon as they got to the van, they agreed to call Coralee's. Tyrone is staying there with the little kids. And Lennie called Coralee's as soon as he got off the train. He says the parents are at the corner of Northampton and Tremont."

Darlene didn't wait for comment. "They've recovered the van, and it's smashed up. They need at least another car over there and a few more people in case the ROAR creeps come back. Someone from the leadership should come."

"That's me." Norberto broke in.

"They didn't think it was necessary to interrupt the dance and take a bunch of people," Lennie said. "The ROAR people have taken off. But they may be back, knowing we have to deal with the van."

"The four of us should go, in two cars," said Darlene. "I told you Lennie's hair was long. He got it cut, and it still looks cool."

Nikkia looked at her with regard. When she herself was sixteen, she couldn't have thought of such a proposal that quickly and kept up a chatter at the same time! The kids in the Boston summer project were acting older than their years. Their political reactions and decision making combined with the swift response of youth. Nikkia could see all at once why the future of the party rested on young people. This summer, built out of the wreck of Boston's schools, would represent the turning point in many of their lives.

Briefly, they discussed such a plan with Don and Yvette and Williams, a GE worker who was on the steering committee of the Boston work during the year. Williams agreed to let Norberto go, and warned, "But if there's any problem, you should try not to be arrested."

Yvette spoke, "I can see what you've been saying, Norberto, about the need to develop everyone into a leader. Russell and Coralee are absent, and Zack's just getting out of jail." She added, "I guess I've been a student too long. I'm in the habit of being told what to do. I think I should go instead of Darlene."

Norberto shook his head. "Somebody who is from Boston is needed to keep the dance together. You'll be needed right here."

Soon Norberto was driving Lennie, Darlene and Nikkia down the streets to the van. Their Volvo was a known car now, so they followed the darker, more residential streets with fewer stop lights. Then they saw the van.

All the windows were broken. The body had been bashed and the tires stolen. The letters KKK and swastikas had been painted on every side as well as the front.

"I think they may return," Norberto announced even before he got out of the car.

The parents of the teenagers were standing in a circle with the two teachers from Connecticut. One couple stood by the Chevy station wagon they had come in, as if to protect it from attack. Members of the community had come out and gathered on the side of the street opposite the van, not coming too close.

Nikkia was frightened. The sight of many white people watching made her think of an audience just before a performance. She couldn't predict how they would react. A few audiences did grow hostile. Nikkia, however, was usually so confident by performance time that she never became self-conscious. She thought only of communicating her physical ability, and that was easy. Today this training made her feel less and less scared as she thought only of getting across their message. She asked the comrades, "May I go over and talk with them across the street?"

Norberto was surprised. At first Nikkia had seemed shy and somewhat awkward to him. Her boldness now made him look at her differently. "I'm glad that you want to. Be sure to take some of the Challenge newspapers with you."

Nikkia had taken up a stack of papers and was headed across the street. Norberto and Darlene went toward the van. Lennie followed Nikkia and waited until Nikkia began a conversation.

The woman Nikkia spoke with didn't hesitate to tell the story. "Them ROAR guys come up screechin', and right away I smell trouble and call my kids in. I don't like them to see no violence." To Nikkia she looked like someone who could stand her own ground.

She had beefy, pink skin and rollers in her dyed red hair that was white at the roots.

"Did you notice what they did then?" asked Nikkia.

"Sure, me and the kids saw everythin' from the window. They must be in the Klan, too, because we watched them write KKK all over." She scratched her scalp under a roller. "What I don't understand is the Nazi stuff. We killed them all off in World War II."

"Their ideas aren't dead." Nikkia showed the woman a <u>Challenge</u> article about the party attacking a Nazi headquarters in Skokie, Illinois. "I think them writing the KKK and swastikas shows it's the same racism. One hundred years ago, forty years ago, and now today."

A man with narrow blue eyes, his shirt unbuttoned and loose over knee-length shorts, joined their conversation. "I won't stand 'em in my neighborhood. They got no business. I'll run 'em out with my bare hands."

"Jim Kilgore, you can't always be a troubleshooter," a tall man with glasses and a beard spoke up. "Let 'em be. Don't listen to that chick. And there's no fighting."

"That's what you think," said the woman in hair rollers. "You think by burying your head in the sand you're gonna solve problems. Well, you ain't."

"They want us to hide," said the man named Jim Kilgore. "I know a couple people right here in this neighborhood who's gonna sign up with them Nazis once they see it's safe to do so. They think we'll all get better off if niggers and Jews are dead. Oh 'scuse me," he apologized to Nikkia. "I get carried away and start mouthin' off like them bastards."

"They know together we can beat them. They knew that a hundred years back," Nikkia added. "After the Civil War, the government of the southern states allowed the Klan to kill whites living near blacks."

"Bull--loney." The man with the beard kicked at a soda can. "Nobody's bothered us. We don't bother them."

As he spoke, two cars pulled around the corner, their lights off. The doors opened, and eight men got out. They carried baseball bats and lead pipes. Ignoring the growing crowd on the opposite curb, they headed for the van. The parents and the teachers around the van had nothing in their hands. Just then they, too, spotted the approaching gang of men.

One of the men shouted. Nikkia couldn't tell which, "We got no room here for fucking niggers."

Nikkia saw one of the women turn. The woman's arms went up to her face. As a bat hit her forearms, Nikkia heard a cracking sound, soft and sickening. She felt paralyzed. She saw one parent whom she only knew as his nickname, Freckles, for his light complexion. He charged at the attackers out of desperation, head-first like a bull.

A man raised a lead pipe and brought it down on the back of Freckles' head. His arms reached out in desperation for the man's legs. Freckles was hit again and again. His wife screamed. Nikkia, from across the street, sensed the action was moving too fast for her body to respond. Each time a bat swung she felt the blow, slow and horrible. Freckles was beaten to the ground.

Suddenly from behind the van, Norberto, Yvette and Don jumped on one of the men beating Freckles. The man, surprised, tried to face them. Norberto grabbed his bat. He twisted it out of the man's hand with the leverage of his weight.

Nikkia felt a cheer rise in her own throat. She was ready. But common sense, louder than optimism, told her she would be no match against the lead pipes the ROAR men carried. And there were three other women in the group of parents and teachers that wouldn't hold up against men who weighed twice as much as they. Even if she and Lennie ran across the street, Nikkia told herself, they alone wouldn't make the difference. Wouldn't win.

Yet the crowd grew around her. There were now more than twenty bystanders. She knew their only chance was to appeal to these men and women. "Are you going to watch innocent people get beaten in front of you?"

Nikkia looked into the eyes of the three people she had gotten to know, however slightly. "Do you want the Klan and the Nazis running your lives?"

She made a pulling gesture toward them with her arms. But she directed her voice at Jim Kilgore. "We can do it," she cried. "Come with me."

"I'm with you," agreed the woman in rollers. But she didn't move.

    The man with the beard stated, more to Kilgore than to Nikkia, "I'm getting the hell out of here." Yet he, too, stayed at the curb of the street.
    Kilgore wavered. He looked at the demolished van. He looked at the ROAR men and took a step toward Nikkia. Then he shook his head and stepped back with the others.
    "This is how it starts," Nikkia continued speaking to Jim. And to them all. "The time to stop them is now." The neighbors, as well as Jim, remained where they were.
    Nikkia found her own legs more than ready to move. She looked to Lennie, also talking with the crowd. A flashing thought came to mind that he, too, had been a stranger only a week ago. And today, out of all these people, she could count on him. He had a young fellow by the arm, too. Not eager, but willing to join them.
    "This is Sean," said Lennie. He introduced a well-built, blond youth. Nikkia realized she would have mistaken the fellow for a ROAR sympathizer. Appearances, she thought. And then a sense of urgency was all she knew.
    "We can't wait any longer!" Nikkia thrust the stack of papers into the arms of a surprised Kilgore. She started running with a sureness she had not felt till that moment.
    By the time Nikkia got across the street, two of the ROAR men were wrestling with Norberto on the ground. They didn't see Nikkia, Lennie and Sean running at them.
    Lennie and Sean lept at their backs. With their first punches, Norberto wriggled free. But he couldn't wrestle the iron bar from the ROAR man. The five of them tossed there on the ground, a tangle of arms.
    Nikkia spied a bat on the ground. She used to wonder what she would do if she had the chance to hurt an enemy. The liberal world of Jeff Gaynor told her that she would only lower herself to the level of a beast. Then she remembered the boy who had been lynched. The memory came at the same time as she saw the sight of a ROAR man before her. He kicked at the breast of a woman in the street, as she lay trapped against a front tire. Nikkia grabbed the bat.
    "You fucking son of a bitch," yelled Nikkia. "I'm going to smash your skull in." The ROAR man, for a

second, was startled. Nikkia moved in blindly, not seeing much of anything distinctly now. She managed to hit the man across his forehead. His hands moved to his head from the pain. But with his face bloodied and one eye closed he lunged for Nikkia.

Nikkia still held the bat. The sight of the man's bloody face coming toward her looked like all the horror films she'd ever seen. She forgot how to swing the bat. She was frightened out of her wits. She could only scream. "You cock sucking pimp you bastard of an ass hole shit."

As he came even closer Nikkia forgot she had the bat at all. She delivered a kick to him in a way she had fought when she was seven years old. Directly into his groin. He doubled over. And Nikkia remembered the bat. She swung it just once, with both hands, to the base of his skull. As he went down, she felt dizzy and had to put her own head down to keep from fainting. The bat rested in her hands across her knees. She could not have swung it again for her hands were shaky and sweaty. It was a moment before she could tell what was going on around her.

She heard a car engine start up. The man at her feet stirred. Two women lay on the ground near the van. Darlene knelt next to them. One woman sat leaning against a tire, crying. Her husband had his arm around her.

Away from the van the fighting continued. It was near the car the men from ROAR had come in. Two of them had managed to get in, and a third was half in the back seat, trying to close the door on Norberto's arm.

About fifty people crowded the curb and stood in the street. Nikkia could hear Jim Kilgore's voice, "Don't let 'em get away." But neither he nor any of the neighbors came closer to the fight.

Nikkia noticed Lennie leaning against the back door of the van. He appeared dazed, rubbing his head. Nikkia could only guess that his light frame had been thrown out from the battle. Two of the ROAR men, who had not been fighting with Norberto and Lennie, now ran toward their other car. Sean ran behind them and tackled one. They both fell.

As Nikkia started toward them, she suddenly saw the two men who remained. They worked like machines with their lead pipes over a body kneeling on the ground. They didn't even look up as the guy Sean had tackled stumbled past them. Nikkia cried, "Over here, Sean!"

Not waiting for Sean, Nikkia hit at one of the men beating the kneeling figure, who was Freckles. Hot tears came to Nikkia's eyes, for she saw that the fingers of both his hands were broken. And she thought of Norberto alone by the other car.

Sean was beside her suddenly and got a fist up under the other man's jaw. He fell backward, and the other headed for the second car. Seeing him get away seemed to hurt as much as the sight of Freckles and the knowledge that Norberto was still alone. More tears came, and she feared for Norberto as the last goon pushed Sean and went for the first car.

"Let 'em go!" Nikkia remembered a word of Spanish, "Dejeles."

Two men in the car pushed Norberto off the door. The car, moving slowly, had dragged him a few feet. Nikkia could not cry out to him again.

Including Nikkia, only three of the people in the fight remained standing. Sean, over there, had taken on the status of a comrade. He walked to her, tears on his face, and she comforted him. Norberto had got to his feet, looking after the disappearing cars.

They turned first, then, to Freckles. "I've called an ambulance," the woman with rollers in her hair said to Nikkia.

"We'll need at least one," said Nikkia. "I think the woman's arms are broken."

"Please move back," said the husband of the woman, Ernesta. He spoke to the crowd of people, which continued to grow.

Some neighbors comforted the injured people, and Kilgore brought ice and clean cloths from his house. He approached Nikkia from the side. "You couldn't a done better."

"Oh yes we could have," Nikkia said abruptly. She stopped herself. She knew it would do no good to get angry at Kilgore. Nikkia turned her attention to Freckles, who was rocking from side to side in pain.

The woman with rollers tugged at Nikkia's arm. "Those of you who are all right better go now, dearie. We'll make sure these folks get to the hospital. The cops'll be here to investigate in no time."

Nikkia nodded but did not reply. She was still

angry that not one of the neighbors had fought. Except for Sean, she told herself silently.

"She's right," said Lennie. "The guys who escaped will go get help from their friends in blue."

"We need to go back to the office and let everyone know," said Norberto.

"I'm not so sure we should go back there," cautioned Darlene. But no one replied, and she was not confident enough to speak again.

Before they left, Sean opened the van, checking the glove compartment and the back. "They didn't wreck everything," he held up a box with a handle. It was Lennie's saxophone.

x x x

Darlene and Lennie rode back to the CAR club house with three of the parents. Nikkia, in the back seat of the other car which Norberto drove, had a strange, child's desire to be comforted in his arms. She began to cry, and one of the mothers next to her, Mrs. Watson, hugged her and wiped her hands with a wash'n'dry packet from her purse.

When they walked in the door of the CAR office the dance music was blasting, the DJ in full swing. Some people quit dancing and stared at them.

Their whole group must have looked a wreck, Nikkia realized. She hadn't given a thought until now to her own physical appearance. She looked down at her torn gauze skirt.

Lennie said aloud, to no one, "I'm dying of thirst." Mrs. Watson was already on her way back from the coolers with an armful of sodas. "You're a mind reader," Lennie told her.

Norberto gathered everyone, and the music quieted to a stop. Bonita translated while Norberto told the story in Spanish. It was as though, in the drama of the fight, he had lost all command of English. "They got away," he concluded. "But one of them will remember us for awhile."

When he pointed to an imaginary lump on his head, the youths, their parents and comrades laughed. Several times Norberto praised the role of the comrades, in particular Nikkia.

"It's a good example of how all of us are leaders," Nikkia was moved to say. "I couldn't convince any of the community people to join us. But Lennie drew Sean here out of the crowd. He fought like a tiger. They had a year-long friendship on account of of the busing." She smiled at Lennie. "Didn't we always say that busing is a good thing?"

A few people clapped. "I wouldn't be standing here if it wasn't for Sean," Lennie told them. Others began to clap, for Sean, for Lennie, the applause grew.

At first no one heard the knocking on the door. Before anyone could get to the door, it was kicked open. There were police, crowding the entrance. With them, four of the ROAR men. One of them had a bandaid on his cheek. A cop spoke to him, "Point out which of these attacked you."

The man pointed to one of the parents. That parent, Jefferson Hill, had been hit with a lead pipe as he defended the women around the van. Bruises were obvious on his neck. He shouted, "It was him put Mrs. Brady in the hospital!"

"Arrest that man." Three cops surrounded and handcuffed Jefferson.

Jefferson looked around as if to ask whether he should protest his arrest. In that moment about two dozen cops crowded into the front office that had been the dance floor.

The ROAR man then pointed to Nikkia. "She wanted to start a race war in that white community," he accused. "She's dangerous." Two of the cops nearest Nikkia grabbed her and pulled her arms behind her back.

"He's a liar," she yelled. "They attacked a child. His parents. Four people are in the hospital busted up because of them and their lead pipes."

"Tell it to your lawyer," said one of the cops. As he shoved Nikkia to the door, she lost a sandal. Lennie picked it up, and they arrested him next.

Sean and Darlene were taken. Some people were seized who had been at the party. They tustled with the police. In all, seventeen people were arrested. All of them were positively identified by the man with the bandaid. Ten of those people had been dancing at the time in the office. One of the DJ's, who was from Puerto Rico, was arrested instead of Norberto.

"I blame myself," Norberto said right after the cops left. He still spoke only in Spanish, and Bonita translated. He seemed to her to have forgotten all the English he had learned. "We never should have come back to the clubhouse. I put you all in danger."

"They would have taken people from here anyway," Bonita was emphatic. "There's nothing you could have done about that."

"We lost this battle because of me," he insisted. "Don't try to tell me we didn't."

Nikkia, on the way to jail, was preoccupied with the battle, too, but had decided not to blame either Norberto or herself. It was not having a relationship with the neighbors as much as not having a better plan or something to fight with. She couldn't wait to get back out and discuss these things with everyone, not only Norberto.

Because of the weekend, however, it took three days before she was released, on a thousand dollars bail. She talked with the other women who had been arrested with her and with the prostitutes in intake. They all encouraged her and wanted to hear the story again and again.

"All you New York City broads is tough as nails," giggled one of the Boston prostitutes. She was a beautiful girl, and she wore her hair in a high pony tail. Her name was Geri, and she looked as if she could be a college freshman at Radcliffe. Her talking made Nikkia feel old and sedate. They became friends during those three days.

Nikkia was very worried about the charges of assault against her because she didn't know how much damage her bat had done to the thug's head. He was not in the courtroom the day she was arraigned. The other comrades told her later that he might have become scared. Or perhaps he was ashamed to have been dealt a hard blow by a woman, particularly a young black woman.

There was a very big chance, however, that he would seek her out. He knew exactly what she looked like. She was advised to give leadership, do visiting work only and not appear at public rallies for the rest of her stay. "He'll even claim you had a gun on you," Zack told her. "And they'll find one in the area to prove it."

Zack himself was facing a trial and charged with aggravated assault of an officer. His wife, Carolyn, was very worried. He would certainly spend several months in jail. Of the seventeen arrested, only the black comrades and community people, five of them in all, faced future trial.

Nikkia was relieved at last to be able to settle into specific tasks. She was glad to be working directly with Zack and Carolyn, both of whom had promised to help her develop more leadership within the Boston community.

For three days she organized early morning leafletting, signature gathering and visiting of contacts, old and new. She felt she was beginning to get to know Boston and to feel comfortable in many neighborhoods. Especially she enjoyed getting to know the comrades from across the country, here for the project.

"This is a happy coincidence," Zack had told her. "It's time you gave more leadership within the party. And it's fortunate for us that at this time it's the best activity for you." He kept Nikkia so busy she had little time to think about her problems with Lawrence. Or her feelings about Norberto.

And one day when she had not been thinking about him at all, Zack assigned her to visit Norberto. "He hasn't been himself the last two days," Zack briefed her. "He got notice on Monday from relatives in California that the Immigration Service has been harassing his wife and children, even though they have green cards. The INS were looking for him, too. As much as he wants to, the comrades think that under no circumstances should Norberto return to California now."

Zack continued, "Norberto feels that the seventeen arrests were his fault. He blamed himself personally for the arrest of the DJ. He has stopped giving as much leadership, though he's still doing the work. Now, with his family in trouble, he wants to go back to California." Zack spread his hands in helplessness.

"Why ask me to struggle with Norberto?" Nikkia asked. "I barely know him."

"If anyone can get him to change his thinking, you can," said Zack. "He told me he thinks you're some kind of wonder woman. I arranged for you both to visit the Freedom School neighborhood tomorrow."

Nikkia thought to herself that she cared a great deal for Norberto. But the way that he excited her could not possibly help her bring him back into the political picture. She might even hurt his commitment if he realized he meant things to her that he should not. Yet no one should know that she was feeling this strongly, and so she must try.

Zack suggested she be very supportive about his family but at the same time realistic. "I talked with him," Zack said, "and he talked as if nothing was wrong. I told him that it might put his wife in greater danger to try to set up a phone conversation. And I told him the comrades in California were in touch with her and helping her children. But I don't think he even heard me."

When Nikkia met Norberto, she noticed immediately that his eyes had lost their intensity. She felt him looking at her. But it was not with the same directness that had attracted her a week and a half ago. They went to see Jefferson Hill and then Maureen McGovern. Norberto talked with them, but at Maureen's he seemed to pause more frequently, fidgeting with his hands.

In one of these silences, Nikkia realized why she had been so drawn to him. His inner political strength had shown him direction and given his body firm, hard lines. Now Norberto reminded her of a wax figure from which the life had been removed.

Nikkia was prepared to be patient. As they travelled to a late afternoon meeting, she sat down on a Metro bench and motioned for him to join her.

"You're thinking about something else today, I notice," Nikkia began.

After they'd chatted a bit, Norberto said, "I suppose you'd like to get me to change my attitude, like Zack. But it won't work. More and more, I feel the black and white workers here won't change. Or it's probably me that's useless."

"What do you mean, useless?"

"Nothing I do is right," he responded. "Let me give you a for instance." He spoke partly in English, partly in Spanish. "Darlene saw the danger better than me by saying everyone should not come back to the dance. That proves it." Norberto spoke rapidly, as though he felt this left no room for argument.

My god, he's so depressed, thought Nikkia. He gives in to it totally. Both in his previous commitment and in his depression now, he's completely without pretense. She felt she was beginning to know him better, but it was like trying to look at the dark side of the moon. Despite her concern, she couldn't help thinking that he must give himself this completely to everything, including his family. But in looking at him sitting stiffly on the bench, she knew how far he was from considering intimacy or even comradeship at this time.

"Everyone makes mistakes. But leaders' mistakes are more noticeable."

"I'm not a leader anymore," Norberto responded.

"You have experience; you've been a good leader because you allow others to develop and urge us to do the right things," Nikkia said. "We need you."

"You need to develop new leadership," said Norberto abruptly.

The trolley came then, and they got on. Nikkia was tempted to continue the conversation in the crowded Metro, but she knew it would only make matters worse. Instead, they spoke of Lennie and of involving more of his friends at a block party near Coralee's. After the meeting, the others wanted to go to Ugi's, a sub shop near the office, but Norberto refused and left to go to Zack's. Nikkia was determined to speak with others about the problem.

It was Yvette, during a conversation late that night, who gave her an idea. "What we think of as personal in people is political, too," she said. "I don't know how that applies to Norberto; he didn't let us know his thoughts on his family before this. But somehow, his confidence in workers and in his ability to lead them was destroyed by this recent struggle, compounded by his personal fears."

The next time that Nikkia was able to speak alone with Norberto was almost a week later. They were leafletting the D Street projects of South Boston. Here, the volunteers went in groups of four. Two to scout and two to leaflet before moving to another building.

Leslie, the woman from Seattle in charge of the South Boston work, filled them in. "We change the canvassing and leafletting routes each time so ROAR can't predict our moves. You can only stay in one place for twenty minutes. That way, no one can catch up to you."

Leslie herself and Don joined them this day. They each carried a lead pipe wrapped in newspaper. Norberto and Nikkia were to be the spotters. The corner of D Street and Seventh crested a hill, and Leslie suggested they stand back to back so as to spot down the hill in either direction.

Nikkia was able to ask Norberto, "What do you hear from your wife, your family?"

"I got a letter. She talks about Manuel working again. She's lonesome for Puebla, where we're from in Mexico. I don't think she cares if I come back."

Nikkia then tried to put herself in the position of his wife. Standing there, with her back to him, she looked down the hill to the bay. "The people in your club, even the new woman, Estrellita, tell me you don't get together for personal talks in between meetings like you used to. Maybe your wife thinks you don't put enough in your letters about her, personally, either."

A group of four teenage girls, all of them with long, wavy hair, crossed the street a block away. Nikkia saw that they were headed for three teenage boys. Four girls and three boys. Odd girl out, Nikkia thought. "I'm sure she misses you." Norberto was so close behind her that she could touch him if she moved her arms back.

"Then why does she talk about everything else?"

"Maybe she's afraid you won't come back. Or if you do, they'll arrest you. Perhaps she doesn't want to upset you by talking about your situation." Nikkia wasn't sure how to proceed. He wasn't helping her.

"I see two guys with dogs," Norberto warned. "They're not just out for a stroll. Those are some bad looking dogs."

"Leslie and Don should be coming out that building any minute. We'll meet them. We can't run towards them."

"Then we'll all go through the other building straight toward the car," said Norberto.

Nikkia was surprised that he could be thinking of so many things at once. Then she realized that she, too, was already planning how she would continue their conversation at their next stop. Then, Leslie appeared.

They had parked the Volvo closer to the second building in case they had to get to the car right away. As soon as they drove off, Nikkia looked back and could see the two dogs straining on the tight leashes, headed right for the building they had just left.

At the corner of G Street and Eighth, the best place to spot was on either side of a corner building. There, they could see the full length of the project. This time, while they waited, Nikkia tried to picture herself as if she were Norberto, thinking of his wife. She found this difficult.

"What you do here, in the summer project," she said, "fights racist attitudes. Our struggle here helps people's awareness of Silvia's situation in California."

"We're dealing here with Boston," he said stubbornly. "My wife is in Delano. Since I can't be there now, I feel split inside when I start to work closely with comrades here."

Nikkia paused, wanting to say the right thing. Instead of continuing to talk about himself, Norberto observed, "I can see an old man with a shopping bag." When he added nothing more, Nikkia did then what she had learned to do in talking with certain depressed patients, and that was to look inside herself.

She remembered that at first she had felt somewhat like a missionary here. She had not believed that such a thing like Boston could ever happen on the upper West Side. Thinking now about the community of Boston that had mainly been sympathetic but not militant around the van incident made her see why she had hoped Manhattan would not become more segregated. She had been afraid that people there--like Lawrence--might do nothing. Nikkia asked Norberto, "What do you think of the people here in Boston?"

"They like the schools segregated." Norberto answered with such anger that Nikkia was surprised.

"What do you mean?" she didn't know.

"The whites like living in slums here as long as the blacks aren't there. And the blacks think they're going to be better off going to those stinking schools." He finished, "They're not like us campesinos. We think alike. Here, they want to fight each other."

Was this how far backward two weeks of depression could take you? Nikkia wondered. This man who led people forward for twenty years? Nikkia sighed. She repeated his words, "Who wants to fight each other?"

Norberto corrected himself, "I don't mean all

blacks. Just here in Boston. You, you're the most militant woman I've ever met."

To herself, Nikkia told him: Flattery will get you nowhere. Her brain began to sift him out more clearly. He's trying to disarm me, she thought. I must be getting close to his real objection.

She stood up and checked her side of the building. The women glanced at her. Then their children argued over a big wheel, and their mothers looked to them.

"You think no one except Mexican-Americans will fight in the long run?" Nikkia pursued, hoping that her intuition was right. "Do you think you'll be killed, and your family will be helpless? And it will all come to nothing. Most Americans--whites--won't fight in a revolution. Is that what you truly believe?"

Norberto was silent a long time. "Well, not just whites," he said.

"O.K., American blacks as well. But for us few exceptions," Nikkia was beginning to regain her sense of humor.

"Ever since I came here in April," Norberto said finally, "I tried not to believe what I was afraid of. I was the hardest fighter for visiting because I know there will be no revolution without all the workers that we can get. And now, with my family worries, I feel the cops can arrest most of us, just like that. They have the guns, the jails, the INS."

Nikkia stopped him there. "That isn't their biggest weapon, the guns." She knew that he was beginning to look to her now that she had discovered his cynicism. But she had to maintain her lead by continuing to draw him out.

"What is stronger than their guns?" he asked finally, unable to help himself.

"When they don't have to use them at all." Nikkia said no more. She waited for his understanding.

"You mean they have beaten me with my attitude," he said, finally.

"Just like that."

"I forgot the main things," he said.

"You managed to forget all the _good_ things that happened the night of the fight over the van. First of all, ROAR and the community know now that ROAR can't do as they please without forceful opposition.

ROAR was more exposed, too. Some neighbors helped with first aid. Sean is now a CAR leader." Nikkia knew that she would not have to say much more.

She found herself admiring his quickness, his awareness of his own contradictions. Nikkia felt instinctively, though, that she had to seize this moment. His cynicism had to be quickly replaced with confidence that comes with doing work. She said, "Dame tu mano."

Give me your hand. It was an easy choice for him. He had only to touch her hand, she thought, and that would be enough. She held her hand around the corner of the brick building, and waited.

Nikkia felt the fingers of his hand slip between each of her fingers until he really held her hand. The palms of their hands met. His thumb touched the back of her hand, and she felt it through her body. She was grateful for the wall, for she had to lean against it.

Suddenly Nikkia wished there was music playing. If she could move with it, her body might not feel as though it were burning. Nikkia very much wanted to sustain her political lead for him, which felt fragile now. He still had not said that he would contribute more to the leadership here. She said, "Time is very precious this summer. You still have well over a month until the first day of school. Do you think you can use your energies well?"

"Right now, I think I have more." She could hear him laughing with a kind of relief. "No one has taken such time with me."

Nikkia replied, "Zack has." To herself she added, you just weren't listening.

"But I did not feel as though I knew Zack all my life."

He loosened his fingers in such a way that Nikkia felt for a moment as if their hands were coming together again. And then his hand was gone, and she withdrew her own. "It's twenty minutes," he said.

"It seemed like five." Nikkia laughed and peered at his face.

It struck her then that within moments he seemed to have begun to renew himself. Nikkia was reminded of how sick children often cure themselves as quickly, while they sleep. Norberto went to the door of the project while Nikkia looked down her side of the building for the last time.

A woman with groceries crossed the street and peered over her bag at Nikkia. Nikkia looked away. The woman kept walking. Nikkia began to tremble. She knew it wasn't just because of the woman's long stare.

Norberto came back and motioned for Nikkia to follow him. They walked behind Don and Leslie toward the car. Norberto held the rolled newspaper in one hand, tapping the heavy lead inside against the palm of his other hand.

She watched the muscles move on his forearms. "I didn't need to remind you that it was mainly white workers who comforted us afterwards. And that Sean is white." Nikkia added. "You knew it wasn't me alone that was fighting."

"I heard you shout. From where I was on the ground I could see what you did," he said.

"The point is, I could have done very little without you and Sean." Nikkia felt a sureness that she had not felt since she left the stage.

Norberto turned to her then, and the directness was back in his eyes. "Now that you know me better, you won't mind if I tell you something?" he began. "If we are truly equals then I can tell you a secret about myself."

Nikkia couldn't imagine what the secret could be. But she felt comfortable with him now. She realized that she could always talk with him about anything that came to her mind. "So tell me," she said.

"When I saw you for the first time two weeks ago in Yvette's apartment," Norberto didn't hesitate, but went on in the same up front manner she remembered so well. "Your face seeing me there, and your body--so very strong . . . You made me forget for that moment that I ever was married."

Chapter 12

When Russell woke Sunday morning, his head throbbed as if a rock were caught in his skull. Twelve stitches, he remembered them. He must have had an x-ray. He didn't remember that. Had they put him to sleep? When Russell touched his head he felt the smooth shaved skin, which hurt.

He had heard that if you wanted to vomit, that was a sure sign of concussion. But he didn't feel bad, only hungry. He saw that it was one o'clock. No wonder he was hungry. He hadn't eaten for more than a day.

"How you feelin?" Renee came into the bedroom, and Russell was glad to see her. "I been lookin in on you. You was asleep all this time."

Russell could see Coralee's face in Renee's today. She seemed to him to stand straighter and more relaxed without her child. And away from Coralee, she seemed more confident. "How's about toast and juice?" He saw that she had made a tray. "I think you're supposed to lay flat for a spell."

She came further into the room. The worn blue denim of her jeans looked soft and comfortable. Renee wore an orange sleeveless knit top. Russell thought how he as a patient would feel more at ease if nurses dressed in old jeans. He had a sudden urge to be taken care of, and he wondered why the house was so quiet. "Where is Coralee?"

"She's got Timothy picking up trash all up and down the block. Thomas mowing the yard." Renee put the tray beside him on the bed, and he could smell the melted butter. The toast was warm to his fingers, and the little mound of strawberry jam made his mouth water.

"Oh, I forgot a knife," she said.

"I'll dip it in the jelly, who cares?" Russell rubbed a corner of the toast in the jam as if to prove his point. He couldn't wait to put it in his mouth.

It was as if his head and his stomach belonged to two separate people. He ate and thought about Coralee and the twins and everyone in the household. He tried to savor the buttered toast and cold juice in his throat, the quiet, and the softness of Renee's presence in her faded jeans.

As if they had known he was thinking of them, Adam and Shukyyirah came into the doorway. Renee glared at them. Adam stopped his movement and put out an arm to hold back Shukyyirah. Obviously, Russell thought, somebody has been telling them not to come in here. For a moment he closed his eyes--imagining the children and their ages: Renee, seventeen; Timothy and Thomas, thirteen; Fay, nine; Adam, seven; and Shukyyirah and Muhammed-Ahmed in the toddler category--wishing he could make everyone but Renee disappear. Again, he wanted to be waited on, if only for a day. Then he heard someone crying, and he opened his eyes.

"I was w-worried about you," stuttered Adam from the doorway, rubbing his eyes before the tears could fall.

"You should have seen him," said Renee. "As soon as he heard you were in the hospital, he was crying all over the place."

"Shut up, you bitch." Adam came through the doorway. "I hate you."

"I didn't mean it nasty," Renee put her hands in front of her as if to defend herself.

Adam's face was bent in rage. "You've always got to make me mad!" He threw one fist behind his back.

"Come here, Adam." Russell held out his arms.

Adam stuck out his tongue at Renee and moved with a sliding motion beside the bed and into Russell's arms. Immediately Shukyyirah ran over and before Renee could stop her, bounced onto the bed. "Ouch," said Russell. "My head hurts, you guys."

"See what you did," said Renee angrily to Adam. "You know Shukyyirah follows you all over the place."

"It's not my fault," Adam said in a smug voice, his head on Russell's chest.

At that moment, Fay came into the doorway. A paper bag was in her hand. "I heard you all up here," she looked accusingly at Renee.

"I've been keeping everybody out all morning. A lot of help you've been spending money at the corner store." Renee's eyes met Russell's, and he felt that she, too, would have liked to spend some quiet time and perhaps tell him things about herself.

Another bounce from Shukyyirah made Russell wince. His head began to throb.

Fay came closer holding the paper bag in front of her. "I brung you a soda with my 'lowance," she said. "It's Punchy Peach: the best kind they have."

Timothy and Thomas, appeared in the doorway just as Fay entered the room, and Russell saw they had a bag between them. Fay turned partly away from Russell, to glare at Renee, "See, I kept them busy for a long time at the store after their chores."

"We brought a honey bun," said Timothy who, Russell remembered, was the taller of the two.

"It would have been more," said Thomas. "But Timothy ate half the Ring Dings."

"To see if they were fresh," Timothy defended.

"And of course Thomas had to eat the other half," Fay said with a sigh. "I said to him that we couldn't give you stuff that had been opened up and messed with because I knew he would cop an attitude if only Timothy got to eat."

Thomas pushed Fay. "You just like to be the big boss all the time. Telling us what to do."

"You both have to be told every minute or you wouldn't do nothin all day," Fay blinked hard as if she were about to cry. "You would've eaten up your whole 'lowance if I hadn't said you should buy him something instead, and you know it." As if to make her point, she handed Russell the soda, still in the bag, but with the straw sticking out. "I can't get it open."

Russell twisted the cap off and took a sip. It was acidy and sweet at the same time, and full of carbonation. He could barely swallow once. He saw that many pairs of eyes were on him. He smiled. "This is great."

Seeing he had accepted the soda, Thomas handed Russell the cellophane wrapped honey bun. "You should have let me hand it to him," said Timothy. "I'll unwrap it for you, Russell."

"No, that's OK," said Russell. "I'll save it for later on." He noticed Shukyyirah reaching for the soda. Thankfully, with the first relief he had known in several minutes, he took the soda out of the bag and held the bottle for Shukyyirah. She drank with slurping sounds.

"She's a pig. Don't let her just keep drinking," said Fay. She made a face at Renee, "<u>She</u> won't do nothing."

For the first time, Renee's mouth hardened into a line. It hurt Russell to see her struggle to maintain her age, for then she lost it. "I'm going to break your arm," she grabbed Fay.

Russell thought, where the shit was Coralee? His head was pounding. He longed for Pat. Her voice on the phone last night had been so reassuring.

He wished to yell at them all, but his head was too painful. And then, because he was the one who must, Russell began to talk. He put his hand to his head as if to draw their attention to the fact that he was ill, and it worked.

"Shhh," said Fay. "His head is killing him."

"Thanks," said Russell. He tucked one arm around Shukyyirah and put the Peachy Punch in that hand so she could suck and wouldn't bounce. "You all have made me feel right at home: Renee by making breakfast and just being quiet; Timothy, Thomas and Fay by spending their whole allowance--and Fay, for making sure it took place; Adam, for taking care of Shukyyirah; and I guess that's it!"

"Let's give us a hand," Adam led them in clapping.

"<u>Softly</u>," yelled Fay. She took Shukkyirah out of the bed. "You shouldn't be in there. He's sick."

"Thanks." Russell motioned with his hand. "For a couple days I'm supposed to stay in bed because I may have a concussion."

"What's a concousin?" asked Adam.

"Tomorrow," said Renee. "Russell has to rest. Now I want all of you out of here." They left slowly and with a lot of arguing. But Russell had drifted off to sleep before Renee closed the door.

When he opened his eyes the sun came in the shadeless window with a white light that left few shadows. It was still late morning, Russell thought, because he smelled bacon. His watch said five forty-five. Then a church bell played a hymn with a mechanical regularity that told him at once that there was a tape being played from a church tower and that it was still Sunday.

Russell raised his head, and felt no headache.

He pulled off the sheet and put his feet on the floor. He was driven by a pain that he recognized as hunger.

He remembered, vaguely, putting his shirt and pants over a chair. Now they were gone. Then another pain--the acute pressure in his bladder--kept his feet moving to the bathroom. Once there, his bowels gave him another message. Afterwards, he looked in the mirror over the sink.

He had one black eye. A cut ran from his left temple to his chin. His lower lip puffed, and the inside was raw. Russell winced, ran the water, rinsed his face and looked again. Every bruise and cut still appeared, but he felt better. He looked at the side of his head, at the shaved area and black stitches. He wondered that Shukyyirah had dared to come near him.

Russell turned on the shower and forgot not to get his head wet, but the warm water felt delicious. And he thought he wasn't going to be sick, that he didn't have a concussion. He rubbed his stomach with the happy thought that perhaps he had lost a couple pounds in only his first weekend in Boston! When he wrapped a towel around his lower half and opened the door, there stood Thomas.

"Hi. How ya feelin?" Thomas smiled.

"I think I'm going to live." Russell, looking at Thomas alone without Timothy, saw that his bare feet were larger than Russell's own, and that he had just begun to grow in height.

"You're going to be taller than me," Russell said.

"Maybe even bigger than Tyrone," Thomas seemed pleased at the thought. "Here are your clothes."

"You didn't have to do that."

"Hey, they were all fulla blood."

At the thought of his own blood-soaked clothes, Russell felt dizzy. He leaned on the sink.

"You don't look so good."

Russell wiped the steam off the mirror and saw himself again. This time, the stubble from a day of not shaving became obvious, and he didn't have the energy to shave now. The blue-purple of his swollen eye made him sick to his stomach, and he had to vomit. It left his knees shaking. The look of it in the toilet made him vomit again.

"You shouldn't a got out of bed, man." Thomas

extended a hand toward him. "Let me get your pajamas instead of these clothes, and I'll help you back to the room."

"Just some clean underwear is good," said Russell, remembering that it was hot. Still, the being sick had left him shivering, and it seemed forever that Thomas was gone. He thought that he should have gone to get his own underclothes, but he couldn't even hold the towel around himself now. He was hunched over with his elbows on the sink when Thomas reappeared.

"Man you look awful." Thomas saw it would do no good to simply hand Russell the pair of shorts. He would have to bend way down to put them on. Thomas shook open the shorts and held them close to the floor so Russell could step in.

"Lean on me," Thomas insisted.

Russell looked down at Thomas' bare back, smooth brown skin with the ribs showing and shoulder blades protruding. He couldn't help putting most of his weight on Thomas, with his hand on his back. The bones felt so frail. It was all Russell could do to lift first one foot and then the other. Steadying himself, he pulled up the shorts. There was a black pressure behind his eyes, and he fell against Thomas.

"I've got you."

Russell closed his eyes, for the light seemed to make him more dizzy as they left the bathroom. He heard an odd metallic sound as Thomas bent to get something, but he didn't open his eyes.

Russell no longer felt faint, but leaning completely on Thomas now, walked--what seemed like twice the distance he had come--back to the room. He didn't open his eyes until Thomas told him the bed was in front of him, and he felt it with his shins. When he lay down again, there began such a pounding inside his head that he leaned over the bedside to throw up once again. Thomas held a metal wash pan under his head.

When he had finished, Russell lay back, completely weak.

"How did you . . . about the pan," he managed to say.

"I had a funny feelin," said Thomas. "You probably shouldn't have tried to get up."

"What time is it? I thought it was the next day when I smelled the bacon."

"Six. Bacon's the only thing me and Timothy know how to cook good. We have BLT's every day in the summer."

"That reminds me, did Coralee ever get back yet?"

"She works private duty whenever she can, but she might be out in the neighborhood someplace. Who knows?"

Russell decided not to show his annoyance. He felt he couldn't blame her in her absence, especially not in front of her children. But the dynamics of all these people pressed him like a physical weight into the bed. What would he do when he heard them fighting and couldn't get up? A nervousness grew inside him.

"I've got to dump this," Thomas took the pan to the door. "Do you want a BLT? No, I don't suppose you do," he answered to himself but waited at the door. "Well, I'll come back and check on you in about an hour." When Russell didn't reply, Thomas knew he was asleep and left, closing the door softly.

The next day, after a couple of eight-hour sleeps, Russell's usual dream woke him. He felt more like company though it still made him nauseous to get up. The children came in, one at a time.

"What _is_ a concousin?" asked Adam.

"Boy, are you stupid," said Fay.

"Why don't you tell him what it is?" suggested Russell.

"I don't know. What is it?" asked Fay.

"That's a good example of what I've been thinking about you guys." Russell felt compelled to deal with the problems they presented. He didn't know if he was up to it. But it was either talk about their troubles or send them all out of the room. "Fay here did a good thing by taking charge of the trip to the store yesterday. But then she sometimes puts people down. They resent her . . ."

"What's that mean, resent?" asked Fay.

"Quit interrupting," Renee was quick to say.

"Shut your face," said Fay. "If I don't know what he's talking about, I can't listen."

"This time Fay is right," Russell came in. "You should all ask questions right away. I don't mind being interrupted. What I do mind is when each of you tries to be better than the next guy."

"What does resent _mean_?" insisted Fay.

Russell tried to answer. It was becoming hard to

concentrate. "I get really angry--I mean I get angry way in here," he pointed to his chest. "When you all pick with each other. I see that you resent--that means you feel insulted--when a person picks on you, like when a boss tries to make you feel small because he only wants to pay you low wages."

"I told you you were bossy," said Adam to Fay.

"Shut up, Adam," Fay said.

"Name calling makes people resent you," said Russell.

"See," Fay made a face at Adam.

"Well she *is* bossy," Timothy broke in.

"She sure is," echoed Thomas.

"Have you ever thought she is that way because she resents, too? Maybe she resents doing a lot of the clean up work, and trying to get other people to help her. You all fight her, and she ends up doing most of it herself." This one little lesson, Russell thought, is getting to be more than I'm capable of today.

Fay put her head down fast, and Russell could see from his lowered viewpoint on the bed that she was crying.

Thomas shrugged his shoulders awkwardly. "We can't help it. It just works out that way."

"You're not sorry," said Renee. "You're *glad* when you don't have to do the work."

"Am too sorry!" Thomas shouted. "Can't you see she's crying. What are you blind?"

"You don't care other days," said Timothy. "That's what he's saying."

"You don't, either," Thomas stuck out his tongue.

"There you go!" said Russell. It seemed to take every ounce of strength he had to speak up. "Now I *am* angry."

"He's angry, and you're all going to make him sicker," Renee grabbed Thomas by the ears. He swung at her.

"Don't forget I'm stronger than you still," said Renee.

"Renee, then you're strong enough to take your hands offa him," said Russell firmly.

Surprised, both Renee and Thomas looked at Russell.

"See all what's happened because you didn't want to look at the reason Fay is crying," said Russell.

"I told you you were blind," said Thomas to

Renee.

"It's all I can do to keep from twisting your ears off," Renee clenched her teeth.

Thomas smiled, a slow smile of victory, knowing Renee wouldn't touch him now.

Russell reached out to Renee's arm to get her attention. He felt too weak to raise his voice again. "Let's go back, to Fay. Do you think it's true she does most of the work?"

"Of course it's true," said Adam.

"I'm asking Renee."

"Why am I not doing it?" Renee questioned.

"That's not what I asked you. Does Fay?"

"She does," said Renee.

For the first time, Fay looked up at them. Russell could see her face was wet. But she had stopped crying.

"Why is that bad?" asked Russell. "Or is it bad?"

"Not for me." said Timothy.

"We get whipped by Mom too much," Thomas said, thoughtfully. "Because we don't do our share."

"Is getting a beating easier than not picking up your room?" asked Russell.

"No, but . . ."

"Dad never beat Renee when he was alive," Timothy informed Russell. "Renee was his pet."

"That true?" Russell asked, putting a hand to his forehead.

Renee looked at them all. "Guess what? This is too much for Russell. Coralee's at the Daley's, and she told me to be sure you guys let Russell rest."

Gratefully, Russell closed his eyes, though he realized that Renee was getting out of the discussion about herself. When the children saw him close his eyes they went out more quietly than they had come in.

Russell opened his eyes the moment he heard the door close. He had pretended to be asleep to avoid saying anything. Missing his own children had become a constant, every time he saw one of Coralee's kids. He didn't want to organize this household; he was physically incapable of it. Nor did he want to even begin getting into the habit of telling Thomas what to do. Thomas seemed better off merely being encouraged from time to time. But the entire house would not simply run itself. If he tried to deal with this family, though, he might get some small sense of accomplishment out of the Boston project.

Lying on the bed, seeing the sunlight slant now, Russell could think of nothing he had ever accomplished. His work in Pittsburgh seemed to Russell to have happened to another man. He had made no friends yet in Brooklyn, he had no prospect of another job, and the thought of going back to sleepless days made his own family just one more impossible burden.

Further pressing on him was the thought of going back without having been active here. Another week might go by before he could be up like a normal person. Perhaps longer before he could do any political work. Then the month would be half over.

Suppose they wouldn't take him back on the job. Pat could not support the six of them while he looked for more work. And soon he would be getting too old to be rehired. He was not yet past forty, but he knew the chances of his getting a lasting job were slim at his age. And what would he do without a pension? He could see the rest of his life slide downward. No matter that millions of other men were in this position. Russell had to admit to the failure of his own unfruitful future. The prospect of living through those years was harder, yet, knowing the best lay behind him.

He turned toward the wall, and his sore scalp made him move back only to force him to stare at the ceiling. He was hungry and too sick to eat. He was sleepy, but his worries made him restless. He turned to the other side and saw the bag with the bottle and straw and could not even get up to throw it in the waste basket. Was he going to spend the rest of his life with other people--women mainly--having to help him get through it?

One thing for sure, he knew, Coralee would be no help in the situation he found himself at present. What he didn't need was another pair of hands bringing him food and clean clothes. Russell also couldn't see himself arguing with her over how to raise the children. In fact--he felt a gripping in his stomach at this thought--she probably thought him one more drag on the functioning of the household!

There was only one thing he had to offer. And being pushed into a corner was the only way he could have thought of it. In the Boston summer project, the party had different study groups to include every volunteer regardless of his or her political level. He could lead a study group with this family, of course!

Didn't the old country schools develop in this way, out of necessity, where the lessons were taught to all, and the youngest helped by the eldest? Russell decided he would start with basics: revolution beyond reform, the dictatorship of the working class, building a base for the party. Growing up in Boston, he thought, had given Coralee's children some of the foundation they needed. The thought of contributing politically seemed gradually to soothe him. Then he slept.

When Russell woke, it was daylight but his watch indicated that the day was Tuesday. He realized he had been with this family four days. Here he lay, flat on his back, and Coralee was never here to talk with or consult about the study group. Yet he felt he was beginning to know the children, these people, around him, and he sensed it was mutual.

Renee peeked in on him. She had some food, and he felt hunger the minute he saw it. Everyone else came in behind her. While he ate, Renee spoke, "Timothy was right. I've been thinking about it. Dad did let me get away with stuff. I guess he didn't want to come down on me cuz Mom was away from the house so much. Maybe it's easier for a father to beat on the boys. I couldn't help that, could I?"

"Easier to do nothing and watch us get beat!" pouted Thomas.

"You should know, you're good at doin nothin," argued Renee.

"Look who's talking," said Fay for the first time.

Renee said nothing.

"You can't blame Daddy for spoiling you now he's dead," pressed Fay.

Renee opened her mouth, but no words came out.

"Everybody felt sorry for you when Daddy died because you carried on so and you were pregnant. They didn't want you to lose the baby. But when Shukiyyrah was born, you didn't take care of her, either. By that time, I was used to picking up for you because I was sorry for you, too. But now I'm mad!" Fay stood up.

"You <u>resent</u> doin all the stuff you do around

here," Thomas stated.

"Fay doesn't do it all," said Renee. "You guys do some."

"She does most," Thomas defended.

"Well, Mom doesn't do any," Renee pouted. "She's always going somewhere visiting when she's not working. Or to a party meeting. The party, the party, the party."

"Somebody's got to fight those people in ROAR," said Adam.

"Our Mom's the best fighter in the family," said Timothy to Russell.

Before Russell could say anything, Fay added, "Ma told me that she used to do everything when she was a girl. She was the oldest of six other kids. When she was nine--just like me--her own mother died. She did everything until she got married herself."

"Nobody's mentioned Tyrone." Renee had been thinking while Fay talked. "You're all picking on me."

"Tyrone pays Mom money," Timothy recalled. "And he hardly messes up."

"He's not in the family, either," said Thomas.

"But he _lives_ here," said Renee.

Russell leaned his head back on the pillow. He sighed. "In a sense Renee is right," he said. "Tyrone lives here, but so do I. I have to learn how to do my laundry so it doesn't take up bathtub space during the day." He chuckled.

Renee smiled then. "I didn't do mines or Shukyyirah's washing for a year. I wasn't a guest here."

"Your head's not busted now, neither," Fay put in.

"Getting back to what happened after your dad died," Russell interrupted. "Sometimes if someone in a family dies, the person closest to them doesn't show they are the most sad. And for the longest time, you can't see their hurt like you can see my injury." He pointed to his head.

"I don't think Mom was sad at all," said Renee quietly.

"She don't show everybody how she feels." Fay was still angry. "She don't like to have everybody feeling sorry for her."

"She's never around to let us know how she feels," Renee said to them all.

Russell was hesitant to say everything he was thinking. Instead he asked, "Do we agree one person shouldn't be doing most of the housework?"

"Or bossing us," said Timothy.

"Or having to be on our neck every minute," Russell corrected. "I'm sure if your mom were here, she'd want the work to be done as equally as each person can. But I also think the job of making busing safe affects everybody in this room. In a sense, what does it matter if this house is spotless if your heads are busted when you go back to school."

"Or right on the streets," said Renee.

"The Daleys didn't even leave their house," Timothy reminded them.

"If you guys did your share," began Fay, "we would have time to talk with the other kids and people on this block. We could make a street fair like Mom has been wantin to do."

"With music!" Timothy cried.

"Street volleyball!" Thomas made a leap in the air.

Renee put her hands on Thomas' shoulders. "No jumping."

"Thank you," said Russell. The vibration from Thomas hitting the floor still made his head pound. It seemed to throb against the food in his stomach. "I've got to sleep now," he said.

"We can work out chores," Renee reassured him. "With Shukyyirah asleep, I can do the whole kitchen." She nodded as if to herself. "I haven't touched the kitchen for three years. Maybe Adam can help me cook supper?"

"I love to cook," said Adam. "But Fay doesn't never let me."

"He makes such a mess." Fay said discouragedly. "But if I'm not in the kitchen, it won't bother me." Her face brightened, "Tell you what. I'd like to do the outside stuff for a change." Her face brightened. "There's junk under the front bushes from the winter. Leaves and rusty cans. Out there, I can start talking up the block party with old Percy." She looked around to see if anyone would object.

"I'm sick of the outside work myself," said Timothy.

"It's fair," said Adam. "The rest of us have been lettin her work while we goofed off."

"I'll make sure she does it right," Thomas put in.

"You. Hah!" Timothy laughed loudly.

"Shut up both of you," screamed Adam. "You'll disturb _him_."

Russell heard Adam's voice rebound as if it were an echo. His stomach was relaxing, and it seemed there was a fog surrounding his brain. When his eyes closed, all sound became haze.

Chapter 13

A loud, hearty voice and a heavy tread on the stairs and Russell knew that Coralee was home and that she was coming up. Seven-thirty in the morning, and the date on his watch told him it was Wednesday. His heart began to pound harder in his chest. He realized that in him this was a sign of fear. Suppose she didn't want her own children taught by him? Perhaps she thought he was trying to show her up in her own house. Or was he afraid because she was probably more dedicated than himself?

"My stars, child, we almost lost you!" Coralee rushed through the door. She smelled of cigarette smoke and a pungent perfume, but her touch on his head was light. Her aqua cotton sundress hung without a waist from its shoulder straps and covered his face as she leaned over him. The dress was filled with her smells, and he could hardly breathe. "I've looked in on you many times a day, but you were out. You've got a head like a rock."

"That's what skulls are for," he tried to make a joke. "This isn't the first time and it won't be the last." Unexpectedly, Russell felt quite cheerful. Coralee's warmth toward him had made him feel accepted. How cynical of him to think that she would put him down for being helpless. He remembered, though, that Coralee had hated the thought that she might have to tell him what to do with the children. She had been quick to assume that he was lazy. Here, her very touch seemed practiced to bring out the happiness in him. He was confused but pleasantly surprised at her complicated personality.

"Thomas tells me you almost went out on him, tryin to take a shower and all." She pushed her weight away from him and crossed her arms in front of her.

"He's a guy you can depend on."

"I wouldn't count on him; he's done some pretty

crazy things just this year. Did he tell you how he fell off the ladder and busted three bones? He was tryin to get in his bedroom window when I locked him out after I said he had to be home at a certain time."

"I see," said Russell. He decided this time not to get into a back and forth argument with her. What was he going to say, that she had been wrong to lock him out? She would tell him the lousy things Thomas'd done to deserve the curfew.

"Did he mention I threw up in the bedroom here, and he had a washpan on the spot?"

"No!" Coralee laughed. "You seem to bring out the best in these wild ones of mine. Good for you!"

Once again, she surprised him. Many people he knew considered children their "private property" and they became touchy if anyone else dealt seriously with them. He hadn't planned how to bring up the subject of the study group. Now seemed to be as good a time as any. But before he could say one word, Coralee spoke.

"You shouldn't try to get up again for a few days--I think they said five, and that makes Thursday. Maybe if you take it slow, you can go to the bathroom. But no more showers. I can wash you myself."

He must have looked surprised for she added, "I've been a nurses' aide for twelve years. I can give a bed bath with my eyes closed and change the sheets while the person stays right in the bed."

"I don't doubt your ability to wash me," Russell smiled, his sense of humor helping him out of his embarrassment. "I'm not sure I can lie still and let myself be washed. I haven't let anybody do that since I was a baby, and I think I wiggled around even then."

"I'll bet your sweet petunias you did!"

"Coralee," he began, afraid she would leave the room and the house before he could make his proposal. "There's something I can do to make things work better around here."

"Anything you can do without getting up is OK by me."

"I want to teach your children some communist principles. If they're old enough to learn how to cope with this brutal society, they're old enough to learn the only alternative."

"Adam won't sit still long enough to finish his breakfast, let alone a lecture." Coralee dismissed the idea without putting him off entirely.

"I've seen kids sit in a fishing boat for hours waiting for a nibble," said Russell.

"That's play."

"Learning doesn't have to be painful work."

"Renee got suspended I don't know how many times. She has a thing against authority. You're not going to get her to agree with anything. I've given up with her."

Russell had no desire to up the ante. Perhaps every conversation with Coralee would arrive into a contest of sorts. Perhaps it happened only with him and her kids. She was stronger, he admitted it. He would never convince her regarding her knowledge of her own children. But he could appeal to her political reasoning.

"They all know there's a future for them out there," he gestured vaguely out the window. "What they don't know is that a communist future is mostly up to them now. My future," he indicated himself," is partly the ruts I get into, the mistakes I keep making," he looked at Coralee.

"You and me," she nodded.

"So I could try?" he pressed.

"Sure, go ahead. Anything I can do?"

"I was about to ask. Can you dig up that recent <u>Challenge</u> article with a few paragraphs on the Paris Commune and make the older kids read it?"

"I'll try."

Something in his stomach unknotted. Russell then had a blade of hunger cutting somewhere there. Why, he wondered, did hunger seem to hit only one part of his very large stomach? He pushed his stomach with his hand, to quiet the juices.

"I'm getting ready to fix you something to eat now," said Coralee.

"How did you know I'm on empty--oh yeah, for a nurse it's second nature."

"For somebody as used to eating regular like you, it just stands to reason," she laughed.

"I could lose a couple pounds, more than a couple," he conceded.

"But you ain't gonna do it by upchucking the little bits you do eat. You'll relax now," Coralee unfolded her arms. "As much as you can around here! So what do you want to eat now?"

"I'd love a bacon, lettuce and tomato," Russell

said slowly.

Coralee reached across to shake his hand. "That's good, because that's all we got!" And then, in a swirl of aqua on muscular shoulders and calves, Coralee left the room. A second later she yelled in, adding, "Some soup, too, OK?" She disappeared before he could thank her.

Russell picked up the Sunday funnies Thomas had left on the chair where his dirty clothes had been. He considered how he might actually enjoy the rest in bed. A BLT and soup he did not have to fix would taste like steak. Even a bed bath in good hands could be a very nice experience.

When the next day came, however, he discovered that Coralee had done nothing to prepare her children for the study group.

That Thursday morning he talked with Renee when she brought him eggs scrambled with cheese. It became obvious that she had no idea what political study meant. He tried to draw the perspective for her.

"You set the pace for this house, whether you realize it or not," Russell told her. "When you brought me my first meal and kept the others quiet, they listened and they watched your example."

When she said nothing, he got right to the point, "You and the younger members of this family have been through a lot, but no one has had the time to give you the big picture. You might all be communists when you get older. It's not going to happen by waving a magic wand. You have to take that day seriously now." He asked, "Have you ever read a book called State and Revolution?"

"I was in a study group once," Renee yawned. "I never did the reading then, either. Lenin takes too long to say what he's got to say."

"Maybe people will say about us one day that we were pretty stupid to take this system for as long as we did. They'll ask themselves why we sat around the house and waited for a revolution."

She crooked her mouth.

"Do you think your mother is gone from the house so much so the people in the future will remember her name?" he asked her, deliberately provokingly.

"I don't know why she does what she does," said Renee, pouting. "I think she just likes to get away from us."

"You feel like she dumps the housework on you girls?"

"Not on me. I won't put up with it."

Russell saw that Renee had made her position in the family known years ago, long before the death of her father. "Renee, a lot of things have happened to you, haven't they?"

Renee was silent. Then "Yes!" she burst out.

"We don't have to go into them. I don't know if I believe in all this psycho stuff too much, but I can guess that you've had a hard time of it and that people think you're just being stubborn for no reason."

"You're right, you don't have any idea." Renee was borderline between tears and anger. "A lot of grandmothers want their grandbabies."

"And a lot of men stay with their women--and vice versa--despite a lot of problems," he said gently.

"I didn't want him, either, after awhile," Renee said, both the anger and sadness broken.

"You know, we're in a similar position, you and I," Russell told her. "I may not get my job back month, and I have children to support. I don't want to pay for daycare. You can't afford to pay someone to take care of Shukyyirah while you work. And neither of us hardly knows what's going on in the outside world. When we get this stuck--like flies in sticky paper--we're targets for things to happen to us."

"What can I do?" Her question was real.

"My wife shook me out of my stuck place," he said. "And now I have time to get you out. With Adam's help I can watch Shukyyirah, read to her, make sure she's down for naps. Get Adam to do the running after that I can't do. But the reason for all of this is so that you can get out to meet people. We need you with us, fighting racism and working for a revolution, so your child will have a better chance."

"People will never listen to me like they listen to Ma."

"They hear her ideas. That's what got her out of the house in the first place. Coralee is one of those people who has a whole lot of common sense. She knows the bosses have the cops and own the TV stations and newspapers. We must be the ones to bring people our ideas. We must train workers to fight against the whole system. She knows that even to beat ROAR we have to get out of the house and organize. But maybe sometimes she can stay at home with Shukyyirah."

"Hah!"

"I mean that seriously. Nobody is so busy with everything else that they can't do some family stuff."

"You're going to have to be the one to talk with her about that."

"I'll be glad to."

He could tell Renee had opened a new line of thought for herself. He didn't want to keep talking at her.

"So what do I have to read?"

"You don't <u>have</u> to read anything. I can't force you to read, just like I can't force you to join the party. You will probably want to read some <u>Challenge</u> articles. Now that I think about it, I doubt I've read much more than <u>Challenge</u>--maybe a few sports magazines--for ten years!"

"Even Adam can read <u>Challenge</u> articles, except for the big words," said Renee. She began to get a little excited. "We can discuss lots of things even without reading. You'd be amazed at how much Adam notices--more than Timothy and Thomas, I think."

"Don't underestimate those twins."

"They like stories. You can tell us stories to discuss. Daddy used to tell us all stories and we would be quiet for hours." Renee had thought back to another time and place, "I used to color while he told stories. Color in coloring books, and I was at least fifteen."

Russell wanted to hold her in his lap, this big girl. He had a need to actually rock her on his knees. But he couldn't sit up for that, and wasn't the whole idea inappropriate? Yet he wanted to. So instead he patted her arm. "Can you help me get them together so we can start in ten minutes?" he asked.

Renee insisted they each bring in a chair. Timothy and Thomas both turned their chairs around so they could lean on the backs, their legs wrapped around. Adam's legs didn't touch the ground. Fay had brought in a stool, and she sat with her elbows on her knees. Renee brought in a rocking chair. Then Tyrone came in, without a chair.

"Welcome," said Russell.

"I told you to bring a chair," Renee stated flatly. "I told the others to bring one each. You have to set an example."

"There are no more kitchen chairs," said Tyrone. "The only other chairs are big stuffed ones."

"I thought you'd be asleep," Russell questioned. "Or I would've asked you."

"Mondays, I'm off. I woulda told you no. I can't stand meetings. But Renee said I had to be here. I can always go back to sleep. I can sleep any time."

"I know the feeling," said Russell. He added, "You can sit on the end of the bed."

"What are we going to read?" asked Fay. "I like to read."

"I hate to read," Timothy objected.

"Let me start by saying this," began Russell. "We are mainly a thinking club, and we will act and plan to act on our ideas. The purpose of my getting you all together is because I want all of you to be communists--some of you may actually join the party before the end of the summer. Many of you are too young to join yet. All of you are old enough to understand the basic ideas of the party, which is why I wanted to meet with you every day that I'm here."

"Can we read books if we want to?" Fay persisted.

"Tell you what, my dear, if you want to read something for tomorrow, I have a long article on building a base in the neighborhood that you can report on." Russell handed Fay a <u>Challenge</u>. "It's about organizing volleyball teams, and how social events are political and fight racism . . . . if that sounds interesting to you, you can tell us about it tomorrow. How about it?"

"If I can read a real book after that, OK."

"Ass kisser," said Timothy.

"Shut up, bean brain," Renee kicked Timothy.

"Let's get something straight right from the start," said Russell. "We're all very different here. I don't like to read, either. I'm not impressed just because someone likes to read. But I'm not going to have name-calling, or kicking or fighting."

"I'm not trying to kiss anybody's ass," said Fay.

"You are, too, bragging about being able to read," said Timothy.

"You're jealous," said Thomas.

"Shut both your damn mouths," said Renee, moving to stand between them. "Can't you get it through your thick heads that Russell can't get up? I'm going to beat you upside your heads if you don't cut it out. I said nobody come who didn't want to come. Do you all understand the rules, or who wants out? Which one of you?"

"Look who's trying to be the big boss now," Timothy put in.

"I'm not trying to _be_ anything. I _am_ responsible to see you behave." Renee made a fist, half-threatening, half-joking. But she was ready to take on both of them, if necessary.

"I don't think it'll come to the physical," said Tyrone, quietly.

"Neither do I," said Russell. "But you know, it takes a lot of concentration not to fight. I plan to learn a lot from all of you by listening. I'm not going to do a whole lot of talking," he glanced at Renee. "Except maybe to tell stories."

"What kind of stories?" asked Adam.

"Depends on what you let me know I should talk about," said Russell. "I'm going to find out from you, who do you think has made the laws we live by here in Boston? Who decides how many schools we have and how much money goes into the schools?"

"The president," said Adam.

"No. The mayor, Mayor White," Fay seemed sure.

"Last week somebody decided to close four schools: Palmer, Wyman, Martin Luther King and Faneuil," said Thomas. "Mom says 'the bosses,' but I don't know who that means."

"Know what? You're all right! And the bosses are the ones who own factories and tell people what to do. They even used to own people." Russell said, and then he asked them, "Why didn't any of you say that we vote for money for schools?"

"Because we don't vote. Simple as that," said Timothy.

"He doesn't mean you, silly," interrupted Fay.

"It's not silly," Russell said immediately. "Who do you suppose decided on the voting age in the first place? Why don't children vote on matters that concern them, if this is such a democracy?"

"I think it's the bosses who decided on the voting age," said Thomas again. "Isn't that in the constitution or something. And weren't the people who wrote the constitution bosses on their plantations?"

"Boy, you've got it all mixed up," said Tyrone.

"I think it is time for a story," Russell decided against right and wrong answers. He would try to let the story speak for itself. He had an atlas on his lap that Fay had found for him, to aid in illustrating geography.

"More than one hundred years ago," he began, "in 1871, the rulers of France went to war with Prussia. They wanted to grab the iron ore-rich lands of Alsace and Lorraine." He showed them these places on the world map and then turned to more detailed maps of Europe and then France by itself. "The bosses demanded work-fines from the workers of Paris to pay for the war. Right here is the city of Paris, in the middle of France. The workers didn't have enough money left to feed their children.

"Really, you had bakers whose children couldn't eat bread. People were thrown in jail forever because they were too poor to pay their taxes." Russell saw that Renee was listening intently, as were Timothy and Thomas. "And many of the French soldiers who were sent to Prussia to fight were upset. They didn't want to leave their own families when conditions were so bad. And they also remembered how, a few years ago, their rulers had sent the French army to kill other workers in Barcelona and in Rome."

"Rome, Italy, is where they invented pizza, right?" said Timothy.

"Right," Russell nodded with a serious face. "The workers in those cities had just fought to overthrow bad governments." He showed them the cities on the map.

"The workers of Paris refused to be part of such an army, to put down other common folk. They revolted. In 1871 they set up a workers government called the Paris Commune. The bosses and politicians who didn't get killed fled to Versailles. Among the people who ran with them were former United States slaveowners. They had left the U.S. to live in Paris with their stolen slave profits after the south lost the civil war."

"You're kidding," said Tyrone.

"Nope. One of the politicians who ran to Versailles had been head of the Cabinet. A man named Thiers, he had given himself a salary of three million dollars a year at a time when France was in financial ruin."

"Three million!" Timothy exclaimed.

"And three million was worth a whole lot more back then. Well, the first thing Thiers did was to send soldiers to demand the National Guard in Paris lay down their arms. But only three hundred out of three hundred thousand National Guardsmen would give up their guns!" When Russell saw a frown on Adam's face, he added, "That's the same as only one person out of every thousand!

"So two generals--Lecomte and Thomas--were sent from Versailles with a bunch of soldiers to fire on unarmed workers' meetings. Instead of shooting <u>them</u>, the soldiers shot General Lecomte! And then they shot General Thomas."

Fay clapped her hands. "Just like Mom told us soldiers did to their officers in Vietnam."

"Exactly," said Russell. "And the commune made its own laws. It reduced the wages of all new leaders to that of the average working man. Priests and parsons were taken off their salaries from people's tax money and sent back to make their own living. All officials were elected and could be recalled--that means fired--if they didn't serve the workers. They destroyed the standing army and the bad police force and armed every working man. The streets of Paris became safe, without the need of police of any kind."

Russell glanced up. He couldn't believe that Timothy and Thomas had been quiet for this long. Thomas' eyes had a glaze to them and did not meet Russell's own. Renee grinned at him.

"Go on," said Fay.

"They stopped forcing nightwork on apprentice bakers--those are beginner bakers--anybody beginning in a job had been treated badly. Not much different from today. Unions for workers were a requirement in every shop. They treated with equality working people from other countries living in Paris. For instance, even though their rulers had been at war with Germany, the commune made a German working man their Minister of Labor. Though their bosses had oppressed Poland, they made some Polish workers head of a fighting group called the defenders of Paris."

Russell took a breath. He had a headache and was getting tired. "And then comes the bad news. The bosses in Versailles made a pact with the armies of Prussia, and together they surrounded Paris. For six weeks they bombarded and set fire to buildings where people lived. They took unarmed prisoners and shot them in cold blood. They buried people while they were still alive."

"The dirty rats," said Adam. "How could anyone do that?"

Russell nodded. "In June they had crushed the heroic workers state. But the world will never forget the Paris Commune."

Fay sighed, "Workers lose all the time." Her face showed how upset she was.

"It's true that almost all the Paris workers were killed," Russell said. "Why, do you think?"

"They didn't have enough soldiers," said Adam.

"Remember that only three hundred of the National Guard gave up their guns," Renee reminded him. "Out of three hundred thousand."

"Maybe because the Prussian bosses ganged up on them," Tyrone put in.

Russell decided to help them, with a political answer. "Less than fifty years later, during the Russian revolution, practically every country in the world went against the Russian workers: the United States, France, England, Japan. The Russian workers still won."

"Well, that was the whole country of Russia with workers deciding what to do," Thomas said right away. "I think they won because Russia was a much bigger place, with all that land."

"You're right that the whole country became under workers' control," said Russell. "Not so much that it was big, but that workers were led by their own communist party and had their own government throughout, and that changed everything. Lenin and Marx called it taking state power."

"I get it. Like the state of Massachusetts." said Adam.

"No stupid," said Timothy and stopped, "The <u>United</u> States government means the state power of this country; we would have to take over the whole country. Sorry I called you stupid."

"You better be," said Adam.

"Thanks, Timothy," Russell spoke, almost in a whisper, for he was really tired now. "You just apologized to Adam, I want to make a big deal of that. If there's nothing else I see from our getting together today, it's that you're capable of treating each other good."

He added, "That was a good definition of state, too. But at another time we'll talk about how that means not only the entire government but the police of a country, as well."

Timothy squirmed. Then Shukyyirah started to dance back and forth, as if she had to go to the bathroom. "I'll take her," said Fay.

"No, I'll take her," Thomas got up and pulled Shukyyirah's arm.

Renee looked at Russell and shrugged her shoulders. "There's plenty of room in the bathroom for all three of you," she said. "What are we going to do without you, Russell, when you have to go back? I'm a little sad already."

"I am, too," Russell's feeling of tiredness left him without a defense for the sudden grip of fear that took hold. What would he do once the month was up? He didn't even think he had the strength to do what he used to do: work all night and take care of the children during the day. After this one study group he had a headache as well as a painful scalp.

"I think I'm going to have to go to sleep," Russell admitted. "I'd like you all to talk about, to plan something you could do in the neighborhood to bring people together. Like the block party. Renee, you've lived here the longest, how would you like to be in charge?"

"Actually, Fay knows most of the neighbors. She has more friends on the block than I do."

Tyrone said, "I agree that a lot of the planning will be based on who will help, of the neighbors. Fay has gone out with Coralee plenty of times. You don't have more friends, Renee, because you watch TV all day."

"I did used to have a lot of friends," Renee mused. "But I get discouraged. Fay doesn't. She'd be better than me. But I'm willing to go out and talk to them with her."

"I'd like to think up some games," said Thomas. "Things that children and their parents could do together, like when two people tie their legs together and run."

"Three legged races," said Timothy. "We could have dance contests, too. Fred Massey has the best outdoor stereo system on the block."

"Let's plan this in the living room," Fay interrupted Timothy. "I think Russell needs it quiet."

"Thanks. And remind me, Fay, later this afternoon I'll give you a book I brought. It's a book of stories about some young Chinese girls after the revolution."

"Not fair," said Timothy.

"I'll let you read it." Fay told him, "<u>After</u> me."

As soon as Russell closed his eyes, he opened them again. "Somebody better be sure to get a permit for this block party."

"Oh boy," said Tyrone. "That may be a hassle. But I'll be willing to go for it."

The block party date was set for three weeks away. That would be Russell's last weekend with them, and after they left the bedroom, Adam suggested they should make the last hour of it a going away surprise party. "If it wasn't for Russell, we wouldn't be having the block party at all."

Fay and Renee started that day to speak to the men and women in the neighborhood. Fay's friend, Pamela was their first stop. Renee noticed that Pamela was about four inches taller than Fay, and although she was exactly Fay's age--nine and one half--she was developing breast buds and had a serious look about her. "My mom is shy about parties," she told them. "I doubt if she'll join in."

"This isn't just a party-party," Fay insisted. "We're doing this so we can always count on our neighbors. So much bad stuff is happening on account of racism, we can never get rid of it unless we get everybody together."

"Mom gets so scared when she watches the news. You can get too scared to trust anybody." Pamela pushed her feet in some yellow "jellies" that were by the door. "I'll come along with you. Mom is shopping now, but I'll talk to her when she gets back."

"How much are we going to charge?" asked Pamela. She mentioned this just before they got to the second house that Fay said belonged to a young couple with a baby. Pamela was busy twisting her hair into two french braids as they walked. She had a no-nonsense attitude that contrasted with Fay's enthusiasm.

"I told you we should have decided on an amount," Renee said to Fay.

"I still don't think we should charge anything,"

Fay replied. "We should do things that don't cost any money because a lot of people don't have extra money."

"We're going to have to have cups to drink out of, and napkins," said Pamela, her sharp, narrow nose twitched as she thought of more items.

"The permit will probably cost something," Renee added.

"We can ask people if they'll contribute money or food or paper things," considered Fay. "But I still don't want to charge. Mom says under communism we wouldn't have money, and I think that's why we should tell people we aren't charging."

"People don't like that word, I keep telling you," Pamela pulled her thick hair into place.

"I don't know how they're ever going to like it if we don't talk about it. They're afraid because they don't understand," said Fay decisively. She was already pressing the doorbell.

Renee and Pamela looked at each other and shook their heads, but before they could say anything further, the door opened.

A small man wearing a knee-length robe held the inside door open but didn't open the screen door. "I just got the baby to sleep," he said somewhat crossly. "What do you want?"

"We'll come back some other time," said Pamela. "Living next door, I know your baby doesn't sleep much at night."

"What we have to say is important, though," Fay, still in front, peered into the screen until she saw the man more clearly and could ignore the metal pattern. "We're trying to build a world community, or commune, against racism right here on this block. We're just asking people to make something or bring their music to a block party three weeks from this Saturday."

"Come back sometime when my wife is home," the man said. "I can't help you." He disappeared on the other side of the door and began to close it.

"A commune helps everybody," Fay stated, somewhat angrily before she followed Renee, who had already started walking toward the next house.

x x x

That Friday, for the study group, Russell helped

Thomas prepare a report on how profit is taken from the price of a product minus the wages paid. Tyrone suggested that Timothy and Thomas go with him to his brother's job at the linoleum and tile company in Somerville. Have them figure out how much profit the company's owner was making off his brother and the other five workers. They would need Coralee's permission to travel the eight miles by bus. And Tyrone would have to bring them home again before his shift began. Russell anticipated a reaction from Coralee.

She came to his room late that afternoon. In her hands was the tin wash basin Thomas had used on Sunday. Over her shoulder was a towel.

"You been makin yourself right at home up here." Coralee's voice sounded flat, but what she said made his heart beat in his head.

"I know I didn't ask your permission about the block party," he defended.

"You might have," she said testily.

"I'm so used to dealing with my own kids all day, I forgot. I'm sorry." Russell wanted to add, 'You're never home to ask,' but he didn't.

"It also bothers me that they've been going out in the neighborhood, at all hours of the day."

"Just a minute," Russell said. "They've been getting their work done around the house." He saw that Coralee had set the basin by his bed and was rubbing a washcloth around the soap. This alarmed him more than anything she could have said in return.

"I'm going to start with your face and work down," Coralee asserted with the same tone that she'd used before. "This house here has been a lot different," she continued. Her voice had neither praise or rebuke.

Russell could not guess her intent. At the moment he was too embarrassed, anticipating the bath. He wanted to tell her to stop, but he wondered if she would be annoyed. He <u>would</u> tell her that he certainly could wash his own genitals. The warm water, though, felt good on his scalp and face, and he closed his eyes all the while she rinsed his face and neck. Then she put his hands in the warm water, massaging them, and he wanted to urinate suddenly, at the pleasure of it.

"Seeing my children go out, not being sure where they are; them making friends with people I know, made me realize how they must have felt seeing me leave the house every day. And I was jealous." She began washing his chest. "I'm jealous of how you seem to deal so well with them. Now roll on your side."

She washed his back, and he felt like giggling. It was all he could do to suppress himself. Now that he was silent, he began to realize that she wasn't attacking him.

"Put this other towel under your bottom." His heart began to pulse again, but this time in his groin. He was no longer afraid yet filled with anticipation.

She continued to talk while she washed his genitals. "You see, I wanted my children to get responsibility. But for the longest, after Rudy senior died, my being in the house reminded me of him. I had to get out, so it was easy to continue my community organizing like I always did when he was alive. And as you know, I get along with adults better than with children."

Russell couldn't speak. The warm washcloth slid behind his genitals, toward his anal area, and around. He knew he had an erection.

"Most mens, they can't help getting a hard on when they're touched."

Russell laughed with relief.

"Don't think I haven't felt 'em all. I mean <u>all</u> lengths and hung in all kindsa ways!" Coralee laughed softly.

Russell chuckled again. And he felt calm.

Coralee continued down his legs and lifted the covers and took the basin down to his feet. She washed between his toes and said, "You done good, with my kids, Russell. I thank you."

"I didn't really do nothin," he stammered. "It's just me being myself."

Coralee picked up the basin, squeezed out the washcloth and put the soap in it. She started for the door. "In two days you'll be able to wash yourself by the sink. You won't need me to give you a bed bath again."

"Too bad for me!" Russell met her eyes for the first time that afternoon.

x x x

By the third day of organizing for the block party, they had gone to every house on their block of Webber St. and neighboring Douglass. Most of the people, who already knew Fay and Coralee, called Coralee to check on the party. Usually, Renee was home to verify that, yes, it was really going to happen. Many neighbors said they would bring something to eat or drink.

One woman who worked at the shipyards thought they should have a letter to pass out, and she helped them write it. It turned out she was a shop steward and knew of a mimeograph machine where she could run it off. Some people read the letter, that talked about the anti-racist purpose of the party, and gave a dollar without being asked for money.

In one family where Timothy visited, three children played musical instruments. They each knew the drums and guitar and got up every Sunday in their church. They agreed to play for the block party.

Adam brought out his wagon and did grocery errands for people while talking about the block party. He didn't agree with Fay about the money part but said the Committee Against Racism in the city of Boston needed money and that she was being selfish to just think about their block. He charged twenty-five cents for each errand and had earned two dollars and seventy-five cents toward the "commune."

Tyrone didn't have as much success with the permit. The Parks and Recreation Department sent him to Traffic Control. They told him he had to fill a petition with fifty-one percent of the neighboring residents to close off the block.

He came back the following week with eighty-three percent. He talked with a Mrs. Raleigh, in the Traffic Control Dept. She was a light-skinned woman with reddish hair. She said there had been too much violence in the city, and she referred to the six black bible salesmen who were beaten up on Carson Beach, South Boston, the previous Sunday.

"We plan a demonstration about that," said Tyrone.

"Your group publicizes these crimes to get yourselves known and to promote violence," countered Mrs. Raleigh. "No one else but CAR talks about <u>smashing</u> racism.

"You're saying you don't believe in fighting

back!" Tyrone couldn't stand these paper pushers in City Hall.

"You groups are always fighting each other. You get innocent people into these things. It's as if you look for trouble instead of walking away from problems."

"What would you know about real problems?" Tyrone spoke loudly.

"I'm going to call security on you if you make a scene," Mrs. Raleigh pulled her wool scarf around her shoulders. The blue paisley was meant for decoration, but Tyrone felt her chill smugness in the gesture.

"I have the signatures."

She just glared at him without answering. He looked at her high red heels and her red suit. Where did she think she was going? he wondered. Tyrone smiled to himself, thinking she looked something like a walking stop sign, warning other people to come no closer. People like her. . . his angry thoughts grew in response to her appearance . . . had the power to stop him from organizing.

When she still didn't say anything, Tyrone wanted to shake her. "We're going to hold our block party, with or without your permit."

"I wouldn't do that if I were you," Mrs. Raleigh didn't smile. Her tone was spoken as if he were a disobedient child.

"You are not me." But she worried him, she bothered him. And he came away without the permit.

When he got to Coralee's, Tyrone suggested, "Let's send somebody who is white in there. I think that damn woman is prejudiced." But Frank Scott, one of the comrades from San Francisco, had no better luck. They decided to go ahead with their plans despite the permit.

"We have to make ourselves known in any case," said Coralee during a planning meeting. "The more people in this neighborhood understand our ideas, the more exposed the cops will be if they attack us for not having a permit."

"We should have done this for the last several years," Una spoke timidly at first. "I know how people think, 'If there's a problem, we'll call Coralee.' Not 'Let's get up a CAR meeting.'"

Una's remark seemed to cut a nerve with Coralee. "I'll be damned," she said. "You should have <u>told</u> me that a couple years ago."

Zack shook his head at Coralee, "I don't think you would have listened."

In the weeks before the block party, Coralee worked more at directing behind the scenes. She suggested that Una be in charge of refreshments and to get specific commitments for food so there would be plenty of variety. She remembered that old Percy Rollins had brought a pot of curried goat to a CAR picnic last year, and thought Una might ask him to make more.

She encouraged a second and third trip to the young couple's house next to Pamela's. They were more willing to discuss their hesitations with Coralee. She found out that the husband, Forest Naughton, had to come up north with his wife, Lilly, because her mother had a stroke. He left a small restaurant that was going bankrupt, and his dissatisfaction with the north ranged from the weather to the rampant racist climate. But he would cook up some blackened fish, he promised, and Lilly agreed to make a German chocolate cake.

Russell stayed in bed through the next Saturday. He had visits from the Daleys, many comrades, and Nikkia, who came twice. In no way did they compare their busy schedules to his own, but their very presence reminded Russell that their contributions to the Boston project were far greater. He was increasingly frustrated with not being able to do what he regarded as his full share of work while he was here. But that Sunday morning he realized on waking that since Thursday, the day starting the study group, he had not once dreamed the recurring dream.

Russell continued the study groups every day, even after he was up on his feet. The agenda was always the same: someone gave a report on a book or article; they discussed it; they talked about their part in the city-wide work, helping with the petition and leafletting. The block party plans continued, and sometimes a person from the block came to the study group. They planned housework, with one person being responsible to make sure everything was done, and dinner cooked.

The day his stitches came out, Russell went over to the Daley's neighborhood. The Daley brothers and Eunice surrounded him immediately. "We think about you every day."

Winston said, "My wife is still in the hospital. The doctors are saying she has some kind of a mental problem. The scum haven't been back since."

Mrs. Chambers came over, hearing that Russell was there, and brought him a huge bouquet of cut flowers. "Son," she cried out. "If only I'd had had a son like you. My own Charles, he's got a name for himself. He's a salesman and was number three last year of all the Cadillac salesmen. But I'm not so proud of him as I was of you, and your group." She gave him a hug, and the soft little hairs on her cheeks reminded Russell of a baby brush.

He hugged her back. Russell heard again in his mind the words she had used about his being her son, and he recalled how his own mother always told him of her disappointment in him. He opened his eyes, and over Mrs. Chambers' shoulder he saw Mr. Daley and his sister and all the children, and the worries he had carried in his guts seemed to melt inside him and diffuse and disappear.

In the next week, his work consisted of visiting people in the neighborhood and the other contacts people had made from the petitioning. It seemed wise during his recovery for him not to collect signatures in the burning summer heat. But in visiting homes, he had a personality that found things in common with teachers and welders, unemployed and, of course, all the children of the households. Especially, he became fast friends with Forest, and the two of them found there was something similar in their marriages. "I often refer to myself as Mr. Lilly Naughton, Forest chuckled. "Seems like I follow her lead in deciding where we live, and even the money matters."

"My wife, Pat, is the one with the steady job in our family," said Russell for perhaps the third time since he'd known Forest. It was reassuring to him to get this out in the open, one of his deepest insecurities. "Often lately I've felt like the one who they say works to keep himself in fancy duds or something. I earn less than Pat, and probably if I added up what I spend in junk food, I would be shocked."

"I understand," said Forest. "My restaurant was failing, I was working just to keep the rent up for the place, and so I constantly felt I dragged us down. I enjoyed cooking for people, and seeing them, though.

I used to go from table to table singing and cooking many things you can make from a grill right in front of the customer.

"We had to move," he said regretfully. "She was pregnant, her mother was sick, and there were no high-enough paying jobs for somebody like me only skilled in cooking. So I got lucky up here at General Dynamics, where they were taking on a bunch of new guys and training them in spot welding. But when I think of never running a restaurant again, singing for the folks, I don't think I can bear it."

"The thought of never working with my friends in the mill cuts my heart out," said Russell.

It occurred to them that they could cook cajun style food right in the outdoors at the block party. It would add to the variety that was turning into a menu from many countries. In fact, Fay, Renee and Tyrone called a meeting of the participants, right in the front yard. Everyone there agreed to the theme of an international, anti-racist commune.

Fay was insistent on not charging any family "dues," and two men who insisted they couldn't cook or make any other contribution were to be judges at the games. It was planned that in several of the races, it was to be those who came in last who would win. Fay herself had a booth called the Paris Commune Design Shop where people would bring clothes that no longer fit their own chidren, and trade them in for larger sizes. Still there appeared to be no chance for a permit.

The Progressive Labor Party and CAR organizers, however, had to mobilize a lot of forces away from the block party. The best possible day for the Carson Beach demonstration was that same date. More groups than PL and CAR were involved in the planning.

On the Thursday before the block party, Russell learned that Pat had been able to switch work with another nurse in order to make the trip up with the children to pick him up and spend the weekend. He was so busy Saturday morning that he had forgotten to look out for them. Pat's familiar face and energetic walk made him blink back tears. He kissed her soft mouth, and knew the intimacy that he had missed at once, for Pat was like his own warm skin. At the same time he was reminded of the ending of his relationships here: of Coralee's family and Forest, the Daleys and Mrs.

Chambers, and of the man in the middle of these wonderful people who was himself.

Next, the children tumbled out of the car. "Daddy. Look what we got," Melvin clamored as they hugged him. "We got us a dog. His name is Hairy. He was free. We missed you so much Mommy let us get a dog. We wanted to surprise you so we didn't write about him."

And a twisting, brown furry mass of legs lopped out of the car window and ran first toward the children and then, distractedly, toward the smells of a tree stump.

"We'll have jobs for all of you at the block party this afternoon. Mostly you'll have fun!" Russell was glad for his children to be able to participate together here. That would mean more for them than a sightseeing visit.

The block was set up with balloons and streamers and big oak tag signs announcing food and activities. Mexican Tacos that Norberto volunteered the moment he heard of the theme. New Orleans specialty dishes. And the Rainbow Rock Stars, featuring Lennie.

Nikkia had said she would give a presentation of classical ballet and modern dance. She also taught the boys and girls of the freedom school a modern dance portraying the stories of John Brown and Harriet Tubman. Then she was needed to be at Carson Beach, and the children arranged an extra rehearsal so they could dance independently of her direction.

Fay had gone around with Pamela to check on food contributions. Two people who had promised to make hamburger patties and cupcakes were not even home. "They went visiting for the weekend," a neighbor said of one family who would have brought the patties. Pamela was angry. "They could at least have told us. We were counting on them."

"You're going to have some disappointments," said Fay.

"You sound just like my mother," Pamela pouted.

It was just noon, the time set for the start of the festivities, and the street was already jammed with eager children. Many of the adults had not yet arrived with their food, but the booths were in place, and a committee had been set up at both ends of the block as security and traffic directors. There was no sign of ROAR or racist gangs. But at five minutes after twelve, six squad cars pulled up at one end, their sirens blasting.

"We want to see your permit." The man challenging Tyrone, who was in charge of the party's security, was none other than the Chief of Police of Boston. His face was close to Tyrone's own and his index finger was on Tyrone's neck. Tyrone felt the heat of his reaction come to his neck and face. He dared not speak. He couldn't, either.

Russell, on security, too, at that end of the block, walked past the chief and over to a man in a suit and tie sitting in a squad car. "What are you doing here," he questioned. "We're having a peaceful block party. I have a copy of the petition signed that gets most organizations a permit. And I don't think you want to disappoint these folks here."

He pointed to the block behind him, and there were more people than there had been fifteen minutes ago. In fact, as they pressed together toward the end of the block, the friends and neighbors seemed to increase in number. Actually, there were more all the time, for word had gotten out that the children were as yet unprotected, and the parents had better drop their cooking and come running.

One woman showed up at the front of the crowd in her robe and slippers. Mrs. Gottchalk was her name. "Either you sit there and direct traffic or you mind yer own business. We're gonna make a stand for our kids' right to this party," she said. "You'll bust it up over my dead body."

The man in the suit got out of the car and put one hand on Russell's shoulder.

"Don't you touch my daddy." Jerry came running behind the barriers of wooden saw horses and raced to Russell. The gangly Hairy bounded behind him. The man in the suit kicked at the dog, and Pat knocked over one of the wooden horses in her rush to retrieve both Jerry and Hairy.

"Keep your feet to yourself," she yelled.

Coralee burst through the crowd just then and announced herself to the Chief of Police. "You may remember me from our little talk in front of the Daley house earlier this summer," she began. "You run the streets, you and your gangs of thugs, in every other part of town. You have bloodied the heads of most of my friends and thrown others in your lousy jail."

Coralee stood out from everyone in a bright gold, billowing outfit that a Persian swordsman might have worn. She spoke for them all. The Chief interrupted her demanding to see the permit.

"We should demand to see your papers," Coralee spoke loudly, addressing the neighbors as much as the chief. "We gathered the signatures you wanted for your permit. And then you wouldn't give it. Now the people themselves are out here. We are our own law. We keep our own order. This is our block today. Are you going to take it from us?"

The Chief went to confer with the cop in the squad near Russell. Russell heard both men curse, and the others got out of their cars. There were twenty-four police in all, and now over three hundred people from six blocks.

A loud voice came from the middle of the crowd, "Power to the workers!" Fay darted to the front, between elbows and around people. Percy picked up a saw horse. Forest had metal spoons in his hands. Fay held up a garden rake.

"Power to the workers," yelled Coralee. She put her arms around her daughter and grasped the rake with both hands. She and Russell took up the chant. "POWER TO THE WORKERS."

The police came out of their meeting and the Chief went up to Tyrone, ignoring Coralee and Russell and Fay. "You won't get away with this, boy. Mrs. Raleigh down at City Hall is pressing charges against you for threatening her with insulting language. The next time I see you it will be to put you behind bars."

Sweat broke out on Tyrone's face as he tried to control his anger. Coralee moved beside him.

"And we will make sure this block party never happens again." The Chief bellowed to the many people who crowded closer and closer. "The next time you try to set up even one booth on this street, you'll all be arrested." The neighbors began to surround the cars. And the cops got into their squads and drove off in an angry screech of rubber.

The music grew louder. It could be heard now by everyone. Coralee began to dance with Russell. Fay wrapped her arms around Tyrone, and he swung her like a top. Neighbors and people who had never seen each other before began to dance as though a holiday had just been declared.

Boston: Carson Beach Swim-in
2,000 Confront Cops/ROAR

CARSON BEACH, Boston, Aug. 10—On May 3, the day of the PLP May Day march, the ROAR leaflet read, "We'll hit them so hard they'll never want to come back here again." Well, we're sure that these racists were somewhat disappointed when on Sunday over two thousand people, mainly black but including hundreds of Latin and White brothers and sisters, participated in a large demonstration against racism and segregation of the public beaches.

Carson Beach in S. Boston has been the scene of xtreme racial attacks against blacks and Latins who have tried to swim there. This demonstration was sponsored by the sellout NAACP and the National Student Coalition against Racism (YSA), who ridiculously advertised it as a picnic. They were forced to call this when they found out that the Committee Against Racism was planning a swim-in on August 17. From the beginning it was made clear that this fight against fascism was no picnic. At the initial rallying point of the "outing," PLP and CAR took the lead when in the presence of a dozen TV cameras a black comrade of PLP interrupted YSA opportunist Maceo Dixon's speech about tuna fish sandwiches and police protection to say that this was a demonstration of anti-racist forces and that if the racists attacked us, we would fight back and not rely on the cops. This speech was met with cheers and helped expose the NAACP and it's buddies. We then leafletted and talked to people, and were confronted by a small group of nationalists who wanted to expell all white people. Multi-racial unity prevented this from happening.

At 1:30 p.m. about two hundred cars lined up for a motorcade to the beach. Upon arriving we saw in the distance what the Boston Globe estimated as a thousand white people, and in between them and us stood about 800 riot geared police. As soon as we reached the front lines, the action began. Bricks and bottles flung by the racists injured several people but easily hit cops. Several people flung the missiles right back. The cops then started trying to move us off the beach but we grasped arms and called for everyone to come to the front lines, which almost all CAR and PLP members did. We stood fast and chanted "Hell no we won't go!" and "racism means fight back." Suddenly a group of ROAR marshalls began running towards our ranks and the cops pretended to stop them. Hundreds of us chanted "Let 'em come!"

Boston, August 10. Fascism's ugly head appeared ever more openly . here as could be seen by the invasion of hundreds of cops at Carson Beach.

These racists then took off and ran back to their line. In the midst of all this, the black nationalist police provocateur dogs began attacking several white comrades, and immediately several scuffles broke out. People on the beach and courageous black and Latin comrades fought like hell defending multi-racial unity. One brother decked three of the nationalists, thus saying we will not be divided. So while these police again were fighting us, the cops were ready to move in, and ROAR was messing behind them. Because of our disorganization, we were not prepared to deal with this situation militarily, and we began to move slowly back to the cars, fighting the nationalist cowards all the way. The police role of the nationalists who made clear when they fought us, having ignored the racists for all these years. Not only did they jump on white anti-racists but they attacked Latin and Black people also.

When people were leaving the beach, one carload of CAR and PLPers accidentally turned deeper into South Boston. Their car was showered with bricks and bottles. They got out and ran, and one black brother was injured when he was attacked by five bat-wielding racists. They were aided by two white women of South Boston. The fact that we went to the beach with thousands of people, Black, Asian, Latin and White despite warnings by Hicks and the police showed a victory of the kind we saw in Selma, Alabama and will see again and again until finally ... through Socialist Revolution!

210

Chapter 14

"It was no picnic, I can tell you." Zack stopped the van in front of Yvette and Don's apartment building as they waited for Nikkia, Bonita and the rest. "But some folks came to Carson Beach with sandwiches and bathing suits."

"Even after those six bible salesmen got beat up so bad?" Darlene couldn't believe people in Boston could remain so naive after a summer of violent incidents, sometimes several of them in one day.

"We didn't plan ahead much better after all our experience," said Zack. He rubbed a long, dark bruise on his upper arm. "We allowed ourselves to get separated from one another at the end. Nikkia got her face smashed up. I think they said her nose is broken." Zack tilted his head out the van window to peer up at the apartment, half-expecting to see Nikkia.

"That's terrible. I didn't know." Darlene felt a sudden sick sensation. She had decided not to go to the Carson Beach demonstration yesterday mostly because of her involvement in the planning of the block party.

The block party plans had been in the making for almost two weeks. Then came the attack on the bible salesmen. Other blacks and hispanics got beaten up on this beach that was formerly integrated. Most of the comrades had to change their commitment for the block party to make a stand on Carson Beach that same weekend.

For some like Darlene, who had helped build the block party from the start, the choice was up to her. She remembered that part of her reason for attending the block party was to hear Lennie play. Lennie's rock group had been scheduled as one of the main attractions. Then he was needed at Carson Beach.

"It was interesting, what happened to Lennie," Zack continued, unaware of Darlene's reaction.

"What do you mean, what happened to Lennie?"

Darlene was barely able to form the question.
Zack pushed on the horn. "Yvette said not to bother coming up, that they'd be watching for the van." He kept looking from the window to his watch, distractedly. "We've got to have this planning meeting before the WNAC-TV broadcast. The program directors were forced to let us attend after the whole city learned about the demo at Carson Beach yesterday."
Darlene thought she must be the only person unaware of recent events. After helping clean up after the block party, she had gone over to spend the night with a girl her age named Rowena, who lived a block over from Coralee.
"So what <u>happened</u> to Lennie?" Darlene persisted.
"Well, after the big fight, he found himself separated. Though he might not have been noticed, on account of his being white, of course, he still had on his CAR t-shirt. This group of nationalists cornered him by the projects." Zack looked up at the window again. "Don is waving to us from the apartment."
"Go on," urged Darlene.
"Oh, yes. Well, a group of five people from the projects, black women--all of them were women--said to these nationalist guys, 'Get out of here unless you expect to get your heads bashed in.'" Zack laughed. "It was terrific. Not only did they know who we were and wanted to defend Lennie, but they were willing to take on the Mau Mau's. They weren't fooled. They probably knew, too, that the nationalists had been attacking us all summer. It's amazing."
"And they were women." said Darlene. But she was still uneasy. "So was he hurt?"
"He was one of the few people who came away without a scratch!" Zack laughed as if appreciating the whole situation once again.
With a sputter of relief, Darlene laughed too.
Just then, a group of people appeared in the apartment building entranceway. Almost all wore backpacks. One of them, Darlene saw, looked as though she had on a ski mask. It was Nikkia, her face in bandages. Darlene ran out of the van and over to her.
"I just heard what happened." She saw the same lovely smile that was Nikkia, but the bandages went around her eyes and over her nose like a ski mask. One eye was puffy and closed.

The two women hugged. "I look awful, but everything is OK except for my nose. It only hurts when I laugh!" Nikkia smiled again, wincing. "Don, Yvette and Bonita are saying I should go back to New York tonight.

"This had to happen," she pointed to her face, "just after I got permission to switch days off with my team mate, Bradley, so I could stay another week!"

Lennie came out of the building then with Russell. Coralee, Don, Yvette and Bonita came out right behind them. Once at the van, instead of getting in back through the rear door with the others, Coralee stopped to talk with Zack at the wheel.

"We've each got a camera or tape recorder with us, so no matter who gets into the TV studio . . ." Coralee patted her backpack. "And we have some handy weapons stashed, too, in case the demonstration gets rough. No more nasty surprises like the night of the dance when the other van got stolen!"

Zack nodded, and Coralee went on. "Nikkia really doesn't want to go home. She was willing to answer the CAR office telephone. Twenty-four hours a day and sleep there, if necessary."

"She gives her total being to what she does," Zack was thoughtful. "I was beginning to depend on her leadership up here. Her judgment. But the office is no place either, for someone who's already hurt. I'll miss her."

"Just imagine how I'll feel with Russell gone." Coralee put one foot on the step below the door and rested her fleshy arm in the window. "I've found a mother for my children, and he's going home today!"

"I never thought Russell was going to do anything much during the project. He sure proved me wrong. The stories I had heard about him in Brooklyn. . ." Zack shook his head. "I thought we were forcing a bear out of hibernation!"

"Pat's the real go-getter in that relationship," said Coralee. "It was her that persuaded him to come in the first place."

"Anyway, I'm real sorry when people leave before <u>we're</u> ready," Zack spoke with an unusual heaviness in his voice. He looked ahead, rubbing at streaks on the inside of the windshield. They both stared at the hot street pavement that pushed a mirage of liquid air under the dusty, drooping trees. "Hey, why don't we get going?" He seemed to need to startle himself out of a daydream.

"We're waiting for Norberto to get off the phone," said Coralee. "He was the person who insisted we involve more parents from the Freedom School at Carson Beach yesterday. Nikkia really turned him around."

"I couldn't have done without either of them this summer," said Zack. He looked over to see Norberto close the door to the building.

Norberto ran, jogging style, toward the van. He wore a backpack and had on new gray sneakers. He carried a clipboard in one hand and waved with the other hand. "Let's go!"

Zack put one hand on Coralee's arm. "The man says 'go.'"

Darlene had gotten in the front seat with Zack as a deliberate move. At first she felt too shy to sit in back, knowing Lennie would be there. But seeing Norberto she sensed his energy, and it seemed to give her courage. "Sit here!" Darlene called to Norberto. She opened her side of the van and angled her body out so she could see over the top of the cab.

Already Norberto was showing Zack some notations on the clipboard, while Coralee held the back door open for Darlene.

The inside of the van was shadowy. Once the rear doors were closed, the only light came from two small windows in the doors. Coralee sat opposite Nikkia, and all she could see was the white mask of bandages. With a jerk, the van started up, and they all braced against the floor and on each other.

"So Russell, you're leaving us." Coralee's voice sounded too loud in the closed van.

When Russell didn't answer, Darlene put in, "Didn't you all have the farewell party for him?"

"Sure, Honey," said Coralee. "But we didn't settle anything."

"What's there to settle?" asked Russell. "I'm going to write to everybody, or at least call."

"It's easy for you to leave," Coralee went on, "you're going back to the life of Riley."

"Who's that?" Lennie puzzled.

"It's a saying," Coralee pushed at Lennie's knee. "Before your time, but Russell understands. It means he's not involved in anything back home."

"You've got a night job, right, Russell?" Nikkia had not been listening and was preoccupied.

"They may not take me back." Russell's voice sounded irritated to Nikkia. "Pat wanted me to ask for a leave anyway."

"Surely you're not going to start getting mad at Pat," Coralee said.

"You're making up that I'm angry." Russell retorted. I've resigned myself to going back to unemployment. Though it's not easy being a child care person and main housekeeper."

"A lot easier than staying here in Boston," stated Coralee.

"I think you're pissed he's not going to work any longer with your kids," Yvette was sharp with Coralee. "I've known you longer than anyone. When I first met you we were both on the unemployment line. You told me then how you hated to stay at home. You haven't changed a bit."

"My mother is the opposite," said Lennie, trying to soften the argument. "She does all the cooking and cleaning--besides working--and never goes out of the house except to her job and to the grocery store. Where would we be, in getting to know people door to door, if it wasn't for Coralee?"

"Or Norberto," added Nikkia.

"And he won't be staying here, either!" Don spoke, as if realizing that fact for the first time.

"Someone's got to change," said Russell quietly.

"<u>Someone</u> has got to do more than just part-time political work," Yvette nudged Don. "We here are going to have a lot more responsibility when you leave."

"Yvette. Don's work has been getting a lot better," Coralee defended. "He's been spending more time on campus getting to know people. His art is becoming more and more political, too. Sometimes it's hard to see changes in the people closest to you."

"Exactly," said Russell. He hit the floor of the van several times with the flat part of his fingers. "And, Coralee, I think you miss the boat when it comes to your own children."

Coralee was surprised, but she answered quickly. "I admit it; I don't have much motherly instinct. I never did like to play dolls as a kid."

"I'm not talking about spending hours braiding

their hair." Russell argued. "Although it's important to do what they enjoy. What I'm talking about is giving them a chance for them to understand what the hell we're all about."

"When you started those study groups you were flat on your back," said Coralee. "I haven't got that kind of time to lay around. I work four days a week. I need to work more, but I can't because Renee won't take more responsibility. She seems to do different, though, with a man in the house. But I'll be damned if I'll get married again to please her!"

"Nobody's asking you to get married again," stated Russell.

"You two argue like <u>you're</u> married for twenty years already," said Lennie.

"Really, Russell is right," put in Nikkia. "Fighting racism, organizing for a world of equality, those are ideas a child can understand. They want to, most of them, because they see their future is at stake. Your kids proved it by organizing the block party practically by themselves."

"I think Renee is willing to do more," said Russell, grateful for Nikkia's support. "My feeling is that you kind of gave up on her after your husband's death. Maybe the thought of getting next to her after the two of them had been so close was too painful."

"You could've asked us to help," Yvette stated.

Coralee had no answer for that.

The van jostled down a cobblestone street. Don bounced against Coralee, and Lennie braced himself on the floor. Darlene held her hands out so no one would bump against Nikkia's face.

"Y'all don't have kids, except for Ilona's family and Zack's. And they're so busy. I figure it's my responsibility." Coralee directed her next comment toward Russell's voice. "Me and Renee's never been close. Rudy, everything about him was an easier child. We fit together."

"They say that about moms and their sons," said Russell.

"Sure, I know that. An' fathers and their daughters." Coralee's voice was sad. "You can't imagine how it hurts, to feel everything you say is wrong to your daughter. I guess I gave up and let Rudy, senior, handle her. It's too late now to get close. I've tried."

"It was probably hard for you, Rudy Jr. going into the service about the time your husband died." Russell spoke slowly.

The others in the van were quiet. They could hear a police siren, away outside, and it was impossible to tell if it was coming toward them or not. Nikkia put her arm out protectively toward Darlene. And Darlene tried to find Lennie's face in the shadowy figure she knew was him.

"I knew my son Rudy wanted to go in the army. We planned that. He went in with his buddy, Malachi. They're organizing in there. I hear regular from him." Coralee smiled to herself. "I miss him, but I'm happy he's doing the most useful thing he can with his life, do you know?"

"I didn't know," said Russell. "Go on."

"And yes, I miss his father, my husband. But I was sorry before he died; I was so afraid of his death."

"What do you mean?"

"He was sick--high blood pressure, diabetes--we all knew, but I knew it the most. An' he wouldn't do nothin about it. He figured if he worked and came home, worked and came home and made the house nice, that it would all go away one day. And one day, sure enough, he died."

They could feel the van pull over. The siren was louder. The van stopped. Louder, and the siren was next to them, and passed them, and became lower and further away.

Russell's heart was pounding. He had a tremendous desire to comfort Coralee. It would ease something within himself, and he felt she needed to be held. But he thought that she might resent his sympathy for losses she'd already dealt with. And that stopped him. Coralee's next statement confirmed his thoughts.

"I was only too glad to talk about my family with neighbors outside the house. And make new friends for CAR. I found they had the same problems I did, many of them. The racism and tryin' to be the breadwinner in this rotten system can crack a man right down the middle. I loved him, but I couldn't fight back on the job for him. I couldn't take care of his health if he wouldn't, you know?"

"I know," said Russell. And he self-consciously tried to cover his stomach with his arms.

The van started up again. Zack yelled back to them, "I pulled over and put my face in a map so they wouldn't recognize me."

"Gotcha," Lennie yelled back.

As the van lurched and moved ahead they all shifted, and Coralee said one thing more. "We might have got together after all, Renee and me, if it hadn't been for Shukyyirah's coming along. Renee wanted the baby, regardless of what happened to her and Malcolm. I could've stopped her, but I didn't want to. I guess I needed that baby in the house with Rudy Jr. and his dad both gone."

"I can understand that," said Yvette.

"Well, everything turned into its opposite," Coralee told them. "Renee hardly lifted a finger with the baby. All I did was argue with her, and she did less."

"The way I saw it," put in Lennie, "You took over that baby. You couldn't help it. My mom would have done the same thing. only she wouldn't have wondered why <u>she</u> needed a new baby around." Lennie went on, "I watched you, though, Coralee. Renee couldn't do nothin right, from the get go."

"You're full of it," Coralee said. "She wouldn't have done nothin whatsoever. "She wouldn't have even nursed that baby if I hadn't thrown away the bottles she bought."

"Coralee, how can you be so smart and so stupid at the same time?" Lennie laughed an angry laugh. "You are so good with people and so bad with your family."

"Lennie, I ought to beat your behind for talking that way to an older woman," Don put in sharply.

"Well it's the truth, ain't it?" said Lennie, somewhat less angrily.

At that point Nikkia reacted. She gave Darlene's arm a final squeeze and immediately made her way to the center of the van. The way she moved, fluidly, with her legs in front and then tucked beneath her, she managed to hold her head with its throbbing broken nose perfectly still. They all could see her mask reflected in the dim light. "Nobody in this whole city does what Coralee does, day in and day out. Not even those of you who don't have family responsibilities."

"She's right, Lennie," said Don.

"I appreciate." Coralee closed one hand over

Nikkia's outstretched foot. "But what Lennie says, and Russell, too, is more right. It's been hard for me to think about the long range with people since Rudy died. It shows in my not recruiting more people into the party."

"This is a tough situation, in Boston," defended Nikkia. "The racism. People here are slow to trust anyone."

"Just a minute, I've seen you going around door to door. Perfect strangers are drawn to you, Nikkia. You pull them out. You'd bring them into the party if you were here long enough. Zack has that quality, too, of developing people into leaders. Then Russell here comes along and amazes me with what he does to bring my own family into action. Me, people see me as getting out and fighting _for_ them, and that's no good."

"We can't all be alike, and there's nobody like you," said Nikkia.

"If it was enough for me or for any of us to do more of the same, we'd never be no further along toward a revolution than we are today," Coralee answered her. But it's easy for me to talk about the need to change my ways with my children. It's another thing to actually do it."

"You sure can't do it alone," Yvette told her. "I could help by teaching them some of my mom's recipes from Nicaragua. Once a week I could come over. But Don is a better cook than me." She directed her voice across to where she knew Don was sitting. "Trouble is, mi amor, you've got no patience with kids."

"She's right. It's a big source of argument with us." said Don. "She's afraid if we get married she'll get stuck with all the heavy duty responsibility. We haven't worked it out yet."

"From what I can see, it would be good for you, Don, to spend more time with families, period." Darlene sounded very adamant. "You spend too much time alone from what I can see."

"Thanks, Darlene." said Yvette.

"Wait a minute," Lennie put in. "Nobody can paint a picture with a two-year-old in the same room. I sure can't practice an instrument without time to myself."

"I suppose you let your mom do all the stuff for Patrick that's gotta be done as well as the housework and her job," Darlene said. "I seen your room. It's a mess."

"I take him around swimming when she asks me to."

"When she asks you," echoed Darlene. "She shouldn't have to ask."

"And if she doesn't want to be bothered with looking at my room, she can close the door," Lennie countered. "She does."

"You going to close the door to your whole house when you get married?" Darlene asked.

Russell sputtered a laugh, and Coralee laughed hard with a contagious ripple that sent them all to join in.

All except for Lennie. "I still say there's a lot of things you can only do alone."

"But raising children is one thing you shouldn't do by yourself, I don't think," said Nikkia. "I can see where many women fall into that, though, men's incomes being higher."

"I may never again earn as much as my wife," Russell thought aloud.

"Is that a reason for buryin' yourself in the house?" When Coralee spoke, her voice was low but angry.

Yvette shifted to sit up on her knees and get closer to the inner part of the circle. "His oldest child is only nine. You had your husband, then Junior, and Renee was fifteen."

"I might have found day care," conceded Russell. "I probably would've found a day job if I'd been more patient. But, the whole situation was brand new. I'd been laid off in Pittsburgh, and we moved from our friends, don't forget. You can't change your whole life, overnight."

"You did here," Coralee said simply.

"This is a summer project," said Russell. "It's all very well to talk about burying myself in our Brooklyn apartment. Here, I can do more because I'm not spending time at a job. We can't afford for me to be out of work. As soon as I get back, I'll at least look into day jobs and babysitting. Maybe I'll go back to UPS part time meanwhile."

"I'm not convinced by what you just said. You're already talking about same ol', same ol'," said Coralee. "I think the bosses have got you believing you deserve that rut. You've gotten beat down like the many thousands of other real mental cases caused by layoffs and firing. Somebody oughta shake you upside down!"

"You're full of bright ideas," Russell said sourly.

"Yes, I am! What's more, I think you and your family should move to Boston. You've already made quite a few friends here."

"Hey, it's only logical!" Don's voice was excited. "From the beginning we talked about some people's staying. But we thought more in terms of students. This makes more sense. For us, and for you!"

"I've even considered it," said Nikkia. "I've seen myself grow in Boston. But back home, my friends on the hospital job are, well, they've become, the center of my life. With the friends you've made here, like Forest, and Coralee's children, it would actually be a mistake for you to leave."

"They're training in the shipyards right now for welders and ship fitters jobs," said Lennie. "I was thinking of getting in up there after graduation."

"I don't think Pat is going to want to leave New York, just like that," objected Russell.

"I know Pat," said Nikkia. "She's mainly worried about your staying stuck at UPS. She's told me you're very hard to live with when you're tired all the time."

"The kids have been pulled out of one school in Pittsburgh already," Russell said. "That's not good."

"Talk it over with them," suggested Coralee. "Just don't do as I do and make them feel like they're being ordered around."

Nikkia couldn't help a laugh. "You're aware you act like a drill sergeant, Coralee?"

"Sure," Coralee said. "Like Russell knows down deep his coming alive in Boston is far better for his children than their staying in one school or another. They need this Russell we see here for a father, not a zombie."

"Whew, you don't leave me much of a choice," said Russell finally.

"Renee's given _me_ no choice but to beg you to stay. You think my home life is going to be the same if you go for good?" Coralee asked. "That triple-layer chocolate delight she presented you after the block party last night was her first homemade cake."

The van stopped, and the front doors opened.

They could all hear Norberto's slapping a little rhythm on the side of the van as he walked to the back door. "We're here!" he announced. "Did you all have a nice ride?"

"We'll never be the same!" spoke Russell, and he rubbed his heavy thighs with a comic movement.

x x x

The meeting, held in the Freedom School building, attracted more neighborhood parents than expected. The news of the fight at Carson Beach had made people angry. Seeing many new faces made a few comrades hesitate to talk about the need for sustained militancy. They were afraid of turning people away.

Most of the volunteers who had come up for August were also afraid. They didn't understand that confrontations went on every day that summer in Boston. "If we simply aren't there when these jerks want to fight, no one can get hurt," said Sam, a comrade from Chicago who had arrived that morning.

"You don't see the daylight," said Norberto to Sam. "If we stop now, there's going to be more children and other people beat up. It just won't be us."

Mrs. Guillroy, a parent from the Freedom School, spoke next. Wearing a purple hat with a peacock feather, she dressed as if for church. "I think they'll have to come up with a law to protect our children. City Hall couldn't predict what would happen when they passed down the busing act."

"The only laws they pay attention to are the laws against people, like immigrants," Norberto answered. "Look how long Hicks and her little committee were able to stop Boston school integration. For nine years!"

Nikkia listened to Norberto. A mixture of thoughts had gone through her while in the van. She had spoken little. Her silence wasn't only because she knew that she looked different. The bandages made her feel like she was on stage, and she was used to being stared at. Something had changed during this month in Boston, where it was no longer significant for her to be noticed as a leader.

What was more important, she was seeing today, was that others had to grow as leaders. Coralee and Russell would make a good team. They, in turn, would develop the leadership in their Boston neighbors. Memories of the people she'd met made Nikkia swallow with sadness, realizing that by tomorrow she would be gone from Boston.

She would be missed, Nikkia knew. But not as much as she would miss them. And Norberto. She knew he would not need her so much now.

Yet Nikkia noticed that Norberto's remark to Mrs. Guillroy implied that she already understood the connections between City Hall, the court's busing decision, and Boston's police. Norberto's inexperience with the English language--and his real concern with the immigration issues--caused him to skip steps in his explanation. Right now, Nikkia told herself, Norberto needed her!

Nikkia realized, too, that if she addressed Norberto, the newer comrade, Sam, and Mrs. Guillroy would not feel put down. She also thought Mrs. Guillroy might well have been insulted by Norberto's assumptions. And so she directed her comment as if to him alone: "Before the politicians decided on busing they were in a bind. First had come the civil rights movement. And the Racial Imbalance Act of 1965. Then countless books and publicity about Boston's crummy schools. They had to do something.

"So they handed down the busing order. But they didn't put a cent in the budget to make the schools better. They even closed two schools. There were no arrests when Andre Jean-Louis was gang-beaten. No arrests when they broke Mrs. Daley's collar bone, threw rocks at children, beat up those six black salesmen at Carson Beach. . ."

"Busted your face," Norberto interrupted. "Nobody got arrested for that."

"Mayor White has pasted the letters ROAR in the city hall windows." Nikkia didn't want a discussion about herself. "He's helped organize the attacks. Do we think he's going to set up laws to stop them?"

At once Norberto understood better how to convey the connection. "If we don't lead the fight to stop them, we're telling people we expect justice from them who want to kill us. We're the only ones they ever will lock up."

Mrs. Guillroy nodded. There was a sense of general agreement. Then Darlene spoke directly to Norberto but loudly enough so that everyone could hear. "And you thought for so long they arrested all the people at the office because of something you did."

"That was messed up," said Lennie, his mouth in a grimace like a small child.

Seeing the emotion in Lennie's face, Nikkia thought that perhaps Lennie was fearful that he, too, might 'mess up' along the way. She realized Lennie cared a lot about Norberto. He was someone older who had spent a lot of time with Lennie this summer. In addition, his being Mexican probably made Lennie take notice. Here was a man from another country who wanted to battle the conditions Lennie had lived with all his life.

Something else Nikkia was aware of: Lennie was moved to talk right after Darlene spoke. She had awakened something within him. Afterwards, Nikkia saw Lennie looking at Darlene. The words to a song came to her mind: "I've had a love of my own like yours." That silly song, she thought; what baloney. As if you're supposed to turn your emotions off at a certain age. Nikkia admitted to herself, I'm jealous of Lennie and Darlene. I want a partner, too!

And for awhile, she only half-heard the discussion about disrupting the WNAC-TV show, Mass Reaction. The dialogue on the cause of violence in South Boston was set up to pose blacks against whites. CAR had requested a speaker proposing unity and their six-point schools program. They had been refused. Zack suggested a plan that a number of CAR supporters be in the audience. Their shouting would interrupt the program, make it impossible to pit white against black.

Most of the women and men from the community, however, voiced their opinions that both sides should be heard. As Nikkia listened, her reaction was more physical. She still felt the effects of racist ideas on her own face. She didn't think she could make her argument understood, so strong was her hatred.

Yet she was uncomfortable in her silence. I can't ease up for a year, like Russell, or even for a couple of weeks like Norberto did, Nikkia thought. In fact, I want to do two things: return to the people on my job and also stay here. The thought of folks at the job gives me a feeling like I am home. But I want to remain active in Boston, too. Here, I can be a part of the sharpest situation in the country, and I am needed. And I need Norberto who is here.

Nikkia was glad for the bandage. She felt her skin twist with sadness. Water coming to her eyes made her nose hurt unbearably. She wanted to cry, and no one else knew.

She would be able to tell no one after the meeting, either. Nikkia recalled that there would be a rally in front of the TV station. Most people would go inside after that, but some of them would not. Those returning to other cities would get in separate cars. Russell and his family would go back to Brooklyn, then, and five of them bound for Manhattan would go back together. Each spin of the wheel would take her further from Norberto as did every passing minute of this meeting. Not once this afternoon, Nikkia realized, had she thought of Lawrence! When she remembered a feeling of home it had been for her job rather than for him.

Meanwhile the meeting became more crowded. People sat on the stage platform. Children saw the opportunity to play away from distracted parents. The disagreement persisted over whether or not to break up the television dialogue. It was nearing time to leave. Coralee interrupted the discussion to ask for volunteers for petitioning. "We don't want to break up this meeting with nothing accomplished."

Zack passed around a list for a telephone chain. Everyone understood that the telephone squad meant a willingness to support others in the streets, and only a half dozen signed. But almost no one wanted to join the party members in taking the offensive to stop the debate.

In fact, Mrs. Guillroy seemed annoyed. "You all leave, and we're still having to deal with the hoodlums."

At that, Coralee gave her a friendly nudge with her arm, and Mrs. Guillroy took back part of her statement. "Well, you're not going nowhere, but things haven't changed enough that I can see."

Three people at the meeting did agree to come with them that evening. One was an energetic young woman from El Salvador, named Estrellita Juarez, that Norberto had met. She was quiet and didn't speak at the meeting. But she had come to two petition rallies. Separated from her husband who had beat her, she had a determined way about her. Nikkia admired Estrellita.

Seeing Estrellita and Norberto talking together now, Nikkia got a rush of confidence. It would help Norberto, she knew, to continue knowing someone so serious and willing to do the work. Nikkia also knew that Norberto was the kind of man who could build this comradeship with a woman. But a part of her was envious of the time they would spend together during August. Time seemed so very precious in these last few minutes Nikkia had in Boston. She looked at her watch: it was already six-thirty in the evening, and they would be gone at eight.

Another person who volunteered to come to the broadcast was Forest. He reminded Nikkia of the man in the stories about the mill that Russell used to tell. The man who had died--what was his name--Quigley? She wondered if Russell himself was aware of the similarities in Forest, a loyal, spontaneous fellow.

Saleem was the third person to volunteer that night. He had joined Bonita on this, her last weekend. "I've decided to stay to go to the TV broadcast," he told the crowd. He hoped that by his statement someone else would join, but no one did.

Nikkia composed a speech in her mind. It would be about the nature of schools under communism. There would be no school buildings as such. Day care for very young children would be near the parents' workplace. And little by little, children would work with the adults in every way they could be useful. They would learn the social purpose of work itself, like the community benefits of the Chinese Revolution's collective farming. Of course, at the same time they would also learn skills like reading, math and safety.

The usual barriers of age and sex, as well as manual versus intellectual labor would be broken down. Results of children's homework would be in front of their own eyes. The work would be geared for them, and the political study would develop communist consciousness and make production better. Their recreation would be frequent, and the children would feel important at the end of the day.

They would study with the adults about how to share equally with each member of every family. Cooperation, not competitiveness, would be stressed in both games and learning. Grades would be a thing of the past. And no child would be labeled dumb.

But Nikkia didn't get a chance to say her speech, for suddenly they were leaving for the TV station. She became angry at herself: was she so used to being on stage that she wanted to rouse applause at her leaving?

Nikkia felt no distinct accomplishment for her efforts, as she was sure Norberto and Russell must have. She couldn't point to one person that she herself had invited to this meeting. It seemed that instead of going home with a feeling of having brought something to the Boston project, she was leaving behind a cherished possession: her deepest emotions.

Darlene was approaching to say goodbye. Then Nikkia hugged her. It seemed as if she were deserting her own daughter, and Nikkia began to cry. Her nose hurt more than when it had just been broken.

Memories flashed of how she had described New York City to Darlene. Had it been a picture of never-ending excitement? From class struggle to the ballet? Or an expensive pile of glitter where thousands suffered the job freeze? Darlene would never get along with Lawrence, Nikkia thought nervously. He would consider her naive, and fat.

The idea made her stomach turn. Nikkia suddenly had a maternal instinct of wanting to shield Darlene from future hurt. She felt very protective, while over Darlene's shoulder she watched the room slowly become empty. Nikkia remembered how she would focus on one spot in a room while perfecting turns. Darlene had become just such an important place for her in that one, whirling month. She straightened her arms, making the decision to invite Darlene to New York. "I want you to visit me soon after the project,"

An image of Norberto going to the television broadcast came to her mind. It was easier, somehow, to visualize his leaving instead of herself. Nikkia let Darlene pick up her suitcase though she could have lifted it. Then there was a light touch between her shoulder blades. Because of the stiff bandages, Nikkia had to turn her whole body around to see what was behind her. Norberto. As she would always remember him--close.

"We didn't say 'so long'."

Nikkia saw lines in his forehead she hadn't noticed before. He looked tired. She wanted to cradle his head. Was this a way of protecting herself, she wondered, that she wanted to mother him, too? Then she was in his arms. Her hands on his back, she felt his hard muscles beneath the soft cotton shirt. The length of her fingers burned, and that was all Nikkia knew until he was touching her lightly again on her shoulders. His arm was around her in comradely fashion, and they were walking. "Thanks for pushing me out of my worries," he said, awkwardly.

For me, Nikkia thought, he has done something more. He has pushed something of me more deeply inside, toward a new center. She found she couldn't say 'so long.' What she wanted to say to Norberto came out with difficulty. "I am sad," Nikkia told him.

"I was sad yesterday," he said.

As the car drove away, Nikkia saw Norberto staring at it. She felt a pull, like a silken spider thread, stretching from herself to him as the miles went, infinitely long.

x x x

In front of the television station at Government Center, there was no place to park the last cars and van. The drivers of each vehicle had to let their passengers out at the front door. Guards blocked the entrance. Una, in front, got into an argument. A guard shoved her. "We were told about you rabble rousers. No more members from CAR go into the broadcast," he said. Cops came up from all sides, surrounding them.

The comrades who had come in the van had most of the tape recorders and cameras. That was a mistake, Una was thinking. Now, they couldn't get in the door. Just then Zack pushed open the front door from inside. Una and Darlene rushed the door but were blocked by the cops.

At that point, Zack asked to speak with the police chief. The guards and cops conferred then and decided to allow him and Lennie to take some of the recorders inside. With five minutes left until the broadcast, they loaded Zack and Lennie with two cameras and several tape recorders. "In case one doesn't work," said Norberto. Lennie and Zack went in.

The eight comrades and CAR members who had been left outside began a picket line. Then, in the distance Una could see a large group of men moving toward the station. As if on a signal, the cops and police cars left, one after the other. Una pointed out to the others what now appeared to be a ROAR crowd. They couldn't tell how many of them there were.

"When we leave, we've got to leave together," said Norberto.

"We've got to leave now." urged Darlene.

They linked arms and chanted, "The cops, the mayor, the KKK; Workers united put you all away!"

Now there was not one policeman in sight. Zack had told Darlene where the van was parked and had given her the keys. But the van was parked in the direction from where the ROAR men now came. Quickly Norberto suggested they retreat to Haymarket Square and take public transportation. They began to run.

Norberto looked back once. Above the door to the TV station building, the American Flag waved stiffly in the breeze. As his eyes darted to both sides of the building, Norberto could see further down the street. He could see perhaps forty or more hefty white men, together on the furthest corner. "Let's get to Haymarket Square fast," he said to Coralee. Coralee noticed that two of the men had already pointed them out.

Haymarket Square was the nearest transit station, where the orange and green trolley lines came together. If they could just make a trolley, Norberto thought, they would be safe. He turned again, jogging sideways, and saw that the men behind them came at a full run. Haymarket Square lay a block away. "Run!" he yelled, half-pushing Darlene, who was slow.

Coralee moved more quickly for her heavy frame. Lennie ran ahead of everyone. In all, they were Tyrone, Una, Forest, Lennie and Saleem, in addition to Norberto, Darlene and Coralee.

They were all at least half a block ahead of the couple of dozen ROAR men. They would make it to the Square in plenty of time. Lennie, furthest in front, could already see there were no trolleys in sight.

They could hear Lennie shout, to no one and to everyone, "I'm gonna die, and I've never had sex."

Una and Coralee laughed in spite of their own fear.

The square was an open area. Not a place to be cornered. No trolley, though, Norberto noticed. No bus. "We'll have to stand and fight," he told Coralee.

"Good thing we're a pistol packin' crew," said Coralee. And she reached in the deep pocket of her backpack for a hammer as well as a wrench.

Tyrone opened his pack and took out a chain welded to a piece of lead pipe. Lennie gave Darlene a tire iron. She held the bar at both ends before hitting the pavement with it, her face showing surprise at the vibrations.

Norberto decided; they made a formation: three in front, two behind them and three in back. "No one is to run," he said.

"We'll get creamed one by one if we do," said Una. She swung her thick-link chain, mostly to make herself feel brave.

Then the first group of men ran up. Including those who came behind them, altogether there must have been fifty. They had counted on surprise and their sheer numbers, with no time to organize their group. Twenty or so men at the back slowed down seeing CAR's weapons. But those in front were still running when ROAR and the CAR people collided.

Coralee and Norberto took on a man with long blond hair. Una tripped another man before he could stop and caught him with her chain. Lennie got a guy on the chin with a piece of pipe.

Darlene was the first of the comrades to get hit--a blow that caught the side of her head--and Norberto couldn't turn quickly enough to stop it. Darlene fell to the pavement. But Coralee caught Darlene's attacker on the back of his neck with the wrench.

Norberto swung a crowbar in front of Darlene, clearing a semi-circle. But still most of the ROAR front line forces fought. Forest and Tyrone worked as a team. They punched with brass knuckles. They worked both sides of a man's head. Three ROAR men managed to run off in the direction from where they'd come. The twenty in the rear retreated further back.

The weapons cut arms, faces. Even so, the diminishing number of their attackers still seemed overwhelming to Norberto. "!No se retiren! !Los mandaremos a la luna! Don't retreat! We'll send them to the moon!"

Darlene got to her knees. She could tell Norberto had forgotten his English. The fight was going too fast for her to follow. She wasn't used to fighting like the others. She was afraid to think about how her head had hit the street. But she could see that if any one of the comrades ran they would get picked off. The twenty or thirty less-brave men in ROAR crowded the opposite side of Haymarket Square. "Don't retreat," she cried.

"Avance!" screamed Norberto. And he took a step forward. But it was impossible. The eight of them could only stand firm there in Haymarket Square. The odds were two to one now. Many of the ROAR men who had not hung back or run were bleeding. Everything had taken place in less than three minutes.

A bus pulled into the square. Its sign said CHARTER, and there were no passengers. The driver's eyes widened. He pulled closer to them.

"El autobus. Ayuden a Darlene!" They all understood, and Una knocked at the door of the bus. It opened. While Coralee swung her hammer, the rest were able to get Darlene on the bus. Coralee got on last. The driver closed the door behind her.

They laid Darlene on a bus seat, and Norberto took off his T-shirt to wrap her head. It became soaked with blood.

"I saw the whole thing," said the bus driver. "From the beginning of the chase."

Just then a bottle crashed against the plastic window.

"Hey, look!" shouted Una. "Look at the damage we've done!"

They had been somewhat stunned with the opportunity that the driver offered and so concerned with Darlene that none of them had looked outside the bus.

They rushed to the windows. What they saw shocked them all.

"Dios mio," said Norberto.

Four men lay on the cobblestones. Twenty or twenty-five men stood facing the bus, their mouths closing and opening, like fish, with curses. At least twenty-five, Norberto saw, still waited at the far edge of the square.

What was most surprising to him, though, was the amount of blood. It shone on the cobblestones in shiny black stains under the night lights. The faces of many of the men standing were covered with blood.

"The Night of the Living Dead," quipped Forest.

One of the men pounded on the side of the bus.

Norberto watched another throw a rock that cracked, but didn't break, the plexiglas. At that moment, seemingly out of nowhere, they all heard police sirens.

The bus driver waved at the sound as if it were a gnat. "We've got to get this girl to the hospital," he said, putting the bus into gear. The bus left the square even before the police arrived.

Norberto felt as if his chest would burst, from the heat and force of his breathing. He told himself over and over: I have led this fight to the finish, and we won. I love these comrades with all my strength.

He felt the fierce pounding of his heart. He would have fought, like a demon, another ten men. Instead, he glared out the window at their enemy as they pulled away. His hot love became hate. Under their feet, the bus transmission ground and churned. They drove away from the scene with a surge of the power of victory.

Norberto grabbed Forest around the waist and let out a yell of pent-up energy. Darlene reached up and hugged Una's waist. Saleem pounded everyone on the back.

"We better go to Metropolitan." Coralee spoke to the bus driver, thinking of more practical matters. "Their emergency room is the fastest."

"The cops may get there first," said Una.

The bus bounced along the street, rattling on every side with the handful of passengers.

Coralee noticed the driver's name, pinned to his uniform. "Dixon, what made you pick us up?" she asked, in her brusk way.

Una laughed at Coralee's way of talking. "You sound like he opened the door in the middle of two bus stops!"

"It's all right," said Dixon. "I saw the whole thing at the beginning of the chase. I was headed near here anyway, to the barn. I knew you couldn't a figured there's not many buses comes in here on a Sunday night."

"She means *why* did you put yourself where you might get hurt." Norberto sensed something more. "And you know the cops'll be all over you for pulling off like you did."

"I saw the guy Andrea Jean-Louis when they beat

him," said Dixon. "I didn't know what was happening at the time. I was on one of my regular runs. Thought it was a fight. If I'd stopped, he might a been all right today."

At the hospital, Norberto let the others answer questions and see to Darlene. Feeling cold from the emergency room air conditioning, he retrieved his bloody T-shirt from Darlene's stretcher and put it on. He leaned back in a nearby wheelchair, suddenly exhausted.

There, he fell into a doze, his mouth open. He dreamed of the three day walk he'd taken once from the hills of Oaxaca to a meeting in the city. He dreamed of pushing up and over more hills, until his knees became weights. While he slept, the stain from Darlene's blood dried on the front of his T-shirt, and that is what saved him from arrest.

The cops came in, immediately recognizing the comrades around Darlene. They arrested six and handcuffed Darlene to her stretcher. Seeing Norberto, with his mouth open, head flung back and chest bloodied, the police mistook him for a derelict near death from a knife fight. And they never touched him.

When Norberto awoke, a nurse was shaking him, and they had moved Darlene. "Borracho," hissed Norberto. "Me drunk, see, borracho." He pointed to himself and grinned.

"Gracias por la dormida." Thanks for the sleep. He waved to the nurse, staggered slightly and walked through the automatic doors.

He could barely see the stars overhead. And he didn't know the names of most of these streets, but living here for three months helped. His good sense of direction led him to a main street that the bus had travelled. On his way, the smaller street lights glowed more dimly and showed him sharper stars.

He thought of his wife, Silvia, waiting for him under a clearer, brighter sky. Walking on this strange street, Norberto missed her and his children so. He felt both tiredness and sadness in his joints. And then he thought of Nikkia, too, the wonderful, warm woman who had gone away and yet still seemed as close as the pulse in his throat.

Racial discussion leads to scuffle, 7 arrests

Boston police reported that seven persons were arrested last night outside of Haymarket Square when a disturbance erupted between a group of black and whites during a discussion of racial trouble on South Boston's Carson's Beach.

Lt. Harry Guilfoy of the Government Center station said three persons were taken to Massachusetts General Hospital where they were treated for cuts and bruises.

Lt. Guilfoy said seven persons were arrested in the scuffle between police and a group estimated at 50. Guilfoy said all those arrested were charged with assault and battery with dangerous weapons: wrenches, garrison belts and bottles. They will be arraigned in Boston Municipal Court today.

Guilfoy said the trouble broke shortly after 8 p.m. after a crowd appeared at the WNAC-TV studio to discuss recent violence in South Boston. Police said the group, blacks and whites, were unable to enter the studio and walked to Haymarket Square, where they began a discussion. That's when the trouble developed, police said.

Police reported last night there were numerous stonings of motorists in the Roxbury and North Dorchester sections.

Police said firefighters were stoned as they attempted to extinguish a fire at Dudley and Magnolia streets in Roxbury. Authorities reported that at 11 p.m. police cars entering the Eustis Street Housing Project were stoned by bands of youths clustered on the roofs. Police reported that windshields of two police cars were smashed, and the officers were hit with flying glass but not hospitalized.

Roxbury man convicted under new rape law

A Roxbury man was given a life sentence and an additional term of 15 to 25 years in Walpole State Prison yesterday after he was convicted in Suffolk Superior Court of the rape and armed robbery of a Back Bay woman last February.

Judge Henry H. Chmielinski Jr. imposed the sentence on Charles E. Welch, 19, of 202 Dudley st., after a three-day, jury-waived trial.

Welch, who was on parole from a six-year sentence to Concord reformatory for armed robbery at the time of the crime, was convicted under the new rape law which includes unnatural acts as rape.

KNOW KIDDING.

We don't fool around. You get a full 5% ann— interest on savin— checking and $—

Chapter 15

None of the people involved in that August 11 Haymarket Square station fight knew what the impact would be on city hall and the organized police. Not the goons in league with the police, nor the bus driver, who was fired, nor the comrades and friends. No one discoverd the result until the remaining days of August unfolded. They revealed the new decision by city hall: there were to be no more attacks on communists by gangs of white racists.

But enough other problems came out. Two of Coralee's children, Fay and Adam, refused to do household work. They felt the major part was being foisted back on them. Timothy and Thomas, just turning fourteen, insisted on their right to hang out more with friends outside the house. Renee needed Coralee at home, and Coralee was torn between trying to turn more community responsibilities over to Una, wanting to spend more time at home and keeping her job.

Norberto, responsible for more new people, couldn't help her much. Developing Forest and Estrellita—in turn to give leadership to the newer volunteers of August—was a job in itself. Zack missed Nikkia's and Coralee's constant community presence deeply. He worked well to develop other comrades but was reluctant to involve many new people. "I'm basically a shy person," he told Norberto.

"You can't stay that way," Norberto answered. "We have not involved enough of the people of Boston." That remained the biggest problem of all.

During the return trip to New York, Nikkia became aware of an unexpected resolution. She thought she might feel divided in her loyalty to Lawrence and to Norberto. Instead, she found herself able to contemplate the experience of both. The space for the two men in her mind, Nikkia thought, was as large as the room for different children in a mother's embrace.

She recalled the years with Lawrence: their

dancing bodies working together, the organizing in Mississippi, their planning a life for the future. It was with a steady kind of fondness that she anticipated seeing him. The rush of emotion she had known with Norberto stayed with her, too, as well as the need for him that stretched the thread back to Boston.

Something else was happening to Nikkia that was born of long training. She began to prepare herself mentally for her work and for living with Lawrence. As she looked down at her muscular forearms and hands she told herself, she would be holding the arms and legs of patients and stroking Lawrence with these hands. She remembered how she used to think about her mistakes in a dance routine and perfect the movements in her mind before going on stage.

She lost this control with Norberto, Nikkia realized. But in a matter of time she would be able to look at the time they spent together as a separate joy. What might marriage--and even sex--have been like with him in his passionate moods? Lawrence and she had learned to have good sex despite their roughest periods. She wasn't so sure, she thought, that Norberto would be capable of that.

Impulsively, she squeezed Bonita's hand. "I'm beginning to get excited about being home."

x x x

They sat in Bonita's apartment the next day, the last day of Nikkia and Bonita's vacation. Boxes full of things were scattered about. Saleem had left them half-unpacked in his partial move. Bonita's own suitcase was open, yawning clothes onto the floor.

Saleem's sudden decision to get further involved at Haymarket Square did not alter Bonita's commitment to the car pool. She and Nikkia heard of Saleem's arrest the moment they got to New York. Then they learned he and the others were released, and that Saleem was taking a plane back in time to get to his job by the morning. Their common worry and pride for him brought their friendship closer, to the point that Nikkia told Bonita about her intimate thoughts of Norberto. Bonita said she thought something had to change between Nikkia and Lawrence now.

I don't agree," Nikkia said flatly. "Those things I felt for Norberto were separate. They have nothing to do with Lawrence."

"But they have to do with you."

"That's romance, and fantasy. It's all in my head." Nikkia insisted. "He's married. He's not about to leave his wife."

"You've changed, though," said Bonita. "I'm your friend, and that's how I know."

"I only look different," teased Nikkia.

"We've been friends for three years now," Bonita reminded her. "You've become different with people in Boston; I've been watching you. You think of more things to bring people in. Things that affect them more deeply."

"Lawrence has grown to understand me, Bonita, just as you have. I'm not going to throw that away for nothing."

"I'm not saying you should, if you're happy."

"Happiness has nothing to do with it," Nikkia snapped. "In America people talk about happiness and love as if they're something you've got to possess like a car."

"Are you trying to tell me that what you felt for Norberto wasn't real?"

"I've also got to live my life," Nikkia stated, thinking that while she talked she was deciding. "I understand Lawrence, too. We've been through a lot of changes together, and we'll go through a lot more, I suppose."

"This all seems so overwhelming," Bonita raised her arm to the cartons and brushed a hand over some dust. "Saleem and I haven't been through half of what you have; we've never travelled together, much less been out of the United States. But now he's moving in. And last night he was more sharply involved in fighting racism than I ever was. I don't know if I'm ready for all this."

"I like Saleem. He's right where he says he'll be. He tells you he's serious. He sees you every night. He says he wants to live with you; he does it."

Bonita decided to focus in on this last statement. "He doesn't have as much stuff to move as Lawrence."

"That's one way of putting it." And it was true, Nikkiarealized. She was glad in many ways she was spending this last day helping Bonita straighten her apartment. Lawrence would not be home from Washington until this evening. It had been lonely looking at an empty apartment after the close companionship and shared living quarters of the Boston comrades.

Saleem's belongings consisted mostly of boxes of records, stereo equipment, a dining room table that came in pieces, with eight folding chairs, and a lounge chair with hassock. "I didn't have any records, and no dining room table."

Bonita handed Nikkia a part of the table, and they began to put it together. "See, you can fold it small, put up one leaf for a couple of people, or spread it out to seat as many as twelve guests. What could Saleem have been thinking of when he bought it?"

"He was thinking ahead, of having a family or company with someone like you," said Nikkia.

"It's funny you should say that, because his personality reminds me something of yours."

Nikkia was surprised. Saleem seemed so cheerful and more able to bounce back from difficult situations than herself. Like today, she felt the demands of getting back to work. Catching up on four weeks of charts. Her life reminded her of these unpacked boxes. Over it all—as if it were the settled dust in her own apartment—lay her disappointment in Lawrence's not being home to greet her. "How are we alike?"

"You can both be as warm and close with one person as with a crowd." Bonita said. "Not me. I lose my sense of humor around a bunch of people."

"It's practice." said Nikkia, but as she spoke, she wondered if she would be able to be light-hearted again, with a hundred people or alone. Was this what it meant to be old? "You take your sense of humor with you, but you become shy. You'll get over that."

"I did somewhat, while I was teaching some basics of nursing to high school kids in the freedom school. Me, a teacher, telling them what nursing school would really be like."

For the moment, Nikkia felt better. Something in her prevented her from sharing this depression. She didn't want to bring Bonita down with her. She could still take pleasure in someone else's enthusiasm. I am a mother to Darlene; a big sister to Bonita, she thought. I wouldn't want to be five or ten years younger again for anything. And it was comforting, Nikkia soothed herself, to know that she could not live with Saleem or Lennie as comfortably as with

Lawrence.

As they unpacked Saleem's cartons and finished assembling the table, Nikkia tried to sort out some of her future plans. That much, she felt capable of talking about. "When Lawrence and I get married," she began, "one of us will have to throw out furniture. Isn't it strange we still can't decide which living room set to keep? His is leather, but mine is more practical for children."

"So he wants to have children, too, now?"

"Well, not definitely. I can see his conflict. He does so much writing at home. And I can't do my work at home, obviously, so he would't get anything done while the kids were small."

"And he's not Russell Brown."

"No, he's not!" Nikkia was grateful to Bonita for making her smile at that.

She heard a key in the door and was more relieved still. That would be Saleem. She was spared from talking about the many unresolved problems she faced with Lawrence: children, managing their work lives. Bonita had a way of cutting through to the difficult questions, and that was exactly what Nikkia wasn't ready to discuss. After all, she thought as Saleem came through the door, I've come such a long way, and these two are just starting out. Everything looks so easy when it's all fresh and new!

"Hi Sugar, hi Nikkia," Saleem and Bonita met each other with an eagerness that was irresistible. Feeling protective, Nikkia watched their kiss as if from a long distance. Saleem was someone with whom she was completely at ease. Even now, as he left Bonita's arms to bend down to her on the floor and touch her cheek, he included her. They both had to hear every detail of the fight and the arrest. After he'd finished the story, Nikkia reminded him that he had not one bruise.

Saleem's wide eyes had taken in Nikkia's bandages but showed no surprise. "Bonita told me yesterday that you'd taken a lump or two at Carson Beach. How are you under there?"

His concern was so genuine that Nikkia got a sudden urge to say 'I'm not ok.' She had not been prepared for his question. Nikkia looked back at Saleem now, and studied his appearance. Saleem was almost hairless on his smooth face, and his wide eyes and broad mouth seemed innocent, even for someone four years younger than herself. The set of his shoulders was awkward and bony with none of the grace she liked to see. And yet she was afraid to answer his question honestly. How could he sense her disappointments?

She answered, "Fine. Really I am. It doesn't even hurt." Nikkia was able to smile at him. He would only get so far as the answer she gave, and the mask.

"Tell me about the union drive," Nikkia added, trying to keep the conversation off herself. "You're not the best of letter writers, you know."

"First thing. Just after you two were gone they announced they were going to cut out the laundry department and have it all done at a private company. Then, they said in order to save the laundry department from complete layoffs they would just lay off a few people from each department."

"What have they done so far?"

"Nothing yet, I think they're afraid of a repeat of the June demonstration. They're testing us, but they could do it soon. Columbia Presbyterian just laid off fifty people."

"We read about the layoffs," said Bonita, "up in Boston." How come the papers never say that represents fifty _families_ who have been cut off of food and rent money?"

"We can say it in _Challenge_ and in leaflets." Nikkia knew a burst of inspiration she hadn't felt since she got hurt. The thought of seeing people at every turn in the hospital halls, people with whom she had something in common, made her feel good. She saw herself talking with Henrietta in housekeeping. She couldn't wait! "We need to have a social event. We never did celebrate what we won!"

"Think of how much we have to tell everyone about Boston."

"And I'm planning to ask several people to come up with us the day of the big march in downtown Boston. That's when we turn in the petitions to City Hall. Or for the first day of school to demonstrate with us." Nikkia continued to think out loud, and so she missed the initial words of what Saleem was saying, which had very little to do with Boston.

He was talking about being asked to work overtime that day. "What can we say when we're faced with patients who've been waiting four hours for an X-ray," Saleem said, "and it's time to go home?"

Bonita heard him. "You told me on the phone that you refused to stay."

"Not only that, Billy Dougherty and me wrote up a petition. The stinking overtime means less jobs. We need more technicians."

"You didn't used to talk like this," said Bonita. "You'd at least think about whether or not you wanted the extra overtime money, remember?"

"I've got a family now," said Saleem. "All of a sudden I've got a future." He folded Bonita in his long arms.

While she sat looking at them, the happiness Nikkia felt for this couple slowly seemed to erase, along with the friendly image of people in the hospital halls. She saw instead a frame of Lawrence as though a slide projector had shown it on her mind. But his face brought with it the problems of their own future. His work required long hours, and quiet. Maybe they would need separate apartments! That image was too uncomfortable. She switched the mental picture to one where she saw Lawrence's arms around her.

She told herself the dialogue: she was asking him to come to Boston for a weekend. He was telling her he could't afford the time away from his new project. The realization came to Nikkia that Lawrence had not, during the month of July, arranged his work so that he could be at her side in Boston. Despite his initial consent--he had meant it at the time, she was sure--he never fully intended to make the trip to Boston this summer! And over the picture of Lawrence on the cozy leather couch showed a patchwork shading of loneliness.

Nikkia wrapped her skirt around her bare feet there in Bonita's apartment. Her feet, those of a dancer with misshapen great toes, were the only part of her body she didn't like. Right now, just when she was feeling so alone, Nikkia had the urge to protect her feet from view.

"You haven't heard my jazz collection. I'm specially proud of Ahmad Jamal's first album, before anyone ever heard of him." Saleem was talking. "I want you to hear it, Nikkia. It'll only take me an hour to set up the stereo."

"Yes, do stay for supper, as well. I want you to." Bonita included Nikkia in a sweep of her eyes over the living room disarray. "You can't go without enjoying the results of all your help."

Do they feel sorry for me, behind these bandages? Nikkia asked herself. Or do they know my loneliness?

"I want to hear about Boston, from you." Saleem said. "I did so much overtime in July that I never made it up there until yesterday. Now that the whole day crew is refusing to stay past three-thirty or work unscheduled Saturdays and Sundays, I'm going up the two weekends in August that Bonita's off. You all blazed a trail; it's the least I can do to follow."

"Saleem told me he was meeting with Tony and some members of the party's hospital collective. I kind of thought his commitment would back away when they got what they demanded. But he surprised me with his proposal to stay in Boston last night for the TV broadcast. As surprised as when he said he wanted to move in here!"

"My motto is, you don't understand something—a person, a political party—without knowing the insides, the good and the bad," Saleem said. "A lot of these parties sound alike: Young Socialists, Revolutionary Union, Progressive Labor. Many people look real good on the outside who're rotten on the inside . . ."

"Is that why you became an X-ray technician?" Bonita was laughing, but it was a real question.

"A comedian. I'm moving in with a comedian to see if I can wake up to a sense of humor before drinking my coffee." He slipped one hand down on Bonita's foot and lifted her leg to his lap, caressing the arch of her foot. "Nobody gives a shit if we pick up something the doc's don't. It's a job, a backbreaking job."

His anger, Nikkia could tell, was unexpected to Bonita. Yet, he modified his outburst by holding her foot in tender stroking. Nikkia wished he would take her own feet from their hiding place. They had become hot under her skirt in the midafternoon heat, as was her face under its mask.

"I think your own bones took a beating this month," said Nikkia to Saleem. "You've always treated your technician label as some kind of a joke. Like the tag that's supposed to record your X-ray exposure." Nikkia thrust her feet out onto the floor. It was a decisive gesture. She wanted to catch Saleem's anger and at the same time show Bonita that her question wasn't lost. "Do you think that you follow your instincts without a lot of planning?"

"I know what she means," said Bonita. "I'm not sure you consider things enough before you jump in, Saleem. Your job, or even our living together. Our relationship shouldn't be a fling. And marriage is one long compulsory overtime!" The little joke seemed to come out of its own accord from her lips.

Saleem smiled at them both this time. "How should you believe me? Most guys, most people, don't make these life decisions so quickly. I'm basically a simple fellow. And I know what I need, in you.

"I think you're smart." He spoke to Bonita as if Nikkia wasn't in the room. "Just as important, you've got the guts to follow your convictions. You believe in equality and in fighting for it. Most women feel they have to marry someone better off." He finished, "I guess I wish I could be more like you."

Nikkia had never heard a man speak so openly about himself. She sensed the communication between the two people across from her, how strongly they knew one another. That's the way it was for a time with Lawrence, she thought. There was that moment he and I were dancing together for the second time in France. He was holding me above him, but it was as though we were lifted together. We both knew we would be close, again and again.

The warm energy of the memory caused her to go to the couch and to hug her friends: the bony Saleem, the vigorously tense Bonita. "I have to go," she said. "Lawrence might be at my place any minute."

"Let him phone around and find you here," suggested Bonita. "Then you're not waiting alone."

"And I can hear the story of what _you_ did. You're depriving me if you don't start now. A month is like a year up in Boston these days, from what I can tell." Saleem added cautiously, "Lawrence may not want to know as much detail . . ."

"The most amazing things that happened never got in the newspapers," began Bonita. "Like how Russell Brown got this family of young kids together."

Nikkia didn't hear the implied warning in Saleem's last sentence. Nor did she respond to the connections Bonita tried to encourage, to pull her in. The urge that had driven her from the couch was too great. "I love you both, but can you understand how I _can't_ stay?"

"Sure I understand," said Bonita, "don't you think you'd be better off waiting here, though?" Her tone echoed Saleem's.

"OK, OK. We'll make a definite date to get together. All four of us. You'll come over." Nikkia reached back for her purse and dug inside for a datebook. She missed the look that passed between Bonita and Saleem. "Is Saturday good? My place?"

"Come here," said Saleem emphatically. "I'll cook the blackened fish Forest taught me. I've never been able to invite Lawrence over to where I live."

"Well, sure," Nikkia responded, taken off balance by Saleem's insistence. She poked her toe into one shoe, the scuffed red huaraches she had worn on the streets of Boston. She noticed the odd shaped strains on the thin leather pieces, which stretched to give way for the lumps on her feet. "Did either of you see my other shoe?"

"If I don't tell you where it is, you can't leave," teased Saleem. His eyes looked for her face, but she was distracted. "There, behind the table leg."

"I'll let you know if Saturday's all right with Lawrence." Not until she could feel the door with the palm of her hand did Nikkia realize the quick sadness of leaving the company of these people she loved, the comrade that had been a part of her for a month. "See you _soon_."

There was no bus in sight. Nikkia felt that walking would be faster, anything rather than wait. The bus passed her in the middle of the block but it was easier to push her legs rather than to sit on a seat. Once in Central Park, Nikkia ran. She ran with a rhythm that gave her second wind, and it carried her through the width of the park. At last she had to stop and pant and go more slowly to her building. Already her mind was thinking ahead to the apartment where her own bedroom needed a dusting.

We'll stay the night at my place, Nikkia told herself as she unlocked her front door. She opened the windows. Then she remembered the leaves of the aloe plant under the light in the bedroom. Lawrence might notice, she thought. Nikkia pulled up the orange and yellow bedspread and checked under the throw rug, a corner of which tucked under the bed. Sure enough, there was more dust. The baseboards of the bedroom from this angle seemed very obviously dirty, too. It was a good thing, she thought gratefully, that Lawrence didn't get here before I arrived.

Her head began to ache, from the bending over. Nikkia realized she hadn't eaten since early morning. She had been working unpacking boxes, then running through the park, and now worring where Lawrence was. Maybe a quick aspirin because she didn't want to eat dinner without him. The medicine cabinet shelves were dusty, too, and had disgusting smears of toothpaste.

Nikkia took the few jars and bottles of first aid cream and bandages off the shelves, rinsed the glass shelves under the tap, dried them and put them back. Even the caps of the jars and bottles were dirty. She had never noticed before how dusty containers got, when closed up inside a cabinet.

As she turned, she noticed the shower curtain had gray soap scum in a fold. She washed that, but there was another, and another, and another, along the entire width of the curtain. The phone rang, and the sponge bounced from her hand into the tub. If she didn't retrieve the sponge now, Nikkia knew herself, she would forget it for sure!

She had put the phone in the hall just outside the bathroom. Sponge in one hand, the other slippery from cleaning, she grabbed the receiver. It fell from her hand onto the table with a bang. She picked it up, embarrassed.

"Hi."

"I've been calling you."

"I was at Bonita's. For awhile. But for the last hour--two hours--no one has called."

"Never mind. When're you coming over. I need to see you."

"I thought, didn't you say when we last talked that you had your project spread out and you would come here."

"I've changed my mind. Organized my files which I should have done anyway." His voice was self-critical. "Besides, I've cooked dinner."

"You have?" How can I possibly say no, Nikkia thought. "Let me get dressed, and I'll be there."

"I can't wait to see you," he said.

Instead of her usual anticipation, for the first time Nikkia became fearful of how she would look to Lawrence. The print dress with its huge vivid tulip pattern that she had chosen, and ironed, seemed too dowdy now. Her delicate high-heeled red sandals, frivolous. Was this what Norberto had done to her, she wondered. Left her so terribly insecure that she no longer felt attractive in her usual clothing? If that were so, she decided, this romantic fling has acted like a poison. I'm not left with happy memories but a gray-tinted world. Not only Lawrence seems wrong; I'm out of sorts with me!

She held the dress to herself caringly. It had been one of the favorites she could count on. She noted her reflection in the mirror. Indeed, the mask looked horrible beside the red tulips--the dress made the mask look sad. She didn't want Lawrence to think she was sad.

Then a thought came to her: Lawrence couldn't tell by looking at her face *what* she might feel this evening! She laughed out loud. No need to worry, Nikkia realized with a glance at the blush pots on her dresser, about how my face looks at all.

That idea made her daring. She remembered a white, skin-tight leotard. Though she knew she had gained weight since she stopped dancing, this month of one meal a day and long hours had made her stomach flat and her hips lean. She put on the leotard and noticed that the fit over her calves was actually smoother on less-muscular legs. The over-all effect with the mask was dramatic.

On impulse, she took the wide patent leather belt off the tulip dress and cinched it on the last notch. That felt good. And now she could wear the red huaraches that had looked too worn for the crisp tulip print. She wanted to wear the huaraches; they reminded her of the good work she had done this summer.

Then Nikkia put her hospital shoes in a plastic bag and her uniform as well into a huge, round red pocketbook. She was sorry she had to work tomorrow. How could she predict that she and Lawrence wouldn't be able to spend this day, the last of her vacation, together? Or that he wouldn't be coming to her place first. How foolish that she had spent all this time cleaning her medicine cabinet!

Nikkia ran her fingertips lightly over the full length mirror on the bedroom door. The glass was cool and smooth, reassuring. No matter that I rushed to polish everything; what's clean is clean. It'll be his turn to come here next.   She did a stretch now, pulling her thigh muscles, holding the big round pocketbook in front of her like a shield. To herself, she looked like a warrior. Why do I feel my heart pounding as if I'm going into battle? Do I want to fight Lawrence? He's not an enemy. Am I afraid of him, then? Yes. No. I love him.

He has cooked dinner. He called me when I wasn't home. Nikkia saw her own eyes smiling at herself in the mask and tossed the pocketbook to one side. She put her hands on her belted waist as she bent in a plie. Nothing like having her body at its slimmest, Nikkia thought, and no one able to see her face! If only her heart would stop pounding with this hot thumping, she would be all right.

Nikkia wanted to walk across town to rid herself of this nervous feeling. But she would be tempted to run and then arrive in a sweat. The idea of a cab reminded her of Jeff and how their common refusal to take cabs was one building block in their friendship. "You miss the art of people's faces from the inside of a cab," he said once.

She suddenly missed his uncritical acceptance of her. In their hours of talking she had been able to bring out her profound doubts about the ballet, as well as the quick silliness they shared. Now on thinking about it, Jeff had helped her decide to quit simply by listening to her. She decided to call him. Tomorrow.

With that, Nikkia took a token from the little dish she kept on the refrigerator and looked forward to riding the bus uptown.

She felt the eyes on her from the people sitting down. The bus wasn't crowded, and everyone had a view of the slim, muscular woman whose skin had darkened further from the Boston summer streets and who wore a ski mask of bandages.

They expected an acting troupe to follow her up the steps, but she was alone. They waited for her to make a speech or to pantomime or to solicit funds. She smiled toward the back of the bus, and they realized she was beautiful. Several people turned to see who it was she might have recognized. Nikkia chose a side seat so she could watch the faces, and a handsome woman with three children politely tried not to look at her. The woman's children stared while the rest of the bus continued to notice her with shorter glances.

Nikkia felt completely at home. This wonderful city full of people, she thought, all different-looking. I could be anyone to them. Their eyes have taken me in. They're used to variety in this big, populated city of garment workers and actors and people whose work I cannot guess with complexions of many countries. We appear to be more different, but most of us are of the same class. I am a communist. None of them is a communist, but here in New York City they have all heard that communists live here, too. And they would show less surprise if I were to pass out leaflets.

Most of them would not agree, but one or two would. And nobody would think it strange. And after this summer in Boston, few of the people there will think it odd that others are willing to fight in the streets against racism. The thought made her smile. The boy-child of the handsome woman smiled back at her.

Slowly bumping uptown the bus emptied. Lawrence lived in one of two high-rise apartments that lofted over the street which became a ramp to the George Washington Bridge. They had argued over his choice, Nikkia aware that she might one day have to live here, too. The buildings were less a part of the community, even, than the growing glass apartments of the upper West Side. Their first floors at least touched the sidewalk.

"I'm able to service the publishing houses of Bergen county in New Jersey with this address," Lawrence had told her. "You've got to admit the location is practical for my business." Yet today Nikkia longed for Jeff's penthouse building. The deco architecture of that thirties structure seemed to penetrate into the very scent of his elevator.

Why did she keep thinking of Jeff, she wondered, and not Norberto? Norberto could not have meant as much to her as she thought, Nikkia realized with a calmness. Jeff had been a friend for far longer--though living another life altogether.

No matter what I've been feeling--she took a deep breath--I'm not a person who romanticizes over a few moments of pretend intimacy. I have changed jobs in order to work with more people. I'm about to marry someone who is practical for me, just as this apartment building is practical for Lawrence. It's only a bunch of glass and cement that I can live in as easily as my own apartment. The building is on top of both the IRT and IND subway lines. I can get to Bonita's even quicker. With a heart full of confidence, she presented Lawrence's business card to the doorman who controlled the stairway to the upper level of elevator banks. He nodded with a face that looked past her own.

An inside doorman pointed to a bank of elevators. Nikkia didn't have to wait for one. The only other person in the elevator was a woman wearing a fur coat and flip-flops. Her hands shuffled envelopes while her eyes stared at Nikkia's face.

The circle for the fifth floor was already lit, and Nikkia pressed the number ten. She stepped to one side and leaned against the wall as the elevator rose. The woman continued to stare at her, so Nikkia stared back until she looked down. At the fifth floor, the woman got out and looked back once quickly as the doors slid closed. Nikkia thought, I bet she was afraid of me!

Somewhere behind the plastic, false-wood paneled walls, a muzak station began to play "Some Enchanted Evening". "It's an omen, Nikkia said aloud to herself, "telling me how my romantic fancies of Norberto were as empty as this song." The door opened at ten.

Nikkia glanced back at the closing elevator doors, and the muzak dimmed. "The things I do for you, Lawrence," she continued talking aloud, "like spending moments in that elevator for the rest of my life."

Is it so easy, she questioned; have I already made up my mind to live here? Lots of people wouldn't consider it a sacrifice, she smiled, pushing the little black doorbell under the peephole, to live in a luxury apartment building! Under her finger the little black button sprang back into position with a click that sounded loud in the green carpeted hall. It was quiet behind the door, and Nikkia looked quickly down the corridor with its triple-gloss walls, silent too. Then the door opened. Lawrence--of course he was here had she ever doubted it--familiar long arms and lean, smooth cheeks. Eyes full of surprise.

"Good god. You look terrible."
"I'm not a beauty queen, if that's what you mean."
"Your whole face."
"It's not my whole face. The bandages hold my

nose in place." Nikkia came closer, her arms ready to hold his chest. Lawrence wore a burgundy silk bathrobe, and she could already imagine feeling his warm skin beneath it.

"No," he said. And then he corrected himself. "You might hurt your nose."

"Well, at least let me in." Nikkia laughed at his discomfort, but a pain of disappointment spread from somewhere behind her lungs, deep in the center of her body. She felt almost too afraid to walk through the doorway. She did it anyway, without waiting for his invitation. He's too shocked to be polite, she told herself.

"You don't know what it does to me, seeing you like this," he held his arms limply at his sides.

"Don't be silly," she said. "Just pretend we're at an all-night costume ball." Nikkia was still hoping she could kid him out of his mood, this reaction.

"Can't you understand," he said, and his hands smoothed the lapel of the silk bathrobe, "in how many ways this hurts me, too?"

He was walking backwards, and his leg stopped at his leather lounge chair. Lawrence sat down, out of reach of Nikkia. She could see now that his reaction was total and not superficial. He was genuinely overwhelmed.

Nikkia saw behind Lawrence as he sank into the big chair. The dining room table was set. There was a thick bunch of fresh daisies, yellow and crisp, in a vase on the polished wood. And a white envelope was propped against one of a pair of candles. Two folded blue napkins. And beyond, Manhattan and the Bronx spread out behind plate glass windows. In the silence Lawrence became part of that urban back drop. As she took in the scene, Nikkia realized that he had gone to some effort.

She put her hand to her bandages and touched the tight paper tape adhesive. It did not feel strange for she had touched it many times. Now it was a part of her. But she could understand in part why the mask was repulsive to Lawrence. It did not fit in with this--she started to smile--rather formal theater setting. Her smile widened under the half-mask of white.

"What in the hell are you laughing about?" he said. "I don't find any of this funny."

She decided to let her impression come out. Perhaps she could lighten his mood. "You're the stage designer," she said, "I'm a naughty actress who showed up in the wrong costume."

"But it's me you're laughing at."

"Not a bit." She was puzzled, though, that she had to explain. "It's the situation. Not you."

"At bottom, it's me. You just don't want to admit it."

She realized it would do no good any longer to try to convince him why she was laughing. Nikkia knew there was a time when she couldn't have smiled at this scene, either. It's as if--and she found herself smiling again--in the month of living with Bonita she had taken on Bonita's sense of humor.

Lawrence could not help but see her smile again. "You're so insensitive right now I could hate you."

His words drove out thoughts of Bonita. What's the matter with me? Nikkia asked herself. I'm only making things worse between us. "I'm sorry," she said.

"Sorry won't change the fact you must have known how I'd respond. You've known me for eleven years, and you know my sensibilities. Don't try to deny it."

She felt wrong. Was it her fault? Truly she was the one out of place here. He had taken so much care with the flowers. The card, too, was certain to be an expression of love, welcome. His wanting to be with her as he remembered her.

She wanted to rip off the bandages. If only they could be removed as easily as a mask. To show that she had been fooling. Certainly she wouldn't ask him to clear his table setting. But neither could she strip away the tape. "I don't think we can pretend the bandages aren't here," she offered.

"You're the one who's trying to operate on business as usual."

Was she, Nikkia wondered. Was that wrong? Perhaps all he wanted was to be recognized, too. Here she realized she had dominated; the mask was so commanding. Weren't Lawrence's feelings equally important? He wasn't an audience or a stage prop. What could she have been thinking? Nikkia felt guilt pour like a warm liquid somewhere between her leotard and skin.

"I've only been thinking how good it would be to see you," she said.

"Don't you think I've been feeling the same?"

"Of course you have," Nikkia said. And then she realized that his seeing her bandages told him at once that she wasn't the same.

"And you knew that tonight I would see beyond the mask."

"What do you mean?" Nikkia honestly wasn't sure.

"You can't be that naive. What must I think when I see you with your face half gone?"

She thought, I feel naked before him. I'm the one that's been injured, but he can't play the protector any longer. He wants me to admit that my broken nose has hurt him even more. I can't do that. But he is pained, or thinks he is, and that's the same thing. I can't deny his pain any more than he can ignore my bandages.

He's playing a game of 'guess what's on my mind?' Her skin-crawling guilt was replaced with a deeper fear--that I'll guess wrong, and we'll have a serious fight on our first night together in a month. Nikkia desperately wanted to stop the direction of their argument.

What bothered her more, though, was that he had to keep protecting some fear of his own. Why is he scared of what's behind my mask? She had to ask, "What are you afraid of?"

"I can't stand people that answer a question with a question."

"I don't want to fight. I know you love me." Nikkia touched the mask. "And this makes you feel powerless." For some reason, she knew this was a good estimate of his feelings.

"Only when I have to look at it."

"But isn't that what matters now, that it's between us?"

He softened his tone. "What would you feel like if _your_ words didn't influence me? If I went ahead and did what I pleased even if it pushed us apart."

"Aren't you doing what you want with your life?"

"I'm trying to build a future for us."

"That's what I'm fighting for."

"I'm not away for a month."

"You never once visited."

"My interviews took place on weekends. I can't revolve my life around your politics. I don't ask you to revolve your life around my work."

"You don't. That's true."

"And do you expect our finances to remain the same? You want children. They'll need daycare, clothes, college." When she made a motion to stop him he continued, "At the very least we'll need a bigger apartment. You think that's going to happen if I just drop everything and chase around after you? If I don't hustle, I'm out of the business."

"I only tried to hush you because something else is happening to us tonight," Nikkia said.

While they talked the slow summer darkness closed the scene beyond the windows. The next time Nikkia looked at the big glass panes she saw scattered orange-yellow lights.

They had not touched. Are we as separate as those lights, Lawrence and I? A new fear grew within her. The longest silence came while they looked at each other. Nikkia thought of the summer project and the separated comrades. They're dispersed, too, she breathed a deep breath. Their windows shine no brighter than other lights of the city. I can't tell where they are tonight.

"I missed you," he said.

That took her by surprise. She knew she should answer him, but a tightening inside her told her she hadn't missed him. She had wanted to feel close to him in Boston, and after their phone conversations she had felt more distant. He was right in reminding her that she was the one who had chosen to go away. What did she expect? That they would clasp together again like magnets. Like lovers?

"Can I light the candles?" she asked. "It's getting dark."

Without waiting for him, Nikkia lit one candle, and as the match went out, lit the remaining candle off the other. The flames merged and became larger when wax fell on the second wick. She stared at the single flame and then put the second candle down opposite the first.

"Why aren't you saying anything?" The shadows and the light played in the cleft that ran alongside Lawrence's mouth. The fullness of his lips made Nikkia want to press the soft skin with her fingers as she came closer. But her own tight stomach muscles kept her from finding an answer to his words. She sat on the floor below him, but silently.

Finally she said, "I missed you, too." It's not a

lie, she told herself immediately. Who did I miss in Boston if it wasn't him? He's been the only man I've known for eleven years. Who is the person for me to love if it isn't the man sitting right in front of me? He isn't make-believe. He isn't committed to anyone else. I must love him. "I love you."

The words frightened her. Perhaps because it's so quiet after our argument, she reasoned. She glanced up at the table where the two candle flames burned without motion. Did she love him for the security of this apartment and the table setting? The thought made her tight stomach cold. She reached for him. The skin of his leg was warm.

"I love you," Lawrence said. But he didn't move to kiss her. His hand rested on top of her hand. She moved her own hand further up his leg. His thighs were spread slightly in the chair, and her hand became warm under the silk robe. She felt that she would rather have kissed him, but was too afraid now that he would lose all desire on having to touch her mask. Her hand made larger, carressing circles on one thigh and then the other and up further, his hand remaining on hers. His penis was already hard and erect. She removed the silk with her other hand so that her mouth could make him wet.

She was cold and hot at the same time as she rose beside the chair and his hands opened and stretched the elastic of the leotard pants and slid them down the sides of her legs. She put her knees on either side of him on the chair. The leather was cold from the air conditioning. His hands were hot on her buttocks and his fingertips warm reaching into her from the back. And still they did not kiss as he pushed up the top of her outfit over her breasts and held her to him and pressed her buttocks again.

She was moist and close around him and did not need his hands to move her on his penis. The thought went completely through her that she was so very moist. Her body was ready, as always. She held his head and circled his mouth with the nipple of her breast, but her own head remained carefully above his. She couldn't see anything but points of light out the windows now.

The windows reflected the candles. Nikkia felt the inside of her press tighter around him; the swaying of her head brought different lights to the windows. Smaller then larger ripples in the glass became opaquely black and shiny as obsidian. She shivered. The tightness in her stomach released a familiar tug that told her that pleasure would rise higher within her in only a matter of time.

Nikkia didn't think about his head in her arms or her nipples growing even harder from the cold air conditioning. Her eyes were wide open above the scent of his soft full hair. She saw the two candles reflected in the windows. Their flames were cold and still. Her pulse began as a thrust and a wave and gripped her pelvis and his hard penis as he pressed her again and again. The rush of his soundless breath told her they had come together. It was too easy, Nikkia thought, and the uncomfortable fear came up stronger now that the orgasm was over.

She tried to make her body relax in the cold, but even the silk of his robe was cool now. The table setting shone as calmly as before, as though nothing had happened. Staring at the candles she took his hand to her clitoris and rubbed his finger slowly back and forth while she blinked at the candles to take away the tears of excitement. Another sharp, thrilling orgasm seemed to pierce her heart because the candles were so bright they made her eyes water and blink as one thought broke: I have become a slut.

As soon as she felt it was decent to speak, Nikkia said, "I'm cold."

He opened up his robe and wrapped her in it, his arms around her. That was a little better, but her feet were outside and icy. She made no move, as if to punish herself for wanting sex without closeness.

Gradually, there came to them both a pungent warming smell of baking chicken. "I can't believe I'm so hungry," said Nikkia, amazed at her body's healthy response. "Can we turn down the air conditioning now?"

"I'm comfortable," Lawrence said.

She went over to the thermostat. "How 'bout a compromise?"

Chapter 16

He had not been back from Boston a full day when Russell felt the pressure to return to his old UPS job. Last night on the drive home, he and Pat had made plans for her to try to get overtime work in preparation for their move. He was to spend his time organizing their belongings and beginning to pack up winter clothing in boxes. But when Russell woke, with Pat gone to work, money problems pushed their recent plans out of his mind.

The first of the month bills were stacked on the corner table by the door. He and Pat took turns writing the checks, and August was his turn. The Brooklyn Gas Company bill carried winter heating charges. The phone bill was high from calls to Boston. His mother had sent a stamped envelope for their late last month's payment on her loan to them. There was no money until Pat got paid in two weeks.

It was Monday, a new work week. The children still slept after their late night ride back from picking up their father in Boston. Pat had already left for the hospital. Russell sat on the couch and through the open window saw cars pulling away from the curb. He heard the rapid steps of people on their way to work. Dirty laundry waited in two baskets for him to start a wash. The rough upholstery of the couch began to itch him underneath his warming skin. Yet he could not move.

Nor was it easy to sit still and listen, between the sound of each passing car, to the whine of the electric clock. The motor made what seemed to him to be a sick buzzing sound every ten seconds. Sometimes the buzz happened more often than that, as though the clock might stop altogether.

Already he could see that the sky had hazed over so he couldn't tell if there was a sun behind the low smog. The activity of comrades in Boston that had pushed him like a spring those July and early August mornings left him now with only memories. The polluted sky, the whine of the clock. The irritating texture of the couch and the thoughts of bills pressed him from without and from within until he squirmed.

At the far end of the couch was a pillow that he had taken from the bed, half awake, when he got up to keep Pat company. He reached for it with a drifting motion. The cotton pillow case felt fresh and smooth, the pillow soft, under his head. He turned his face to let his cheek rest on the cool surface, and his eyes closed.

He dreamed of dressing for work in the brown UPS uniform. The buttoning of the shirt one by one let his mind sleep. He looked for a shoe. He found it at the bottom of the laundry. Then he sorted the laundry, light and dark, and put it in the wash of his dream.

Later that morning Russell gathered the children, went down to the UPS and found they would take him back. He felt a strange sense of gratitude. The place seemed like home. The children and he made a day of it, seeing where daddy works. They all met two of the guys that had worked his shift, Moberly and Johnson, who were covering for the day shift of August vacations. "C'mon back to the barn, kids, and see where we load the trucks."

Russell had not gotten along so well with Moberly, whose own children were grown--in their middle twenties--but still lived at home. He seemed to Russell always to be complaining about their lack of responsibility. Yet he continued to shoulder their car insurance and his younger son's two children. His frame, over six feet, was stooped so that he appeared shorter, and older. Russell didn't like the fact that Moberly gossiped about his fellow workers. Here he was still at the barn, though, his shift over, and Moberly was taking the time to show Russell's children around.

The drivers weren't back yet from their routes, but there were several of the brown trucks parked around the barn. Moberly found hats for the kids and let them play on a truck. Russell found himself telling Moberly about Boston.

"Yer nuts to come back here, then," said Moberly. "For the little bit more money . . . ." His blue eyes squinted even in the dim light of the loading barn, and he looked sideways at Russell. "Get out while the gettin's good. You got your family behind you."

Perhaps for the first time, Russell felt the unhappiness of this man. What did Moberly have to look forward to? He finally understood why he hadn't liked him. The gossip was secondary. He'd even stopped doing it around Russell after Russell had made it clear he wouldn't tolerate it. Russell knew that twenty years from now he was terribly afraid of becoming Moberly.

"What else can I do? I'm used to working nights." Russell shrugged. "We need the cash."

"You'll never get out from under," said Moberly. "Just accept that."

In this last month, Russell had forgotten about the pessimism he had grown to live with working the night shift. "We have to clear up _some_ bills," he insisted.

"There'll be others to take their place," said Moberly half-jokingly. "There's always something."

Russell hated that phrase. He didn't want to think beyond a few weeks from now. He was already tuning out Moberly.

"School clothes," said Moberly, unaware that he was now talking to himself.

A flood of thoughts about his children starting school in Boston made Russell's mouth dry. How could he have been in such a hurry, he thought, to push his children into a racist situation. They, too, would be bused, along with the black children of their new neighborhood, to a school where none of them would be welcome. Maybe the boys would be OK, he considered, with the exception of Jerry. Tammy. He felt very protective of Tammy. How would she feel when they called her 'nigger lover?' Would she have to fight no matter what she said?

"Always something," said Russell aloud.

He spent everything but the subway tokens he had on ice cream cones for the kids, and for himself. For a brief moment he forgot everything but the hard, chewy, cold chocolate.

"We want to go to the beach now," Jerry insisted.

"We didn't have a beach in Pittsburgh," Al reminded Russell. "You promised we'd go soon's you got back."

Marvin joined in, cagely, "It's free."

Russell wanted to get home and managed to put the beach trip off until Sunday. It came to him that by working he was giving up some of the quieter week days at the beach. Tammy and the boys would have him there all week long! Well, he figured, they'd just have to be satisfied with a day here and there.

Pat greeted them at the door. "I just got home myself. I've signed up to work some double shifts. This is a perfect time because of vacations. I start tomorrow."

A dull numbness hit Russell's stomach. He felt the same as he had when as a child, caught with a ten dollar bill from his father's wallet, he pretended he had found it on the street. There was nowhere to hide. "We went down to UPS, just to see what was going on. And guess what?"

"No you didn't." Her face was hard.

"Well, I saw the bills, and we couldn't pay a one!" Russell went to the little table and picked them up, as proof.

The children sensed an argument.

Al said, "I'm going over to Ronnie's."

"Can Jerry and me play the tape recorder? We'll do it soft," asked Marvin.

Only Tammy remained. "Play cards." She reached for the bills. She was thinking of the game where she and her dad matched the previous months' bills with the new ones.

"Not today," said Russell, and put down the bills. Lifting her over to the couch, he gave Tammy her Raggedy Andy doll.

"You were supposed to start packing," Pat stated. "We made a decision last night."

"I completely forgot when I saw the bills. I'm sorry," he added.

"Well you're just going to tell them that you won't go back. Period."

"I can't do that."

"There's no law. I certainly can't tell my job that I can't do the overtime I've committed myself for."

"It's the same thing. You can't expect me to sit by and watch you work."

"Who's going to take care of the children?"

"I didn't know for sure you were going to be working sixteen hours a day."

"That was our decision," Pat sighed. "Well now you know."

"You're being unreasonable. Maybe I agreed last

night to moving. But I've thought it through. We can't afford it now. Not with moving expenses on top of bills."

"You didn't think the bills were automatically going to stop, did you?"

"Always something," Russell muttered.

"What did you say?"

"Nothing."

"You did, too, say something. I resent your going off on your own when we had an agreement. It's like you retreat into your own little world when I leave the apartment, as if I never existed." Pat walked back and forth in her white clogs, from the rug to the wooden floor and back again. "And now you're mumbling so I can't understand what you're saying."

"There's always something!" he shouted. "First I get laid off, and then we move to Brooklyn. And then we decide to move again. I think we ought to save for it, like my mother said. They never did anything until they had the money for it. Maybe you like living hand to mouth."

"If we waited for us to afford to move here, we'd still be in Pittsburgh. It's a good thing we moved. It's good you went to Boston, right?"

"You're making a lot of noise for the people downstairs," he said.

"Why is it," Pat asked, "that when you and I talk about your political work, you get so touchy. Like it's your private property."

He looked at Pat. She seemed so put-together to him with her hair in a french braid and her tunic top and pants uniform. She was not slim; she had big bones. But she was solid. Russell felt uncomfortable seeing her looking so trim, as he always had these past couple of years that he'd gained the weight. Today he felt ashamed, too, as if he'd been caught stealing money from her for candy: a fat little kid.

"I couldn't help going to UPS," he said. And as he said it he realized how hopeless he sounded. But it was the truth.

"What a crock." Pat stared flatly into his eyes. "You tell me you see the bills and your feet start walking out the door like a robot. The kids tell me you bought them ice cream with the last money you had. Does nothing pass through your brain these days? You see something, you go for it? Don't you stop to remember anything we talk about?"

He tried desperately to remember why he bought the ice cream. He had seen no ice cream cones on that block of Gould Avenue. Three hours since lunch they all felt hungry. The sun was blinding and made their skin prickle outside the dim cool hub. "It was hot." Russell said weakly, trying not to look at or to touch his stomach so as to bring it to the attention of them both.

"Don't you understand I could care less about the few dollars?" Pat seemed to be really trying to discover what was going on within him. "It's the whole trip I object to, and the fact that what I say doesn't make a dent with you."

"I went to Boston, didn't I? You wanted me to do that."

"Didn't you get a lot out of it? Didn't you start becoming involved again?"

"Our children weren't there," Russell protested. But even as he spoke he didn't know why he mentioned the children. "Your mother can't live with us in Boston as easily as she did this past month here in Brooklyn."

"I can work nights. I thought we'd settled that. Something else is bugging you, and I wish you'd tell me what it is."

"I think I'm afraid for them up there."

"I don't get it," said Pat. "We come to a decision, and then you slide back into your shell. You never mentioned our children; you just up and went to UPS like an old horse." Pat clapped her hand over her mouth. "I'm sorry."

"You're not sorry. You're just hurt I didn't talk with you first." But Russell felt the pain of her words. He did indeed feel old, and out of shape, and some great weight pressed him further into the corner of the couch. He tried to joke. "Maybe I can't hear you because of my shell."

"You're making me angry," she said. "There's something going on with you, and you're trying to pin the blame on the children."

"You're wrong," he said, but he didn't know exactly how. The more Russell thought about it, going to his old job seemed the right thing to do. He didn't have to wait for them to process applications; they had his physical; he knew the guys he liked, and those he didn't like. He might as well be comfortable. Between the softness of the couch and the weight of many things, Russell settled and watched Pat grow more upset.

"I tell you what's happening with me. I tell you every little thing about the job." Pat walked back and forth from the kitchen to the couch and away again as if she, too, wanted to leave for somewhere and do something on her own. She was probably tired of supporting him, Russell imagined; perhaps she saw herself as the work horse in the family. But to him she didn't look old or even tired after working all day. Her jaw line was prominent and firm. "I deserve to know what's on your mind, don't you think?"

"I don't know myself," Russell said.

"But you went back to the job. To do that you had to know <u>something</u>. Pat sat beside him on the couch. "You didn't even call to tell me."

Russell wanted to tell her he had tried to phone so she wouldn't be quite so angry. Then he quickly considered saying UPS had called him. But he wasn't a good liar. He didn't plan ahead for her response. She would find out in a minute. Her closeness demanded an answer. But he had none. "You would have told me not to go," he said.

"Absolutely."

"Don't you see, how was I to know you'd be working overtime? I couldn't see the harm."

"Just who do you think is going to watch the children?"

"We'll get someone. It can't cost a paycheck." Russell began to smile. He smiled when he was embarrassed. With the smile came a sense of relief that made him grin more.

"Very funny. Perhaps you just thought my mother would stay on."

"I didn't think you'd be working overtime so soon. You didn't tell me that." As if to get even he said, "You didn't call <u>me</u>."

Pat's response was immediate. "But I can call my mother. And I'm going to call my mother." Her eyes darted to the kitchen phone. She knew that he was aware it was only a threat.

But he could tell he had made her angrier. "I'll just let UPS know I can't start tomorrow." That was also an empty challenge. He didn't mean a word of it.

Pat's gaze rested on the telephone now. "There's the phone," she said.

"I can't tell them I won't start."

"I'm not backing down on my overtime. I have to face those people who'll be going on vacation."

"I'm not staying home and twiddling my thumbs."

"You didn't give one thought to the children."

"You didn't care how they'd react to another move."

"How do you think they react seeing their father a zombie?"

"Forget Boston entirely."

"And watch you rot away?"

"Why don't you just let me lead my own life?"

"Your own life! Your very own?"

"Well, the <u>children</u> are ours, then."

"Are you telling me you can shelter them from reality?" "I'm telling you I don't want to put them in with those racists."

"They've had fights with school kids here, black as well as white."

"I know what I'm getting them into. Boston is worse."

"You said yourself the white kids were learning a lot up there about integration."

"It's not the white kids I'm afraid of."

"The ROAR adults, then."

"No, goddamn it. We'll fight them like we been doing."

"So, we're going where there's high-paying day jobs AND where you've been organizing. Where you've turned back into the guy I married."

"You go, then. I'm not ready. Won't be ready for a year or so."

"So you're going back on your word."

"If it makes you feel better to say that."

"I'm going to say even more." Pat's face was red. She got up and threw the couch pillow across the room at the lamp. It broke. "I'm calling Coralee. I'm calling Nikkia. And I'm going to talk with Zack."

Pat left the room without another word. Russell slowly got up off the couch and began picking up the pieces of the lamp. Of all the things Pat had said, he was most ashamed that she would call Coralee. Zack, he thought that maybe Zack would understand his position. But Nikkia. What would she say? For sure, it would be worse than this argument with Pat.

Two days later, Pat's mother came back to live with them. Though she slept on the couch, Russell had the impression she spent the night lying between him and Pat. She was very friendly to the kids and barely spoke with him.

x x x

"You got to finish what you started up here," Coralee told him bluntly. "Fay has been crying for you."

"I miss all your children, and you, too." said Russell. "Believe me, I wish I could be in two places at once." Russell knew the real truth was that he was overcome by the needs of his own children this summer now that he was back. The beach. Tammy and the boys needed to get outdoors. He couldn't think about the two households at one time.

Coralee. He imagined her in a bright, full dress. Her voice brought her close like a technicolor dream. Their apartment, with its beige sleep-away couch, seemed drab to his eyes while he spoke to Coralee. Yet he was used to it, he thought, half-consciously. It seemed to hold him steady. He watched his mother-in-law move through the apartment while he talked. Florence in her sleeveless housedress. Seeing her work, he felt more bound. For he knew she resented being here.

"Forest and I have been looking for an apartment for you in the neighborhood, and I think we've found something big enough."

"Stop!" Russell realized immediately that his shouting wouldn't halt the situation. But maybe it would end the conversation, he hoped. "I'll be there, but I can't say when." The indefiniteness reassured him at the same time as it made him more afraid.

x x x

Zack did seem to understand. "There's no rush," he said. "Of course we need your leadership up here, but nobody should panic."

"Pat seems to think I'm hopeless."

"Well, she's a take-charge person. She goes about things in a different way than you. You wouldn't be good as a hospital nurse. You don't move as fast. But you have your own speed; you'll get here. I have every confidence."

I wish I did, thought Russell. I only wish I was as sure. Already the three days of loading at UPS had made his bones heavy. The thought of moving himself, let alone his family and the furniture to another city, seemed out of the question.

x x x

The day Nikkia came to see him Russell felt unprepared. He had never been comfortable in her presence. She was too attractive. She reminded him of all the times he sat in Junior High School homeroom near a girl named Iva Irwin.

Iva looked like the country with her green eyes and freckles. She never wore makeup like the other girls did. Russell lost himself in her Shirley MacLaine smile with a crinkly nose. He felt too inadequate to ever approach her. She looked too perfect, like Nikkia.

Nikkia's smokey complexion needed no makeup, either. Now, with her mask of bandages removed, her beauty made him so ill at ease that he wasn't sure where to sit in his own house. So they stood together in the kitchen: Nikkia with one foot propped on the side of her other leg, her arms folded. Seeing the sinews of Nikkia and her readiness for life, Russell couldn't bear the contrast of his own flabby stomach. He wished Pat were there, to add her solid flavor.

Then he noticed that Nikkia's full lips were a natural lavender color. Russell felt hypnotized and was sure he would have believed anything she said. But Nikkia only asked him questions. "What do you do? What do you like about UPS?"

"It's busy," Russell answered readily. "I like not having time to think about myself. There's always a big rush. Unfortunately, the company cares more about saving time than about the packages getting there in one piece." He went on. "Right when I get there, we concentrate on the hot sort . . ."

"The what?" Nikkia laughed. He loved to watch her laugh, for she gave in to her laughter. And he was drawn closer to her.

"The hot sort is for all the tractor trailers

that go to trains, the midway points like the Meadowlands. Some drivers have to be in Connecticut by midnight. After they leave, we begin the midnight sort. That's for the brown trucks, the ones everybody sees on the streets." Russell looked out the window as if expecting to see a UPS truck.

"What's your job. You did the loading?"

"After three months of loading they made me supervisor. I guess that was because I can tell guys what to do in such a way that they want to do it. I don't ride them."

"Was it hard to quit to go to Boston?" She tilted her head, trying hard to understand him.

"Not really. 1 thought it would be just for a month. Probably you're curious as to how I could say I'd agree to move to Boston."

"No. I almost did it myself, but for different reasons." Nikkia paused, her full, lavender lips open. Russell wondered if she was aware that a person standing next to her could want to dive between her open lips and disappear.

But Nikkia was focused on Russell's life, and her next question partly revealed her own story, so as to make his easier for him. "I thought I could leave behind my personal life and become a part of the Boston work," she said. "So I can understand. You found, though, that you had to return to something that had been a part of your life. Even though it may not have been the best job for you."

"You know, I practically ran all the way to UPS with the kids, like a dog following a scent!"

"I understand. I ran to Lawrence's apartment--rather, to my apartment--thinking that was where he was going to be, and I was in such a hurry . . ."

"I didn't even stop to decide whether it was right. I didn't think about our talk the night before. I guess I didn't _want_ to think. So when Pat questioned me about it, I had no answer for her. She was right. I really am a jerk."

Nikkia ignored his last comment. "When you were in Pittsburgh, how were your wages as a steel worker?"

"Now there's a job where the hourly rate is deceiving. It was relatively high, as jobs go, but more dangerous, too. We'd look at them ingots and know how much they were worth and how much me and the other workers'd been ripped off.

"I admit, I was bringing home enough money to cover our expenses. Pat didn't have to work. The boys were really small, and it would have been crazy to pay for day care for all four kids. Then later she started working a few weekends, but I was still . . . ."

"The main breadwinner?"

"Isn't that a stupid expression if you ever heard one?" Russell started laughing for what seemed the first time in a long time.

Nikkia laughed but didn't give in to the humor as before. Instead she waited for him to continue.

"I was happy," Russell told her. "I was always in trouble with the boss for instigating this or that. Guys would come over after work to talk. We'd plan what to do next to the foreman. I'd cook spaghetti, and they'd call up their wives or girlfriends. We'd have a party in the middle of the week! And then a whole lot of us got laid off." Russell's eyes drifted with his thoughts. "Some guys didn't want me to get in touch with them after awhile. Then we had to go someplace else to find work . . . ."

"And you found yourself in a new town, with your wife being the breadwinner."

"I never was aware I didn't want her to work full time," said Russell. He reached for a can of ground coffee and pointed, questioning Nikkia, to the percolator. When Nikkia nodded, he put water into the percolator and went on, "I just went and got me a job nights so I could cover the homefront for her, for us."

"It sounds like you felt guilty as shit for making the family move and your wife earning more than you." Nikkia reminded him, "When we were kids, only one parent usually worked. Times are changing to where every family has to have both working, not just yours."

"You're right," Russell acknowledged. He stopped talking for a moment to measure coffee into the metal basket. "Look at your, situation, too. A black woman gets a job in a ballet company because of the changing times of civil rights. So now you feel equal to Lawrence and want to keep working even though he certainly earns enough money . . . ."

"There's more to it than my not wanting to be just someone's wife. I want to be there socially and to organize. It's hard for him to understand that."

"He hasn't come around to anything we've done in the last six months," said Russell.

"But I had to run back to him," Nikkia reminded herself.

"And after I ran back to UPS, I felt like celebrating," Russell chuckled. "I bought everyone ice cream, and I couldn't help that, either!" He patted his stomach.

"I couldn't help being intimate with Lawrence," said Nikkia in a whisper. "Even though something between us is gone." Her soft eyes filled with tiny red lines, and Russell saw a rim of water that never turned into tears. He put his arms around her and laid one hand on her head.

Nikkia breathed a long breath. "I hadn't meant to say that," she admitted.

Russell was silent. Then he stepped back to look at her. "Listen, I've been wondering how a fighter like you can stay so loyal to a guy who's so comfy in his own little niche."

"He's not so satisfied," defended Nikkia. A knot formed in her chest.

"Now wait. Are you both changing so that you can become more fulfilled? Or is he trying to become more comfortable and you're accommodating yourself more toward him? Which way are you going?"

Nikkia recognized that the knot in her chest seemed to rock back and forth, as if it had a weight. Then cool, damp air rushed from her lungs. "Oh, you're right. I know he's bad for me."

"Maybe I asked you that because being back at my old job isn't making me feel as good as I thought it would," said Russell. "The fellows I know best are on vacation. I'm working with this down-in-the-mouth guy who distrusts everyone. I'm too tired to go to club meetings. I can't even read a paper. Every ounce of energy I have I give to my kids."

"What is it you're giving them?" Nikkia prodded.

"Not a very good example, I'm afraid. When you started talking about my last few years, it got me to thinking. I was giving my kids more when I was happier. The time I spent with them was less, but better." Russell poured their coffee and then sat down heavily on a kitchen chair. "What worries me is what they will think of a father who makes his wife work."

Nikkia reminded him, "You're saying that, not

them."

"We'd be spending so much of our money on the move, for me."

"What's money for?"

"I'm disrupting the lives of the children."

"Temporarily."

"It's like I'm a quitter."

"You're following a decision to be more of a leader."

"All right. All right. So why haven't you quit Lawrence?" Russell felt he owed Nikkia this much.

"I can't."

"Because he hasn't broken off with you?"

"We've made a decision, too. To get married."

"What do your friends--like Bonita--think of that?"

"I can't compare her choice of men. She's five years younger."

"I didn't ask who she would choose. What does she, as _your_ friend, think of Lawrence?"

"They argue. I don't think she trusts him. And her boyfriend, Saleem, doesn't seem to like him for some reason." Nikkia stopped, remembering them hinting her first day back that she stay awhile with them rather than rush home to Lawrence. "What are you saying?"

"What're _you_ saying?" Russell asked.

"That I've changed? That Lawrence is changing?" Once again, Russell saw that Nikkia's eyes carried water, but she didn't cry. Instead she looked at her coffee cup.

Russell no longer wanted to protect her. Rather, he felt that they shared similar problems. "What are you going to do?" he asked.

"I don't know. When I came over here, I intended to convince you to work in Boston. Now I'm up in the air about my own future. I only know things don't stay the same, and I can't pretend that we didn't have this talk."

"I didn't say anything."

"You said plenty. Enough to help me see that Lawrence and I are moving in opposite directions. It all seems so obvious now. I thought he and I were going somewhere all right, but together instead of separately. It's hard to know when you're on the inside."

"You're telling me. I have trouble looking over my whole life, and it's tough enough living it!" Russell sighed. "I go back to my old job without thinking twice, and suddenly I'm further back from where I started. Pat is mad at me. My mother-in-law is living with us. And I never see my kids, which was the whole point. I was holding off on moving to Boston for them!"

"You thought."

"OK. I was scared. If I wasn't making money I wasn't any kind of a father. No kind of a man, huh?"

"You're one step ahead of me. You've got Boston." Nikkia thought suddenly of Norberto. His face appeared in a floating image, like a balloon. She couldn't find a resting spot for him in her mind. Nor any place for him to quiet the desire in her body. Certainly not in the air of this poorly-lit Brooklyn apartment. Still she did not cry, although she had to confide in Russell, "I've got no other love."

Chapter 17

"Why in hell are you getting married?" Coralee had not told Nikkia who she was when she called, but Nikkia recognized her voice. "I'm worried about you, Girlfriend."

"Don't be," said Nikkia. "You taught me something in Boston, watching you, I'm sure I can live with or without a man!"

"We're talking about Lawrence and you, not you and nobody." Coralee laughed softly. "You won't ever have to worry about Mr. Nobody."

"I learned that I don't have to have someone at home to cheer me on," Nikkia explained. "That was an important lesson for me."

"That sounds lonely. Rudy was very supportive of me. You wouldn't <u>rather</u> to have someone who shared your views?"

"I can't have everything in one man. Lawrence has a life of his own. I can do what has to be done at that hospital and spend time after work with people. He's not going to expect me to be home cooking dinner. How many men understand that?"

The other end of the phone was silent for a moment. "Rudy cooked better than me. Day and night, there was always a pot of somethin' smelling good. I could bring anyone home and we could pull up a chair in the kitchen, and it would be homey." Coralee stopped, as if waiting for another memory. "Then Rudy would find some excuse to leave the kitchen. He could find things to keep him away from meeting people. I didn't want to be bothered with most of the house stuff. We made excuses for each other."

"I think Lawrence and I could work out an agreement like that."

"I'm telling you it's not so great to start out on separate paths."

"But we're managing so far."

"So long as you don't interfere with his work."

"What do you mean?"

"You told me, when you were up here. Lawrence wants to get ahead."

"It's only natural, when you think like he does that he's making a way for more blacks to follow."

Without the pause of a second, Coralee said, "Of course the truth is just the opposite. There's only more room at the top for daydreams."

Nikkia could not answer right away. She knew again a tightening in her chest. "But he's not a bad person."

"I didn't say he was."

"I can live with him, with that."

"What I want to know is," Coralee asked, "Why do you want to?"

"We go way back, a long way back. I don't know anyone else who has travelled that road with me." Maybe, she thought, sadly Coralee is so used to being alone by now that she can't understand the fear.

The sadness in Nikkia's voice came through. "Child," said Coralee, "What place was you at when you started that road?"

"You know I was dancing," Nikkia felt somewhat annoyed.

"Lawrence kept you company in this, he was your partner?"

"You have different partners; he was hardly ever my partner. You don't see, the ballet is a whole world."

"You liked being on stage?"

"Not me." This question Nikkia could answer from what she felt was a solid place inside her, a place of no fear. "I liked the dancing."

"I remember you told me how much about it you didn't like: the jealousies, the being scared of injuries, the being a pet poodle of the liberal rich. Doesn't leave much room to like the dancing."

"You have people all around you afterwards telling you they liked your dancing."

"You could have been a star, so why didn't you?"

"You know why." Nikkia was annoyed now. "I learned through the civil rights movement that voting still results in unemployment and a premature death for too many blacks. I couldn't keep dancing and pretending that life was going to be better for my brothers and sisters."

"And for Lawrence?"

"He was more practical. There're even fewer positions for men in the ballet."

"You mean he needs to earn money. Then it follows that he's got to be one of the best black writers and editors in the business?"

"Well, I guess he could do other kinds of work. But then he wouldn't be himself."

"And this himself, it's OK with this himself that you have another whole life, that you don't share with him?"

"He's worried. That I'll get hurt."

"You did get hurt; what did he say?"

The evening with Lawrence came back to Nikkia. He had said all the right things, Nikkia remembered. But he could not kiss her with her face in bandages. Their love making had been more separate than their dancing ever was. She might as well have been alone. But still, she thought, wasn't that better than not doing it at all? "He said, he is worried about me."

"Not concerned enough to come up and see you once during a month."

"He couldn't. He had business in Washington."

"I see."

"He does what he has to do. I do what I have to do. But we can live together. How many men can you live with?"

Coralee didn't respond for a moment. "Did you ever think, there're maybe millions of men more compatible out there?"

Nikkia smiled; Coralee certainly had a different way of looking at things. "You never remarried with any of them."

"The ones old enough for me are too set in their ways. But you, you have the whole field!"

Nikkia was thinking, we have our past, me and Lawrence. And if the past is not so important, then today we can go to the ballet together and see the same things. And if we hardly ever go, why, then, "We have our commitment to each other. And you just don't walk away from a commitment."

Coralee interrupted her at that point. "Do you have a date yet?"

"A date?"

"For the wedding ceremony?"

"Why. . . no. But it's soon. Funny, he didn't

talk about the date. And we talked about the date before I went to Boston. In fact, it couldn't be soon enough for him before I went to Boston."

"Do you think he's waiting to see how your face comes out?"

"No!" Now Nikkia found herself very angry at Coralee. "He's not like that. It doesn't matter. I'm not dancing. We're not on stage!" She wished she could shake Coralee's shoulders. "He's not that kind of a person."

"I didn't say he was. I'm only asking you questions."

Nikkia realized that Coralee was being as pushy as her mother had been. Maybe that was why she was getting upset. Nikkia tried to remember Lawrence's face when he saw her bandages. Was he concerned that she could be ugly? Nikkia was very unsure.

She tried to calm herself. Coralee was probably wrong about Lawrence. In fact, suddenly, Nikkia realized that this call was probably costing Coralee money she didn't have. "I appreciate that you called me," she said.

"I care about your being happy, Honey."

Nikkia heard Coralee's warmth. She felt now as if she were standing next to her. Coralee did care. That was the whole reason for the call. Though it had hurt, and she still had no answers, Nikkia trusted Coralee's probing of her. As a woman and as a comrade. "I love you, Coralee. Thanks."

"We'll see you in two weeks. When we have the big rally to turn in the signatures."

"Oh, you're right! I did remember to ask for that weekend off. And the weekend two weeks after that when we want to be there for the first day of school. I think my supervisor is scared of me right now after our picket lines. She gave me both weekends that I asked for."

"Speaking of your job, your friends on the job. Bonita was just up here. In fact, she's who said I might call you. I'd been wanting to anyway."

"Hmmmmm." Nikkia realized she hadn't talked with Bonita since Bonita got back yesterday from a follow-up weekend in Boston. So Coralee and Bonita must have got their heads together . . .

"Her and Saleem, they've got a surprise for you."

"They're getting married?"

"I promised I wouldn't tell."

"They're pregnant!"

"No fair guessing."

"All right. All right. I'll see you. I'll see you in two weeks!"

"I can't wait."

Immediately Nikkia dialed Bonita and Saleem's number. She had to talk with a friend. Either of them would do. There was no answer. She dialed a number she hadn't called in three years, but she knew it still. Jeff's sister, Iona, answered.

"He's no longer living here, Nikkia, but I'm sure he won't mind if I give you his new number. He's living with Earl Klein presently." She makes it sound like she hopes it's only for a short time, Nikkia thought as she dialed the number. She anticipated Jeff's voice.

"Darling!" And then, briefly. "I'd have throttled my sister if she hadn't given you our phone number."

"I think she knew that," Nikkia bantered. It had been so long since she had spoken with Jeff that she forgot there was always a hint of a game in their conversation.

"You have to see our apartment," said Jeff. "It's me, it's us, it's we!"

Nikkia laughed. How Jeff could turn on the affectations whenever he chose! He did it often when he was in a good mood, and today his good spirits were contagious.

"There is art in every corner that Iona would never allow. I'm collecting artifacts of the pre-Columbian period. There's an absolutely gorgeous vase that we suspect is of the fourth century. It's up for auction on the seventeenth at the Midtown Gallery, and I must have it. I don't care how much it is, the values of green that he has created--whoever the artist is--are priceless. You must see it to believe it. You don't know how I've missed you!"

"Jeff. I just want to see you. I've got to talk about . . . I've got to talk about Lawrence with you."

"You're perfect for each other, darling. How many heterosexual men are there who love the ballet as much as you do?"

"That's just it, I don't, anymore, Jeff. Working in the hospital I feel so removed from that whole scene."

"So come over and talk, right this minute. I've missed you like crazy. Just because I haven't called doesn't mean I haven't thought about you." Jeff caught his breath. "I've changed a lot since I saw you last. I mean, I'm the same, but my surroundings are a lot different."

Jeff insisted on his point, "That's what I'm trying to say about you and Lawrence. You can't change something you've been doing your whole life. You and Lawrence have each been dancers longer than you've been anything else! Radicals or no radicals!"

"Jeff, I'm a physical therapist now. I've been helping other people move their paralyzed limbs. I'm not dancing at all! I have changed!"

"I bet you do stretches every day. I'll bet you still walk like an angel stepping on flower petals."

"My feet are as messed up as they always were, if that's what you mean!" Nikkia teased. She thought to herself that she wasn't ready to admit to him that she still found herself doing exercises.

"I can remember the first time I saw you in Paris. I predicted your success. Was I wrong?"

"No, Jeff, you weren't wrong. You aren't wrong now. I'm the one who's out of kilter."

"Nonsense. You're still just caught up in the fad of being left wing. Everyone else who was out there during the Vietnam war has realized they've got to go back to the real world. For most people that means work, but not me!"

Nikkia had always liked the way Jeff joked about himself and his wealth. Money, too, she thought, was a game to him. That was at least better than taking it as seriously as the rest of his family. And Jeff wasn't hurting anyone. And neither, Nikkia mused, was Lawrence.

"Please come up and find out what you've been missing. Earl feels as if he knows you. Your picture is on my dresser!"

"Oh, Jeff. Of course I'll come." But it was odd, she thought as she walked down Seventh Avenue to the West Village apartment, how the conversation with Jeff had turned around. She was going to satisfy Jeff's need for her rather than to gain any insights at all into her and Lawrence. But she kept walking.

The visit with Jeff, like the telephone conversation with him, was unsettling. He still refused to look at her as anyone but the Nikkia he had known. It was as if he wanted to preserve her love for Lawrence so as not to arouse unaccountable feelings in himself. He was so happy in his new life.

Rather than ask questions, as Coralee had done, he shared stories of his new love and a very expensive bottle of champagne. But the bubbly feeling quickly evaporated in Nikkia. She decided to leave before getting annoyed with Jeff for not being able to listen, and she walked home earlier than planned.

It was a hot, beautiful hazy day, and yet already a few leaves had fallen off the New York City trees. Nikkia thought that the nights weren't cool, and yet the trees knew the season was changing. As always, she felt, the first leaves to hit the pavement are the most painful for me to see.

x x x

The next day at work there was no time for thoughts about Jeff, nor of anything outside Nikkia's patients. Administration in the nursing department, under which the physical therapy section came, obviously had decided to counterattack the leaders of the strike.

In engineering, the new contract had a provision which allowed the supervisors to change the workers' shifts. And they did, at random, to harrass. Clarissa, one of the strike leaders in dietary, was moved to the psych unit. In psych the kitchen staff had to cook in the kitchens on the unit and serve the patients. Clarissa's mother was mentally ill, and her supervisor knew that she couldn't face psychiatric patients. She cried that entire day.

Nikkia's new patient assignments consisted of a drug addict who had had a third stroke, a four hundred pound woman in spinal traction and an entire family who were victims of an apartment fire and required extensive therapy due to scarring tissue. After writing up care plans, Nikkia was transferred off these patients to seven others the next day. It was within the union contract.

"The patients are the ones getting the short end of it," said Nikkia to Jacmel, the aide in the coronary unit.

"And we too often get impatient with them,"

Jacmel agreed. "Take Sampson over there," he referred to the man with three strokes. "Why didn't he take better care of hisself, I figure, in that world out there? And then I get mad at <u>myself</u> for thinking that way."

Nikkia realized how she'd been annoyed with the patients who were so overweight. All her life she had worked to keep her own muscles in tone. Here in the hospital stayed many people never able to discipline themselves to a good diet. How could she undo those years of their having no exercise and eating the wrong foods?

So many people had physical problems that hurt their friendships and their love! Ads and popular magazines encouraged bad health and illusion, Nikkia knew. With a feeling of guilt, she recalled pictures of her and Lawrence which had appeared for months in <u>Jet</u> magazine. The articles made their lives into the love affair of a god and goddess.

Some of these very patients had probably gazed at their pictures and read about their highly publicized relationship. Nikkia realized that some of the patients probably had become jealous. The very idea made Nikkia feel no better.

Not until she saw Bonita at the end of that dreary Tuesday did Nikkia know the relief of sharing her day's experiences. Strolling outside the hospital, Bonita and Saleem walked together the way she and Lawrence used to walk, Nikkia noticed. Their arms draped on one another's hips, they moved loosely and closely. Nikkia had not spoken to them since she'd talked with Coralee last night. She wondered what news they might have. Bonita certainly didn't look pregnant. But then, at first, who did?

She wanted to be cheerful, so she wouldn't deflate their youthful good spirits. But the day had been hard. Nikkia had strained her back some way. Not working with heavy Mrs. Hausmann. She had done it while assisting Stephen Pilowski, whose limbs were frail. A little twist while leaning over the bed had caused a brief warning pain. And Nikkia was getting her period. Perhaps that's the reason my back hurts now, she reassured herself.

She greeted Saleem and Bonita, and tried to smile, "I think after a few more days I'll be ready for traction myself--in fact I'll welcome the rest!"

They walked away from the hospital. Nikkia suggested a stroll behind the branch library of the Jefferson Market, around the collective neighborhood garden. It was a triangular block, where Greenwich Avenue and Eighth Streets came together. Late summer bluebells, sunflowers and tiger lilies bloomed there. The unexpected loveliness of the communal effort never failed to lift Nikkia's mood. She decided not to ask what the future held for Saleem and Bonita; she would let them surprise her.

"You know that last weekend was Saleem's fifth trip up to Boston," said Bonita.

"Two hundred miles seems like nothing to you two," smiled Nikkia.

"Four hours is no time at all," Saleem stated.

"Go ahead and tell her," said Bonita.

"I've known you both for two years," said Saleem. "But not until I went to Boston with Bonita did I realize something. I loved Bonita even more when I was watching her talk with people. We went to that fucking supermarket--Blair's--on welfare check day, and she pushed harder than the rest of us to get shoppers to fight the price increases! Bonita comes alive!"

"We chased the manager. He ran into the refrigerator! Bonita closed the door on him!" After a day of work, Nikkia could see that Saleem was reinvigorated.

"And we're making progress." Saleem put his thumbs in his T-shirt in a proud gesture. "After that battle of Haymarket Square, the fascist pigs have stopped attacking."

Nikkia waited for him to finish.

"I joined the party up in Boston this weekend," Saleem said with a grin.

The news made Nikkia happy, and she hugged Saleem. But while she held him another feeling came from somewhere inside. She had the sensation that her own feet no longer stood on solid ground. Underneath her spread a quicksand of jealousy. She would never know the kind of bond that Saleem and Bonita shared. She, Nikkia, who had seldom known the twisted stab of wanting, felt it now.

There was something else, that Nikkia couldn't identify. Perhaps it came with the unsteadiness. Or triggered it. Yes! From Saleem's neck drifted the same scent of soap that Norberto used!

The quicksand below Nikkia turned into loneliness. Nikkia could hardly bear to hold the scent so closely. Behind Saleem, she noticed again the flowers. Their very beauty persuaded her to hold Saleem at arms' length so that she could get them both and the garden in her view.

"You're pale," Saleem said. "Don't worry, I know what I'm doing."

"Nothing you said could have surprised me more." That sounded inadequate to her, and Nikkia found one more thing to say. "All my confidence rests in you both."

x x x

Nikkia asked Lawrence to come over to talk. He said he was in the final draft of his article. Couldn't she wait until he was at a stopping point? No. She would come there. He couldn't spare more than an hour. Couldn't *it* wait. No. Perhaps it wouldn't take longer than an hour.

An hour, Nikkia thought, to discuss an eleven year relationship. Of course, he doesn't see the problems I do. He can't know that I'm thinking of ending this time we spend with each other. He will laugh. I'm not so sure I can bring this up and then drop it until the weekend. He won't be able to write if I do. But I can't wait four more long days.

"You've never been this eager before," he said. "That journey up to Boston was some aphrodesiac."

"You're a lousy mind reader." She looked crossly at the phone receiver as though it were his head.

"Sometimes you don't say what's on your mind," he countered. "What are you going to do when I go to Africa in October?"

"When did you decide to do that?"

"I just found out yesterday, but I was waiting until the weekend to tell you about it."

"Perhaps I can wait as well."

"That's more like it."

"What's more like it, that I should wait to talk?"

"I didn't want to come right out and tell you, but this notion that we can build a future on *your* comings and goings. . . You go to Boston when you choose. Now that you're back, you want to see me the moment it suits you."

She decided not to argue about going to his place. But she couldn't pretend he'd said nothing about this new assignment of his. "I'm not going with you to Africa."

"For five thousand dollars you might consider the trip."

"They're paying you five thousand dollars?"

"Do you see why I didn't want to get into a discussion until the weekend?"

Nikkia ran a finger over the telephone. How quickly dust collected, she thought. I should wait. His future and the African contract depend on how well he writes this article on the investment cycles. Maybe I'm an idealist: throwing away someone who loves me because he's a success in the bourgeois world? Do I expect him not to be as single-minded about his career? She couldn't answer herself, let alone Lawrence's question. "Sure. Talk with you later."

Nikkia hung up and then promptly called him back. "So what's the article about?" She had decided to listen to him before getting around to herself.

"It's to be on the biography of Nkrumah and the development of the third world nations."

Despite her resolve to hear him out, she found herself asking, "How can you write about someone who's selling out the people in his own country?"

"That's not a foregone conclusion. Neither one of us has been over there. You can't believe what you read in the U.S. papers; you of all people should understand that."

"They're praising him to the skies. Is that what you'll be doing?"

"Mine is going to be a balanced viewpoint."

"If you're writing about the man who has taken military aid from both the United States and the Soviet Union and used it to get the two major tribes fighting each other, how can you be balanced? He's half bad and the other half worse."

"These rivalries have been going on before he came to power. You had better learn your history." He corrected, "We both have a lot to learn, and I intend to put in my own opinion, however subtly. My ideas will be there, too."

"I've changed my mind," Nikkia said suddenly. "I must see you today."

"I never thought you weren't coming."

"I considered letting you work."

"Most of your conversation with me takes place in your own mind. Like our first night after a month apart when you were laughing and never told me why. That's one of your problems."

"That's exactly why I'm coming over."

She didn't bother to change from jeans and a sweatshirt. Lately, since the bandages were removed, Nikkia found herself looking in the mirror less and less. She didn't know if it was because she was more confident or less concerned about her appearance, or both. But she was out of the door one half a minute after she hung up the phone.

The way to Lawrence's seemed to go slowly this time. I was wrong to tell him he couldn't write an objective article, she thought. Here in my brain are two completely equal halves: he is part of my life; he is no part of my life. Lawrence and I move well together; we're going in opposite directions. I love him; I don't love who he is.

The elevator creeped, the muzak played low, and two men each wearing black loafers with tassles rode the elevator with Nikkia. She looked at their suits, and their neckties. Nikkia smiled to herself: they're going to a necktie party.

Their faces were different shades of bronze, and as the words necktie party swung in her head, she saw the boy in Mississippi hanging from the tree. She looked down at their manicured hands, and she thought of her father's broad, working hands.

Inside the soft fleece of her sweatshirt, her feet in springing sneakers, Nikkia was relaxed during the elevator ride. But as she pressed the round black button and heard the metallic cling of Lawrence's doorbell, her knees were shaking.

"Sweetheart," Lawrence was dressed in jeans, sweatshirt and moccasins. She saw that his Levis were as worn and wrinkled as her own. His arms were warm. Why had she worried, Nikkia asked herself. Everything was the same.

"Sorry if I sounded abrupt on the phone, but I'm trying to work through this second draft, and the interview with Allen-Spencer has got to sound smoother than what actually took place."

"You've put a lot of work into this Fortune magazine series." As she spoke, Nikkia was aware of two levels within her, one that spoke the words she felt Lawrence wanted to hear, and the other that remained deeper, and silent.

"It's the kind of work I've always wanted to do. I miss the exertion of the ballet, but you know, in a way this free-lancing is similar. You communicate with your audience, but still you work in such a way as to leave you free of actual contact. And in this business, I'm the director!"

Nikkia thought of her own daily contact with patients and how often her skin touched theirs. But what she said to Lawrence was, "You can do something they can't."

"You should see how poorly these financial wizards write. They're brilliant, but can barely use the English language. Some of them can't even speak with proper grammar."

Nikkia guessed that Lawrence had to develop a kind of arrogance to operate in a world where he was writing for people that earned five times what he did. In the hospital she herself was brought down a notch or two every day. There she was forced to realize that some of the people she was training in simple range of motion had been at one time stronger than she. On the job injuries and automobile accidents claimed the arms, legs and spinal cord of people who had run the cities' buses and subways. They had built the buildings and bridges and run the assembly lines. And now they lay flat on their backs.

Nikkia's imagination drifted above the image of subways and buses as she pictured New York City. On top of what her patients built rode the magic carpet of Wall Street investments. She pictured Jeff and Lawrence riding on that carpet, high above the buildings. She felt uncomfortable and tried to find common ground again. "I'll bet you find ways all the time to make fun of these guys shuffling their stocks and other worthless paper."

"It's serious business, and the competition is so fierce that you'd think of a jungle as having fewer daily casualties!" Lawrence laughed. "I get along best with the other black executives and ad men, naturally. We're just coming into our own and we're more articulate, often, than anybody out there. We're professional speakers and writers. We have to be."

Nikkia took a breath, "Where do I fit into your

new life?"

His eyes widened in genuine surprise. "Don't you know? Without you, none of the rest of my plans make any sense. You're the reason for my doing what I do."

"I think you do it for yourself mainly." Nikkia sat on the floor. She studied the movements of his body.

"Isn't everything we do for ourselves?" He swayed on his feet, weighing his point. "Don't you want a better world for you and your family?"

"It's going to happen by fighting for it, not by earning more money at the top."

"In the meantime, before this revolution, we have to live within the system."

"We have to live together, too," said Nikkia. "And I've been feeling further from you, even when we make love." She felt she had to say this. Seeing him flinch, though, she tried to explain. "I don't love what you do . . ."

"You love what an auto worker does, I suppose. A coal miner. That automatically makes a person more worthwhile, if he works for a boss." He stepped a pace toward Nikkia. "A grape picker--he's got two bosses! I suppose that makes him twice as good."

Nikkia stared at him. He couldn't know about Norberto! Did he know about the part of her that honored most workers beyond basic respect? She wondered. What she said was, "You're not the average professional writer. You wouldn't be the average . . . farmworker, or campesino. You've got a program." She continued to press him, "Your program is black nationalism."

"Then I have to be in the party for you to marry me." He came another step closer.

"Not necessarily."

"I have to work in the garment center."

"No." She felt herself retreating.

"I don't see any callouses on your hands."

Nikkia fought her need to snap back at him. She was determined to get to a level beyond petty attack. She went to what she knew best.

"We've been two separate people for months now. Maybe the last year."

"I don't notice that you've been pushing to move in here. You were going away to Boston with or without me."

"Let me put it another way." She was more determined than ever before. "I can't see myself going to cocktail parties with executives. You went to Washington and will have to cater to these business people. I found I couldn't lead the life of a dancer partly because of that. There are nice people. Jeff is a nice person. But I couldn't spend half my life entertaining them."

"We blacks laugh behind the backs of the white upper class."

"At the same time as you mimic their lives."

"I'm a writer. I'm never going to be rich."

"Look at this building. Look at the people you spend your time with."

"Most of my time is spent alone. I like it that way."

"That's another question. Being in Boston and Saleem's joining the party made me look hard at my whole life style as a communist. You and I are not pulling together, or even in the same direction."

"I would rather say that we're independent. I think it's healthy." He planted his feet wide apart. "I barely have time for politics, as you describe it. But what I do, I do for you, in the long run."

That was the second time he'd insisted that what he did was for her, she realized. She did not trust this altruism. "Neither of us should build our life around one person."

"You're going to live in a commune, I suppose?"

"Come on, you know I don't believe in utopias." She bit her lip. No more abstract discussion if she could help it! "Let me tell you what I do believe in. My best friend, Bonita, and her boyfriend, Saleem, live together. They split their incomes. He just joined the party. We don't share any of those things in common. Not a solitary one."

"Everyone is going to be just alike in your society. You'll all be clones." His voice grew louder. "Mirror images of one another. You're not facing the fact there are many kinds of people in this country, in this world. Under communism everyone isn't going to be just alike, either."

Nikkia caught herself smiling despite the tenseness. She was used to anti-communist arguments, though not from Lawrence. "But like under communism, we've got to start out in agreement over basic principles.

You're building a little castle in the sky here. I can't be a part of this kind of future."

He sat down in his lounge chair. "So you don't want to give us a chance."

"I think we would learn to hate each other." Every word was difficult for her. "At least now we might remain friends."

Lawrence stared at her in silence.

So this was their last night together? Nikkia felt the fear of loneliness again the way she had by the Village garden. She spoke to reassure herself as much as for him. "You'll find someone that wants the same things as you. You're becoming one of the country's most desirable bachelors." She tried to make a joke, but neither one of them laughed.

"Are you trying to say you heard of something that went on in Washington, with me and another woman?"

To Nikkia, he sounded unreasonably angry. She expected a reaction to their break-up, but not like this. She tried to make him feel better. "I'm just saying that successful black men are at a premium."

"Your flattery could be a coverup for your own guilt."

Nikkia didn't like this turn of the subject. She sensed he wanted to bring out something. "Did you--I'm asking you--meet someone? Is that why you never came to visit me? Was it in Washington?"

"She was a wall street lawyer." He didn't seem to take satisfaction in telling her. "Worked with a big firm in the world trade center building."

Nikkia was shocked. "You had time for an affair but no time to see me!"

"I wouldn't call it as much as an affair. She was separated, practically divorced. I wasn't about to get involved in something like that."

"Why would you do _anything_, when we were most serious about finally getting married?"

"It's very common." But his voice was sad. "Many people have a fling before taking a big step. Maybe you also had time in Boston to find that out for yourself."

A cold doubt seemed to take the floor from under Nikkia. She felt as shaken as she did when Saleem told her he had joined the party. The fear must have shown on her face.

"You did," Lawrence stated.

It was Nikkia's turn to remain silent. She thought about the possibility that her desiring Norberto stemmed from a fear of commitment to marriage.

"There was someone," Nikkia began.

"So."

"I was very attracted to him."

"Of course it was mutual, and you couldn't help yourself."

"This wasn't an ordinary physical attraction."

"That's what they all say. That's what I thought, too."

"He had an enthusiasm for the work. A burning enthusiasm."

"That's attractive in some people. I feel that way when I meet a confident woman."

"A successful woman?"

"You were that way."

"Was?"

"You never realized how secure you looked. Nothing could touch you when you were dancing. And you had men all over the world wanting to touch you."

"And now, you found another women more appealing?"

"You didn't deny making love with your Boston buddy."

"I'm telling you now. We didn't. I wouldn't have unless we meant something to each other."

"You had a lot in common. Wasn't that enough?"

Nikkia thought of her conversation with Coralee. "I have a great deal in common with millions of people, but I am only one," she said. She didn't want to discuss Norberto.

"Wasn't he a comrade?"

"He was married."

"That stopped you?"

"Yes. It stopped both of us."

"I'm surprised. But I suppose that's what a communist is expected to do."

"You're making fun of me."

"I'm just telling you in my own way that you're a woman first. You have natural tendencies."

"Are you trying to excuse <u>yourself</u>?" Why else had he mentioned the woman tonight? she wondered. Especially after he must have realized their engagement was broken. "You were engaged to be married to me. Did your lawyer friend know that about you?"

"Of course."

"She didn't care?"

"Why should she? We're friends! We have an understanding."

"How long would this understanding go on?" Nikkia asked, thinking he had to know he was still capable of hurting her.

"The intimacy is over. That part of it. You were to be my wife when you settled down from your side trip to Boston."

"You did it to get back at me?"

"Absolutely not." He hesitated. "But in one of your letters you wrote about joining the summer project next year in Delano, with farmworkers. . ."

"So you are angry."

"I'm a man with needs. That's what I am."

"And what was to prevent you from doing this if we got married?"

"I wouldn't." His words were sincere, Nikkia could tell. "Maybe you're right. Maybe I was upset at your being gone. Sometimes you don't seem to need me."

"I'm sorry. I really am. Yet if you recall, you were drawn to me because of my independence. I don't feel guilty about doing what I know I have to do." And she didn't.

"You can feel anything you want. But you can't make a big deal out of the woman in Washington. No one got hurt."

"How do you know that?"

"I know her."

"Maybe you can shut your feelings on and off. Maybe she can. But I believe in commitment."

"That's why you fell for a married man, I suppose."

"You can't twist my words around. For a long, long time to come I think there'll be commitment between men and women. I don't think that we can just trade around partners without someone's feelings being hurt."

"I'll feel that way if we get married. See how much we still have in common? Then I'll be content with my fantasies." He attempted to lighten their mood. "Some people stay married having jobs in two parts of the country, seeing each other once a month. Some stick it out through real affairs, career changes. Can't you see, I've stayed with you through a kind of career change? A prima ballerina to a communist? What more can you expect of me?"

"It's a lot." He was fighting for her, Nikkia realized. She began to feel a sorrow that went deeper than pity.

"More than most men, most any man, would have put up with."

The sorrow left her, like a passing cloud. "Is that the way you feel, that you put up with my politics?"

"You have to admit, it's a lot more to swallow than a housewife getting a job, even a career that keeps her out of the house for long hours, sometimes overnight. You may get fired, thrown in jail."

"Would you hold that against me?"

His body straightened in the chair. "I just want you to understand my point of view. You don't have a clear picture of yourself. How different you are."

"You and I are different," she stated. "Becoming opposites; can't you see?"

"Opposites attract." He tried joking again. "We don't have to get married tomorrow. We could stick it out until the revolution."

"We're not going to last any longer than today." Nikkia felt her eyes sting. She walked over to the windows, turning her back on him.

Lawrence came over and put his hands on her shoulders. They felt like a grip, as if he were trying to hold her back. She turned to face him, and the tears were on her face. "I have to go."

"I won't let you."

There by the window, for a moment she felt fear. It was irrational, she supposed, but she was afraid he would push her. "You can't stop me. We're two people now."

"We always were," he said with a cynical tone.

"Not always." Nikkia looked at his face, and she was distressed to see the fear in his eyes, too, as well as the anger. "But I still want to be your friend."

"I still want you to be my wife," Lawrence said. "That's the difference between us. I love you. You're the one who's changed."

"So be it," said Nikkia.

Chapter 18

The first day of school in September 1975 brought a light chilly rain to the city of Boston. The children didn't seem to notice the drizzle. Their parents turned their own heads away out of annoyance. With no evidence of obvious raindrops, water collected on windshields, and the driver of the schoolbus flicked on the wipers again.

The bouncing bus came to a stop, and the children laughed as they slid about on the slick vinyl seats. Fay wiped the window next to her bus seat with the palm of her hand. Her feet hurt in the hard school shoes after a summer in sandals. This was one reason that riding the bus was better than walking to school, she thought. Why was my mom so old fashioned to buy me leather shoes and not sneakers? She bet Russell would let her buy sneakers.

With the windowpane clear now, she could see only five hecklers. Fay noticed their mouths open like they did in silent movies, but the closed windows shut out their screams. Knowing that somewhere Coralee was riding toward them with other INCAR members in a similar school bus, she felt secure. Six-year-old Jeanette sitting beside her did not feel so safe. "I'm a-scared. Those white people's faces are so mean."

Fay put her arm around Jeanette. "Dumb and stupid is all they are," she said confidently. "They're too stupid to go and fight the mayor for more school money."

"But they can hurt me," said Jeanette. "The cops don't do nothin to them for it, neither."

"I know," Fay wanted to let Jeanette know she understood. At the same time she realized it was hard to tell someone so young about the city council and, for that matter, the whole government. "My mother and INCAR are coming soon with more people than ROAR or the cops."

next bus to unload."

Where was her mom? Fay was becoming as concerned for her mother and friends at this point as for herself. They should have been here by now.

x x x

About two miles away on another crowded schoolbus, Coralee sat angrily and impatiently. "I hate the feeling of being trapped in this stuffy rattletrap," she said aloud to no one in particular.

She struggled with the metal pull on the window latch. Norberto, sitting on the same seat with Coralee, reached over behind her and pushed from another angle. "They must have sealed them up," muttered Coralee. But as Norberto pushed the window up to the limit and rocked it back, it came loose. With each of them holding one of the two spring levers the window came half-way down. No further. The window was blocked; one of the few safety regulations observed.

"You're sweating like me." Coralee ran the palm of her hand over Norberto's forehead. Norberto smiled and extended to her his handkerchief to catch trickles of water that ran down Coralee's temples from her hairline.

Other people, pulling and pushing together, managed to open several windows. As the bus started up again, a wet but cool breeze brought some relief.

"Only another couple of miles," Zack announced, just as the bus hit a large pothole. Sitting next to Russell and in front of Coralee and Norberto, Nikkia braced her arm in time to prevent another bash to her nose.

"You OK, Honey?" Coralee put one arm on Nikkia. "Fuckin' dangerous seats. Our kids need seatbelts on these contraptions."

Hearing the sudden fury in Coralee's voice, Norberto sensed there was something else troubling her. "You thinking about Fay, Thomas and Timothy?"

"I am. Right this minute they could be getting hurt." Coralee turned in the seat to look into Norberto's face. She liked the steadiness of the way he looked at her when she began to answer. "But I'm not as afraid of them being out there on their own as I was last year. Thanks to him," she confessed, indicating Russell. "The boys especially grew up a lot this summer."

"They understand more."

"And they might not have. I was wrong to leave them alone so much. Too much freedom." Coralee shook her head.

"Only the bosses have freedom." Norberto was very serious but he also wanted to make her laugh.

Coralee chuckled. "They were taking over the house." And then her face became troubled again.

Seeing her concern, Norberto encouraged her to talk. "I thought maybe Renee would be here today." This was a question, but Norberto made it sound like he was just thinking scattered thoughts.

Before answering right away, Coralee gripped his forearm. She noticed, from her years working as a nurses' aide, the smoothness of his skin. In his turn, Norberto was astonished how much his arm hurt under her grip.

"She's sick," said Coralee. And then as his eyes waited for her, she went on. "Renee's pregnant again. Same damn guy."

"I'm sorry."

"<u>You're</u> sorry."

Una, sitting across the aisle from Russell, had been talking with him and Nikkia, but she overheard Renee's name and put in, "She thinks this time Malcolm'll stay with her. She doesn't want an abortion."

"He's not with her now!" Coralee protested.

"Try telling that to her stubborn self. He's with her in that baby, in her mind."

"Renee's always wanted most what she couldn't have," reflected Coralee.

"Maybe you can convince her, Norberto," suggested Una. "You're so direct."

Norberto hesitated. A look passed over his face that changed his eyes to a glaze. He said, "Something has come up at home and I must leave the U.S. soon. My wife has taken the children to Mexico."

The bus jerked to another stop, and this time Zack got off the bus. Seven police cars were parked at various angles in the middle of the street in front of the schoolbus. Zack was only a moment in talking with the chief of police. He climbed back on the bus and picked up the microphone of a bullhorn. "They want us to wait here for half an hour," he announced. "There's not a lot of choice."

At once an angry sigh came from most people on the bus. The ride had been long and frustrating. It was a hell of a thing to be trapped on this bus, knowing that the children would be going into the schools without them. "We've organized all summer for this?" someone blurted out from the front.

"When they wouldn't let our Dorchester marchers take a single step today without being arrested--whether or not they had a permit--we had to have several plans." Zack spoke openly though the three plans had been previously discussed only by the leadership: a small, open march, the busload to specific schools and a much smaller, secret contingent to a single school.

Zack had a way of presenting the situation so that most of those who had not been part of the planning understood the reason for the secrecy. "Our Dorchester group decided to march anyway. The chief informs me he just had them arrested. I think he meant that as a threat."

This time people laughed. Nikkia, who had a lot more on her mind than she expected to have, laughed despite her own tension. She had been a part of the over-all planning and knew that by now the smaller group of people should have arrived at the school where Fay would be going. The police were too much aware of Coralee's role in the community for her to have been a part of this contingent. The demonstrators would arrive in ones and twos. If stopped on the way, they would be telling the police they were followers of ROAR. While Nikkia considered this action, yet another thought demanded her attention: Norberto's recent announcement that he would leave.

At this moment, though, Nikkia saw a need to assist Zack in the leadership, and she stood up. "The cops, the mayor, the money men of Boston, they want to take more and more away from us and our children," she said. "That's their only plan no matter how they twist and turn to hide it. And that's why they will fail! But we must be around to point the way out."

Then there was still the wait, and several people rose to talk of the changes they had seen in the people of Boston. And what few forces of ROAR had been on the streets this school day.

Nikkia did not wish to be rude by not entering the discussion, but at the same time she had to know more of Norberto's sudden decision to go to Mexico. The idea of his leaving the country forever created within her a vacuum. The empty space seemed deeper than the place that Lawrence had occupied, just when she thought she could feel no more loss.

She looked back to see Norberto's eyes on her as though he had expected her reaction. "Won't it be difficult for you to cross the border?" she began, not wanting to open herself entirely, for she still had told no one but Bonita of her feelings for him.

"It's easier to go back," Norberto said.

"How could she leave, knowing you're still here?" Nikkia spoke to him now like there was no one sitting near them. She couldn't help herself asking the question, and yet when she saw Norberto's face, she regretted putting it in that way. He looked as though he had been slapped. She knew immediately she should have asked him if his wife's family was there, or at least made some comment less revealing, but it was too late.

When Norberto spoke, his answer was equal to her question. "She came to the United States for different reasons from me. She hoped for a better life for her and the children. I came to work closer with comrades here."

"I'm continually surprised at how close I can get to comrades," Nikkia murmured, "and how quickly."

Coralee, listening, gave Nikkia a knowing look. She suggested, "Nikkia, why don't you sit here? Switch seats with me."

When Nikkia shook her head, she pressed in a tone that was not to be argued with, "I have to hear the discussion up front anyway, about what we're going to do."

Nikkia shrugged her assent. If Coralee understood the need she had to be closer to Norberto, how many others could tell?

When they made the switch, Coralee asked Russell about a leaflet he had announcing ROAR in the borough of Queens.

Nikkia only briefly speculated how Coralee managed to focus Russell's attention so quickly, away from what Norberto and she might have to say to one another. She was aware of a certain urgency, knowing there might not be another chance to talk with him.

ROSEDALE
FOREST HILLS
CANARSIE

What do these 3 New York City communities have in common with Boston?

These are the homes of various White Ethnic Americans, the "Forgotten Minority," who have been relegated to the status of 2nd class citizens.

It seems our communities, comprised of hard-working, middle income men and women, whose main concern is trying to support home and family as honestly as we can, with little or no time to get involved in interests outside our homes, are being crucified, and branded racists and bigots when we finally do speak out and take action on issues that concern us and affect our lives and our way of living.

WHERE ARE OUR CIVIL RIGHTS?

Are we not allowed to realize our American dream? To send our children to the schools of our choice, (busing), to live in a community free of fear, crime, violence and filth? Is it not our right to speak out and be heard when we feel threatened? Don't we have the right to have our side presented in a dispute?

Why are you, the media and the politicians not affording us these rights? Why are you taking these rights from us?

IS IT BECAUSE we are so involved in our work and families that we've become passive and submissive, and have been afraid to speak out? IS IT BECAUSE you takeus, the backbone of America, for granted? IS IT BECAUSE we can be counted on to turn the other cheek? IS IT BECAUSE we are not radicals or the real bigots who have nothing but time to burn, loot and often destroy businesses, while the media and politicians stand by and ignore these acts (even rewarding the leaders of these groups with well-paying jobs) while all the time trying to make us feel guilty for the lawless acts of these people?

Or is it because you of the media and "our" politicians are living in a world apart from ours?

Most all of you offer rhetoric and condemn us, while at the same time you live in safe, lilly-white high-income neighborhoods, and send your children to private schools.

WE ARE TIRED of watching our mothers and fathers, after long years of seniority, lose their jobs in order to protect those of newly-hired "minorities." WE ARE TIRED of standing idly by while our brothers and sisters are denied entrance to law and medical schools, in favor of less qualified "minorities," and most of all . . . WE ARE TIRED of having our children bussed out so that "minority" children may be bussed into our schools

WE DEMAND THE RETURN OF OUR AMERICAN RIGHTS!

ROAR was formed because of these inequities. Our purpose is to awaken middle class Americans and get us back on the track to true Democracy, where majority rules. If you want to help ROAR get our message across, and help pay for this and future ads, please send your donation to:

ROAR of Rosedale

"Isn't there more danger for you in Mexico than for her in the States?" Nikkia was afraid of his acting impulsively. And she was equally afraid of never seeing him again.

"Possibly. Yes. The police killed two of our comrades in Puebla. I'll have to work quietly for some time." He reflected, appearing to be recounting memories. "But I have many, many friends I left behind in Puebla, and so it will not be like starting all over."

"How can you go back to her after she just took off on you like that?" Nikkia's own insistence embarrassed her. She glanced over at Bonita and Saleem, who sat in animated conversation. Was it so wrong to want to be as close with someone as they were to each other?

"She must have left out of fear for what the INS might do if they sent her back. I'm sure she didn't think of it as leaving me."

"Do you <u>know</u> that?"

"No," he admitted. "But I know her. And her ways of protecting the children."

"But she was confident that you would follow her. Even knowing it would be more dangerous for you there."

"She knows I wouldn't want to give up being with the children," Norberto turned his hands palm upward. "She's aware how close I have always been to our fifteen-year-old, Manuel. I wouldn't leave him."

Nikkia's breath became still. She spoke the words without thinking, "Are you in love with her?" Once she asked this, she thought about his family and the problems he and his wife had to face together. The question sounded strange now, almost childish.

"I love her," he said, in his straight-forward way. "But I am not in love with her. Our, what's-his-name, goals are different."

Relief spread across her body like a wave. She looked down, afraid the language from her body would say too much. And as if to reprimand herself, she thought it sad that she should rejoice that he wasn't in love with Silvia.

"The plan was for me to return eventually," he continued. "This is just sooner rather than later."

"Plans change," Nikkia motioned to the others in the bus, and to the police outside, by way of example.

The chief had engaged Zack once again.

"We half-expected this move on the part of the police." Norberto made a dismissing gesture as if the impending arrest was insignificant. "They can't change the party's long-range strategy."

Nikkia tried to bring order to her thoughts. It seemed to her there must be a way she could persuade him to stay. The setting appeared like the high drama of a stage scene. Here, sitting in a bus filled with the people she had worked with, Nikkia felt the pull of their personalities--the best friends she would ever know. The bond between Coralee and Russell as they talked. The strength of Una beside her; thoughts of Renee.

Outside, milling in their riot gear, the police went back and forth between the gray paddy wagons. Zack got off the bus once to speak with them. A hazy curtain of rain dimmed the apartment houses around them all. For these forty minutes, this setting became the world.

Her leaving Norberto at the end of July, she thought, had been simple compared to this latest chapter in her life. Last month, his marriage responsibility and farmworking job seemed as acceptable to her as the three thousand miles that would stretch between them. Now, as Nikkia's anxiety for Norberto grew, her first thought was of Silvia's worst possible motivation: a game of power. Might she be using his loyalty to pull him back into a difficult situation? But Nikkia wondered if she was being fair to Silvia. Could she be fair? All she knew was that Silvia couldn't love Norberto as much as she did.

Nikkia tried to imagine the reasoning of a person who had expected the U.S. to offer her the good life. Silvia <u>couldn't</u> have been thinking of Norberto so much as of her own aspirations. Was she possibly angry when Norberto left her and the children for Boston? Nikkia compared herself to Silvia. She remembered she had left Lawrence for needs of her own: comradeship and, yes, loyalty. She had to have both now.

All this, Nikkia realized in a few seconds. She looked around the bus and outside, and down at the gold ring on Norberto's hand. Many men, many Mexican men, didn't wear a ring. The fact that Norberto did was significant. He was as much wedded to Silvia--Nikkia recalled her name with anger--as to the idea of fidelity no matter what. And he was married to his children, particularly his eldest son, Manuel, who was most like him. This was the man whose feelings ran so deep in his commitment that the thought of Silvia's danger had immobilized him.

Would she, Nikkia, ever be able to command such loyalty in a man? Why not in Norberto, for more positive reasons than those of Silvia? Did he understand that for her to be able to work him out of his depression in July she had to know his mind almost as well as his wife of nineteen years?

"But you aren't regarding your life seriously enough," Nikkia began to argue. "If you were to stay here, you could send money to your family--to your children. That way you'd be helping your family, without putting yourself in danger." She had given up asking herself what it was that she wanted more: his safety or the possibility of his staying in Boston. Somehow, it had become one and the same.

"I can't be pulled in so many directions. I do better when I have my family in the same place where I do my political work. Then I am more effective to help with my country's problems. You saw the way I got this summer. I plan to bring my family back if I can't do what I want in Mexico."

"What if your wife leaves again?"

"That's too far off in the future."

Neither could Nikkia see that many years ahead. But she could not tell him how much she needed him. Not here on this crowded bus. Not when it wasn't mutual.

"If you don't do something differently now . . ." Nikkia began, and stopped. She realized that there was really only one option open to her at the moment. She had yet to tell him of her own life's decision. "I've stopped seeing Lawrence."

Norberto's face registered surprise. "I thought you were definite about marrying this man."

"I was. I mean, we no longer have enough in common." Nikkia felt herself close to tears. She couldn't look into Norberto's eyes. He would be able to see right through her the desire for him. She was embarrassed, feeling almost subhuman.

So she looked away from Norberto and saw Saleem and Bonita, their arms around each other's shoulders. It hurt to think that she herself might never know what it would be like to enjoy their kind of future.

"You told me you and he had danced together, had been organizing in the South. That he works alone now, and that he is ambicioso." Norberto's tone was sympathetic but somehow disapproving. "I don't know why you stayed with him."

Why do you stay with your wife? Nikkia said to herself. Maybe he's putting me down because he's a man and expects less political commitment from his woman. What's the difference between our circumstances? His piece of paper? She couldn't help asking, "Don't you wish your wife were interested in the party?"

"I wasn't in the party myself when we got together. Would it have made a difference if we'd married after I became involved?" He asked, not fully expecting an answer.

"Well, I changed," Nikkia admitted, resting one arm behind him on the seat. "I found our life together harder and more separated--physically separated." Surely Norberto should be able to understand this.

Opening herself up to Norberto, especially when he seemed to disapprove, made her feel vulnerable. Was he trying to make her feel uncomfortable so as to keep a power over her, like a lot of macho men she knew? "He cheated on me this summer," she finished with an anger that was partly directed toward Norberto.

"Oh, I'm so sorry," he said, with a very light touch on her arm that to her was, again, like fire.

"I'm over it now," Nikkia said abruptly. Above all, she didn't want his pity.

"I hate him for hurting you." From between his soft parted lips Norberto almost whispered the words, full of passion.

Nikkia realized he had never shown any sign of emotion toward her, but had made simply a flat statement once that he thought her attractive. And now, hatred of Lawrence's actions seemed to arouse the depth of feeling that he couldn't permit himself about her. So this is one way, she thought, with a resurgence of love, that he shows his capacity to care.

"He didn't hurt me so much as he made me cold," Nikkia told Norberto. She tried to remember how that evening with Lawrence had left her feeling.

"Out in the cold?" Norberto tried to understand. "We say abandonada." He pronounced the word slowly, and Nikkia watched the anger in his eyes turn into a well of pity.

"He didn't leave me in that way." Nikkia fought against this tendency of his to pity her. She looked around the bus to see if anyone was listening. Then she went on, "I think I began to leave him first. I stopped caring when I heard him talking down to my best friend."

And for a moment, her anger matched Norberto's. Unable to stop her outpouring, she clenched her fingers.

Norberto's eyes widened, and he no longer showed any pity. "Don't waste such powerful emotions on him," he said. "It is certain you will meet someone. You have so much to offer."

I have met someone already, Nikkia thought. But to Norberto she said, "And you, you have so much to offer the movement here. You were just beginning to share in the leadership."

"I will give more leadership in Mexico than I did before."

"In Pueblo there is no party club. It may be a waste," Nikkia said. But she was thinking that it was much more a shame that his passion should be driven to a woman who chose to run away rather than wait the few days for his return.

"Nothing is ever wasted," he said. "I will build a club. The auto work demands one."

He is leaving, Nikkia thought. He is leaving, and nothing I can say will change his mind. She dug her fist into the back of the seat, causing Una to turn around.

"Why are you so upset, Nikkia?" Una thought Nikkia too strong to be so angry, as Una perceived, over the delay.

This fear is mine alone, Nikkia realized. No one can know. The more I talk with Norberto, the more I think that even if I meet someone, like he says, I won't be able to love two men: Norberto and him. She shook her head at Una, dismissing her comment with a gesture of her hand, and Una turned away.

"I will miss you, Nikkia," Norberto said.

Was there to be no more than that? Nikkia couldn't respond. Something stopped her from saying she would miss him, too, as she had said in July. Missing had become a word far too simple.

"Are you so disappointed in me that you can't say

anything?"

"Not exactly." Rather, Nikkia felt helpless. Did he say that because despite what he says he, too, has considered other choices? And if I insist I'm not disappointed then his decision doesn't have to be difficult. I'll be damned, Nikkia thought, if I'll make it easier for him.

"Here in Boston you've already proven that your leadership goes beyond Mexico," she said. "This is a retreat."

"Zack said something like that. I don't agree. I know myself."

Nikkia turned to face him directly. Her thoughts seemed at once more clear than ever before. "You'd return to Mexico even though it's more dangerous. You said you'd organize there even though there's no collective. What you're saying is you're a better individual organizer in Mexico than a leader here. Norberto, Los obreros no tienen fronteras. Workers have no borders!"

"I am not a nacionalista. We are an international party," insisted Norberto. "You just said it." A little smile came to his lips.

"You're hearing what you want to hear. International does not mean 'individualista.'" Nikkia smiled too, but more broadly. She felt confident that he was beginning to understand, even if he wasn't ready to admit that to her, or to himself. "The Mexico City comrades are many miles away from Puebla." She added a bit more lightly, "That's not much of a collective for you."

Norberto stared out of the window before answering. "I guess I understand, but I have to think about what you say. I don't agree with everything." He looked at her then.

Her eyes met his. Nikkia saw the brown of his eyes soften. Their warmth let her all the way inside. She drew a sharp breath. Norberto looked abruptly down at his hands.

"I will miss listening to you," he said after a moment. It's hard to tell you goodbye, even after we argue."

"There's a word close friends use when they don't want to say goodbye," Nikkia said slowly. "Ciao. Ciao, Norberto."

x x x

    In an identical cheese-colored school bus two miles away, Fay's voice sounded over the jeers outside the bus. As the driver pulled on the door handle, the insults grew louder. With a fervor that came from wanting to protect, Fay stood up with her arms circling her young friend, Jeanette, like a long necklace.
    She yelled at the top of her lungs at the faces outside: "MOTHERS, CHILDREN, TEACHERS, TOO. BLACK AND WHITE WE'LL MAKE IT THROUGH." The students on the bus caught up the chant, partly out of relief at something to do in the stuffy, crowded bus.
    Parents waiting alongside the line of buses expected their children to exit with bowed heads, anticipating drizzle and pelting rocks. Instead they heard the chanting, and it excited them into shouting, too. They added words they had learned over the summer. "MAYOR WHITE; LOUISE DAY HICKS. WE CAN BEAT YOU AT YOUR OLD TRICKS."
    The ROAR people began to throw rocks at the bus windows. Their faces showed shock and anger at the boldness of the children. Parents wasted no time in throwing their own rocks and bottles over the heads of the cops into the crowd of ROAR. The police responded by trying to push the parents further from their children. Two cops began to arrest the father of a boy behind Fay.
    The boy began to cry and ran into the crowd. Other children started running, too. The police dispersed as they attempted to restore order to the departing children. ROAR gathered themselves once again, and screams of "Get Out Niggers" became louder. A large rock broke the window and grazed Jeanette's head.
    The parents pushed and broke through the line of police at that point. One woman picked up Fay's little friend, who was more frightened than hurt. Another parent found a rock that had landed outside the bus and threw it back into the ROAR crowd. A new demonstrator threw a full can of soda. Backing off from fighting parents, ROAR screamed louder yet.
    Someone else threw a soda can, too, shouting, "The only solution is communist revolution." That woman was arrested. The chant continued. "THE ONLY

SOLUTION IS COMMUNIST REVOLUTION!" A ROAR follower threw a brick at the boy whose father was in the crowd.

By now the first children were entering the school. More went in. As Fay got to the door, she turned around and shook a small fist. Then she stuck out her tongue.

x x x

"Fay must be scared to death wondering why I'm not there with her." Coralee knew she must be the most frustrated comrade on that bus. She only partly listened to Zack's announcement:

"The police have decided to arrest all the people on the bus."

"They're afraid of the attention we'll attract," said Russell to Coralee, "sitting here in the middle of the street for six hours until school is over." Already curious residents and their neighbors were gathering. They stood on the other side of the line of squad cars and paddy wagons. They were talking to each other about the CAR school bus.

A woman pointed at the signs which said, "SMASH RACISM. UNITE FOR BETTER SCHOOLS."

Suddenly someone cried, "There's Hicks herself!" And for a brief moment, Louise Day Hicks spoke with the police captain and got back in her car to drive forward to the targeted schools.

Coralee almost ran off the bus saying, "Fay's waitin' for me!" But Russell held her. She pictured Fay crying as she had done last year when Timothy got beat up. Would Fay think her mother had found something better to do this day? Coralee looked at Russell and noticed that he appeared more disturbed than she.

"You're not havin second thoughts about moving up to our charmin burg, are ya?" Coralee stared at Russell feeling the relief she'd always found on leaving her own house. Outside, sharing her thoughts with neighbors, she seemed to be able to get away from herself.

"We haven't grown in numbers that much this summer," he reflected aloud. He, too, was worried about Coralee's children. But it wouldn't help them for her to go running off the bus into the arms of the cops. And so he tried to divert both their attention.

"I think about the movement we've created. Somehow that's the easy part, the battles. The hard part is getting people to see they have to join us permanently. I see our work as just starting." Russell no longer paid attention to the others on the bus, aside from Coralee. "The building of deeper friendships will be slow. When most of the comrades have gone back there'll be just us."

"Many of the younger, college comrades, are going back much stronger than when they came." Coralee spoke in her melodious voice that calmed patients and was so soothing now to Russell. He smiled, remembering the bed bath at her fingertips. She went on, "But they aren't seasoned, like you."

He felt filled with a sense of confidence and well-being.

"I've talked with some of them, and I must tell you I lose patience sometimes. They think the revolution is just around the corner."

"I used to think that, too," Russell said, "before I started a family and got to know other people with families. The students don't know much different because most of the actions this summer involved only us." He shifted in the seat. "I only hope I can help you turn that around. I'm rusty. Been out of circulation for more than a couple years."

"You've dealt with workers," was Coralee's response. "Once you know how to talk with workers and gain their respect, you don't forget how." She grinned. "A lot of our new comrades in college--some of the most militant men and women I've ever seen--have never worked a day in their lives."

"That's not their fault," said Russell, "but I admit I get along better with high school kids."

"<u>Other</u> people's kids. Period. For me," laughed Coralee. "But Nikkia there, she seems to be able to talk with everyone."

"She even seems to have broken the language barrier completely." Russell referred to the concentration between Norberto and Nikkia as they spoke together.

"I felt she should talk with Norberto a bit, so I got them to sit together," revealed Coralee. "She's more upset than she realizes about having broke up with that man she was about to marry. Norberto seems to understand her."

"Maybe it's the other way around," hinted Russell.

Coralee found herself liking more and more this man who saw behind people as well as a woman could. "I'm still worried about Fay just now," she said, "more than Renee or the boys."

Russell turned his heavy body to face her, so that he was sitting half off the seat. "I'm not going to tell you I think she's OK. I can't even tell you I think she can handle herself--though I've seen her do it in some circumstances. But I know one thing for sure. You need to spend the next few years making friends with her so you'll be more sure of how she's doing in years to come."

Coralee thought about that for a moment. "It's good you and Pat are moving here," she said. "Pat don't take no bullshit from you, and you don't take none from me."

Then as Zack spoke again from the front of the bus he held both their attention. "We have to leave the bus one at a time," he announced dryly. "So they can search us."

His lean body adjusted the weight of the bullhorn. Darlene realized she wasn't the only person to have lost weight this summer.

Zack went on, "I suggested to the cops that they should have started with Hicks when she was across the street. They told me we'd caused them more problems than ROAR had caused them for years." He smiled, "I'd say that was a compliment!"

Everyone on the bus laughed, including Nikkia this time. As she watched people move into the aisles, she realized she had needed to be reminded that they'd worked together well this summer. She had dismissed her own contribution as she might a brief performance. Now she looked over to Darlene, standing up beside Lennie. She caught her smiling eyes and a blown kiss. Darlene stopped in the aisle to hug her, and Nikkia felt what she couldn't see in the baggy clothing--Darlene, along with the weight loss, had a whole new set of proportions.

"There's less of me to love, right?" said Darlene, seeing the amazement on Nikkia's face.

Nikkia laughed, "I'd say more! I bet everyone in the project has complimented you," she added, her eyes darting significantly in Lennie's direction.

People halted in front of her, and Darlene confided, "I don't think Lennie's noticed. He tells me we're just friends," she said quietly. Then she said with more confidence, "But I'm coming up here to live and go to welding school, and the heck with what he thinks. I'm not going to live for that."

Though Lennie didn't hear what Darlene said, he must have caught the emphasis in her voice, for Nikkia noticed an admiring look from him--if not for her appearance, for her determination. At the same moment Nikkia felt happiness for Darlene, her own wanting crept in beside the joy. Within her, stiffening her neck muscles, envy sat hunched.

Darlene was much younger than herself, Nikkia knew. But she had as much confidence as Nikkia ever had. Nikkia thought that despite her own past accomplishments, organizing history and experience in the life of love--Darlene had something going for her. And Darlene had another thing in her favor: she could work near Lennie without being as nervous as Nikkia felt around Norberto. First Bonita and now Darlene, Nikkia mused. It hurts to compare my life to theirs.

She sensed the mood of the other people on the bus. If Nikkia generalized, it seemed to be one of steadying resignation. Some comrades already stood outside, leaning against the wall of a building, their hands up, legs spread.

Nikkia, too, deferred some of her stronger feelings before this show of force. But underneath was a repugnance at the thought of someone feeling over her body. She liked to be in control. Could the lack of control that Norberto aroused in her be the reason, she wondered, that she would never be able to forget him? Or was it simply realizing that she was unable to control the circumstances of never seeing him again? Or both.

Underneath the shivering anticipation of the hands of the women cops, Nikkia cried inside for the loss of this one man. Because she cried alone and without tears, her neck muscles clenched so that she felt her jaws begin to lock.

Nikkia gradually realized the implications of their mass arrest. In theory, she had always known that the rulers of Boston, in order to hang onto every dollar, ultimately would exercise their power. But now she realized this force stopping completely their small action. The logic of this reality told her that schools could never be much improved. And the bosses would not rest until they tried to seed Boston's racism in every part of the country. Including Manhattan's upper west side. She knew a terrible sense of pressure, accentuated by the fact that, for the day, they were all being held back.

She waited while Coralee and then Russell climbed out of their seat, their large bodies comfortable and slow. "We're in no hurry," Coralee smiled and transmitted the confidence of an older comrade. Seeing these two friends move in front of her as though there was all the time in the world, Nikkia felt herself relax a bit.

Oddly enough, she thought even her neck muscles seemed to be loosening. Then she was aware that sure, warm fingertips behind her were massaging her neck precisely where the muscles were the tightest. The fingers massaged one side especially, where she had been turning toward Norberto, the side she didn't realize herself was stiffening more. Only a person touching her neck and massaging it carefully could know that. Norberto.

Nikkia would not allow herself to turn around before descending the steps of the bus. She was so completely conscious of her own high-strung responses at this point that she could not possibly acknowledge him. She knew that if she were to face him, thinking that perhaps it would be for the last time, she would cry uncontrollably. As out-of-control as she had been when she had danced with him that night too long ago.

She reached back to lay her hands on his carressing fingers. They went down the steps of the bus that way, together, before the cops separated them for the search and the waiting paddy wagons. She didn't even flinch as the woman cop went over her breasts, for her mind was elsewhere.

x x x

Mr. Cooper reported that *** and shortly after class, laid tribute *** there were some attempts to *** there antibusing *** in *** Tom *** were same attempts to *** 1,000 students leaders who urged a student *** 75 youths *** away down a steep *** was a school boycott. *** had not reached the aggressive jol *** a crowd of white youths *** and chanting, some *** among blocks today. But its *** reported to The School Department had *** adults gathered in front *** by motorcycles and nd most black parents were *** a special center. projected an enrollment of *** the drab brick housing *** weary-looking Tactical Patrol against such action. But in Charlestown, only 66, 63,000 in the Boston public project on Bunker Hill Street Force police who shoved residents off corners. At one point, Tom Johnson, a leader of R.O.A.P. (Restore Our Alienated Rights, the antibusing organization), who had been acting as a peacemaker, was arrested

As the police lined up to escort the buses from the high school shortly before 2 P.M. the band of white youths marched around the far side of the monument grounds, then suddenly broke and ran down a side street.

As they went, they turned over three Volkswagens parked by the roadside, and, some distance away, turned over and burned another car.

South Boston Arraignment

Meanwhile in South Boston, state and local police cleared away crowds that had begun to gather for the arraignment of 14 members of the Committee Against Racism, a group allied with the Progressive Labor party.

The party has been attempting to organize here for some time and has attracted the wrath of South Boston residents, who consider the party members "Commies." They were seized on disorderly persons charges as their bus attempted to enter the neighborhood early this morning.

They would have been slaughtered if we hadn't arrested them, said John Cuffey, an Assistant District Attorney.

The opening and closing of South Boston High School was quiet today, with only a few people standing on corners or sitting on their stoops, in contrast to a night of stone and bottle-throwing last night that left a policeman and a National Guardsman injured.

On the other side of Boston, many miles from the tensions in Charlestown and South Roston, calm prevailed in Boston's last upper-middle-class stronghold, West Roxbury. Federal marshals and policemen were seen in this leafy neighborhood of rambling homes and expansive lawns on the western edge

Police in South Boston lining up prohusing demonstrators near neighborhood high school. They were arrested a few blocks from the school when they refused to obey orders to leave the area.

United Press International

Once inside the jail, the thirty women were put in another building from the men. They went through fingerprinting, endless waiting and photographing. It wasn't until one-ten in the afternoon that the women were placed in two cells.

"You just missed lunch," smacked the light-skinned matron through heavily lipsticked lips. She sat at a metal desk, opened a drawer and got out a stand-up mirror. "I don't expect no trouble out of you," she went on loudly, her voice directed toward the mirror. "Just sit tight, and you'll be out of here by four o'clock. Long after the kiddies have gone back home on their buses."

None of the women gave her a response. Nikkia thought about how she had fixed breakfast at 4:00 AM for the people staying at Zack's, while he and Carolyn picked up more people. No one had wanted to eat at that hour, but Nikkia had forced them. "You never know what's going to happen today," she had said. "You'll need your energy." At the time, she hadn't been hungry, either. But now she was ravenous again.

Nikkia looked around her. One sink and one toilet stood in a corner of the large cell. There was one metal cot suspended from the wall. Odd, she mused. The cell is too large for one and too small for the fifteen of us. Then she noticed unpainted rectangles on the walls where two bunks and another cot had been suspended. Overcrowding more folks into jails had turned a cell for four into one for fifteen. After first checking the condition of the floor, which appeared to be dry at least, Nikkia sat down. Emotionally, it had been an exhausting day.

Everyone felt the frustration of not being on hand when the children would leave school. Coralee looked at the clock and paced the length of the cell, walking around people, looking at the clock again. There wasn't enough room for everyone to walk around, and by some tacit agreement, the people in Coralee's cell allowed her to be the one to pace.

"They think they're trying to fool the people of Boston," Coralee called out to no one in particular. "Do you see any ROAR dogs in jail today? Is anybody going to tell me the cops didn't see kids getting hit by stones?"

Nikkia could feel the built-up anger of those closest to her on the floor. In one corner she could see Zack's wife, Carolyn, organize a game with her neighbors who had joined them. Zack and Carolyn are good for each other, she remembered. They make their home always open. Nikkia reflected a bit on the strengths of people in this cell and the cell on the other side of the matron's desk.

The other cell held white and hispanic comrades, mainly students from other cities. They had two sinks and enough chairs for everyone. Darlene had yelled over, "Look: we've got the Plaza suite!" And they had all laughed. Now Nikkia waved to Darlene and smiled again at the endless attempts of the Boston justice system to discriminate.

She was beginning to take in the whole situation and to sense there must be something she could do to alter the mood of their having been trapped. She knew that ordinarily she excelled in such tense conditions, when she wasn't preoccupied with her own problems. Somehow the ugly gray walls and bars beside the comrades she loved brought her to her feet. She whispered to Bonita and indicated the matron, "There's more prostitutes on the police force than behind bars."

Then Nikkia noticed Una, whom she hadn't seen before because her head was in her arms on the cot. "Hey, dream boat," whispered Nikkia.

The way Una opened her eyes gave Nikkia cause for alarm. She didn't seem to be able to rouse herself from a daze. "You don't look yourself."

"I thought I'd be OK," Una mumbled. "I didn't remember to take my insulin injection this morning." She stopped, weakly putting her head back down. "I didn't remember on the bus. Then they took my medicine. 'Druggie,' they said. I didn't tell anyone cuz I was afraid they'd keep us here longer count of me."

Nikkia saw beads of sweat on Una's forehead. Her own hands were sweaty as she took Una's pulse. Immediately she called to Coralee. "Talk to everyone on this half of the cell. Una forgot to take her insulin this morning. She looks like she's about to go into a coma. They took her medicine."

"You don't have to say more," said Coralee. "Una had to pick up everyone in the Freedom School this morning in two trips." Coralee grabbed Nikkia's shoulders. "We're going to give this matron a time she'll never forget."

It took eight seconds to organize the cell. "The other folks'll catch on quick once we begin," Nikkia told Bonita.

"Matron," Coralee then called sharply. "We have a sick woman here. She needs immediate attention."

"An old trick," said the matron, without looking up from her TV STAR magazine.

"You'd better get your butt over here," said Coralee.

"That language is going to get you at least an overnight visit," sneered the matron. "What's your name, girl?"

"None of your business," Nikkia returned. "Take a look at our friend here or you're the one's going to be up on charges."

The matron straightened her blouse and peered between the bars at Una. "That's the junkie they warned me about," she shrugged.

Hearing them talk, Darlene shouted, "You better see to her right now. She needs her insulin. That's why she had a needle on her."

"Get us her medicine," Nikkia yelled.

"And orange juice," Coralee added.

"Medicine now!" all fourteen voices surrounding Una shouted.

"MEDICINE NOW," joined in the fifteen voices from the other cell.

"MEDICINE NOW!"

The matron stood up. "Shut up!" she screamed. "They'll hose you all down if you don't shut up."

"She's afraid what her boss'll think of her if she can't keep us quiet," said Nikkia. "Let's show her what noise really is."

The women took off their shoes, as they had planned, and banged them, in unison, on the bars.

A student in the other cell started to sing in the same rhythm, The International. "ARISE YOU PRISONERS OF STARVATION . . ." Coralee and Nikkia laughed, and everyone who knew the words sang, too, and kept banging on the bars.

The startled matron fled the room, leaving the door to the cell block open behind her.

"THE EARTH SHALL RISE ON NEW FOUNDATIONS . . . WE HAVE BEEN NAUGHT; WE SHALL BE ALL . . . ." Within minutes the matron was back, flanked by two officers. One of them scolded her for leaving the door open while the other, holding a needle, a vial and a glass of juice, motioned to Una's cell. "One of you in there know how to give injections?"

Coralee stepped forward. She gave Una the juice and then the insulin.

"We need a doctor," insisted Nikkia.

"I don't know if that's possible," said the other officer. "You are all going to be out of here in less than an hour, or more, and . . ."

He was interrupted, "'TIS THE FINAL CONFLICT; LET EACH STAND IN THEIR PLACE. . ." and the pounding of shoes.

All three officers left to the cheers of twenty-nine women and a smiling Una. Soon a doctor came.

Still, it was four-fifteen before the women were released. The men had got out first, they soon discovered. "Guess the cops were afraid of the ruckus we'd make to get them out," said Coralee.

Zack laughed, "We could hear you all singing The International way in the next building!"

Nikkia smiled, but she was distracted. She saw all the others who had been arrested. But where was Norberto? She had more to say to him. She asked around.

"He's at the airport," Zack informed her. "We had to get him out before they hauled him back for another look at his green card. The black comrades here will be sentenced. But that will be nothing compared to Norberto if he comes up for trial."

Distress appeared on Nikkia's face. "He shouldn't go back to Mexico," she glanced wildly from side to side.

"There's nothing you can do now." Zack tried to calm her.

"He wants to do work in Puebla. By himself," she agonized. "It's impossible!"

"We all want him to stay," Zack reassured further. "I think the comrades in California will be able to convince him to wait for us to help his family across again."

"You don't understand," Nikkia said at last, pulling Zack aside for she knew she could trust him. "I'm afraid I'm concerned much more personally than I should be."

The two of them stood outside a Blimpie's sandwich shop. Most of the other comrades and friends had gone in to eat their first meal of the day. Coralee and some others had rushed home instead.

Since Zack didn't seem shocked by her statement, Nikkia decided to tell him more. "Maybe I care for him because I was breaking up with Lawrence. Maybe not. But there's no one in the whole New York party--or in the hospital where I work with thousands of people--who I feel so close to!"

"I don't think of you as a kid on the rebound," said Zack.

Hearing his kindness, Nikkia wasn't sorry she had confided in him. This man, she knew, could read between the lines. "Just don't lecture me," she cautioned.

"For two years I was in love with a woman who went with another man," said Zack.

He looked at her with patient eyes. Slowly Nikkia realized that all this time she had never known she was the other woman. Her eyebrows raised as she remembered all the insignificant reasons she had given herself, and her mother, for wanting Lawrence over Zack.

"Yes," he said simply. "And then I met Carolyn. And she was and still is the sweetest person I know."

Zack held out his arms to Nikkia, and she embraced him. She could feel the bones in his shoulders. He had the build of a young boy, she thought tenderly. "I needed this," she said. "Thanks."

Cyril came up behind Nikkia and teased, "Zack! You already stole Russell! You better not convince Nikkia to stay in Boston. We need her in our little hick town!"

"Are you kidding?" Nikkia said. "We've got to do our damndest to beat them away from my own front door!" She took one arm from around Zack and hugged them both.

"We've done it," said Cyril. "Even with half the Boston comrades we had last year."

Zack and Nikkia looked at each other. "Yes, but we still have to measure success in terms of our recruitment," Zack said seriously. "One or two people are a lot closer to the party here. Forest. Una. Sure, quite a few joined who came as volunteers, and they'll work to build the party where they live. Or here, like Darlene. But realistically, throughout the country we're barely holding our own."

Nikkia shook her head. "Cyril is right. Even a small party can do a lot." She reminded Zack, "The Chinese revolution began with a few guys talking about it in a rowboat."

Cyril chuckled. "All of you here in Boston were giving the rest of us inspiration a ways back. Chasing around racist theorizing professors, like Jensen and Herrnstein. Those blokes will surface again. It'll be jolly fun giving them a good belt."

"I hear Zack, though. The schools are still falling apart." Nikkia was thoughtful. "Our kids will have to suffer for years to come in these prisons they call schools. None of us'll get a fair shake until we get these parasites off our backs once and for all."

"That's a long row to hoe. I don't know if people here are ready to spend the time it's going to take." Zack couldn't seem to get his mind off the party clubs in Boston. "The pace will be a lot slower this fall. I think many of the comrades expect a revolution around the corner."

"Are you blind, man?" Cyril shook him by the shoulders. He pointed to their laughing friends, walking out of the sandwich shop onto the city sidewalk. "Understand the quality of these people, their caliber. We're dealing with human beings of the future, my mates!"

Appendix

The reader, on glancing through this appendix of <u>Challenge-Desafio</u>, <u>Boston</u> <u>Globe</u> and <u>Herald</u> articles, will immediately note gross distortion. Not only did the <u>Herald</u> and <u>Globe</u> lie about many facts, but in most cases chose to blatantly omit the role of CAR and the Progressive Labor Party. The truth of the class struggle in Boston that summer rests in the pages of <u>Challenge-Desafio</u>, which was distributed and conveyed to the communities where the actions occurred.

This appendix is included, therefore, not only to give an overview of their organized activities but to highlight some of the sharpest struggles. Reproducing the <u>Globe</u> and <u>Herald</u> articles demonstrates how much control the Boston rulers had over the media during their own attempts to organize racism.

First, we find there were many mass actions the Globe refused to publicize. On July 19, for example, Louise Day Hicks staged a 'sleep-in' during the Mayors' conference. This event had full page write-ups, with no arrests (Hicks was greeted warmly by the Mayor's son). The previous day, PL led a demonstration of one hundred people in front of the headquarters of the conference--for more schools and an end to segregated parents' meetings (see p. 327)--which the <u>Globe</u> did not see "fit" to print.

The <u>Globe</u> was careful, however, to make ROAR appear invincible. On August 11, seven CAR members held off fifty ROAR thugs in Haymarket square, and the <u>Globe</u> (see text p. 234) reported only that the seven CAR members had been arrested. Not one ROAR member got arrested that day. The <u>Globe</u> failed to report that out of two hundred fifty arrests the entire summer, just a handful belonged to ROAR. The only convictions came to black and hispanic members of the Committee Against Racism. Nor did the Globe ever indicate ROAR's losing trend, from fifteen thousand at their anti-busing rally in 1974 down to three thousand in 1975.

Second, no connection is made in the <u>Globe</u> between ruling class led violence and national Klan-Nazi publicity. The murder of Tom Medjerec, a white working class youth who tried to break up a South Boston gang fight, is only one example of the casualties of fomenting violence. In the pages of <u>Challenge</u> the fact becomes clear that racist and fascist violence is part of a nationwide movement. The June 23 action (p. 328) against the Nazis at City College in Sacramento is pasted up side by side with a ROAR cartoon. The Detroit fight against the Nazis on July 16 stands alongside the Boston CAR Round-up in the July 31 <u>Challenge</u> (p. 329). Also striking is the obvious attempt to build the Nazi Party with nationwide coverage on ABC-TV (p. 330). There was no equal--or any--time for an anti-racist speaker on the Boston summer project.

Just as important is the direct link between ROAR in Boston and ROAR in Rosedale, Queens, N.Y. (p. 295). In addition to Rosedale, the Morris Park Association in the Bronx (p. 331) was yet another offshoot of the same racist movement.

Only in the <u>Challenge</u> articles do we find a) the anatomy of ROAR, including their police connections, strike-breaking activities and all their political affiliations. They received cushy jobs within the Boston city government. Tip O'Neill put forward their anti-busing program as part of his platform (p. 321); b) accounts of ROAR's gang violence (pp. 333, 328, 334 and 335); and c) their sound defeats by anti-racist fighters (pp. 334, 333, 330, 336 and 337).

The incident at Carson Beach (p. 210) provides the best mass example of a mass racist action--combined with liberal groups, nationalists and the cops--contrasted with our commitment to fight racism. In all, perhaps two thousand anti-racists, many of them under the direct leadership of PLP and CAR, were committed to putting an end to Jim Crow racism. Although CAR and PLP were overwhelmed by the eight hundred cops and hundreds of racists, many blacks defended us against the nationalists, and our protection by local community members was never published.

Similarly, the largest anti-racist march on August 18 through downtown Boston never was covered in the bourgeois press. On that morning, no permit for the march existed. (See letter, "When a Permit is not a Permit." p. 338). But PL and CAR were determined.

The marshalls stood toe to toe with helmeted police. And police forces not in uniform waited in the wings to see if the march would take place. A priest walked beside the waiting marchers. The cloak covering his head blew open with the wind to reveal a police radio.

That morning, hundreds of communists and non-communists, workers and students, citizens and immigrants stood ready, too, to march together toward the Government Center from Boston Commons. The summer's petitioning had gathered more than thirty-five thousand signatures. Their petition demanded the maximum from the education budget, more money, teachers, smaller classes and an end to racist divisions with the parent-teacher organizations, with more busing if necessary. Note that the <u>Globe</u> (p. 339) claims this was a demonstration to indict Hicks rather than publicize the constructive demands actually on the petition. But even according to the lip service given CAR in the Globe and Herald articles that summer, CAR appeared as the only organization with a platform. ROAR had been exposed.

The court was forced to grant a permit at the last moment. The permit represented not so much a victory as a milestone in the weeks of sharp struggle. At that point a 'legal' roadblock would have exposed the courts even more for their role in maintaining racism. The keynote speech (p. 340) echoed down the corridors of downtown Boston's financial center and was heard by more than ten thousand spectators, many of whom joined the march. The march itself was a victory, and like all victories under the capitalist system, only temporary, but branded in the memory of workers forever.

ROAR Speaker Forced to Flee

BOSTON—Avi Nelson is talkmaster of a nightly 4-hour radio program here. He is also an arch-racist and a regular speaker at all the anti-busing rallies organized by ROAR (Racists on a Rampage). On Tuesday, April 15, he came to spread his racist—"blacks are getting everything"—lies at Boston State College.

BUT MEMBERS OF THE COMMITTEE AGAINST Racism (CAR), the Afro-American Students Association, and PLP attacked Nelson's Nazi-lies and disrupted his speech for over half an hour. Finally, security guards and outside cops were forced to take Nelson to another room and bar all but a select few people from hearing him.

The action won support from a lot of people who felt it was about time we started putting racism on the run. Many students said it was too bad we couldn't run him off campus completely.

ROAR—the main "anti-busing" organization in Boston—is now a national organization, and it is showing its fascist nature more and more clearly. During the past couple weeks members of ROAR have (1) busted up a hearing on the Equal Rights Amendment (ERA), chanting "Stop ERA." They claimed that "forced busing" is the only real issue women should be concerned with; (2) inspired violent assaults and attempted murders against black people (A black worker narrowly escaped death when pushed in front of an oncoming subway train by two white South Boston youths; several black families in a Dorchester apartment building have had bricks thrown through their windows five times in recent months.); (3) endorsed George Wallace's view that the U.S. is losing in Indochina because liberal politicians were intimidated by the anti-war movement into selling out to the Communists. (Wallace has some of his close friends scouting out whether he should run in the Mass. presidential primary next year.)

U.S. bosses need Wallace and groups like ROAR to prepare the ground for fascism. We need to organize **now** to destroy these fascists and the capitalist system they serve. This summer hundreds of students from all over the U.S. will be coming to Boston in the CAR Freedom Summer project. This project can go a long way toward stopping the fascists in their tracks and building a new anti-racist climate in the city to bolster united multi-racial struggles for jobs and better schools. We urge all students and workers to build and join the project by coming to Boston or by providing housing to the volunteers who do come.

Boston CAR Demands,
R.O.A.R. Out of Dorchester

BOSTON, April 19—A group of anti-fascist demonstrators was greeted by cheers and clenched fists of solidarity by white, black and Latin workers as they marched through the Dorchester community here today after having picketed the local fascist headquarters.

Dorchester Avenue threads its way through an integrated community of black, white and Latin workers. Many of the shops bare the imprint of ethnic background—Irish, Puerto Rican, Italian, Slavic. A new storefront has just been thrust forward into the shopping scene. It sells racism. Its front is anti-school busing. Its intention is fascism.

A group of black, white and Latin men and women marched vigorously through the street demanding an end to racism and unity against fascism. They came up to the storefront to find a group of fascists ready to defend their "heritage." Many people came out onto the street and 17 cop cars turned up within a matter of moments. The back of one squad car bore the ugly face of two German shepherd attack dogs barking their anger.

The group outside the R.O.A.R. ("Restore Our Alienated Rights") headquarters shouted abuse at the demonstrators: "Hitler was good! Yea racism! We need fascism!" They were letting it all hang out. Gone was the facade that "We're worried only about our children's education." The fact that had massacred black children since black people had been brought here as slaves and the face that had slaughtered millions in the death camps of Europe was now facing the anti-fascist fighters of the Committee Against Racism (CAR) in Boston. the "cradle" of U.S. "democracy." More police cars started arrive. but the 30 who were demanding an end to fascism and racism continued picketing. Their sounds— "Hitler— Hicks, same old tricks!"—resounded against the R.O.A.R. office and made those who were fascists go even more crazy. They screamed like wild beasts.

After a while the CAR group marched smartly back along the route they had come. A half block away groups of black, white and Latin people, obviously overjoyed some organized force would

Boston, April 19. Workers and students led by CAR picket R.O.A.R. office in Dorchester.

take up the banner of direct confrontation with these racists, cheered and raised fists in solidarity as they eagerly took leaflets. The 30 marched on to the huge nearby shopping area and collected names from people interested in joining CAR's Summer Project Against Racism.

While all this was happening. Gov. Dukakis was making it clear that the main enemy of white. black and Latin workers was those who rule and not those who work. The Boston Herald-American reported that he warned "the relatively young. collecting welfare will have to go to work even though it may not be 'the most pleasant work.'" The Governor's drive to cut welfare allotments by $311 million was to include forcing unemployed people to work on jobs "paying between $2.15 and $2.50 an hour." Dukakis' definition of "young" is "40 and under."

What unity to U.S. economists saying that 10 per cent unemployment is "acceptable" into the 1980s and Gov. Dukakis forcing people to work for almost nothing. racism and fascism is just the thing to insure that white and minority workers starve and kill each other for the next 10 years. Only unity to fight for jobs. a 30-hour work-week for 40 hours pay and for money for all schools will win needed gains for all workers. A huge May Day march. joined by thousands of Boston workers would start the steamroller moving towards these goals.

PLP On Busing

U.S. bosses are consciously promoting and backing the violent movement against busing in Boston and elsewhere as the battering ram of their strategy for fascism. In order to counter the rulers' plans, workers and their allies must adopt and act upon an unwavering class position that will enable us to maintain vital unity within our own ranks. Therefore, the Progressive Labor Party offers the following program on the question of busing and the schools:

—The public school system in the U.S. is generally rotten. Classes are overcrowded; basic skills are not taught; buildings are antiquated and unsafe; materials and textbooks are often unavailable; food and health service are non-existent or woefully inadequate. In addition, to the extent that the schools do teach anything at all, they systematically promote the foul ideology that maintains the ruling class in power: racism, anti-working class notions, male supremacy, patriotism-for-profits, etc.

—At the same time, racism creates by far the worst overall conditions in ghetto schools and in schools where a high percentage of students come from minority groups. This is overwhelmingly the case everywhere in the United States. Given this situation, many minority parents may reach the conclusion that their children would receive a better education in a school with a higher percentage of white children, where the effects of racism are not as devastating. THE PLP SUPPORTS THE UNCONDITIONAL RIGHT OF THESE PARENTS TO SEND THEIR CHILDREN TO THE SCHOOL OF THEIR CHOICE.

—However, many parents may not want to see their children transported long distances to schools outside their neighborhood. They reason, logically, that the schools should be improved where they live. THE PLP SUPPORTS THE RIGHT OF THESE PARENTS TO KEEP THEIR CHILDREN IN ADEQUATELY STAFFED AND MAINTAINED SCHOOLS IN THEIR OWN NEIGHBORHOODS.

—The bosses are able to use racism to build an anti-busing movement in cases where white parents oppose the arrival of new groups of minority students into their children's schools. These parents justify their action on the grounds that too many new students will create inferior conditions in the schools. This viewpoint is a trap. It can lead only to worsening the conditions in everybody's schools. To these parents, we say: DON'T BE A SUCKER FOR THE BOSSES. NOTHING—ABSOLUTELY NOTHING—CAN EVER JUSTIFY WANTON ATTACKS AGAINST ANYONE'S KIDS. WHEN CHILDREN ARE BUSED INTO YOUR SCHOOLS, WELCOME THEM. MAKE FRIENDS WITH THEIR PARENTS. UNITE WITH TEACHERS TO BUILD A MOVEMENT THAT CAN FIGHT TO WIN SIGNIFICANT IMPROVEMENTS IN EVERYONE'S SCHOOLS. DISUNITY AND RACISM ARE CERTAIN ROADS TO DEFEAT. HOW MANY SCHOOLS HAVE HICKS AND KERRIGAN BUILT FOR THE CHILDREN OF SOUTH BOSTON? HOW MANY JOBS HAVE THEY FOUND FOR UNEMPLOYED TEENAGERS?

—Ultimately, decent, non-racist education that teaches important basic skills and that prepares children for useful, productive lives is impossible under the capitalist system. We can have it only under socialism, after we have wiped out the big bosses and taken power by ourselves. Smashing the obstacles that block our way to this goal therefore becomes a primary task for our class. The greatest of these obstacles at the present time—particularly in the mass movement to improve the schools—is racism. The most virulent racism manifests itself in the anti-busing movement. The fight for socialism, the fight for survival, and the fight to win more and better schools depend on our ability to wipe out racism. DON'T FALL FOR THE BOSSES' PLANS TO SPREAD DISCORD IN OUR RANKS. THE ANTI-BUSING MOVEMENT IS A DEADLY TRAP—REJECT IT! WE MUST ACT IN BOSTON AND ELSEWHERE TO GUARANTEE THAT NOT ONE SINGLE HAIR IS HARMED ON THE HEAD OF ONE SINGLE BUSED STUDENT. THOSE WHO ATTACK CHILDREN VIOLENTLY ARE FASCISTS. THE WORKING CLASS WILL MAKE THEM PAY FOR THEIR CRIMES.

INCAR's Program For Boston

1. Build 25 new schools in working-class areas now. Upgrade all schools, starting with those in black and poor areas. Hire at $200 per week 5000 unemployed people to work on this upgrading plan.
2. Hire hundreds more teachers, especially minority teachers. Double the number of janitors for proper school maintenance.
3. Expand bilingual programs.
4. Indict John Kerrigan and Louise Day Hicks for conspiracy to violate the civil rights of school children.
5. End the practice of having parents' meetings segregated on the basis of race, now taking place at many schools. Multiracial groups of parents, students and teachers must form to fight for better schools. Integrated parents' meetings are the key.
6. Establish cafeterias and hot lunch programs in all schools.

Boston ROAR: Liberal Bosses Tool
Racist Union Buster

BOSTON—As the opening of the 1975-6 school year approaches, the racist anti-busing forces in this city are intensifying their violent attacks against both black and white people who act to oppose racism.

The organization known as ROAR (Restore Our Alienated Rights) is the main instigator and organizer of these attacks. At this point, it is the most significant and dangerous open racist organization now functioning in the U.S. For this reason, Challenge-Desafío readers may be interested in knowing a bit more about what makes ROAR tick.

WHO BELONGS TO ROAR? By now, most people have heard of Louise Day Hicks, the head racist of Boston who is ROAR's chairperson and founder. Others in the ROAR leadership include various political hacks like wild man "Dapper" O'Neill, School Committee member John Kerrigan, and various other ward heelers. Nine of the ten School Committee members are in ROAR. The organization's secondary leadership is made up of various patronage-grubbing racists like "Pixie" Palladino and Janet Palmariello. **There isn't a rank and file worker in the whole bunch.** More to the point, there are very few, if any, rank and file workers in ROAR's so-called "grass roots." The fascist thugs who have thrown rocks and bricks at school children, who have savagely attacked black families in Hyde Park and elsewhere, and who on July 27 ganged up on six black Bible salesmen from out of town on South Boston's Carson beach—do not come from the shops and factories. They are drunkards, perverts, junkies, the parasites—the "lumpen." As is the case with all fascist movements in their initial stages, ROAR's contingent of storm-troopers is recruited principally from among the unemployed who become lumpen (there are thousands of unemployed in South Boston who are not lumpens), and the families of policemen. Last week's **Challenge** editorial dealt with the collusion between ROAR and the cops. Nothing could be more accurate. On

Boston. Wherever ROAR forces appear, the uniformed fascist are there to protect them.

December 12, 1974, the Boston Police Patrolmen's Association donated $1000 to help ROAR hire a constitutional lawyer.

At the ROAR convention on May 18, Louise Day Hicks told her followers: "You **are** the labor movement." This is pure demagoguery—straight out of **Mein Kampf.** The fact is that ROAR is a union-busting, scab organization. Take the case of the Amalgamated Meat Cutters Packinghouse Division Local P575, which is presently located in Andrews Sq., South Boston. This local's logo shows a black and white hand clenched together in a gesture of class solidarity. The local is integrated. For months, its meetings have been harassed and, in some cases, broken up by "unidentified" (who else?) racist goons from South Boston. The local president is so fearful of retaliation that he will not issue a statement denouncing these attacks. Local P575 is now looking to sell its building and move out of South Boston. Furthermore, ROAR goons attacked pickets during a recent strike on the South Boston docks. Emulating the grand tradition of Hitler, Mussolini & Co., ROAR's action prove that **racists are inevitably union-busters.**

DOES ROAR HAVE A FRIEND AT CITY HALL? You bet. Kevin White, the liberal Mayor of Boston who got his start in life as corporation counsel for Rockefeller's Standard Oil of California in 1955, is on excellent terms with ROAR's Executive Board and has concluded a not-so clandestine political alliance with Louise Day Hicks herself. In October 1974, ROAR endorsed a No vote on a referendum that would have given the Mayor control over the schools instead of the present School Committee. The referendum lost. Six days later, ROAR Executive Board member Janet Palmariello's husband went on the Boston payroll in the Department of Weights and Measures. Other jobs have been channelled from White through Louise to ROAR E-Board members under the federally-funded Comprehensive Employment and Training Act (CETA). 9,000 Bostonians have applied for these jobs. Thomas Johnson, a ROAR E-Board member-at-large, is on the CETA payroll in the Public Works Dept. Nuncio Palladino, husband of Pixie (who, it should be noted, keeps a picture of Mussolini in her office), has been on the CETA payroll in the Housing Inspection Dept. since March 7 of this year. White, who just laid off 600 teachers, has a fondness for putting ROAR in nice jobs.

On November 20, 1974, White met in his office with the ROAR Executive Board. He announced that he would provide the Home and School Assn. with city funds to represent it in Judge Garrity's court. The Home and School Assn. has three regional representatives on the ROAR E-Board. White gave the ROAR leaders a typed list of twelve services he had provided for them. These included: hiring former Nixon mouthpiece James St. Clair to represent the School Committee in its legal fight with the State Board of Ed. (a cost to taxpayers of $250,000); authorizing funds for School Committee appeal to the Supreme Court; and ". . . asking my staff to assist you as much as possible in staging your rallies."

In return, except for the recent farcical sit-in at White's Mayoral Conference headquarters, ROAR has never publicly demonstrated against White. The mayorality is up for grabs in Boston this year. ROAR's leadership has refused to endorse any candidate, thereby in effect throwing tacit support behind White.

If all this collusion between the liberals and racist ROAR weren't enough, Tip O'Neill, the House Majority Leader and the prime figure in the Massachusetts Kennedy machine, has now stated that he will support an anti-busing constitutional amendment.

What is ROAR? A nazi organization of racist bums, sadists, and policemen; a fraternity of scabs and union-busters; a fascist movement protected and patronized by the ruling class: the scum of society paid to do the big bosses' dirty work. A united working class will destroy them.

"With all the help we're getting from our friends the mayor, Big Business, and the police, we still can't stop the PLP! What the hell is going on? It's not safe to hold a meeting anymore. Workers are telling us to get lost! Even a few of our closest, racist supporters are afraid to crawl out of their holes!

U.S. bosses are promoting the violent movements against school busing in Boston and elsewhere as a key battering ram of their strategy for developing fascism. The main anti-busing organization, ROAR, is seriously attempting to constitute itself as a nationwide group. **The ruling class wants the racist attacks against schoolchildren in Boston to serve as the springboard for similar attacks in dozens of other cities.**

THE INTERESTS OF THE WORKING CLASS DICTATE THAT THIS strategy **be smashed.** In order to counter the rulers' plans for fascism, workers and their allies must act upon an unwavering class position that will enable us to maintain vital unity within our own ranks and at the same time go on to the offensive. Therefore, the Progressive Labor Party offers the following program on the question of busing and the schools:

—We support and fight for the concept of **quality, integrated education.** Segregation in the schools, which prevails in ghetto schools else, harms the entire working class. It divides us, promotes racism, and therefore weakens our ability to fight back against the bosses. From a class standpoint, the fight for integration is inseparable from the fight for more schools, more jobs, higher wages, and more benefits for everyone, especially minority workers and their children who are hardest hit by segregation and racism.

—The public school system in the U.S. is generally rotten. However, because of racism, the worst conditions overall prevail in ghetto schools and in schools with a high percentage of minority children in attendance. Given this situation, many minority parents have reached the conclusion that their children will receive a better education in schools with a higher percentage of white children, where the effects of racism are not as devastating. These parents should be able to send their children to any school they choose. They should be provided with adequate busing service to accomplish this. When busing is used in this way, it can help to integrate the schools. **The PLP supports busing for integration.**

—The bosses are able to use racism to build an anti-busing movement in cases where white parents and students oppose the arrival of new groups of minority students into their schools. These parents justify their action on the grounds that black, latin, and other minority children will create "inferior" conditions in the schools. This viewpoint is a nazi trap. It can lead only to worsening school conditions for everyone. Those responsible for the disgusting conditions in the schools are the bosses, the politicians, and the school administrators. To the white parents who oppose busing for integration, we say: Don't be a sucker for the ruling class. Nothing—absolutely nothing—can justify wanton attacks on anyone's kids. When minority children are bused into your schools, **welcome them. Make friends with their parents. Unite with teachers to build a movement that can fight to win significant improvements in everyone's schools.** Disunity and racism are certain roads to defeat. Hicks, Kerrigan and ROAR have yet to build a single school for the children of Boston—and the Boston public school system is one of the worst in the country.

—At the same time, liberal politicians like Kennedy, Boston's Mayor White, and others, who represent the center of power in the U.S. ruling class, deliberately use the issue of busing to provoke as much racism and discord as possible in the ranks of the working class. When Judge Arthur Garrity (who was a high-ranking JFK campaign worker in 1958) issued his busing orders last year and this year, **he made it illegal to build any new schools in the city.** This is standard operating procedure when the liberals organize any busing program: they actually intensify racism by making integration appear contradictory to improvement of the schools. At the same time, liberal Mayor White stood by while the Boston police under his command let the ROAR-inspired fascists viciously attack black school children all year long. If we want to build a united movement that can win significant reforms in the schools and that can fight back against racism, we must smash both the open ROAR-type racists and the liberal bosses and politicians who stand behind them.

—Ultimately, decent, integrated, non-racist education that teaches important basic skills and that prepares children for productive lives is impossible under the capitalist system. We can have it only under socialism, after we have wiped out the big bosses and taken power by ourselves. Eliminating the obstacles that block our way to this goal therefore becomes a primary task for our class. The greatest of these obstacles at the present time—particularly in the mass movement to improve the schools—is racism. The most virulent racism manifests itself in the anti-busing movement. The fight for socialism, the fight for survival and the fight to win more and better schools depend on our ability to wipe out racism. Don't fall for the bosses' plans to split our ranks! The anti-busing movement is a deadly trap: reject it! We must act in Boston and elsewhere to guarantee that not one single hair is harmed on the head of one single bused minority student. **Those who attack children violently are fascists. The working class will make them pay for their crimes.**

A Progressive Labor Party Editorial

Boston CAR Summer Project Launched. Plans Include:

In Roxbury: Set up a Freedom School to work with community students on reading and math, conducting anti-racist courses, and help organize to stop the gross police brutalities. Roxbury CAR will work with South Boston CAR to set up welcoming committees.

South Boston CAR will begin by publicizing the fact that ROAR means nothing more than racism, and that racism keeps everyone from getting decent schools.

Boston State CAR will hold rallies on different campuses and busy shopping centers.

If you are interested in taking part in this BOSTON CAR SUMMER PROJECT, call 617-277-0232.

Dorchester. Boston CAR demonstrates

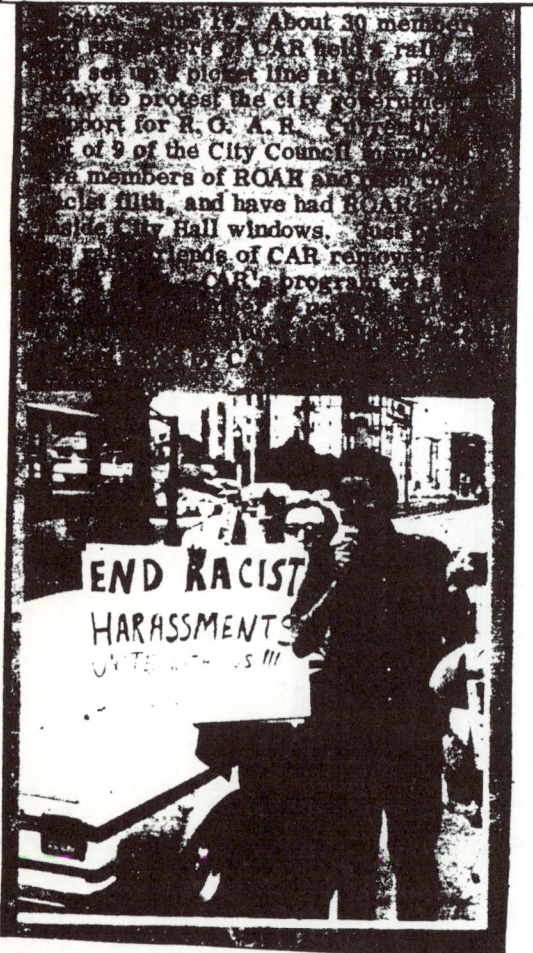

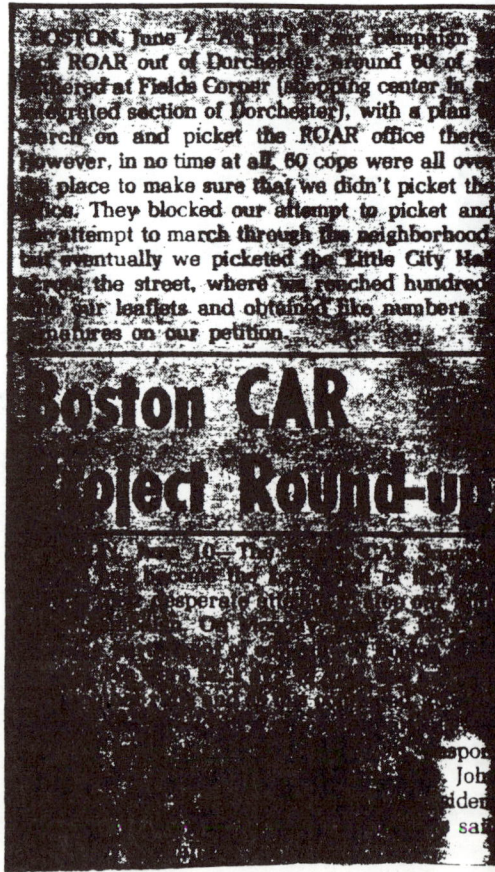

BOSTON, June 7 — As part of our campaign to kick ROAR out of Dorchester, around 60 of us gathered at Fields Corner (shopping center in integrated section of Dorchester), with a plan to march on and picket the ROAR office there. However, in no time at all, 60 cops were all over the place to make sure that we didn't picket the office. They blocked our attempt to picket and our attempt to march through the neighborhood but eventually we picketed the Little City Hall across the street, where we reached hundreds with our leaflets and obtained like numbers of signatures on our petition.

Boston CAR Project Round-up

COURSES/CURSOS

MATH/MATHEMATICA

1. Basic Concepts/Elemental
2. Algebra/Algebra
3. Bookkeeping/Contabilidad

SCIENCE/CIENCIA

1. Basic/Elemental
2. Chemistry/Quimica
3. Biology/Biologia

HISTORY/HISTORIA

1. Anti-racist History/ Historia antiracista
2. History of Black and Irish Working Class/ historia de la clase trabajadora negra e irlandesa

SPANISH/ESPANOL

1. Basic/Elemental
2. Conversational Spanish/ Conversacion

ENGLISH/INGLES

1. Reading/Lectura
2. Writing/Escritura
3. Literature and Drama/ Literatura y Drama

ART AND CRAFTS/ARTE

1. Painting/Pintura
2. Drawing/Diseño

RECREATION/RECREACION

1. Basketball/Basquetbol
2. Volleyball/Valleybol

SE NECESITAN FONDOS Y MATERIALES URGENTEMENTE.
Si a usted le gustaria contribuir, participar act-
ivamente o registrar a su hijo, por favor comuniquese
con la Escuela de la Libertad:

MONEY AND MATERIALS ARE URGENTLY NEEDED.
If you wish to contribute, participate actively
or register your children, please contact the
Freedom School at:

      CHARLES A.M.E. CHURCH
      551 Warren Street
      Rexbury, Mass.   442-7010

Freeedom School Opens July 7

ROXBURY, Mass.—The following article was prepared by the Committee Against Racism, Rosbury Chapter. The quote is from an interview with CAR member Barry Blackstone, a Boston student who was bused from Roxbury to South Boston last fall.

"**BOSTON CITY SCHOOLS ARE NO DAMN** good. Many of the teachers and principals are prejudiced against black and latin people. When they teach history about black and latin people, they don't tell it like it really happens ... They send you to a class "developmental reading"—there is a high level, low level, and a middle level—the high level is mostly white and the low level is mostly black. Sometimes it is just called the black level and the white level. I never remember taking a test for this program and when I asked to see my tests they told me that I had taken one but that I could not see it.

"At the South Boston High annex where I was bused last September, the conditions were just as bad as in any school in Roxbury. The cafeteria was nasty, the toilets were always stopped up and running over, the stairway was broken down ... When I was in school I could not talk to any of my white friends, because they would get beat up for seeing me. Wasn't anybody going to make friends too fast with the other races because they were afraid. A lot of kids did not want to fight but if they didn't, they got beat up by some of the older kids ... I think that if the parents stopped coming to the schools to picket and fuss about busing and stopped telling their kids what to say and stopped telling them lies about blacks, that busing and everything else could be worked out. I think that all parents should get together like CAR says and fight for better schools."

There is a new school in Boston this summer, and unlike the schools described by Barry, it will emphasize multinational unity. The Freeedom School is one of the major focuses of CAR Summer '75 in Boston. The Committee Against Racism believes that not only can a school with children of all races succeed, but that it can also teach a relevant anti-racist and pro-working class curriculum. Courses in multiracial history, Spanish, French, English, remedial math and science, music, art and physical education will be offered. Unlike the racist public school system here, the Freedom School will not be run by a small group of self-seeking politicians. Parents, teachers and students have worked together to develop a curriculum and will work jointly to carry it out. In the Freedom School no one is an expert: teachers are students, and students are teachers.

To date over 20 people, black, latin and white, from ages 9 to 19 have enrolled and we are expecting many more. The school will be in operation from July 7 to August 29, from 9 a.m. to 2 p.m. Free lunch will be provided. For more information about the school and the Committee Against Racism in the Roxbury area, call 442-7010 or drop by the school at Charles Street A. & M. Church at Elmhill Ave. and Warren St., from 9 to 2. We are located in the basement.

Boston CAR Round-Up

DORCHESTER, Tuesday, July 1 — Plans were made for speakout against racism, to be held late July at a meeting at Marshall School. A construction workers from the Dominican Republic offered to hold meetings and a block party in his house.

—July 2: CAR and the PLP hold rally in Codman Sq., a predominately black neighborhood of Dorchester.

—July 5: Rally at Upmann's Corner, beginning of citywide petition campaign demanding CAR's program of 25 new schools, upgrading of existing ones, multi-racial parents' organization and indictments of Hicks and Kerigan. Over 230 people signed the petition during the 2-hour rally.

CAMPUS — Boston State College campaign against cutbacks and racist like John Kerrigan with petitioning, leafletting. CAR party for Boston State stidents, well attended. Rallies at North-eastern and Harvard Sq.

HYDE PARK, Monday, June 30 — Contact was made with another black family, the Pages', living in Hyde Park and harassed by punks. A Page child was chased by a white teenager with a torch. Forty or 50 kids were around. But Mrs. Page found out who had done it and "kicked his ass." Punks also came around, saying "we got rid of the Daleys (they haven't; see last week's C-D), and we are going to get rid of you." Members of CAR met with Mrs. Page to decide how to stop the racist violence and to build for a meeting July 9. On Saturday, July 5, CAR held a rally in Cleary Square in Hyde Park. We leafletted and circulated the citywide petition for CAR's program. The cops who say that they cannot protect black homes from attacks, told us we would have to leave because we were "creating a disturbance." Two women came up to us at the rally, one said, "You have a fight on your hands, but I'm glad you're here." The other was a neighbor of the Pages. She took leaflets and helped hand them out, and when ROAR supporters honked their horns, she went out into the street and blocked their car.

MATTAPAN, July 5—Over 100 copies of **Challenge** were sold. The workers of Hyde Park like those from South Boston are obviously open to antiracist and communist ideas.

S.F. Paras Win Back Pay

S.F. June 30. The Board of Supervisors here has been forced to release $1.4 million in back pay to paraprofessionals. Mobilized by the TAC (Teachers Action Caucus) parateacher committee, the paras have been pounding on the city bosses door for the past month demanding the back pay.

Boston, Mass.
Upsurge of Anti-Racists

BOSTON—The ruling class is moving full speed ahead to turn this city into a racist blood-bath by the opening of the public schools in September. Local bosses, liberal politicians, open fascists represented by Louise Day Hicks and her organization "ROAR," and the cops are all acting out their roles in a deadly scenario that has already seen the murder of one working-class youth and promises to bring more. Meanwhile, the forces of anti-racism, represented by the Committee Against Racism (CAR), the Progressive Labor Party, and thousands of Bostonians who want class unity, are beginning to go on the offensive.

WITHIN THE LAST TWO WEEKS, SEVERAL important developments have taken place:
—Judge W. Arthur Garrity, the mouthpiece for the Kennedy wing of the Massachusetts ruling class (he was JFK's top campaign worker in 1958), finally released the plan for "Phase II" of school desegregation. In essence, it doesn't differ from Phase I, and therefore gives the racists a blank check to organize more violence in the schools. More children will be bused in 1975 than in 1974. Which is fine in and of itself, but the liberals have organized the busing to create the maximum possible havoc in an already collapsing school system. The "secret" clause of the Phase I ruling that made new school construction and significant expansion or improvement of existing facilities illegal is still in effect—with a vengeance. Under the guise of "reducing travel time," three schools (Elmer, Faneuil and Wyman) will be closed down. By the same token, some of the less dilapidated facilities, like the relatively modern Martin Luther King School, will be deliberately **underutilized**. With Phase II assignments now being delivered under these conditions, the racists are having a field day deluging the School Board offices with complaints, threatening to boycott school again in the fall, and promising more violence.
—Meanwhile, ROAR is more and more in the limelight provided by the liberal-owned media. Virtually every time Louise Day Hicks or her cronies blow their noses, a TV camera, radio mike or **Globe** reporter is there to record the event for posterity. The latest historic occasion was a sleep-in staged by Louise & Co. at Mayor White's hotel suite during the Conference of Mayors. The event had the authenticity of a pro wrestling match. Hicks and her cronies were graciously admitted by the Mayor's 5-year old son, who left after finishing an ice-cream cone. The **Globe** made this farce front-page news for all day and dwelt at length on Louise's dramatic complaint that the Mayor hadn't provided her with adequate room service. Not one ROAR member was arrested. The day before this ludicrous charade, PLP led over 100 demonstrators in a militant picket line at the front entrance of the racist Mayors' Conference HQ. The cops threatened to arrest all the demonstrators, and the **Globe** didn't think it worthwhile to report on this action, which demanded an end to mass layoffs and racism.
—ROAR's direct connection to racist violence has been clearly exposed in recent weeks. After a series of unsuccessful goon attempts to intimidate CAR

BOSTON, July 8—About 100 members and friends of PLP picketed the Mayor's Council meeting here

and prevent CAR organizers from conducting street agitation in Dorchester and South Boston, the anti-communist **Real Paper** ran a muckraking story that laid the blame for these incidents squarely on ROAR's doorstep. Led by Dan Yotts, a retired South Boston cop who is now a ROAR marshall, the racists have formed a vigilante squad which, by their own admission, requests and receives aid from the police. The **Real Paper** story identified the ROAR thugs in this squad as the men who viciously attacked a June 14 CAR rally in Dorchester and who have been present with bats and oars at other CAR actions. Since the appearance of this expose, the ROAR leadership has gotten jittery about placing their non-violent image in jeopardy and have told Yotts and his storm troopers to cool it temporarily.
—However, despite the provisional retreat by Yotts & Co., racist violence **inspired** by ROAR is increasing daily. At least two black families in the Hyde Park area have been brutally assaulted by racist street gangs. The July 10 **Challenge** reported on CAR's successful effort to organize a unity meeting to protect one of these families. Gang fights against black youths are occurring more and more frequently. On the night of July 4, a gang fight among white punks, the same kind of gang fight started daily by the racists, took place in South Boston. Tom Medjerec, a white working class youth who had just graduated from South Boston High, tried to break it up. The punks beat him with a bat. He died the next day. This is the logic of racist violence. Tom Medjerec was killed by racism. Louise Day Hicks and her bosses can be proud of their handiwork.
—While the liberal rulers and their puppets in ROAR are speeding up the preparations for fascism

in Boston, one bright ray of hope has emerged for working people and their allies here. In a few short weeks, the CAR Summer project against racism has met with overwhelmingly favorable mass response and can already count several important accomplishments. Over 100 CAR volunteers from all over the U.S. have launched a Greater Boston-wide petition drive to build more schools, hire more teachers (with preference to minority teachers), improve existing schools, and indict Hicks and the ROAR leadership as criminals. From Dorchester and Harvard Square, thousands of people are lining up to sign this petition—a good indication of what the working class of this city really wants. CAR plans to collect 50,000 signatures and then stuff them down the throats of the City Hall crooks at a demonstration on August 18.

In addition, the Freedom School organized by CAR in Roxbury has already enrolled 60 pupils in its first week of operation, and more are coming in every day to study classroom subjects and anti-racism.

THE PROJECT IS BRANCHING OUT INTO the mass movement with endorsements from several religious organizations, academic figures, and most importantly, the labor movement. The national office of the American Federation of Government Employees just sent a warm letter of support. Much more can and must be done on this score.

A steady flow of anti-racist volunteers is joining the Progressive Labor Party. The sharpness of the class struggle in Boston is enabling many to see that racism and its logical development, fascism, can be prevented or smashed only by destroying the profit system and the moguls who run it.

Sacramento
Students Rout Nazis at City College

SACRAMENTO, Calif., June 23—Sixty people demonstrated today against Nazis who were attempting to increase their ranks by preaching white supremacy on Sacramento City College campus.

The Nazis, in full uniform with swastika armbands, had a sixteen foot banner bearing a swastika, the white power slogan, and the location of their San Francisco offices. Cars at City College had been leafleted with Nazi slogans and announcements of their speaker.

Eight Nazis arrived: four in uniform, two men in suits, a girl about seventeen years old, and their speaker in a suit. Campus security guards and the Assistant Dean of City College were there to protect the racist Nazi mongrels.

The assistant dean was questioned why fascist racist Nazis were allowed on an integrated college campus of working class people. He replied with the usual "Right to free speech" bull, threatening to arrest demonstrators if they entered the room where the Nazis were speaking.

The sixty demonstrators, including members of Sacramento's Progressive Labor Party and the Committee Against Racism picketed, carrying signs with anti-fascist slogans, and chanted "Death to the Nazis," "No free speech for Nazis," and "Fascists No, Racists No." After a half hour of picketing no one had entered to hear the Nazis speak, except two reporters—one working for the Nazis paper.

Then PLP and CAR members stormed into the room chanting "Death to the Nazis." The Nazis ran out the back door, too scared to face the crowd in front.

Nazis and racists must be stopped wherever they surface. They have nothing to offer the working class except genocide and oppression.

THE CUSTODIANS OF ROARING RACISM

Chicago: CAR Wins Child's Return Home

CHICAGO—The Chicago Committee Against Racism went to bat for Nancy Johnson. Nancy was wrongfully charged with suspected child abuse. Her two-year-old son was taken away from her by the Department of Children and Family Services. After 3 months, Nancy was unable to even learn the specific charges against her, nor was she given the chance to defend herself against any charges.

When twenty members of the Committee Against Racism met with Children and Family Services, the social workers knew we were serious about getting Nancy's child back. The social worker changed her attitude right away and recommended that the child be returned. At a hearing on the matter, all charges were dropped, and the child returned immediately!

The racist doctor that made the charges against Nancy knew he was wrong. To prove this, he didn't even sign his name to the charges against Nancy. This victory was a giant step for CAR.

Detroit: PLPers
Send Nazis Flying

DETROIT, July 16—At lunch time yesterday, the cops had to rescue ten punks of the American Nazi Party from a furious crowd of workers in downtown Detroit. The Nazis, complete with boots and swastika arm bands, had come from as far away as Washington State to sell their filth for a few hours he day before and for nearly an hour yesterday, but when dozens of workers jumped on them, sending a couple of them to the hospital for stitches, the cops marched them into the nearby police station under custody.

At the same time they arrested two PLP members who had just arrived with four other members and friends to carry out what dozens (figure taken from the TV evening news), of workers had already done. The cops tried to get one of the Nazis to press charges against one PLPer but they had to release him when the Nazi declined, due to his living too far away.

As they were being escorted the Nazis chanted "White Power" but many onlookers, both white and black had their responses, ranging from "racist scum" to "I hope you bleed to death!" Only one onlooker said he thought the Nazis had a right to sell their trash, but he was quickly set straight by PLP members who pointed out that the ovens in Germany during WW2 proved that it was either them or the rest of us. Many workers bought **CHALLENGE** in agreement with this answer.

Today ten PLers and friends returned to the downtown area to make sure that none of the Nazis escaped hospitalization, but the Nazis didn't show up. Apparently they decided to lay low with their camp in nearby Port Huron, where no doubt they are trying to figure out which idiot among them suggested Detroit would be a friendly town.

Roxbury, Mass:
Freedom School: An Alternative

ROXBURY, Mass., July 16—"While public education deteriorates, Committee Against Racism poses its alternative." This is the slogan of the Committee Against Racism's Freedom School and on the morning of July 7th, when the doors to the school were opened wide, members and friends of CAR began to make the slogan a reality.

The first days of the school were filled with numerous activities, events and classes which clearly demonstrated that an integrated anti-racist school was possible. In one class for instance, a number of students read and discussed a CAR leaflet entitled "Racism Hurts Us All!" A group of 20 students in a history class taught by a member of the communist PLP, wrote and performed a skit called "Strikers and Scabs" (the skit was based on an article from **Challenge-Desafio** about the Pennsylvania Social Service Union strike). In addition, students took courses in Art, Math, English and Spanish all of which were received extremely well. Trips to local parks and swimming pools were organized and a "Freedom School" basketball team was formed. As the days went by the enrollment swelled and by week's end there were over 60 students involved! And more are expected.

One of the most important tasks of the school is to involve parents in the program. Only by building multi-racial parents committees within CAR will we be able to stop the racists this fall. A parents meeting will be held Thursday, July 17th and on Sunday, July 20th there will be a school picnic at Franklin Park (for info. call 442-7010).

Boston CAR Round-up

SOUTH BOSTON, July 17—CAR held a bullhorn rally at a large printing plant, Court Sq. Press, in South Boston today. CAR's 6-point program for better schools, stopping racists attacks on minority workers at Cort Sq. by ROAR goons and support for the unionization drive going on there were topics of the rally. Workers leaned out of their windows and cheered, many of them-minority and white-signed our petition (during their lunch break).

MISSION HILL— The area surrounding the CAR office has been the scene of a number of attacks on individual black people by racists groups over the past week. However, on Friday, the 18th, these racists were met by an enraged community. Ten racists were sent to the hospital. Four are still there.

DORCHESTER— CAR has planned a speakout for August 9th to unite parents into multi-racial welcoming committees for the fall. The American Federation of Government Employees, which has endorsed the summer project, and Children In Crises, Inc. are co-sponsoring the speakout. Four community people joined C... this week. Rallies were held everyday at Codman Sq., Uphams Corner and Fields Corner. Dorchester CAR meets every Wednesday at the Marshall School, 35 Westville at 7:30 p.m. Everyone invited.

HYDE PARK— The past week has seen continued canvassing of the community surrounding black families that have been attacked by racists gangs. A community meeting has been planned for the next day.

BOSTON— This past Friday, July 18, 20 members of the Committee Against Racism sat-in at Mayor White's office, in City Hall, for two hours while 70 members picketed outside to protest a 30 million dollar cutback in the educational budget. White says that these cutbacks will affect 1,200 unnecessary teachers aides, bus monitors, and others important for the functioning of schools. The mayor was away at the time, but we will return to meet with him to demand that he rescind the budget cutbacks and grant CAR's 6-point program.

Boston. CAR leads picket line which led to two-hour sit-in in Mayor White's offices.

Thus far the Freedom School has been a big success. However, with the rapid expansion of the program we're in desperate need of money for supplies, to meet the growing number of students. We need books, paper, pencils, art materials, etc. Therefore, we must ask our brothers and sisters from all over the country to reach once more into their pockets for funds to keep the Freedom School and Summer Project going. Please send all contributions to Committee Against Racism, 896 Huntington Ave., Boston, Mass. 02115. If you wish your contribution to go directly to the Freedom School, please note so on the check. Make all checks out to Committee Against Racism. If you would like to enroll your child or come to the Freedom School, please call 442-7010.

San Francisco
ABC-TV's Cop Violence Protested by PLP

SAN FRANCISCO, July 22—Over 150 people demonstrated outside ABC Channel 7 against the fascist and racist police attacks on Progressive Labor Party and the Committee Against Racism at our picket line two weeks ago. Chanting, "We don't like ABC, workers will smash racist TV," "Cops and Channel 7 say 'attack'; we say FIGHT BACK," we made it clear that we will not tolerate ABC's use of police terror to protect their advertisements for the Ku Klux Klan.

Our demonstration was in response to a prearranged fascist attack on our picket line of two weeks ago. We were protesting Channel 7's national coverage of the KKK. They showed the "new image" of the KKK, without masks, having a "friendly" community sing—also where to send for the Klan's White Power tee shirts and how to join. All this was for one of the most hated organizations in this country, with a long history of vicious racist lynchings and terror.

Ten members of PLP and CAR originally went to Channel 7 to demand equal time for an anti-racist speaker. We wanted to talk about the fights going on on the job and on campuses, and especially the Boston Summer Project—where workers and students are organizing against racist schools, working conditions and lay-offs. But news editor Charles Biggs flatly refused.

We organized a picket line to protest ABC's racism and to intensify our demand for equal time. ABC bosses were so worried about preserving their racist campaign that they arranged for our picket line to be attacked and broken up by the cops. Four people were arrested, one nearly killed when he was pistol whipped against the police car and his skull fractured. Two of these comrades are still facing felony charges for defending our demonstration.

Both the racism pushed by ABC and the attack by the police are parts of the ruling class' plan to bring fascism to the U.S. They want to continue and increase their racist policies and programs that are helping bosses in this country make bigger and bigger profits at the expense of the working class and our conditions. In San Francisco, ABC can't be so ready to advertise the KKK and the Nazis without expecting to be attacked for it. We must take the offensive, then we can win.

"ATTENTION"
(All You Forgotten People)
The Morris Park Community Association

Invites Everyone to Attend this Very Special Meeting
To Discuss:
(Are You Tired of Being the Forgotten Minority)

- **WE ARE TIRED** — Of being passive and submissive.
  Of fear, crime, and filth.
- **WE ARE TIRED** — Of unfair tax burdens placed on our backs by our government to cover budgetary deficiencies and just plain freeloading.
- **WE ARE TIRED** — Of being branded racist and bigots. When we speak out and take action on issues that concern us and affect our so called American dream of working hard for what we earned.
- **WE ARE TIRED** — Of having our children used as cattle so that minority children may be bussed into our neighborhood schools.
- **WE ARE TIRED** — Of standing idly by while our sons and daughters are denied entrance to certain colleges in favor of less qualified minorities.
- **WE ARE TIRED** — Of losing jobs after long years of seniority to unqualified newly-hired minorities.

WORKING WITH YOUR POLICE DEPARTMENT
"GUEST SPEAKERS"

Meeting to held at: PS 83, Auditorium
950 Rhinelander Ave.
Between (Radcliff Ave. & Bogart Ave.)
Bronx, N.Y.

Time: 8:00 p.m. Date: Tuesday, May 27, 1975

PROTECT YOUR FAMILY & PROPERTY NOW

ATTENTION NEW AND UNPAID MEMBERS: $5 per year
Please fill-in and return the following Membership Form. Upon receipt, we forward you a Membership Card.

MEMBERSHIP MORRIS PARK COMMUNITY ASSOCIATION 1801 RADCLIFF AVE., BRONX, N.Y. 10462	-CHECK- RENEW ☐ NEW ☐
NAME:_____	
ADDRESS:_____	
PHONE NO:_____ DATE:_____	

Boston: Anti-Racist Movement Grows
Desperate Bosses, Cops Can't Stop CAR

BOSTON, July 28—The inroads that the INCAR Boston '75 have made in their anti-racist project thus far, has the Boston bosses and their cops making desperate attempts to stop an ever growing movement.

RECENTLY RACIST PUNKS BROKE THE windshield of the canvassers in Hyde Park and threatened to attack if we did not leave the area, with cops telling CAR to get out of the neighborhood.

On July 23, about 50 fascist ROAR members attempted to invade a Hyde Park community meeting called by CAR. They were ordered out of the meeting by the 12 CAR members present. ROAR surrounded the building and locked everyone inside. Due to the pressure from residents attending the meeting, the cops were forced to escort us out of the building. While ROAR outnumbered CAR by at least 4 to 1, they begged to be hit. They called CAR "rich Jews trying to mislead the poor black people."

Meanwhile a van load of CAR's security people, who had come to aid those at the school, were followed by three carloads of ROAR filth. When the van stopped at a member's house in Hyde Park, a ROAR member attempted to assault the people. The anti-racists defended themselves, teaching the fascist a lesson. The van left the Hyde Park area.

Boston: Members of CAR and PLP picket and rally outside of courthouse where the 17 brothers and sisters who were arrested during the cops' fascist round-up are being arraigned.

followed by ROAR members, who pulled away as the CAR office was approached. The cops moved in fast, surrounding the office.

A crowd of 30 Mission Hill residents came to CAR's aid, but were ordered away by the cops. The cops, and ROAR who were led in by the landlord. Seventeen CAR members (mainly non-white) who had been singled by the ROAR thugs, were arrested and charged with assault and battery with a dangerous weapon. A CAR member who was doing his laundry across the street was also arrested.

The arrested were brought to the Hyde Park precinct, where a crowd of 300, organized by ROAR chanted "we want the niggers."

The next morning, at the West Roxbury Court House, 100 members and friends of CAR gathered to picket during the arraignment. Chants of "Attica *(continued on page 7)*

(continued from page 3)

means fightback" and "Boston '75, the racist won't survive" rang out as the CAR members climbed out of paddy wagons and joined in chanting with clenched fists.

The judge was forced to release the 17 on their own recognizance and they marched out of the courthouse, chanting to join the rally which was continuing outside. One long-time resident of Hyde Park spoke of the negligence of the District 5 police force, for arresting CAR people while failing to do anything about ROAR thugs. A PLPer reminded ROAR punks who were standing around, how communists had led the charge that smashed the fascists on Columbia Point, on May 3.

Boston CAR Round-up

HYDE PARK. CAR has recently expanded its work into neighboring Mattapan, an integrated section of Boston, with rallies held at Mattapan Square. The trial date for the 17 arrested at Hyde Park has been set for August 19.

CAMBRIDGE. In the past three weeks, thousands of residents have signed CAR's petition at Harvard and Central Square with hundreds of copies of **Challenge** sold each issue. CAR gave picket line support for striking city workers and is preparing for a campaign at Harvard to kick Edward Banfield off campus. Banfield, in *Unheavenly City*, says that blacks like to be poor. Banfield's returning to Harvard and increased governmental attacks against Portuguese and Haitian workers in Cambridge showed that the bosses are trying to make a racist offensive.

ROXBURY. This past Sunday, CAR held a picnic, with 15-20 families of Roxbury school children. More parents have become directly involved in the operation of the Freedom School, including one who will teach a course on carpentry.

DORCHESTER. On Wednesday, July 30, 11 community residents attended a CAR meeting. On Saturday, August 2, a unity block party saw close to 100 people joining in. The following day, we spoke at church about CAR.

MISSION HILL. CAR helped organize the Huntington Avenue Association, which was formed to protect the neighborhood from racist attacks. 20 residents attended the founding meeting. The Huntington Ave. Assoc. meets every Tuesday at 7:30 PM in the Hennigan School, 200 Heath.

SOUTH BOSTON. On Tuesday, July 29, South Boston and Roxbury CAR held a parent meeting which included people from South Boston, Charlestown, and Roxbury. A speak out against racism and for better schools, was called for Thursday, August 14, at the Roxbury YMCA, on the corner of Martin Luther King Blvd. and Warren. These parents meetings are held every Tuesday at 7:30 PM in the Marshall School, 35 Westville, Dorchester.

This past summer has seen increased attacks by racist gangs against black and latin on Carson Beach, in South Boston. On Sunday, July 7, 6 black men were beaten and chased by a gang of 100 racists. A ROAR spokesman stated in the Boston Globe, that "good colored people are welcomed," but "radical blacks and communists" are not, adding that "good colored won't come to South Boston," and blamed CAR and the PLP for the racial tension.

The August 4 Boston Globe, in a front page article, reports that 300 white youths, armed with bats, attacked a black taxi driver and a Puerto Rican family going by the beach, saying that it was in response to a leaflet supposedly put out by "outside agitators" in CAR and PLP, which called for not letting "honkeys use the beach." Even though a number of anti-racist groups and individuals had been discussing a beach liberation from racism, nothing was actually planned and this article is another step in the ruling class against CAR and the PLP, the main point being that outside agitators call a demonstration, increase racial tension, and don't bother to show up themselves.

Boston 75 forces have canvassed several factories in South Boston, using CAR's 6-point program petition for better schools and received a very favorable response from workers who see that racism is not in their interest and that uniting with other workers and CAR, is.

Committee Against Racism; Summer Project

BOSTON '75

Dorchester

BOSTON, June 26—Thirty militant and spirited people from the Committee Against Racism and members of the PLP, chanting "In Boston '75—the racists won't survive," "CAR is for schools—ROAR is for fools," in a demonstration today at Dorchester Little City Hall, demanding the shutting down of the ROAR office and for more schools.

In the past few weeks of canvassing around the community with petitions, demanding the ousting of ROAR from Dorchester, 2,000 signatures have been obtained.

During the demonstration, 15 goons heckled us, after 50 cops arrived. It was clear by an earlier incident at Upham's Corner (where cops rushed to save ROAR when goons with bats were disarmed by unarmed CAR members), that they weren't pacifist. That's why the cops put up a pretense of protecting CAR in order to create an illusion that fascists like ROAR are invincible.

The viciousness of the racist is such that one black man was beaten by 15 men with bats in broad daylight; houses and places where minorities are employed have been fire-bombed. These are some of the incidents that have occurred in Dorchester. Only a mass organization of workers and students in Dorchester can rout the racists.

To begin to correct one of our basic weakness in the Boston '75 project—not mobilizing enough people into our base to take an active part in combatting racism—we held an Open House at the CAR office for people who live in the neighborhood. You can be part of this growing anti-racist movement. For information call 617-277-0232. Send contributions to Committee Against Racism, 896 Huntington Ave., Boston, Mass. 02120.

Round-up

ROXBURY, June 30—Freedom School scheduled to begin July 7 will offer tutoring in Math and English and an anti-racist Irish and Black history course. For information, call 277-0232. Freedom School: 42 Hawthorne St.

SOUTH BOSTON—Leafletting at the Broadway subway station. With the High School students and one of the three black teachers at South Boston High. Church groups in the area have been contacted about supporting Boston '75 activities.

DORCHESTER, July 26—Demonstrators at Fields Corner presented petitions (see article) to the Little City Hall. Petition drive will continue, especially around Fields Corner and Uphams Corner. Speak-out against racism being organized. CAR meetings held every Tuesday at the Marshall school, located at 35 Westvil Ave. Self-defense organizations and welcoming committees will be set up at these meetings.

BOSTON STATE COLLEGE—Petition drive against racist cutbacks and racist John Kerrigan has begun. Faculty press conference on the cuts was called by Al Leisinger, a member of CAR and the Boston State Faculty. Leafletting about the Freedom School continues there.

HYDE PARK—CAR committee being set up in this predominately white working class neighborhood. The Daleys, a Jamaica family moved into this neighborhood in mid-June. Since then they have been harassed by gangs of punks, many of them cops' children. Mrs. Daley was stoned and her collar bone broken. Since learning of the situation last week, CAR has worked with the Daley family. An open letter to the community written by the Daleys was distributed by CAR. CAR has also leafletted and canvassed the area to stop the violence. Security has been arranged, with members of CAR guarding the house and the gangs have been stopped from breaking windows. A weakness in the security has been the failure to involve more people (especially from the Hyde Park area) in protecting the Daleys. Clearly, it is in everyone's interest to join in this project as several white families have also been harassed by the racists.

COLUMBIA POINT: ROAR has been attacking people in the projects here for a year. A self-defense unit is needed now.

BOSTON, June 30—20 Residents of Hyde Park came to a meeting called by the Daley family and CAR to organize against the terrorist attacks against the Daleys. Not intimidated by the carloads of goons driving around, we set up a crisis phone line and organized neighbors to patrol and canvas the area. We are meeting again on July 9 at the same place (Pius the Tenth Church).

Of Cops And Crime

During this period of municipal crisis, the bosses are letting a few cops go and many cops are trying to preserve their ranks, saying that without them "crime will increase," raising a racist fear campaign. McFeely, head of the N.Y.C. Police Benevolent Association (PBA) had gone as far as to demand that other workers be fired instead of cops because cops are "more important."

But an interesting thing has again proved what PLP has always said: cops are actually the main protectors of crime and the more cops the more crime.

—From 1965 to 1971, police personnel increased from 25,000 to 31,000 in N.Y.C. During that same period crime rose more than 30 per cent.

—The police are virtually powerless to prevent many of the serious crimes that most alarm the public—murders, rapes and burglaries. (**N.Y. Times,** July 23).

—During the 10-day strike ended last week by the Albuquerque, New Mexico police force, crime actually went down. Mayor Harry E. Kiney said that criminals feared armed citizens protecting themselves more than they feared the police. (**N.Y. Times,** July 24).

—During the 1971 cops' strike in N.Y.C., crime actually went down.

—The Knapp commission investigating N.Y.C. police corruption and the revelations by ex-cop Frank Serpico showed that police actually control the drug traffic here (the cause of a great percentage of burglaries and other serious crimes).

Capitalism causes crime. Unemployment, drugs, misery and other evils of capitalism create lumpens (or criminals who leech on working people). Cops only protect those lumpens and use them to enrich themselves.

The main role of cops is to make sure that workers don't rebel against capitalism and to protect the capitalists. The biggest racketeers and crooks are in the government and they seldom get caught (and when they do, as Nixon and his gang, they get off easy). Cops are scabs, e.g., they used their horses when hospital workers blockaded Brooklyn Bridge on July 24 protesting hospital cutbacks in N.Y.C., the workers got them out of the way (see article) and took over the bridge for more than an hour. When one cop passed out and was taken away unconscious by his buddies, the crowd cheered, chanting "Hope he dies."

The reason the bosses have fired a few cops is because they got plenty of cops already to do their dirty job of keeping down the workers and they can afford to let go a few thousands. Cops are enemies of all workers as they prove everyday. We don't need the parasites!

CAR Round-up

SOUTH BOSTON, July 23—A bullhorn rally organized by CAR in downtown South Boston, three blocks from the ROAR office, followed previous canvasing and petitioning which was well received. Many people listened as CAR spoke of its 6-point program and plans for a joint Roxbury-South Boston Charleston speak-out to organize welcoming committee to protect bused children. After 15 minutes, the cops made us turn off the bullhorn. The presence of the cops intimidated friendly and neutral people. The cops did nothing to stop the small group of racists that were heckling. We leafleted and petitioned for 10 more minutes and left.

CAR's lead is being followed in South Boston, where two black men were attacked by a racist gang. Seven elderly white women came out of their houses and chased the gang away, calling them animals and saying they should be shot. These women surrounded the two men, protecting them until an ambulance arrived.

ROXBURY, July 26—Rally at the American Legion Highway shopping center brought over 200 signatures on the petition. Over 70 students are now enrolled in the Freedom School, which has been advertised on a number of radio stations as a public service announcement.

DORCHESTER—Speak-out on racism being organized to be held on Saturday, August 9 from 4 PM to 10 PM at the American Legion Hall, 10 Dunbar Ave. For more information call 282-7655.

Rebel Against Cop Harassment

FLASH. Boston, August 11. On the heels of the swim-in at Carson Beach, the fascist Boston police have stepped up their harassment of black residents, terrorizing the communities of Mission Hill, Eustif Projects on Harrison Ave, Washington St. in Dorchester, and Upmans Corner and Roxbury.

Police attacked minority workers with clubs and dogs. In the Eustif Project, the cops invaded the buildings like gestapo, pounding doors with clubs, breaking windows and attacking passersby.

Workers fought back with rocks and anythings else they could get their hands on.

Earlier in the evening, about 50 ROAR thugs attacked 7 black and white CAR members who had come to Government Center for the TV show, Mass Reaction. A white bus driver attempted to help out the anti-racist forces who were being attacked. The cops arrested the 7 CAR members on felony charges, but did not touch any of the ROAR thugs.

The stepped-up harassment is clearly an attempt by the bosses here to whip up a race war, which they can use to stop the busing plan. Opening school day has now been set back to September 8.

Liberals-Fascists-Police: Partners in Crime!

It is about mid-way in the Boston Summer Project. This project, led by the International Committee Against Racism (ICAR) has involved about 175 students and others from around the country. The Summer Project was launched to combat racism, which in Boston combines mass terrorism against the black community—especially children. Prior to the summer the racists organized around the stopping of school busing for integration.

During the past six weeks the CAR and Progressive Labor Party forces have reached tens of thousands of Bostonians with their anti-racist ideas. INCAR and PLP have linked terrorism and racism to the development of fascism. Boston has become the scene for hundreds and often thousands of semi-armed hooligans roaming the streets attacking black people. Now ROAR attacks whites who dislike their racist-fascist ideas.

Not only have the INCAR and PL forces reached thousands with their ideas, but they have organized many more anti-racist fighters into struggle. Larger and smaller skirmishes have been held against the organized fascist group called Restore Our Alienated Rights (ROAR). In most cases, when INCAR and PL were attacked by the hooligan bands, the fascists were repulsed. In some cases citizens in the immediate locality have come to the aid of the anti-racists. Because ROAR has not been able to smash the Summer Project, and because ROAR is losing much ground amongst many white forces in Boston, they are desperate. INCAR and PLP have gotten under their skin! The fascists are losing ground as the fight has been carried right to their doorstep by a relatively small group of anti-fascists.

It is worthwhile to digress for a moment and point that you can't defeat fascists by looking the other way, or by ignoring them. Some groups talk about fighting fascism, but this is reduced to press releases and chatter in their papers. The Boston Summer Project has shown that one of the best ways of fighting the fascists is to win away or neutralize the people whom the fascists can either convince or intimidate, on their own turf.

In desperation, ROAR has now been forced to rely on the full power of the state. Unable to *break the will* of their enemies, *defeat* them on the streets, or even to *isolate* them from the general community, they have been forced to call on the uniformed police. We say uniformed, because much of the ROAR base is amongst the police and their families. The police have just arrested 17 CAR and PLP people for felonious assault. These charges have been pressed by ROAR. The CAR and PLP people were arrested at gun point. Even this *stopped nothing!* The next day, INCAR and PLP were on the streets. They conducted the Roxbury Freedom School, and demonstrated at the court house against the arrests.

In all cases in which ROAR has attacked the anti-fascist forces, the police responded with arrests and attacked the anti-fascists. Not once

Progressive Labor Party Editorial

was a ROAR member treated likewise. Obviously, the police and their liberal Mayor White stand full square on the side of reaction. And why not? Only days ago the Mayor lopped 30 million more from the school budget. The liberals need the overt right-wingers to divert and split the workers from liberal mis-deeds. These forces which expose, attack and organize against any of these anti-working class actions are hit by both liberals and their right-wing partners.

As the ranks of the anti-fascists grow the police mask of supposed objectivity will be dropped. The police force is a willing adjunct of the fascists. However, if the anti-fascists grow vigorously they will be more than match for them. In the final analysis the workers are the many, and they the few. How can one compare the strength of a few bullies against the fury of oppressed workers? This is the direction that the Boston Summer Project is leading to. There will be no other end to the story.

When A Permit Is Not A Permit

Dear CHALLENGE-DESAFIO:

The attempt to revoke the permit already granted for the CAR (Committee Against Racism) march on Aug. 18 was a study in ruling-class hysteria. On Friday, Aug. 15, at 4:30 P.M., three uniformed cops arrived at the CAR office here with a 1-sentence letter from the Traffic Commissioner (on obvious orders of liberal Mayor White) canceling the march permit. They figured this would accomplish three things: 1) a "march" forced onto the sidewalk, if attempted, would be seen by a lot less people; 2) now the press could print the "story" that there would be no march, without a permit; and 3) they hoped this would scare a lot of people from marching at all and cause many sympathizers to think it was being cancelled.

But CAR had no intention of backing out, not with the positive response they had been getting all summer whenever they initiated militant struggle. CAR's lawyers and legal committee were in court early Monday morning demanding the judge revoke the ban. The judge called for a city lawyer to appear, so one was sent over from the Traffic Commissioner's office. His "defense" was that the court should "respect the Traffic Commissioner's wishes." This was too much for the embarrassed judge who sympathized with the rulers but felt it had to be made to look better than that. He called for a second lawyer.

This one accused CAR of all sorts of "crimes" but that also fell flat. Then he said that it was "suddenly" discovered on Friday at 3:15 P.M. that the police were against this march due to its "potential" violence. From where? From the events around the picnic at Carson Beach two weeks before! But if that were true, how could it "suddenly" be discovered 12 days after that event?

Finally the exasperated lawyer fell back on the idea that, with the cops "not now expecting" a march, there wouldn't be enough police to handle the situation! This said while hundreds of cops were massing outside the City Council and along the route of march. Even the businessmen in court that morning on their own cases laughed out loud at that one.

The judge, although openly sympathetic to the racists, had to choose between allowing the permit or brazenly admitting that a fascist situation existed in Boston. He was forced to choose the former and granted a restraining order against the city, even as hundreds were preparing to march and thousands more were sympathetically awaiting them.

These ruling class antics show how fearful the bosses are of the burgeoning anti-fascist, anti-racist, pro-working class movements arising in Boston. Even now the press is starting to compare it with the massive anti-war movement of the Sixties.

—A Boston PLP'er.

200 march on City Hall
CAR seeks indictment of Hicks, ROAR officers

More than 200 members Committee Against Racism (CAR), chanting and carrying placards, marched from Boston Common to City Hall this afternoon, with a petition seeking the indictment of City Councilor Louise Day Hicks and the executive officers of the antibusing group, ROAR.

The march took place after the Suffolk Superior Court overruled the city's revocation of CAR's parade permit.

Members of CAR already were gathered on the Common when word of the court's action came.

A group of Boston Police Tactical Patrol Force officers stationed at Beacon and Park streets to maintain order and prevent the march disbanded.

Prior to the court hearing, Finley Campbell, CAR cochairman, told his group: "We'll march anyway whether we're allowed to or not. We'll take the Freedom Trail instead of going to City Hall.

"We don't consider our march permit to be revoked," he added, "until it is done by a judge."

He noted that the revocation came in a one-sentence letter signed by Boston Traffic Commr. William Noonan.

Campbell said his organization is seeking the indictment of Mrs. Hicks and executive officers of ROAR (Restore our Alienated Rights) for "conspiracy to violate the civil rights of school children."

Members of the group carried signs protesting racism, demanding the hiring of more teachers to reduce class sizes and call for the expansion of bilingual classes.

In a press release, CAR charged that certain politicians "are using the issue of outside agitators to cover up their segregation policies."

Police have cool day at Carson Beach

The cool weather, the presence of about 800 policemen, and the concentrated efforts of the people themselves all blended yesterday to help provide Boston with a quiet day — a sharp contrast to the last three Sundays which were marked by racial disturbances in South Boston.

At one point yesterday 50 of the policemen gathered in a corner of a police staging area at Bayside Mall in Dorchester to attend a Mass celebrated by Rev. James Lane, a Boston police chaplain.

Later in the day, about 100 Boston, state and MDC policemen took part in patrols and training exercises near Carson Beach, scene of a confrontation last Sunday between blacks and whites hurling rocks and bottles at each other. There were no reports of trouble yesterday.

Overcast skies and cool temperatures also helped keep most of the usual weekend crowds away from the beach.

A spokesman at the South Boston Information Center, a neighborhood center, a point of antibusing activities, said: "The word is out to avoid confrontation."

unsigned leaflet, circulated in parts of the city and calling for an assembly of "veterans" at Roxbury's Franklin Field yesterday, as a factor that generated some concern.

"Fortunately, that march did not materialize," he said.

Snedeker said he visited the South Boston Information Center shortly before noon to ask if "anything was up." After being told there were no problems, he praised the "mutual working relationship" that has developed between the center and his officers.

Warren Zaniboni, chief marshal at the Information Center, said 150 persons associated with the center were in the streets of South Boston yesterday "keeping kids from gathering in groups."

Meanwhile, three black Dorchester men were to be arraigned today in Dorchester District Court on disorderly person charges in connection with disturbances on Geneva avenue and Corona street in Dorchester yesterday.

Ralph Searcys, 36, and Carl Searcys, 25, both of 50 Corona st. were arrested at 11:30 a.m. after police said they confronted with baseball bats a group of whites similarly armed. The Searcys said the whites vandalized Ralph Searcy's business, Cris's Auto Body at 451 Geneva av.

Ely Henderson of Charles street, was arrested about 8:30 p.m. at 451 Geneva av. Police said he was apparently taking part in a demonstration staged by the Committee Against Racism (CAR).

Police said they confiscated six molotov cocktails from the roof of the auto body shop entrance last night after receiving information from neighborhood residents.

Police did not know who placed the bombs on the roof. The Searcys said they were unaware of the bombs.

About 50 members of CAR went to Station 11 on Gibson street, Dorchester, to protest what they called "police brutality" in Henderson's arrest. There were no incidents at the station and the crowd dispersed after Henderson was released.

Meanwhile, police at Station 3 on Morton street, Mattapan, reported three incidents of whites' cars being stoned last night in Dorchester. Two of the drivers were treated for facial and head lacerations at Carney Hospital and released.

We helped a kid in Needham sell a dog in Foxboro.

Give one million people a chance to buy what they're selling. Call Globe Classified. 929-1500

Boston Anti-fascist Forces Unite:

March Inspires Workers' Anti-Racism

BOSTON, August 18 — Tens of thousands of Boston's workers, black and white, lined the streets of the downtown area and cheered over 300 militant members and supporters of the Committee Against Racism (CAR), as they marched from the Boston Commons to the Government Center today, rallying for better schools and against racism. The well-integrated march had defied an attempt by all the rulers of Boston to stop them and, even more important, to stop the overwhelming sentiment of the working class here to express itself against a cop-provoked race war and for unity of black and white.

The liberal mayor and the cops had revoked the march permit at the last minute; the press had announced nothing would take place; the cops had been on a rampage for weeks and were now massing at the City Council steps and along the march route. In the face of all that, the march took place (winning reversal of the permit ban hours before). It was cheered by thousands and 35,000 signatures of Bostonians on petitions for better schools, busing and against fascist ROAR were brought to the Gov't Center.

When the marchers assembled at Boston Common, one young black working-class woman was so impressed that she grabbed the mike and announced she was "joining CAR immediately! This is what we need here!" At least two dozen other Bostonians signed up for CAR after that.

As the marchers wheeled down Tremont Street, chanting anti-racist slogans and demanding better schools for all, workers left their desks, shop machines and sales counters, looking out windows of buildings on both sides of the march, watching intently, cheering and giving the clenched fist salute. Tens of thousands of black and white workers, plus 35,000 who had signed the petitions, gave lie to the rulers' claims that "outside agitators" were the only anti-racists in Boston.

A Nazi who tried to "lead" the march carrying a sign about "red jew Gerrity" wound up in a four-foot ditch with his sign destroyed.

Defy Racist Cops
Rebels Counterattack

BOSTON, August 15— With the memories of years of racist police brutality, and Carson Beach on their mind, thousands of young black and latin rebels took to the streets for three days here, barraging the cops with rocks and bottles, and anything else they could get their hands on.

Monday, August 11 began the first in a series of nights of defiance of the cops, sellout black leaders of ROAR, and the city government. It all began about 8:30 PM in the Eustif Project in Roxbury, when during a fire several firemen who had allegedly been stoned called in the Boston Police, who im-

apartment. Working people's anger mushroomed when the cops beat a young brother on the roof of one of the apartment houses. Upon observing this, angry workers bombarded the cops with stone missiles and threw bricks at moving cop vehicles. This energy became misdirected however; when rebels began to make indiscriminate attacks upon white people driving near the area. The cops moved in rapidly in full riot gear with carbines, shotguns and dogs. The Tactical Police Force (TPF), the elite of the Boston gestapo, took the lead in this offensive. Just as five of us in PLP arrived on the scene we saw

CAR March
continued from page 3

When the marchers arrived at the Gov't Center, they found thousands of government workers waiting outside for them, ready to listen and cheer the speeches and events that followed. These government workers had read about the CAR Summer Project and the march in their union newsletter, the American Federation of Gov't Employees, whose district leader had endorsed both. He later withdrew the endorsement. The papers said "nothing would take place." The permit was revoked, but these workers waited their lunch hours and beyond to greet the anti-fascist militants. This was the true sentiment of the trade union movement rank and file expressing itself and shows the potential of mobilizing the working class's feelings against racism.

The Gov't Center where the City Council has its offices was like an armed camp. At least 150 cops, motorcycles and horseback were lined up in front of the steps. Hundreds of other jack-booted, riot-geared cops were in the area, many with attack dogs. The City Council members—9 of 10 are ROAR members—had canceled their meeting in which they were discussing how to screw the workers of Boston and were watching furtively from the windows. In these windows, from fascist Louise Day Hicks' office to racist Dapper O'Neil's, were the letters R-O-A-R, brazenly advertising this racist outfit (two of the letters having been put back up, after CAR members had torn them down, earlier this summer).

This was the fascist-like scene that "greeted" the marchers and their supporters as they arrived at the Gov't Center. But they then proceeded to turn it around. Findley Campbell, chair-person of International CAR, made a fiery speech in which he contrasted the bicentennial ravings of the ruling class with the actual facts—the 200 years of popular struggle of black and white workers in this country. He attacked Mayor White, the liberal, along with the Hicks gang with whom he is working, comparing them all to "dinosaurs—big teeth with brains like peas. They're on their way out," declared Campbell, to the cheers of the assembled throng.

At this point the marchers all turned to the racist

continued on page 5

CAR March
continued from page 4

City Council members at the windows behind their armed guards and in unison gave them the finger. "We will turn ROAR into a meeow," Campbell shouted, to the delight of the crowd.

A black worker from Dorchester spoke about how he had been harassed by racists and arrested for defending himself. A Progressive Labor Party member explained how the bosses use racism to divide workers and prevent them, minority and white, from winning their demands, how we must fight for socialism to smash racism once and for all. Initially, at Boston Commons, the CAR Freedom School had put on a skit showing how the only way to improve schools is through multi-racial unity.

Then 12 members of CAR attempted to present a representative amount of the 35,000 signatures on the anti-racist, pro-busing petitions to the City Council. When racist O'Neil saw them coming, he became frantic. He immediately turned to the 15 ROAR thugs guarding his office and screamed, "I deputize you!" The CAR members left and re-joined the rally.

This event marked the end of CAR's Boston Summer Project, but it marked the beginning of the organized anti-racist and anti-fascist movement in Boston. Many Boston workers and students have joined CAR and are preparing to welcome and protect bussed students on the opening day of school, Sept. 8. Workers and unions are being contacted to come to Boston Labor Day events (see announcement page 3). All this is becoming the basis to counter-attack against the plans of Boston's rulers for a race war here, an attempt to whip up racist hysteria and there-by defeat attempts to have integrated schools.

The response to the Summer Project, the 35,000 signatures gathered in less than six weeks by a relatively small number of people, the tremendous outpouring today supporting anti-racist sentiments, all point to the fact that probably 90 per cent of Boston's working class is ready for a rank-and-file-led, united movement of black, latin and white for working-class demands, for jobs, against racism, for better schools for all, and for the smashing of the ROAR fascists and their liberal counterparts in City Hall and Washington.

GENERAL DYNAMICS STRIKE:

Company Scabs Face 'Fight to the Finish'

GROTON, Conn., Aug. 26— Workers at General Dynamics (GD) are in their eighth week of a long and bitter struggle against the company's Electric Boat Division here. The bosses have tried many tactics to smash the solidarity of the rank-and-file members of the New London Metal Trades Council (MTC). One is phoning workers urging them to come back to work and scab, saying "Oh, you don't have to worry about the union, we'll take care of that."

THESE SCUM OF THE EARTH WHO CALLED workers knew well that scabs are **never** forgotten. (Recently an article told of a coal miner who shot his brother-in-law who scabbed on a strike 23 years ago!) These bosses know once a person scabs he or she is marked for the rest of their life. But only about a dozen scabs crawled in out of 10,000. Most have quit or re-entered the union. The company's strike-breaking attempts are not bearing fruit.

But there is a strong possibility GD will organize strike-breakers from elsewhere. For instance, they have intensified their "training programs" in other facilities. Reliable reports indicate they have an excessive amount of trainees for the immediate area. This means that the MTC must be prepared to mass picket and fight these scabs, if the company chooses to bring them in to break our strike.

If our union officials don't respond fully, we must mass picket to save the unions despite what the leaders say, despite what the "law" says. There is no law that can save a union. Look at Dow Chemical, now a non-union sweatshop. The "law" destroyed that union.

Remember well, unions were originally "illegal." Workers fought and died for the right to unionize. If we are to win, we too must be prepared to fight, and die, if the company chooses violence to crush us. The other alternative is to die the slow, murderous death of a non-union death house. That is the COMMUNISTS HAVE SAVED LIVES WHEN companies and governments choose to crush workers. When bosses choose to kill us slowly on the job, communists have saved lives by attacking corrupt union leaders and forcing union and government codes to protect workers. Communists are not blood-thirsty. We thoroughly understand that we, as communist workers, must be prepared to fight to the finish to win a good life.

PLAY REVIEW

GROTON, Conn.—Striking members of the New London County Metal Trades Council put on a show for their brother and sister strikers at the plant gates here, under the very noses of the General Dynamics bosses. It consisted of the brilliance and talent of rank-and-file workers who are striking GD, with a natural humor and wit that would surpass any playwright.

DESPITE RED-BAITING, DESPITE THE bosses' agents cackling about the "Commie peril," the rank and file surged ahead. The final number was the entire audience becoming the "cast," and together singing **Solidarity Forever** with fists raised high in defiance of a company camera trained on the show from the top of a building across the street.

It is this unbeatable unity that will forge our union into the fighting tool that we need to win a better life. This solidarity can smash the bosses, their scabs, the fascists and the rest of the anti-communist scum.

Gen. Dynamic Strikers Use Skits To Expose Bosses

GROTON, Conn. — The strike at General Dynamics, Electric Boat Division is now in its seventh week. The bosses have refused to talk. Relying on stalling and bribes from the federal government, they plan to starve the workers out. Since the beginning of the strike, the Progressive Labor Party and other rank-and-file fighters have won respect from many of the 10,000 workers holding the fort.

RANK-AND-FILE COMMITTEES HAVE SPRUNG up. One such committee—some strikers linked up with members of the community and PLP'ers—wrote a skit.

The skit was performed in front of the Engineering Building, with some 1,000 Marine Draftsmen Association members and members of the striking Metal Trades Council watching. The skit depicts J. D. Businessmen, no relation to J. D. Pearce, general manager of Electric Boat who owns the governor and the state police, but who is a humanitarian as he belongs to the Boys Club, Girls Club and the Home Journal and gives blood to the Red Cross. Workers' blood. He "was once a worker himself and hates to kill workers for profit."

In the second scene he is addressing the workers who are on the picket line. The workers are actual pickets, with some holding the script. J.D. talks his propaganda, until they get so angry they attack him and kill him. And one worker says, "Business will always be in the way. Was this a crime? Or was it self-defense? This is not the solution, it's not even a revolution. It's a play, with workers power all the way." Then the whole cast points at the audience and says, "We are many" and points at the corpse of big business and says, "They are few."

The bosses' media was there and on the 6 P.M. news, channel 3, they cut it so that it was politically impotent. A rally will be held to discuss this "editing" and how fearful the bosses are of any group that shows militant rank-and-file leadership, especially with the fighting leadership of communists in PLP.

Over $57.00 was collected towards a rank-and-file talent show to take place Sat., Aug. 23, at the Thames St. Parking Lot across the main gate. The show will be put on by the strikers to show the bosses that "the longer we are out, the stronger we will get."

General Dynamics PLP'er Wins Back Union Rights

GROTON, Conn., August 13—This past spring militant PLP member Bruce Burns was attacked by the bosses' agents in the Painters union, thrown out of the hall by the bosses' police and politically attacked by a bosses' lawyer in the Connecticut State Labor Council. This fascist lawyer, Norman Zolot, attacked the U.S. labor movement by trying to get a Federal judge to stop the voting rights of rank-and-file union members.

IN A BRIEF SUBMITTED BY ZOLOT, HE stated the vote of one member was "not that important." In fact the votes of the 600 members of Local 1503 of the International Brotherhood of Painers and Allied Trades were "not that important."

Rank-and-file pressure was exerted on the Federal government; over 10,000 leaflets were issued to workers stating that the U.S. government was in bed with the Nazi Zolot. And the failure of this Judge to issue a restraining order against the cops and the boss-led union leaders indicated his alliance with them.

Because of this pressure the Judge granted Burns the right to attend union meetings.

The decision came after the 10,000 members of the Metal Trades Council struck General Dynamics and defeated the Conn. State Police in a well-disciplined and well-organized battle. This struggle was led by PLP ideas and militant rank-and-file comrades who believe in a good life for workers. This growing popularity of the PLP and the interest in the Party during the strike has led the U.S. government via Judge Zampano to take notice.

There is no doubt that PLP has won respect from the workers in Groton, Conn., and the fear of the Federal Courts.

Dump R.O.A.R. in Rosedale Queens
MARCH & RALLY AT RACIST'S DOORSTEP
Sat., Sept. 6, 12 Noon

Fascist cops attack workers—PLP members—at transit hike protest (see p. 4).

For months fascists operating out of the racist R.O.A.R. group in Rosedale have been attacking a black family in the community. Many white families have sympathized with their black neighbors. Let's back black-white unity. The fascists like to dish it out. Now let's see if they can take it! Join Progressive Labor Party in demonstrating at this fascist's house. If we workers don't destroy these fascists, they will destroy us!

ASSEMBLE at corner of Merric Blvd. & Francis Lewis Blvd. in Laurelton, march to J. Scala's house and rally at near-by school. By public transportation: "E" or "F" train to 169th St. & Hillside Ave. station (next to last stop); then take Bus No. (Rosedale Station bus) to Francis Lewis Blvd.

Carson Beach, Roxbury, Dorchester:

BOSTON REBELS BATTLE RACISTS

· FIGHT FOR SOCIALISM ·

See Page 3, 4

Members of CAR and the PLP were among the anti-racist forces that confronted the cops and racist at Carson Beach in South Boston. Prod used by cops was just one of many used by cops who were there to insure that the South Boston Beaches remained segregated.